BARBARA CLEVERLY was born in the north of England and is a graduate of Durham University. She now lives in the middle of Cambridge.

The Palace Tiger is her fourth Joe Sandilands novel; her first, *The Last Kashmiri Rose*, was named by the *New York Times* as a 'notable book of 2002'. To find out more about the series, visit the website www.barbaracleverly.com.

Praise for Barbara Cleverly's Joe Sandilands series

'Spellbinding début mystery.'   *New York Times*

'Cleverly draws an India so vivid you can smell and taste it.'   *Poisoned Pen*

'Captivating and enchanting. Attractive, duplicitous women grab all the best roles. Between the natural beauty of the setting and the seductiveness of the women, it's a wonder that Joe Sandilands gets out of Simla with heart and mind intact.'   *New York Times*

'*Ragtime in Simla* contains enough scenes of smashing action in and around the marvellously invoked Simla to delight even Rudyard Kipling.'   *Chicago Tribune*

Also by Barbara Cleverly

The Last Kashmiri Rose
Ragtime in Simla
The Damascened Blade

Forthcoming

The Bee's Kiss

THE PALACE TIGER

Barbara Cleverly

ROBINSON
London

Constable & Robinson Ltd
3 The Lanchesters
162 Fulham Palace Road
London W6 9ER
www.constablerobinson.com

First published in the UK by Constable,
an imprint of Constable & Robinson Ltd 2004

This paperback edition published by Robinson,
an imprint of Constable & Robinson Ltd 2005

A copy of the British Library Cataloguing in
Publication Data is available from the British Library

ISBN 1-84529-048-8 (pbk)
ISBN 1-84119-812-9 (hbk)

Printed and bound in the EU

1 3 5 7 9 10 8 6 4 2

For Stephen and Rebecca

Captain Sandilands of 'The Fighting Fifth'.
Quo Fata Vocant

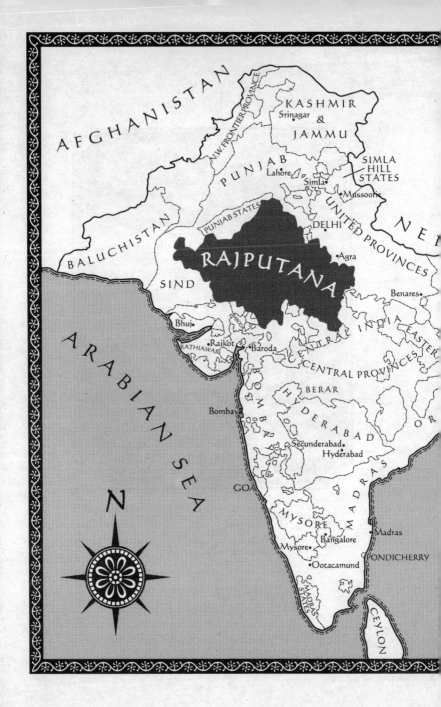

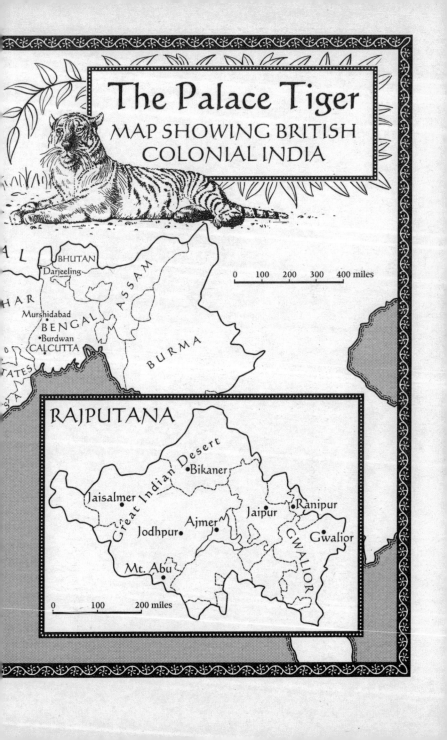

The Palace Tiger
MAP SHOWING BRITISH COLONIAL INDIA

0 100 200 300 400 miles

BHUTAN
Darjeeling

ASSAM

Murshidabad
BENGAL
Burdwan
CALCUTTA

BURMA

RAJPUTANA

Great Indian Desert

Bikaner

Jaisalmer

Jaipur

Ranipur

Jodhpur

Ajmer

GWALIOR

Gwalior

Mt. Abu

0 100 200 miles

Chapter One

Northern India, 1922

Putli's mother, her hands on her hips, straightened pain-fully, glad after two hours to break the rhythmic co-ordination of arm and shoulder, glad to stand back and count the mounting bundles of tall cut grass that had fallen to the steady swish of her sickle. The weight of the coming baby was beginning to unbalance her and slow her down. There was no doubt of that, but an early start while the oat grass was still wet had paid off and she was pleased. She called out a practised musical cry answered by her daughter working a few yards behind her on the steep slope that led up to the forest beyond the village. Glad to share this pause, mother and daughter smiled with word-less tenderness.

Her mother looked with satisfaction at the eight-year-old girl. Yesterday had been the most important day of her daughter's life. She had been fêted and spoiled by the whole village and fed to bursting with puris and rich milk and sweetmeats. It had been her wedding day. Putli's mother had been proud to see the pretty girl, her eldest child, dressed for the first time in the costume of a married woman. No longer the infant in simple cotton dress, she was now wearing the tight blue bodice, the short skirt and the chaddar of the women of her tribe.

Putli's mother remembered the two small brown right hands clasping each other as the bride and groom made their marriage vows and she had been happy to see that the boy chosen from a neighbouring village was as strong

11

and handsome as her daughter. The bridegroom's mother, a distant cousin, had earned her approval too and this was very important for Putli's mother. In a few years Putli would leave her family home and go to join her young husband as his wife and become a part of his family. This was the way of it with girl children. Putli's mother acknowledged and accepted it but she would be sad. Oh, she had two good sons who had come after Putli and of these she was rightly proud, but it was her oldest child who was secretly her joy. She had a loving husband who had allowed her without question to rear Putli although not all mothers of first-born girl children were so lucky. And her care had been rewarded by the constant good humour and energy of the child. She would miss her sleepy smile as she rose uncomplaining in the early morning to help with the meal and polish the cooking pots; she would miss her chatter as they brought back the cows or harvested the wheat. The light of her life would too soon be shining at another woman's hearth.

Putli opened her mouth to shout something to her mother but her mother never heard the words. In deep and stealthy silence a gold and black shape detached itself from the grass behind Putli and leapt at her. An iron-clad paw scythed through the air and severed the slender neck with one blow. The dark head, still entangled in its chaddar, fell to the ground and the tiger, seizing the body in its jaws, turned to make off through the long grass towards the trees above. With a despairing howl, Putli's mother swung about. Rage, disgust and hatred gave strength to her slim arm and she hurled her sickle in a glittering arc at the savage face. By the grace of the jungle spirits, the spinning blade hit the tiger in the eye and, half blind, his shattering roar changed to an almost human cry of pain and affront. Releasing his prey, the beast shook the sickle from his great head, turned and in a second was again a shadow amongst the grasses. The crumpled body of Putli lay at her mother's feet.

Chapter Two

Simla, May 1922

Ambling down the Mall, Joe Sandilands steered his sweating hireling through the thickening crowds to return it to the stables at the Chummery, enjoying, as always, the early morning sounds of the waking town. Simla, the summer capital of British India, rose early and went about its business at a brisk pace. Uniformed men were striding between the military establishments along the Mall, red-coated chaprassis, message boxes on hips, were speeding from Post Office to government buildings, their energy fuelling the flow of information spreading out from this unremarkable street and pulsing around the world. Joe shook his head half in admiration, half in disbelief. The eccentric little town perched in the Himalayan foothills half-way between the scorching plains of India and the frozen summits of the Tibetan mountains looked like nothing so much as a displaced Godalming. And yet, between March and November, the mighty British Empire was governed from here and that meant half the world, Joe supposed, conjuring up a memory of the pink-coloured lands he'd studied on his globe as a child.

Already the first nursemaids pushing baby carriages down the street were greeting each other, their fluting voices a treble accompaniment to the distant pounding of marching feet. As he wove through the purposeful crowds, Joe felt a stab of puritanical guilt to be at leisure when this small world was at work.

Not all of this small world though! He took comfort in

the thought that his own temporary lack of occupation was as nothing to the endemic sloth he would find at the house he was about to visit. Eight o'clock. The four inhabitants of the Chummery would most certainly be still in bed sleeping off whatever had been the indulgence of the previous night, or, at best, tremulously astir. With any luck he would be able to sneak off back to the Residence without announcing himself. But then he remembered that there was in his pocket a telegram. He had been charged by Sir George Jardine, his host, the acting Governor of Bengal, to deliver this to Edgar Troop. Edgar, the leader of the louche côterie that inhabited the once grand house on Mount Pleasant, earned his position in the group by being the oldest, the most enterprising and the most unscrupulous. Unaccountably, he seemed to have Sir George's confidence. He did not have Joe's confidence and though they had stood shoulder to shoulder in dangerous circumstances in the wilderness with that instinctive understanding and trust that two military men fighting towards the same objective experience, Joe found Captain Troop enigmatic, his style of living repellent. When he asked himself why he continued to spend more than a polite five minutes with the man, he had to admit that Edgar's cheerful cynicism and his appetite for life were ultimately seductive.

'You'll be returning your horse to the Chummery? Well now, when you get there I'd like you to deliver this to Edgar in person,' Sir George had said. 'Don't entrust it to anyone else in that hopeless establishment! Why? I don't often call at the Chummery but the last time I did so there were two telegrams on the mantelpiece. One was a year old and the other – goddammit! – was nearly two years old. Both unopened and one was from me! This could be important and I don't want it to go astray.'

Joe didn't want to do this. He knew that if he was intercepted it would be nearly impossible to avoid a second breakfast leading to a drink or two, a morning of inconsequential gossip shading off into tiffin and imperceptibly into an afternoon moving lethargically round the snooker table. He wondered whether, if he rode round the back, he could hand his horse over, leave the telegram with a servant and make a discreet withdrawal, and this he resolved to try. To no avail. He had hardly turned into the compound before a window banged open and a cheerful voice summoned.

'Must have smelled the coffee, Sandilands!' Hospitably, the beaming face of Jackie Carlisle appeared at the window. 'Come on board and tell us the latest news! You who have the ear of the great and good must have something interesting to tell us in this otherwise uneventful town.'

Joe knew that he was caught and Jackie continued, 'Heard someone say the other day, "Where Sandilands goes, trouble follows." Come on, Joe, live up to your reputation – enliven our dull lives.'

Reluctantly, Joe handed his horse to a syce who had hurried forward on hearing the hooves on the gravel. In the Chummery, Joe had discovered, the grooms knew their business, but the house servants, of whom there seemed to be a number varying from day to day and from two to ten, seemed to take their pace from their employers. He let himself into the house and made for the breakfast room. Here at least there was order. The table was laid for four with piles of bread and fruit and a large steaming bowl of porridge. A large pot of coffee too – good coffee. That you could count on. Three of the inmates were already gathered around the table and dressed in their usual crumpled white linen suits. Jackie Carlisle entered clad in a silk dressing gown and made his way to the sideboard. Joe watched in awe as Jackie poured himself out a drink and threw it down in one gulp. His eyes bulged and his purple face took on a darker shade. He crowed, he stuttered as he fought for breath.

'Christ!' said Joe, impressed. 'What was that, Jackie?' and he waited while Jackie spluttered on.

'Oh, for God's sake – someone loosen his stays,' muttered Edgar.

15

'Only thing that gets me going these days,' Jackie managed at last. 'Want some?'

'I'd need to know what it was,' said Joe guardedly.

Edgar intervened. 'Don't touch the bloody stuff!' he said. 'It's wormwood. Absinthe.'

'Absinthe?' said Joe, surprised. 'I thought it was illegal?'

'Yes,' said Jackie, wiping his mouth and looking round vaguely, 'I believe it is.'

'So it should be,' said Bertie Hearne-Robinson. 'It'll kill him sooner or later.'

Edgar picked up the glass and sniffed it. 'This is nothing,' he said. 'When I was in the Russian army, most of my fellow officers imbibed it nasally.'

'Edgar, is that linguistically possible?' Joe asked.

'Possibly not. But certainly *physically* possible! Witnessed it many times. They'd pour out a little cupful and snuff it up. Jackie may be in a bad way but he's not quite as bad as that. Not yet.'

'It's boredom,' said Johnny Bristow. 'Poor old sod! Who can blame him? Nothing much happens. I know how he feels. When Joe's been up here a bit longer, goodness knows into what he'll be driven by boredom.'

'Or into whom,' leered Bertie. 'Couldn't help noticing that Margery Phelps was showing more than common interest at the Gaiety last night . . . and Colonel Phelps is in Burma, I understand. Like me to fix it up for you, Joe?'

'Oh, come on!' said Johnny. 'The Commander can do better than the garrison hack! Handsome young chap like him, chestful of medals, friends in high places, all the charm in the world, he can have his pick! Let's think . . . Now, little Maudie Smithson's still unbacked, I believe. She's quite a strider! What about it, Joe?'

The conversation diverted into an informed comparison of the attractions of the available ladies of Simla and much speculation as to the attractions of the unavailable.

'This is nothing but talk!' said Edgar. 'Not one of you

16

has anything going if the truth be told. Young chaps like you ought to be making things happen. When I was your age –'

Bertie hurried to cut him off. 'When you were our age, you were Emperor of all the Russias! Don't tell us!'

This was beginning to turn into a mild Chummery quarrel and Joe didn't want to listen. Mercifully, he remembered his telegram. 'Oh, by the way, Edgar – telegram for you. Or rather a telegram for Sir George for passage on to you. It's probably nothing but he said I had to put it into your hand. Hold out your hand!'

He passed a buff form across. Not much privacy here. All crowded round to read over Edgar's shoulder. As he watched he wondered very much how the leaky ship that was the Chummery stayed afloat. He knew that Jackie Carlisle was paid a substantial allowance by his wife's family to stay in India. He knew that Johnny Bristow carelessly but seemingly successfully bought and sold horses, had horses for hire and carriages for that matter. Bertie Hearne-Robinson was widely believed to have contacts over the border and not to be above a little gentlemanly smuggling in concert with a number of gentlemanly Pathans and all under the cover of the house lettings and sales agency he ran from an office in the Mall.

Then there was Edgar. What about Edgar? An accomplished shikari, he managed shooting trips for passing visitors. He arranged contacts and some of the contacts he was fabled to arrange were of a rather dubious nature. It was widely known that Edgar enjoyed shares in a prosperous and select brothel in the lower town. Perhaps it was no wonder that the respectable did not care to be seen to be associated with the Chummery, but at the same time perhaps it was clear why the adventurous sought their company, admired their style and, on annual return to Simla, found their way there. Want a game of polo? Johnny would fix it. Want to dispose of a few stones? Bertie was your man. Want to raise a small holiday loan? Jackie might

17

be able to help. Easy terms, only needing a promissory note.

It was clear to Joe that demand would always create supply and when you had a town full of men – full of women too – on pleasure bent, the procureur, the middle man, would always prosper. That was what kept the Chummery going!

'Could we,' he enquired mildly, 'have a look at this fabled telegram? And could we – I beg your pardon, gentlemen – have a little privacy to do so?'

All were at once contrite. 'Yes, old boy, of course. Good gracious! No problem at all!'

They rose in turn from the cluttered breakfast table and left Joe and Edgar alone.

Joe considered the once handsome square face opposite as Edgar studied the telegram. He seemed to be spending a disproportionate amount of time on such a short missive and had clearly read the text three times before Joe asked impatiently, 'What's it all about, Edgar?'

'Ranipur,' said Edgar. 'They want me to go there. Happens sometimes.'

The name was familiar to Joe. Ranipur. Familiar, but amongst so much unrelated information about India he couldn't place it.

'It's a princely state,' said Edgar and he lifted a framed map from the wall and set it on the table between them. 'It's about three hundred miles away. Here's Simla. And down here there's Delhi. Now follow the railway line from Simla down to Kalka and Umballa. That's the way you came up last month. It's not shown but there's a branch line, a private line, connecting with the main one at Umballa. Here,' he said, pointing with a splayed finger. 'There's a narrow gauge railway like the one up to Simla. It was put in by the maharaja of Ranipur to improve access to his state.

'His state's big. Oh, not when compared with some of the states of Royal India like . . . Hyderabad, for instance, but big enough. About the size of Norfolk, I'd say. It's prosperous too. The maharaja is said to be the tenth richest man in the world. When you look at some of the competition that's quite a proud boast. He doesn't exactly get himself weighed in diamonds but he's not down to his last hundred million. In his youth he was quite a tough! He needed to be to keep his feet on the steps of the throne of Ranipur, slippery with the blood of half a dozen immediate predecessors. I never quite understood the ins and outs but I tell you – his early years in Ranipur would make *The Duchess of Malfi* sound like one of Gilbert and Sullivan's jolliest!'

'Tell me some more,' said Joe, reading the telegram Edgar handed to him. 'Tell me about this peremptory prince.' He read aloud, '"Kindly make Troop available Tuesday 15th to Tuesday 22nd. State time of arrival Ranipur."' He waggled his eyebrows in mock astonishment. '"Make Troop available"! What's he take you for? Sir George's errand boy?'

'Oh, he's a good man, Udai Singh. We've done a lot of business together. We trust each other. Hard to believe. You wouldn't imagine that the respected ruler of goodness knows how many millions, the confidant of the British Raj, model innovator and blah, blah . . . you can't imagine why such an individual would associate on intimate terms with a rascal like me but so it is.'

'Oh, I don't know,' said Joe slyly. 'I expect there are goods and services you can supply.'

Edgar laughed, leaned back and lit a cigar. 'When I first moved here I was contacted by a tourist, a tourist who wanted to shoot a tiger. Would I arrange it? Well, the long and short of it was I did arrange it. This ass, Brigadier Montagu Wickham-Skeith, duly bagged his tiger but I made a mistake. Didn't know the country so well in those days and I'd strayed into the Principality of Ranipur. The Brigadier and I were caught by the border guards and thrown into the deepest dungeon below the castle moat as it were. More than a possibility, thought I, that we'd be trampled to death by elephants! A custom that had only just died away. At least, I think it's died away . . . Anyway, I knew that the ruler still had powers of life and death over his own subjects and certainly over suspected poachers.

'But, by the mercy of Providence, the prince had a big shooting party arranged – the Viceroy, ambassadors, visiting royalty, God knows who! Now there's one thing I'm good at – well, many things I'm good at – but pre-eminently I'm good at organizing a shoot and the wild duck of Ranipur are famous the world over. The Brigadier and I were led out, still in manacles, I guessed with the idea of getting us identified by one of the British grandees present, and we can't have been looking very sharp. Hadn't had anything to eat for twenty-four hours.

'We were led, blinking in the sunlight, over to a couple of chaps standing about with guns. An Englishman and his Indian aide. The Englishman was a very impressive fellow but unfortunately a fellow I'd never set eyes on before, so – no use to me. He was tall and slim with a neat waist, equally neat moustache and that commanding, super-cilious air you British are so good at affecting. He turned around and gave us the benefit of it. Someone with that amount of confidence I calculated could be none other than the newly appointed British Resident, Claude Vyvyan. Know him, Joe?'

Joe shook his head.

'Well, he certainly didn't know me. His icy blue eye passed over me with the same interest he'd have paid to a pile of camel dung but he did brighten up a bit when he saw the Brigadier. "Monty! What the hell?" The Brig danced about with relief. They knew each other well and release and explanations swiftly followed. And, of course, wouldn't you know, Edgar Troop was found much to blame! My hunting expertise was decidedly being called into question and to break the rhythm of all the "But how on earth was it possible to do such a stupid thing? . . . Monty, old boy, in future, always refer to me for advice!", I decided to assert myself. I looked up at the sky with what

20

I thought to be a disparaging, dismissive and cunning air and made a remark.

'Now, in Ranipur the climax of a duck shoot was to drive what they call the Long Pond and I can tell you – the wild duck come off it as thick as bloody sparrows! It really is the most impressive thing when they start to move. I said, addressing the remark to no one in particular, "Why on earth do you suppose they take the Long Pond from east to west and stand the guns along the south side when they could take it from north to south and everybody would get a second shot, a third or a fourth?"

'Now the Indian aide in European clothes who'd been standing at Vyvyan's side and listening, answered me. To my astonishment in perfect and unaccented English he said, "Say that again, will you? It sounded like an inter-esting idea – if a bit obvious, perhaps." Well, I began to realize that this must be a person of some importance so I said, "Get me a drink and I'll gladly repeat it." As you've probably guessed, this insignificant figure was the maharaja of Ranipur. Without much discussion he adopted my revised plan for driving the Long Pond. It worked beautifully, just as I'd said it would, and Udai was very impressed. From that moment on – though obviously we've had our tiffs from time to time – I could do no wrong. When I'm in Ranipur he puts a guest house at my disposal and although Ranipur is what you might call his principal residence, there are others. The moment he wants to get away from the formalities of court he moves away into a more secluded part of his state and I've accom-panied him many times.'

Joe looked back at the telegram once more and frowned. 'And this enables him to order you to come and go at a whim, does it?'

'Bit sharp, isn't it? But that won't have been sent by Udai. That's Claude's style. He usually sends the tele-grams. Claude. The British Resident I was telling you about.'

'Resident?' Joe queried. 'A political appointment?'

'Yes. This is usual with the princely states. The rulers have all signed treaties with the British Government. They support the crown and in return we leave them largely alone to get on with ruling as they see fit. But, just in case, we send a trusted civil servant or military bloke of some standing to reside in the state and see that the ruler stays on the straight and narrow. He's a sort of permanently-in-place ambassador.'

'And does this system work?' Joe asked doubtfully. 'Surely autocrats like the maharajas resent someone peering over their shoulders all the time?'

'Yes, it works. Mostly. These fellers manage to steer a clever course. Some of them have done a great deal of good, making just the sort of social improvements a chap like you would approve of. More than one ruler's been persuaded to haul himself and his state into the twentieth century and build roads, hospitals, schools. Some are only too pleased to pass the running of the state over to a pair of capable hands.' He paused. 'Of course there are some rulers who are incorrigibly medieval in their behaviour.'

'And how does a Resident deal with medieval behaviour?' asked Joe, intrigued.

'Decisively,' said Edgar with relish. 'Ever heard of the maharaja of Patiala?'

'Heard of him? I've seen him!' said Joe. 'In Calcutta last December. He was in the parade to welcome the Prince of Wales when he opened the Victoria Monument. You wouldn't forget seeing *him*!' Joe remembered the impression the maharaja had made on the crowds. He'd swaggered about in scarlet tunic, white leggings, black thigh-length leather boots, the whole topped off with a daffodil yellow turban fastened with an emerald cluster. Well over six feet and built like a bear, he wore his luxuriant black moustaches tucked up into his turban. 'An impressive figure,' Joe added.

Edgar grinned. 'Couldn't agree more but did you know that this friend of the Prince of Wales, this loyal advocate of the Pax Britannica, this member of every polo club from

Hurlingham to Isfahan has been in hot water for what I can only call medieval bad behaviour?'

'I didn't know,' said Joe. 'What did he do? Drink from his finger bowl?'

'It was discovered,' said Edgar gleefully, 'that the chap had been deflowering virgins. Oh, not just the odd one but on a gargantuan scale. One a day for no one knows how many years! And all that on top of having hundreds of concubines in his harem!'

'How tiring!' said Joe. 'Come on, Edgar – you don't believe all these stories, do you?'

'His people certainly do! They're actually proud of their ruler's prowess!' Edgar smirked and went on in a confiding tone, 'There's a yearly ceremony in Patiala. People travel for miles to see it. Went myself one year and saw it with my own eyes so I know this is no story! The maharaja parades through the streets of his city naked but for a waist-length vest encrusted with a thousand and one diamonds, acknowledging the cheers of his subjects with what I can best describe as a priapic salute!'

'Good Lord! Seems a bit excessive!'

'Not one to go off at half cock, Patiala!' Edgar laughed. 'But too strong for most tastes and someone – the Resident, it's assumed – had a quiet word with him and told him not to do it again.'

'A quiet word, Edgar? Would that be enough to bring about the required change in behaviour?'

'Depends on the word,' said Edgar. 'If, amongst all the finger-wagging, wrist-slapping and minatory phrases a slight emphasis were put on "deposition",' he grinned, 'it would do the trick. Or perhaps – horror of horrors! – HM Gov. threatened to reduce his gun salute from nineteen to eleven. Now that would have a decidedly deflationary effect! But, whatever the persuasion used, the Resident achieved his end, which was to placate the memsahibs who've infiltrated the state as they have all over India bringing their dire baggage of morality, religion and social justice.'

Joe knew Edgar was likely to get the bit between his teeth when the conversation moved to the modern woman. For him, the India of the East India Company was the ideal: a glamorous, masculine world of traders, fighters, opportunists, men who, discarding Western influences, took Indian women as wives and mistresses, spoke their languages and exploited their country. The world of John Company, according to Edgar, had come to a regrettable end when sea travel improved and droves of English-women found themselves able to make the journey out to the East and fish for husbands in India. He hurried to divert Edgar from the anticipated diatribe.

'I take it the Ranipur Resident has an easier life? What sort of man is Vyvyan? You speak of him with modified rapture?'

'Oh, Claude is very good. Brilliant even. Gets on well with the prince, knows when to look the other way, works tirelessly for good relations between Ranipur and the Empire. Model situation, you could say. And far from being a strained relationship as you might expect, Claude has become his friend and confidant. It's a tricky balancing act being ruler. Lonely too. Most of Udai's relations are only waiting to step into his empty shoes, most of his subjects are standing round trying how best to make money out of him. Claude helps him keep balance and authority.'

'And what role does Edgar Troop play in all this? Which of your many talents do you lay out for the ruler?'

Edgar looked pleased. 'In my way, I suppose I'm a sort of safety valve. Udai enjoys his drink, shooting, polo, expensive trips to Europe, female company, occasionally getting married. In fact the perfect life of the Rajput gentle-man that he is. I couldn't sympathize with him more! I wouldn't like you to know all the things I've done for him in my time. I wouldn't like to mention some of the things he's done for me. But that's what's given rise to this telegram. It probably means he's bored and wants me to spice things up a bit for him.'

'What sort of a place has he got in Ranipur?'

'Think Buckingham Palace and multiply by ten. Perhaps a thousand rooms. Ancient. Beautiful. Parts very dilapidated, parts immaculate. Parts inhabited by storks and bats, snakes too probably. The Old Palace is kept for formal occasions and it's home to many of his relations and all the women of the household. Udai has the sense to live elsewhere – in the New Palace. Every modern convenience! And he's built himself several guest bungalows. He usually sets one of these aside for me.'

Servants were beginning to hover round the disordered breakfast table.

'I think we'd better take the hint,' said Edgar and, giving orders as he did so, led Joe out on to a cluttered terrace. He waved a hand vaguely at the overgrown shrubbery in the courtyard. 'Must do something about this,' he said absently. 'Trouble is, things either grow to four times their expected size or die off and, as you see, we've got a fair sample of both here. Sit down. Ready for a beer now?'

It was the Chummery routine to move straight from coffee to a foaming glass of chilled ale and a servant was standing by with a tray already loaded. Edgar gulped down half his glass, wiped his moustache and looked at Joe with speculation. He leaned forward. 'Look, Joe, I can see you're getting fed up with Simla. Damned hard work being on enforced vacation. Why don't you get Sir George to sign an exeat for you and come to Ranipur with me?'

Chapter Three

When Joe's rickshaw dropped him at the Governor's Residence a servant was smiling a welcome.

'Sir George is in the gun room, sahib. He wonders if you could join him for a few moments before tiffin?'

'Yes. Certainly. I'll go straight there. Thank you, Karim.'

Nothing happened in Simla without Sir George Jardine being aware of it, very often for the simple reason that he had instigated the action. Joe guessed that he was now about to be questioned closely but with a show of casual lack of interest about the contents of Edgar's telegram and his immediate travel plans. Joe had no doubt that Edgar was Sir George's eyes and ears in the state of Ranipur as well as in many a darker corner of the Empire.

He swung open the heavy door to the gun room and went in, enjoying as he always did the smell of leather and gun oil and Trichinopoly cigars. Sir George was working on a gun. Its silk-lined case lay open on the central table. Joe knew that gun. The lid of the oak and leather case carried a coat of arms and in florid script the words, 'Holland and Holland. Gun and rifle manufacturers. Bruton Street, London.'

Sir George looked up to greet him with a hearty bellow. 'There you are, my boy! Glad to see those villains didn't shanghai you for the afternoon. Now we haven't much time. Remind me when you're off . . . Tuesday, is it? That gives us four days to prepare.'

Joe had been amused to discover from the flyleaf of a

borrowed book that the Latin motto of the Jardine family was *'cave adsum'*. The Romans hadn't made use of punctuation but if they had, they would have needed two exclamation marks adequately to convey the flavour, he thought. The confident 'Here I am!' was always preceded by the warning 'Watch out!' Joe found it useful to bear this Highlander's challenge in mind in his dealings with Sir George.

'George! How the hell –'

'Edgar never turns down an invitation to Ranipur and if there's anything Edgar enjoys it's involving someone else in his schemes. He was bound to ask you to go with him and I guessed you wouldn't be able to resist. Of course you can go. I'll square it with Sir Nevil in London. He's aware of your achievements in India. I've sent him a complete report. Mentioned you in dispatches, you might say. In fact, Joe . . .' George turned his attention back to the gun barrel and rubbed it thoughtfully with his cloth. 'I ought to tell you that he's agreed to your staying on a little longer. He'll be quite happy if you take a boat back in time to be at your desk in September. Look, why don't you pick up a cloth and give me a hand?'

Joe stood, silently taking in the sudden reshaping of his career, resentful of the ease with which these two old comrades, so similar in autocratic style, moved him around like a chess piece. It occurred to him that Sir George might be expressing a more than polite interest in his forthcoming trip.

'Anyone in Ranipur you'd like me to arrest while I'm down there, by any chance?'

'As a matter of fact, I can think of at least half a dozen who'd be better off behind bars. But, seriously, Joe, we do have a problem in the state. A problem with the succession.'

The door opened and Karim came in carrying a tray of whisky, sherry and glasses.

'Sherry, Joe?' George poured out a glass of sherry for Joe and a large whisky-soda for himself. 'The situation is very uncertain. I'd like to have my own man on the ground to keep an eye on things over this next bit.'

'But you've got Edgar to report back to you should there be a problem.'

George took a careful sip of his whisky. 'Edgar may be part of the problem. He's very attached to that old rogue, the maharaja. Soulmates you might say. I'd like to think there was a pair of sharp and unbiased eyes watching out for our interests.'

Joe found the cloth being offered to him and with reverence took the gun from Sir George. He stroked the oiled, finely grained French walnut stock and admired the richly engraved steel. Automatically he tested the balance of the gun then held it to his shoulder and squinted along the barrel.

'This isn't a weapon! It's a work of art,' he murmured.

'It's both, you'll find,' said George with satisfaction. 'Don't be taken in by the beauty of it. It packs a huge punch! It's a Royal double rifle, 23-inch barrel. Quite simply the best in the world. Theodore Roosevelt took one to Africa with him and was very impressed. Wonderful for heavy, fast-moving game. Points with ease and speed and can fire two shots almost simultaneously. Great knock-down effect and it's got a fast reload should your first two shots miss a charging buffalo.'

Joe laughed. 'Sold! Have a dozen sent round to my suite at the Dorchester!'

George put on a pair of spectacles and eyed Joe carefully. 'Fusilier, weren't you? Thought I'd got that right. Put it to your shoulder again, Joe,' he said. 'Thought so! Could have been made for you! You know that each of these guns is made to measure? You go along to the gun shop and have more parts of your anatomy measured than they'd bother with for a suit in Savile Row. Height, chest, length of arm . . . and the result is an individually tailored gem. Extraordinary! You fit that gun exactly!'

'I've never felt so comfortable with a gun,' said Joe. 'But, George, for whom was this made? Not you, I think?' He looked speculatively at the rangy figure of Sir George, now growing a little portly but a good two inches taller than Joe and with longer arms.

'My younger brother, Bill. It was a gift from our father on his twenty-first birthday. 1907.' His voice took on a gruff tone and he added, 'Killed at Ypres. He'd have been amused and pleased to see you standing there hefting it. You're very like him. Look, Joe, take it. I mean have it. Gift from Bill. You'll make good use of it in Ranipur and it'll give you a certain standing amongst the shooting classes. The maharaja may have its equal (I believe he's got Purdeys) but no one else will.'

Joe could hardly find the words to stammer his thanks. He knew there was no point in attempting a polite refusal; George Jardine said what he meant and always got his own way.

'I shall go to Ranipur well equipped to shoot something, then, but what or whom have you in mind, George?'

'With the rifle: tiger. There have been reports of a wounded tiger that's developed a taste for human flesh terrorizing the villages in the north of the state. And while you're about it, I'd like you to take that pistol over there on the rack with you. Bit more up to date than your Scotland Yard issue blunderbuss.'

Joe took down the pistol George was indicating. 'Haven't seen one of these before,' he said, impressed. The weapon was small and businesslike, pared down to its stark essentials. In contrast with the rifle, there was not a curlicue, no decoration of any kind, to relieve the elegantly blunt 3½-inch barrel surmounting a sculptured butt which housed the magazine.

'No, you won't have seen one of these. It's a Browning M, this year's model. Magazine holds eight bullets. As you see, it's discreet and as lethal as it looks. You could slip it into the pocket of your dinner jacket and no one would be any the wiser. I thought we'd spend the afternoon popping off the guns, getting the feel of them, putting in a bit of target practice.'

'George, are we about to start a war?' said Joe in sudden alarm.

George considered. 'I hope not. But there could be bloodshed. Best be prepared.'

'You said something about the succession? Is it in doubt? Is that going to give rise to difficulties? And why now? I understood from Edgar that the prince is only in middle age. He's just married a third wife in fact, hasn't he?'

'This is something even Edgar hasn't got wind of yet. And I suppose I'd better warn him before you go off down there. Poor old Udai Singh has got cancer. He's dying, Joe. The medics, and he's consulted the best, give him six months at the outside. Heard of Sir Hector Munro? Former Royal Physician? Forefront of the profession. He's staying with the prince in Ranipur for an unspecified time, treating his condition as far as he's able and, of course, keeping us informed of the progress of the disease. The succession – and this is always at the ruler's whim, you understand – is of considerable interest to the British. It's usual, though not mandatory, to nominate your eldest son as heir and, last month, Udai had two sons so you would think it was straightforward. No longer.'

'George, you'd better tell me what happened last month,' said Joe with foreboding.

'A disgraceful scene! The elder son died. Now what was his name? Bishan, that's it. Any coroner would have said death by misadventure, but the circumstances were, to my mind, a bit mysterious. Oh, no loss! We assumed he was the heir and we weren't happy with that. Chap was a sort of walking sponge. Alcohol, opium, absinthe, he took it all aboard. Not the slightest interest in anything but his own gratification and consequently a rather unpopular man, but his cause was espoused by his terrible old mother, the First Her Highness. She was twenty when she married Udai thirty-odd years ago and he was a lad of thirteen. An enterprising lad because she presented him with a son in short order. A few daughters followed but I don't know their names; they've all been married off to neighbouring princes. One or two sons who died in infancy, I believe. He married a second wife years later and she too has a son. Must be in his late twenties now.'

'So there's no immediate problem then?'

'Not so sure of that. Everybody heaved a sigh of relief when the elder son met his sticky end but that left number two next in line and he's hardly any better from our point of view. A drinker like his brother – though they say reformed – but what has really annoyed his father is that he's recently married (whilst on a trip to the States) a very unsuitable girl. An American. Dancer of some sort. Some say she's a circus girl. Very beautiful by all accounts but a menace. Refuses to join the other ladies in the zenana and insists on having her own accommodation. Drives around in a cream roadster with scarlet trimmings, drinks too much champagne and swears like a trooper.'

'Sounds fun!' said Joe, unguardedly.

'A rackety pair but – they say – devoted to each other. Prithvi has held out against all his father's suggestions, commands even, that he marry a decent Indian girl as second wife to ensure the succession. There's a law, you see – British law – that any children of marriages to Western girls may not inherit so Prithvi has really upset his father! Cut off the line, you might say. The pair met on an airfield, I understand. And that's another of number two's passions. He's mad about flying. He's got a plane in Ranipur and flies it, recklessly I hear, about the place. Not a good insurance risk!'

'Is there an alternative?'

'As it's quite in order for the ruler to nominate whomever he likes – and never forget Udai was himself a village boy, a distant relation, when he was nominated as ruler against all the odds – there must be hundreds! He can pick and choose. Doesn't even have to be a member of his own family. His older brother, over whose head he was promoted so to speak, is his Dewan, his prime minister I suppose you'd say. Very sound and sensible chap, Zalim Singh. Statesman. He must think he's strongly in the running. And we would not be displeased if he were. But there is another serious contender. Had my eye on this one for some time.'

Joe waited, wondering whether he ought to be making a few notes.

George went on with relish, 'The prince has a third son. Illegitimate. Son of one of his concubines. The lad's only twelve years old though.'

Joe was not deceived. 'Twelve years old? Impressionable? Malleable? In need of a highly principled regent to show him the ropes?'

'You've got it! He's bright as a button! I've met him. Sounded him out, you might say. Interested in science and astronomy. Good little hunter too. Shot his first leopard three years ago. Speaks good English, gets on well with Claude and that's important. If he succeeds, as you suggest, he'll need a regent to supervise him during the years of his minority and – who better than Claude? We were planning to send the lad to Mayo College near Jaipur next year to complete his education. Or to Eton and then Sandhurst if he wishes.'

'So, the stable money's on son number three. But you haven't told me, George, what exactly happened to put number one out of the running permanently?'

George hesitated and took a large gulp of his whisky before replying. 'You have to understand, Joe, that this is quite an, er, alien culture we're dealing with here. Until very recently these chaps were – and I have to say still largely are – Rajput warriors. Very special breed. Hindu by religion with some Moslem attributes. Many of these Rajput tribes fought off the Moghul invaders with suicidal bravery. Some, like Udai's mob, even managed to hang on to their independence. Tough nuts to crack! They're very fierce, very proud, quarrelsome and quite intractable. Imagine a Scottish chieftain, if you will, but unconquered and with oodles of cash in the treasury.'

'Not easy, but I get the idea!'

'They put great store too by physical courage and

strength. Now they can no longer show their prowess on the battlefield, they demonstrate their power through sport. Hunting, wrestling, polo, elephant fights, pig sticking, that sort of thing. You must get someone to show you the armoury while you're down there – it's very special. Well, it was apparently son number one's charming habit to show his strength by wrestling with panthers.'

'Good God! I'm surprised the heir to the throne was allowed to do that!'

'Not quite as dangerous as it sounds. I'm unhappy to say that this chap fixed the odds. He had a black panther kept in a large cage in the palace courtyard. He'd had it declawed and its jaws sewn up. He'd go down every morning and wrestle with it to the fawning admiration of the courtiers. It was his custom to use a panther in this way and then turn it over to the elephant pens to give the beasts trampling practice.'

Joe's mouth was a tight line of distaste but he remained silent.

George went on, his joviality fractionally strained, 'One day, this charmer rolled out of bed, said his morning prayers, consumed his customary dose of opium to give him strength and courage and went down for his pre-breakfast wrestle. Trouble is, this time the panther won. During the night, someone had replaced the declawed panther with a fresh and very angry beast who wasn't playing by the rules. It tore him to pieces.'

'Appalling!' Joe murmured. 'Did they find out who'd replaced the animal?'

'I don't suppose anything like a Scotland Yard enquiry took place but there was retribution. The Master of the Hunt and all his assistants disappeared at once and haven't been seen since. It's assumed they were quietly executed.'

'Didn't Claude Vyvyan have something to say about that?'

'Apparently not. I'm still awaiting his report.'

There was something in George's tone which alerted Joe.

33

He knew him well enough by now to be able to pick up his unexpressed thoughts. Certainly time he got out of India! Almost resentfully, he followed where George was leading him.

'A man you can trust, Vyvyan? It sounds as though you're going to need to trust him, the way things are going in Ranipur. A regency is no small matter. Calls for a skilled and loyal servant of the Empire and one who's prepared to put in a concentrated effort over a period of time . . . Is this what we have in Vyvyan, Sir George?'

'Highly qualified fellow. Talented . . . thorough . . . ambitious, you'd say. But, well, you understand, I'm always glad to have an unbiased pair of eyes to spy out the land. Let me know what you make of him, Joe. That's another reason I want you down there, my boy. Find out, if you can, what's really going on in Ranipur, will you? Look on this in hunting terms, shall we? We're out in the jungle, unseen danger lurking behind every bush, and some helpful forest creature gives a warning cry. What do you do? Well, you interpret the cry and check your gun's loaded. Then you wait and watch and see what comes creeping out of the undergrowth. Come on, let's go and have lunch then we'll get our shooting practice in.'

He turned to Joe and looked at him steadily. 'My boy, there are man-eaters about in Ranipur, certainly one with stripes and four legs but quite possibly another prowling the palace corridors on two legs. Be careful, Joe!'

Chapter Four

Joe very much enjoyed Indian first class rail travel. He liked the comfortable buttoned black leather upholstery, he appreciated the block of ice sharing a tin bath with a dozen bottles of India Pale Ale, strong and hoppy, and he watched as one by one their labels floated off. He listened with half his mind to Edgar's anecdotal conversation and was glad enough to have escaped from Simla.

It was late afternoon before they arrived at the junction with the private rail link with Ranipur. 'Say goodbye to comfort,' said Edgar. 'From now on we're on the narrow gauge, colloquially known as the Heatstroke Express. I keep talking to Udai about it but he never travels by train himself and he doesn't know how the rest of the world suffers. You would think that some of the nobs who use the little railway would have told him.' He rose to his feet, began to button himself up and committed his cigar to a deep ashtray. Joe joined him to look out of the window.

'Behold the powerful state of Ranipur!'

'Powerful? Would you say powerful?' Joe asked.

'Well, it's all relative, isn't it? Some would say prosperous, successful, untroubled.'

'But having a bloodstained past?'

'Yes, indeed, and possibly a bloodstained future as well.'

Joe gave him a sharp look. 'You sound a bit ominous. Ancestral voices, do I hear, prophesying war?'

An unaccustomed look of uncertainty passed briefly over Edgar's florid features and he paused a moment before replying. 'Nothing as definite as that but I'll answer your question properly when I find out why, I mean really why I've been summoned by Udai. Devious old twister that he is!'

They stepped down into the extreme of an Indian summer's day.

'Heatstroke Express!' said Joe. 'I see what you mean!' And a little train whistling and steaming sweatily stood by on another line to receive them.

'Only an hour,' said Edgar. 'We'll probably survive. People mostly do.'

But they didn't have to make the experiment. As they walked across the station forecourt they turned to look at a large white car approaching them at speed and trailing a cloud of dust.

'Ha!' said Edgar with satisfaction. 'A great honour! They've sent the Rolls! I wonder if it's for you or me?'

'Can't be for me,' said Joe. 'He didn't know I was coming. Did he?'

'My dear chap,' said Edgar, 'you haven't begun to understand Udai if you imagine he doesn't know who's come, who's gone, who to expect, who not to expect and what you've got packed in your luggage!'

For a startled moment, Joe had a vision of the dark metal of the snub-nosed gun nestling amongst his dress shirts and hoped he'd remembered to lock his trunk. Joe's eyes followed it anxiously as it was moved with Indian efficiency along with other luggage from the mainline on to the waiting narrow gauge train. For a moment he regretted not keeping the gun tucked away in his belt in spite of the discomfort. He turned his attention back to the open-topped Rolls Royce Phantom and looked and looked again at the two people in the front seats.

The passenger seat was occupied by an Indian wearing a smartly tailored but dusty chauffeur's uniform. Hatless and dishevelled, he was holding on to a leather strap, bracing himself as the car came to an abrupt halt at their feet. The driver, a slim figure in khaki trousers and white shirt, applied the handbrake and jumped out to greet them. She took off the borrowed chauffeur's cap, releasing a shining fall of fair hair, and knocked the cap against her knee to shake off the thick layer of dust.

'Edgar. How nice to see you again.' Her tone was formal rather than warm and her attention moved rather more quickly than was polite from Edgar to himself.

'And this is your English policeman? Cops finally got wise to you, did they, and put you in custody?' She stared at Joe with undisguised appreciation, her expression now warm and playful. 'Well, lucky old you! . . . My! If I weren't already spoken for I'd put my cap right back on and set it at you, mister!'

'Hello, Madeleine,' said Edgar stiffly. 'May I present my friend and colleague, Commander Joseph Sandilands? Joe is in India on secondment from Scotland Yard. Joe, this is Madeleine Mercer – as was – now the first wife of Udai's second son, Prithvi. What the hell are you up to, Madeleine? Still trying to astonish, unnerve and upset? Udai won't like this display, you know!' He waved a hand theatrically at the onlookers beginning to gather round the Rolls. 'Quite a decent crowd you've drummed up . . . thinking of going round with the hat?' The sarcastic edge to his voice made Joe uneasy and he waited for Madeleine to reply in kind, but she ignored the gibe, smiled sweetly and put out a hot, sticky hand to shake Joe's.

'Hello, Joe, and welcome to Ranipur. I'm Maddy. Oh, and I'm not the first wife – I'm the only wife.'

Clearly there was little respect or liking between these two and Joe thought he could understand this. Loyal as he was to the ruler, Edgar would share his disappointment with the heir to the throne's odd choice of bride. And Joe suspected that Edgar had an innate mistrust of any woman who did not conform to his idea of her role in society, Indian or British.

And this was a nonconformist, Joe decided, liking her at once. She was pretty, even beautiful. The first impression of youth and innocence given by the shining blonde hair and widely spaced brown eyes was belied at second glance by the thick straight brows, knowing expression and determined chin. He would have guessed her age as mid-twenties, a year or two younger than himself.

'I've never driven a Rolls,' Joe offered in an effort to distract them from pursuing their show of mutual dislike.

'Have a go on the way back if you like,' said Madeleine easily.

'Thank you, but I'd hate to wrap it round a peepul tree,' said Joe. 'Not had much practice with motor cars. I do rather better with horses.'

'It wouldn't matter much if you crashed it. My father-in-law's got nine more like it back home.' Was there disapproval in her flat American drawl? 'I'll give you lessons if you like. I'm pretty good, you'll find.'

'Madeleine's father was a racing driver,' Edgar explained. 'And he passed on his skills – along with his modesty – to his daughter.'

The disapproval was unmistakable.

While they talked the chauffeur had taken their hand luggage and stowed it away in the car. He was now standing hopefully by the driver's door.

'Oh, go on then, Gopal! You've had enough excitement for one day, I guess! You can drive us back to the palace,' said Madeleine. 'Edgar, you sit in front. I'm going to cosy up with your friend and colleague in the back and tell him about Ranipur.' She grinned at Joe. 'All about Ranipur. The lid off Rajputana! Though I'll have to work hard to counter some of the impressions Edgar's given you, I expect. A woman's-eye view of the principality is never going to be the same as a man's.'

They settled down into the leather upholstery and the sleek car moved off at a sedate pace into the interior.

'Just irritating Edgar,' Joe guessed as Madeleine fell silent, allowing him to register his own impressions of the countryside uninterrupted by commentary. He looked about him eagerly. Desert scenery gave way to orchards and cultivated fields; strips of corn and millet and other crops Joe didn't recognize filed past. Here and there patches of jangal, which Edgar explained meant uncultivated land, intruded into the tame landscape, small thatched villages sheltered under ancient fig trees, plough oxen plodded their desultory way under the relentless sun. In this dry countryside Joe was pleased to notice sleeping tanks of jade green water and here and there a turning water wheel and evidence of irrigation. And everywhere there were people working, the men standing out against the dun background in white dhotis and richly coloured turbans of saffron and magenta.

Their way was blocked for a moment or two in a village by a flock of girls as bright as birds of paradise in their saris of pink and acid green and yellow. Chattering and laughing and, Joe was quite certain, making rude remarks about the white faces in the white car, they moved off the road, heavy copper pots of milk balanced on their heads, backs straight and swinging along with a lithe grace.

Joe was enthralled. 'What beauties!' he remarked.

'Village women,' said Madeleine dismissively. She gave Joe a look full of speculation and amusement and added, 'If it's female beauty you're interested in you'll find a fine sample at the palace. Well, at least, the ones you're allowed to see . . . the respectable ones are still in purdah.'

'I had understood that the ruler wasn't in favour of purdah? It's a Moghul tradition, isn't it? Not Rajput?'

'That's so. The Rajputs adopted it from their conquerors – the Moghuls. It was the fashionable way to live your life. The women got used to it, I guess, and most of them at court would refuse to give it up if you gave them the choice . . . and, to be fair to Udai, I think he has. His first two wives both stay firmly behind the slatted screens of the zenana. They haven't been seen by a man apart from their husband since they were married. And before that – only their brothers. Can you imagine! They spend their whole lives guarded by eunuchs, in the company of other women, most of whom they can't stand, squabbling and intriguing all day long. Their chief topics of conversation are who's been given the most valuable necklace and how many times has the ruler slept with them that month. What a life!' Madeleine shuddered in a showy way. 'I have nothing to do with them. As far as I'm concerned, they're dead. Dead to the world!'

'A very short-sighted and ill-informed view, if I may say so,' drawled Edgar. 'First Her Highness and Second Her Highness are very intelligent women who not only rule the zenana with a rod of iron but manipulate events on the outside as well. First Her Highness, in particular, is very influential. Anyone affecting to be ignorant of that would be foolish indeed.'

Madeleine rolled her eyes and sighed.

'And how do you rate the Third Her Highness as I suppose she's called?' Joe asked hurriedly before Madeleine could snap back a reply.

'The Princess Shubhada?' Madeleine fell silent for a moment, considering her response. 'I hardly know her. We're not exactly bosom pals. I'm American and what I do is flying. She's Indian and what she does is hunting. She was educated in England and hobnobs with the aristocracy and the royal family. You should have seen her showing off when the Prince of Wales visited last winter! "Oh, Eddie darling! Do you remember that soirée at the Buffington-Codswallops in Henley Week? Pogo was so smashed I thought he'd drown when we chucked him in the Thames!"'

Her imitation of upper-class flappers' slang was unnervingly good.

Joe nodded seriously and replied in the same accent. 'What a perfectly ghastly stunt! Poor Pogo! Too many pink gins aboard?'

Madeleine laughed and squeezed his arm. 'You've got it! But you can imagine that we haven't got much in common. Her natural milieu – as she would put it – is the polo field and mine's the flying field. Hurlingham meets Kitty Hawk? Never!'

Their road led onwards and upwards and they caught

occasional glimpses of the little train as it chugged along in their wake.

'What are those hills ahead?' Joe asked.

'Outrunners of the Aravallis,' said Edgar, turning and pointing. 'And the reason for Udai's wealth. Those unimpressive – and if we're being honest we'd say down-right ugly – bleak hills are a gold mine. Well, better than that – they're a precious gems mine. They're full of minerals from onyx up to the finest emeralds. Millions of pounds' worth of gems have found their way into the Ranipur treasure house for generations. The city's up there. It's not at a great height but enough to lower the temperature a few degrees. Now prepare yourself for a surprise when we round the next bend!'

What Joe saw in the distance was the fabulous palace of Ranipur. A cliff of fretted, carved and decorated pink stone seemed to extend for a hundred and fifty yards on either side of a grand central entrance and to rise upwards and backwards in a cascade of balconies and pavilions, of garden, dome and temple and, over all, pencil-slim cypress stood on guard on every hand. At its feet frothed and surged a small town, the houses painted white or pale blue. Joe was enchanted. Without an instruction given, the car drew to a halt and the chauffeur put on the brake.

'A thousand rooms!' declared Edgar. 'Udai says he's been in every one of them but I bet he hasn't.'

'Who lives here?' Joe asked.

'Well, the state rooms are kept for use only on special occasions. Udai has more sense than to live here himself. You'll see the New Palace in a minute. He's got a large family. Aunts, uncles, sons and daughters, his wives if it comes to that. They all have their apartments. Each apartment has its servants and I could go further and say that each servant has his servant. The last time the Ranipur army went into action each fighting man was accompanied by two armed retainers. You need a big house if you're going to accommodate that size of entourage, and pension them and feed them. There must be upwards of three

41

thousand people living within the palace walls, each as careful of his or her dignity as it is possible to be, quarrelling, tale-bearing, eating, stealing I shouldn't wonder, plotting and planning . . . Sounds awful, doesn't it, but really, on the whole, I think they have a pretty good time. But I don't think it would suit me.'

'I don't think it would suit me either,' said Joe.

'Damn sure it doesn't suit me!' said Madeleine with feeling.

Edgar ignored her. 'Doesn't always suit Udai. I'll show you the state apartments tomorrow. In the meantime, the idea of a bath is beginning to appeal to me.' He turned to Madeleine. 'Shall we continue?'

'Sure. But first, prepare yourself for another surprise!' said Madeleine. 'You're about to get a welcome, Texas style!'

She pointed up to the sky above the flat foothills separating them from the town and palace where a small aeroplane appeared to be lazily circling. Catching sight of them, the pilot turned and made towards them at speed. He swooped low and everyone in the car ducked as the plane sheered the dusty air only feet above their heads. Joe squinted into the sun as it passed over to the west behind them. In the two-seater plane the front passenger seat was empty, the clearly silhouetted figure in the rear position raising an arm in salute.

'Who the hell's that?' Joe shouted, startled.

'Best pilot in India or America or anywhere,' said Madeleine with pride. 'That's Captain Stuart Mercer, ex-Escadrille Américaine. My brother.'

'Your brother? What's he doing in Ranipur?'

Madeleine's eyes never left the small Curtiss Jenny as it began a series of stunts. 'Well, I'll never know for sure whether it was me or Stuart that Prithvi fell for!' she said with a smile. 'He met us on an airfield . . . well, it was more of a cow pasture . . . in the States where we were performing. Came backstage at the end of the performance, you might say. We have – we had – a family business. We're barnstormers. Ever heard of the "Airdevils"?'

Joe nodded. So that was what she was – a wing dancer in an aerial circus! Had Sir George got it wrong deliberately? He'd heard of many flying circus acts, even seen some of those that made the trip to Europe. Their suicidally daring exploits left him breathless. The young pilots, many of whom had survived service in the war, had been turned adrift in a dull and unrewarding world which had no appreciation of their talent. What they craved was some way of earning a living using their flying skills and they soon caught on to the entertainment value of those skills. People would pay to see them perform, even pay to go up for a flight themselves. Joe shuddered at the idea. But, inevitably, as the public grew used to the spectacle, they became jaded and pilots had to devise ever more daring stunts to keep their attention. Death drops, flights into the heart of Niagara Falls, leaps from racing car to low flying-plane, even leaps from one plane to another in mid-air, they were all attempted with the aim of making money from their audience. Some of the daredevils got rich but most had trouble raising meal money and some died.

'Planes were going for six hundred dollars when Stuart got back home. No shortage. They were stockpiled all over the States. The military were glad to get rid of them. Spares were no problem either. So he bought a couple and cannibalized one of them to get the plane he wanted and we set up in business. Dad helped with the mechanical side and I soon learned that too – I can fly and maintain an aircraft as well as dance on the wings.' Madeleine spoke with pride and a touch of challenge.

Joe guessed she had probably run into much male criticism for involving herself in such unladylike pursuits. She would hear none from him; he was fascinated. Madeleine Mercer was a very unusual and attractive girl, he acknowledged, and it was no wonder to him that she should have caught and kept the undivided attention of a maharaja's son. He tore his own attention from the smiling, chattering girl at his side and looked up again at the pilot, who was performing a manoeuvre which Joe had never seen before. 'I thought being a policeman was dangerous,' said Joe, 'but it's nothing compared with this!'

'It's dangerous but it's safer than flying the mail routes,' said Madeleine laconically. 'And it beats liquor smuggling over the Mexican border which is what we were doing as a sideline before we left the States.'

Joe smiled. 'Do I gather you and your brother were one step ahead of the law when you skipped off to India?'

'Something like that . . . Some would say, "Captain Mercer, dashing young air-ace with twenty kills chalked up on his fuselage, accepted the job of personal flying coach to his brother-in-law and accompanied him home to Ranipur. The maharaja's second son, international socialite Prithvi Singh, is said to have in his stable a collection of no fewer than ten aeroplanes all of which he is able to fly."' Madeleine was obviously quoting from a society magazine. 'See what he's doing now!'

Joe hardly dared look. The plane was flying over their heads, upside down, the pilot waving a cheery hand. No – two hands.

'Oh, my God!' breathed Joe.

'Now that is dangerous!' Madeleine said with pride. 'These Jennys – you can't trust 'em! The engine cuts out sometimes when they're upside down and then you've got trouble! They were never intended to be stunt planes but Stuart's a fabulous mechanic as well as pilot and he's worked on his planes until they do what he wants when he wants it. Now look at this!'

The plane was spiralling upwards, gaining height. As he climbed, the pilot threw out a shower of shiny tinsel that fell, sparkling against the sun, drifting lazily down over the plain.

'This is the Eastern bit of the welcome,' said Madeleine.

Edgar caught a piece of tinsel and looked at it closely. 'Gold?' he said.

'Of course,' said Madeleine.

'Um . . . how high is he proposing to climb?' asked Joe nervously as the pilot continued his upward spiral, releasing more tinsel as he went.

'Oh, he's barely started,' said Madeleine comfortably. 'Stuart tried for the altitude record a couple of years ago. Just kept on going until he ran out of gas then freewheeled back down. He made over twenty-five thousand feet but he was still a hundred feet off the record. He'll do it one day.'

They watched in silence, mouths open, increasingly tense.

'Okay, Stu, that's good enough . . . We've got the picture,' Joe heard Madeleine mutter.

As though hearing her, the pilot stopped his ascent, levelled out and began an abrupt dive.

'What's he doing now?' said Edgar uneasily.

'He's going into a loop,' said Madeleine. 'Never seen a loop before?'

The plane's nose pulled up and the frail fuselage fought its way upwards, the engine screaming a protest.

It was her gasp that alerted him. At the moment of maximum effort, half-way into the loop, the plane had suddenly stopped rising. Its nose dropped and the plane flattened out. At the same moment, the engine appeared to stop.

'Now why the hell would he do that?' she said to herself. 'That's not in the script!'

To Joe's horror the plane began to drop out of the sky. This was no lazy, calculated, gliding descent.

'He's going to crash!' he blurted out and wished he'd kept silent.

Madeleine's face was anxious but she replied confidently enough. 'Not this plane. Not this pilot. This'll be some new stunt he's been working on for our benefit. He's supposed to scare us! That's what he does! Oh, come on, Stu! Pull out now!'

'But the engine's cut out,' said Edgar. 'How can he pull out? Idiot's leaving it too late!'

Madeleine rounded on him. 'Well, you sure know a lot about planes! These crates can have the whole engine drop off and you can still land them. Done it myself!'

But Joe noticed that she was climbing out of the car and beginning to run towards her brother's plane. In a few strides he had caught up with her and grasped her by the shoulders. 'It won't help to have us cluttering up his landing space!' he shouted. 'Come on, Maddy, let's get back!' But they stayed, frozen together, unable to run in any direction as, inexorably, the plane continued its uncontrolled descent. Joe thought he saw the pilot struggling with the controls a second or two before it crashed on to its belly in the dust about fifty yards ahead of them.

The fuselage fell apart, the wings crumpled in on themselves, the tail section broke off and dropped away, trailing steel cables. The machine Joe had admired dancing like a dragonfly only minutes before was a pile of matchwood.

Edgar lumbered past them. 'God's sake, Joe! Shift your arse, man! He may be alive still! Madeleine – stay back!'

They set off to sprint the short distance to the plane, one thought in both their minds. 'Fuel tank! Can we get him out before it blows?'

Joe reached the plane first. He went straight for the pilot, who was slumped sideways in the open cockpit, blood pouring from him and down the side of the fuselage. Joe grasped him under the armpits and pulled. He was aware that manhandling of this kind was likely to do further damage to a battered and broken body but every pilot he had ever known had had the same fear of being trapped in a burning plane. Any man would rather be hauled away from a wreck at the risk of leaving limbs behind, Joe reasoned, and he gave another desperate tug.

The body moved an inch or two. Good, there were no obstructions in the cockpit. But a splintered wing had come to rest just above the pilot's head and there was no way Joe could complete the manoeuvre. Just as Joe emitted a curse, the wing creaked up into the air and he turned briefly to see Edgar, purple in the face and muscles cracking, heaving the heavy wooden wing out of the way. Joe eased the body out, avoiding loose cables and torn fabric covering, and with Edgar grasping the feet, they scrambled to what they judged to be a safe distance from the wreckage.

'Is he dead?' Edgar asked.

'Hard to know with all this gear on him,' muttered Joe. 'Let's get his helmet and goggles off.' He looked keenly at the young face, dust-covered, blood streaming from his nose and mouth but apparently lifeless.

They were hurled aside by the arrival of Madeleine, screaming her brother's name. Gasping and distraught, she elbowed them out of the way and began with expert fingers to unbuckle the helmet and goggles.

'Gently! Gently!' Joe warned. 'He could have head injuries.'

She threw down the leather gear and stared at the body in silence. Rigid with shock, she sank to her knees, gazing down at the dirty face. Gently she stroked his cheek. Joe watched, aghast, as the eyes fluttered open slightly and he did not imagine that one hand reached out and moved an inch towards Madeleine before flopping back lifeless. Still Madeleine did not move or speak. Joe sensed that, even in these horrific circumstances, there was something off-key about her behaviour. Had she gone into shock? What should he do? He looked at her uncertainly, waiting for a lead.

Finally, Madeleine said one word. 'Prithvi.' Then she threw back her head and howled in grief and rage.

Chapter Five

Her shriek was obliterated by the whoosh of the exploding fuel tank. With a roar that thumped on Joe's eardrums the fabric covering, doped with cellulose, caught fire and went up in a sheet of flame. In seconds it had been consumed, leaving behind a scorched skeleton. So swift had been the conflagration, the spruce ribs, the broken wooden limbs, remained for a moment standing in blackened and stark outline against the sand before they too began to burn. To Joe's consternation, Madeleine started running towards the smoking plane. For an agonizing moment his mind was filled with the image of Rajput women throwing themselves on to their husbands' funeral pyres and he hurled himself after her, catching her by the arm. She turned on him, shouting desperately, 'The tail plane, Joe!' She pointed to the wreck. 'The tail plane! Can you pull it away? It mustn't burn!'

Instant understanding and the surge of outrage it brought with it sent Joe recklessly on towards the plane. Through clouds of black smoke he spotted the tail lying several yards behind the main body and still intact. He tore off his jacket as he ran and using it as protection from the heat and thick fumes he grabbed the nearest section of the tail, already almost too hot to hold, and dragged it away, trailing steel cables with it.

At a safe distance, he straightened, gasping and choking, the super-heated air burning his lungs. He turned to look back at Madeleine. She was standing, a tragic figure, the last remnants of the festive tinsel mingling with black smuts from the burned canvas and swirling down on to her head, a surreal confetti, Joe thought grimly, not for a bride but for a widow.

Madeleine joined him, white-faced and staring but gaining a measure of control. With a supreme effort to keep her voice calm she said, 'Examine this with me, will you, Commander?'

It was the use of his rank which confirmed Joe's suspicions that the scene they had just witnessed was not an accident. He had little experience of aeroplanes but had listened for hours with interest and pleasure to the stories of Squadron Leader Fred Moore-Simpson in the time they spent together as guests of the fort at Gor Khatri on the North-West Frontier, had even gone up with him once or twice, and he remembered his terror when Fred had demonstrated with mischievous relish a stall at five thousand feet over the Khyber Pass.

He thought he knew what to look for. Kneeling in the sand he hauled in the lengths of twisted steel cable that had linked the controls in the cockpit with the elevators. He picked up the two ends, brushed away the sand and looked at them closely.

In a formal tone he replied to Madeleine's request. 'I observe that the control cables are both broken. To the naked eye – and I will need to have a magnification of this, of course, to verify my observation – it appears that several strands of the wire have been cut through. The cut is clean and straight, the section recently severed. Two . . . no, three, strands were left intact. These subsequently snapped, I presume, when placed under the stress of the final manoeuvre – a loop – before the plane crashed. These strands are stretched and ragged at the break point.'

Tight-lipped, Madeleine listened and looked carefully at the cable ends.

'What are the chances of damage like this happening accidentally?' asked Joe.

'Accidentally?' said Madeleine. 'No chance! No chance at all!'

She fixed him with desperate brown eyes, 'Commander, my husband was murdered.'

Left alone at the scene of the crash, Joe looked down at the broken body in speculation. He had sent Edgar and Madeleine off in the Rolls along with the tail section and had settled to wait for help to be sent from the palace. Udai, sick unto death himself, if George had it right, had lost his two oldest sons in the space of a few weeks. Edgar's fears were being realized. Joe had just witnessed the second act of a murderous tragedy and his policeman's mind was asking the usual questions beginning with the glaringly obvious 'Who stands to gain from these deaths?' He tried to remember what Sir George had told him about the other possible heirs to the throne and number three in particular.

With relief, he noticed that a rider was making his way at a gallop from the town. He paused briefly to exchange a word or two with Edgar and Madeleine as he passed the Rolls and then came on down the road. The man approaching rode well but with none of the stiffness of a military man. He was wearing a solar topee, khaki drill jacket and trousers, and his horse was a fine, tall sorrel. Looking about him with a keen eye he dismounted and, leading his horse, came on towards Joe, hand outstretched.

'How do you do? Claude Vyvyan. British Resident at Ranipur.'

Joe extended a blackened hand and tried not to flinch as Vyvyan grasped it firmly. 'Joe Sandilands. Commander, Scotland Yard.'

So formal and ridiculous was the exchange, Joe almost expected Vyvyan's next utterance to be 'I see you've been having a spot of bother?'

What he did say was, 'What a bloody awful mess! Thank

God you were here. Though I'm sorry you ran into this shower of shit.' He batted away a straying strand of tinsel and grimaced apologetically.

Joe smiled and looked with interest at the man who was the power behind or, more probably, beside the throne in Ranipur. Vyvyan moved with an athletic grace unspoiled by the parade ground. In his early thirties, he was as tall as Joe and, as the portly Edgar had not failed enviously to notice, had a slim and elegant figure. Seeing that Joe was bareheaded, Vyvyan swept off his topee and the two men stood for a moment assessing each other. Cold blue eyes, Joe remembered, had featured in Edgar's description. Not cold, he thought, not cold to him at least, but intelligent and penetrating. The nose was commanding; he'd seen its like on a portrait of the young Duke of Wellington. The lips, at the moment slanting in a rueful and discreet smile, were thin but well defined under a neat brown moustache. His hair was well barbered, dark brown and plentiful.

Under the other's gaze, Joe felt suddenly aware of his dishevelled appearance and unconsciously ran a dirt-caked hand through his own thick black hair. Vyvyan smiled again. 'What a welcome to the state! Pity it had to be like this! I've been so looking forward to meeting you, Sandilands.'

'What would I say if I'd just been told this man was my new commanding officer?' Joe asked himself, applying his usual test when meeting someone in authority for the first time, and he decided that he would be reassured, even pleased.

They went to stand on either side of the corpse, each wrapped in his own thoughts. Finally Vyvyan said, 'Two sons in six weeks! Coincidence? I think not. Is there any chance, Commander, that . . .' His voice trailed away.

'Every chance,' said Joe. 'We witnessed the crash and have inspected a key part of the wreckage which luckily was undamaged. I've sent it back to the palace where you can inspect it yourself. Are you familiar with aeroplanes, sir?'

Vyvyan shook his head.

'Well, I haven't much experience but – look, I'll speak plainly: I suspect the plane was sabotaged. Someone meant to kill the pilot.'

'Yes. The pilot,' said Vyvyan slowly. 'But, Sandilands, you should know that it was generally understood that Captain Mercer was to undertake the flight. You should put that in your notebook if you're going to investigate this . . . this . . .' He waved a hand over the body. '. . . occurrence. But I leap ahead. Are you aware of Captain Mercer?'

'I only know what I heard from Madeleine on the way here. Don't assume I've had any briefing or have any professional interest in events past or present in Ranipur, sir,' he lied. 'I'm down here for a tiger hunt.'

'Is that what he told you? Scheming old bastard! George Jardine can smell trouble coming across a continent! There was a time when he would have appeared himself to sort out a crisis like this but now I hear he's found himself a young and active alter ego to do his dirty work while he gets on with running India.' He smiled to lighten the comment and added, 'Am I right? Still, I think I can promise you'll get your tiger hunt.'

A thin crowd of onlookers had begun to leave the road and fields and gather round, staring from a distance at the scene of disaster, chattering volubly and scuffing in the dust to pick up handfuls of gold tinsel. Claude turned to them, gesticulating and shouting in Hindi. 'Get back, you buggers! Nothing to see! Ah, at last! There we are. Reinforcements on their way.'

Several motor vehicles and men on horseback were coming down the road towards them. 'We'll get you back to the palace and then perhaps you can give a formal written witness statement? Not often the investigating officer is invited to do that, I'd guess!'

52

'Is that what I am?' said Joe lugubriously.

'Oh yes. Certainly.' Vyvyan allowed himself a broad smile. 'I'm appointing you.'

Joe looked back with guarded friendship at his new commanding officer.

Chapter Six

The late afternoon sun was slanting down on the sculpted and fretted façade of the Old Palace, creating a complex shadow play on the pink sandstone, an effect which would, in other circumstances, have held Joe's delighted attention as they entered a vast courtyard and paused in front of the ceremonial entrance. Once again he was in the back seat of the Rolls, accompanied this time by Claude who had handed his horse to a syce and joined him. He turned to Joe as they came to a halt.

'This is Govind,' he said as a tall and impressive Indian stepped forward to open the car door. 'He will see you to your suite in the New Palace. Govind will look after you during your stay – he's your khitmutgar, your personal butler cum valet. He is Rajput, of course, and he knows everything there is to know about the palace. He speaks better English than you or I and is very used to European ways; he always accompanies His Highness on his trips to Europe and had his training in a ducal household.' Govind bowed and smiled. He had a luxuriant black moustache and was wearing a spotless white uniform and an impeccable saffron turban. Joe suddenly felt very grubby and weary.

Reading his thoughts, Claude said, 'Bath first, I think? And then your written report if that's not too much of an imposition, then I'll ask you to come down to dinner with a selection of the guests. If you're feeling up to it, of course! His Highness, in view of the dreadful events, will not be joining us, I assume. Not that he ever does dine with his guests – a religious thing. He usually greets them and has a drink but, today . . . who can say? Let's play it by ear, shall we, Sandilands? See you later, then. Oh, and enjoy the plumbing!'

He turned to leave but, casually, over his shoulder, added, 'By the way, we usually wear white tie . . .'

He flashed an unspoken question at Joe who picked it up and replied genially, 'I would expect so. Don't concern yourself, sir. I've just spent a month in Simla. I'm not straight off the beat! I even have a snooker jacket in my luggage,' he confided. 'Black velvet. With frogging! At Sir George's insistence!'

'Good Lord! Bury it!' was Vyvyan's reply.

'I was planning to do just that!'

'But look, Sandilands, we're the same size – anything you want, just mention it to Govind.'

Left alone with Govind, Joe shrugged off his weariness to make contact with his new mentor. He gestured towards the ceremonial gate which led from the courtyard. 'A splendid entrance, indeed!' he said. 'I had heard that Rajputs were tall but this is surely of an extraordinary height?'

Govind smiled. 'Not extraordinary at all, sahib. Rather ordinary you will find for Rajputana. We build our gates to accommodate the elephants which pass through them and, of course, the elephants are surmounted by a howdah.'

'Oh, yes, of course,' said Joe, feeling foolish.

'Guests frequently enquire about the emblem of the sun which you see alongside the gate,' Govind prompted.

Joe's eyes followed his gesture and took in a large golden smiling face which radiated good humour and the literal rays of a sun from what appeared to be a shuttered window let into the palace wall, many feet above the ground. A plaque of some sort?

Seeing his interest, Govind went on, 'The Rajput race is descended from the sun . . . to be precise, from Lava, the elder son of Rama. The people gather here in the courtyard each morning to see the rising sun reflect from the golden face you see above you. Then they know that all is well. The god is with them and remembers his offspring.'

'And if, one day, the sun does not show his face?' said Joe. 'I mean, you do have a monsoon season, don't you?'

He guessed from Govind's slight smile that he was not the first to ask this question.

'When the weather is inclement, sahib, and the sun is not visible, then the ruler himself opens the window and shows his own godlike features to the crowd. They are reassured that the sun in one form or another is always with his people. And now, sahib, if you will follow me . . .?'

Joe followed Govind through a maze of courtyards and corridors, finally crossing a lush green lawn and standing to gaze, shrugging off his fatigue and heat-exhaustion, at the building adjoining the Old Palace. The New Palace, he presumed. New in Victorian times, perhaps. He looked with pleasure at the English country house now confronting him and wondered about the architect. Charles Voysey? Edwin Lutyens? No. He looked again, seeing now a distinctly Eastern element to the design which was a harmonious blend of Eastern and Western style, and a name came to mind. Sir Samuel Swinton Jacob. Surely his was the hand behind this formidable pile?

Govind had stopped, sensing his charge was lagging behind. With an apologetic smile, Joe waved him on and followed him through an imposing entrance and down a marble-floored corridor, along which, unaccountably, a cooler, if not cool, current of air flowed. They crossed an internal courtyard which Joe reasoned was part of the simple but cleverly designed and natural cooling system for the house. The courtyard was full of raucous peacocks and fluttering white doves, its grassed centre green and well watered. Surrounding shrubs echoed the mix of East and West, thoroughly English roses stoutly holding their own against extravagant bougainvillea, cascading in shades of purest white to deep purple. A drowning perfume, intensifying in the early evening air, enchanted Joe. He stopped again and asked what it was. Govind reached up and plucked a flower from a tall shrub and handed it to Joe. The small, bell-shaped flower was cream and white and looked as though it were carved out of wax.

'Frangipani, sahib,' said Govind. 'Delightful, is it not? Though I find it becomes a little overpowering if it is allowed to grow too abundantly.'

Joe's rooms were down a corridor off the courtyard. Govind pushed the door open and showed him inside. Joe took a moment to look about him. The Ritz? The Savoy? As good as either, he thought with satisfaction. An electric fan overhead seemed to be dealing effectively with the residue of the day's heat, the bed, piled high with silken cushions, looked inviting, the furniture was the best that Waring and Gillow had to offer and his trunk was standing at the bottom of the bed. Magically, his travelling bag seemed to have made the trip in safety also.

'My gun case?' he asked, anxiously.

Govind hurried to reassure him. 'It is already in the gun room, sahib, where it is being checked by our Master At Arms to ensure that your gun has been unaffected by the journey.' He pointed to a bell pull and invited Joe to ring when he wanted anything. He led him through an archway to a further room which was laid out as a study with a fine writing desk, two chairs and a low table, illumination supplied by elegant electric lamps. A door off, Govind told him, led to the bathroom. 'Your bath has been drawn, sahib, and awaits you. Please ring when you are ready to summon help with dressing.'

'No need for that, thank you, Govind. I'm accustomed to dressing myself.'

'Many military gentlemen are, I find, sahib.' Smiling and salaaming, Govind left the room.

Joe helped himself to a large glass of mineral water from a silver tray on his bedside table, then he unlaced his boots and kicked them off. He took off his socks and put his feet with a groan of satisfaction on cool marble tiles. He sat down on the bed and gave an experimental bounce or two then, throwing off his jacket and shirt, stretched out and closed his eyes. Probably a foolish thing to do but it had been a long day. A few moments to calm his racing mind before he got into his bath?

A shiver in the air, the slightest sound of a stealthy movement and a sharp metallic click brought him back from the edge of sleep and alerted his swimming senses to the fact that he was not alone in the room. He opened his eyes and looked straight down the black barrel of his own pistol pointing steadily at the space between his eyes.

'Well, aren't you the careless one! If I had a gun like this I wouldn't let it out of my sight!' said an Indian voice speaking in cultured and fast English. The voice was male, young, unbroken. A child?

Breaking free from the hypnotic fascination of the barrel, Joe looked along it to the small brown hand holding it so unwaveringly steady. Beyond that, an impish face looked back at him with scorn. A boy of ten or eleven, Joe guessed, dressed in a white silk buttoned coat, white trousers and a blue and white striped silk turban.

'And you're supposed to be a policeman, they tell me!'

'And what are you supposed to be?' said Joe, annoyed. 'A burglar? The palace dacoit? No, I know what you are – you're one of those thieving monkeys that break into guests' rooms and steal their hairbrushes! Well, you left the window open, monkey!'

Surprised, the boy looked sideways at the window and opened his mouth to make a rude reply, distraction enough for Joe to knock his hand away, grasp his wrist and with a quick heave, flip his slight frame over the bed, grabbing the gun from him as he rolled.

'Get up, monkey, and sit down in that chair!' Joe snapped.

The boy picked himself up, straightened his turban and sat down, eyes fixed on the gun.

'Never point a gun at someone unless you intend to kill him,' said Joe, 'even if, like this one, it is unloaded! And never pause to have a conversation with your victim. It shows you're not serious. Anyone who needs to hold a gun to a feller's head to make him listen is likely to bore his target to death rather than fill him full of lead.'

The boy swallowed, glared at Joe and said haughtily, 'As you are speaking to me at some length, though I would hardly call it a conversation, I assume that you have not been sent to murder me?'

'Sent to murder you?' Joe was stunned. 'Who are you? And, perhaps more important, just what do you take me for?'

'My name is Bahadur Singh. I am the son of Maharaja Udai Singh. The third son,' he said with a pride that could not be concealed even by his obvious terror. 'Bishan is dead and now Prithvi is dead. I am the next son. I think you have been sent to kill me.'

'Why on earth should you think that?' said Joe, putting the gun down on a small table by the door.

'I searched your luggage and found the gun hidden. Who but a hired assassin would hide his gun?'

'Is it a custom of yours to go through guests' things?'

'Yes, of course,' said the boy, puzzled. 'How else can I decide who I am going to like? Shall I tell you,' he said, relaxing now that the gun had been put out of reach, his tone changing to one of confidence, 'what Sir Hector Munro has in his smallest black bag?'

'No!'

'Well, then, what Mr Troop keeps in his shaving kit?'

Joe was ashamed that his second 'No!' was a betraying split second slow.

'And besides,' the boy went on cheerfully, 'you have the face of a killer.'

Joe must have registered dismay at being so described because the boy hurried to add, 'Oh, it's a nice face. A very nice face but you look as though you are accustomed to fighting. Like Yashastilak.'

'Yasha who? Who's that?' Joe felt he was beginning to lose the thread and the initiative in this exchange.

'Yashastilak. My father's favourite fighting elephant. He is old and ugly with many scars but he has won a hundred fights!'

'Well, that's something, I suppose,' said Joe. He grinned, sat down on the bed and put his hands on his knees in an unthreatening posture. 'And you're not far wrong. I was a soldier, Bahadur, in the recent war in Europe. A piece of shrapnel – that's the casing of a shell – sliced through my face . . . here.' He touched the unsightly scar which cut through his eyebrow and skewed the left side of his face. 'And now I have to be careful not to scare the horses but that doesn't make me a killer. I've killed men. But I'm no threat to boys who behave themselves. I'm here, if anything, to protect you. Sir George Jardine sent me and he asks to be remembered to you.'

'Sir George! I have only met him once when he visited my father last year but I know he is my friend,' said Bahadur. 'I wish he would come again. He knows nearly as much about astronomy as I do and he taught me conjuring tricks.'

'Ah, yes,' said Joe drily, 'he does that to us all!'

'And he is very jolly!' Bahadur went on with enthusiasm. 'And full of mischief, my nanny says. He took a pot of treacle and a pot of honey to the top of the palace and poured them both out into the courtyard. He made me stand below and note what happened. The treacle won the race. It fell on to my turban! The purdah ladies in the zenana were watching and laughing. I told them it was a scientific experiment but they thought it was just a bit of fun.'

'No reason why it can't be both,' said Joe.

There was a catch in the boy's voice as the memory of the past faded and the seriousness of his present situation came back to him. 'I think I would feel safer if Sir George were here! You say you are his friend but how am I to know that is true?'

'Sensible of you to ask the question,' Joe remarked. 'Look, I've got something in my bag for you. George sent it and he's signed his name in the front.' He unbuckled his bag and produced a book. *One Thousand and One Cunning Card Tricks for Clever Boys*, was its whimsical title.

It seemed to work its magic as Bahadur's next question was, 'If it's not you, then is it Edgar Troop who's going to kill me?'

Joe could only guess at the depths of insecurity, the loneliness and the fear behind the question, and his sympathy and his heart went out to the boy. Soon he would be fatherless – did he know that? – and he would be surrounded by people out to manipulate him, perhaps even get rid of him. What reassurance could Joe give – a stranger in the palace? A ferret being thrust down an unexplored rat-hole where any menace might lurk? The next Heatstroke Express might be ferrying a hired gun to the palace, though he might well be already in place. And, Joe supposed, there was no lack of home-grown talent who might oblige.

'Not Edgar,' he said. 'No, not Edgar. He works for Sir George too. We're both here to help you and to find out what happened to your brothers. I've no idea yet what's going on here in Ranipur but there is something wrong. You seem to have the run of the palace,' he added speculatively. 'Help me to find out what's happening as far as you can – without putting yourself into danger, that is. Breaking into strangers' rooms and sticking a gun in their face is a good way to get yourself killed!'

He was struck by a worrying thought. 'Bahadur, tell me, whereabouts do you live in the palace? Have you got, er, safe living quarters?'

The boy shook his head. 'This is a problem for me. I will tell you that there is nowhere that is safe. I have been living, as do all young boys of the princely family, in the zenana but I do not like it and I have left that place. My mother has her own apartment there but it is very crowded. The maharanees also have their apartments in the zenana. Their sons sit higher on the carpet than I do and they despise me. When Bishan died his mother, First Her Highness, was heard to say that it was unfair that her son, the rightful heir, the Maharaj Kumar, had died when "that little low-born, crawling insect" was still alive. She was speaking of me. And now Second Her Highness will say the same thing. Their Highnesses are not friendly with each other in normal times but I think that now they have both lost sons their hatred will combine and fix on me. They will do whatever is in their power to keep me from sitting on the gaddi.'

'Gaddi?'

'You would say throne. The ceremonial cushion the ruler sits on.'

'But would ladies of their station – maharanees both – stoop to kill a child?'

Bahadur gave him an astonished look. 'Oh, yes. They have tried to have my mother killed many times. But my mother is clever and well served by the palace servants who always bring warning. She is called Lal Bai. They hate her because she is a village girl and speaks only her village tongue but mainly they hate her because my father has always spent much time with her.' Bahadur looked doubtful for a moment. 'Until Third Her Highness came to live here. That was a year ago and my mother and I have seen very little of my father since then.'

'So, where have you found a billet? Where do you sleep?'

'I sleep anywhere and everywhere. Never in the same place twice.'

He paused and looked at Joe, wondering how far to trust him. Joe arranged the features of his killer's face into what he hoped was a reassuring and receptive expression and waited.

'There are people watching me. Everywhere I go I feel I am being followed. I hear footsteps behind me in the corridors and when I turn, there is no one there. Figures I have noticed ahead of me disappear. In the night, I hear noises I don't understand. Govind finds me places. There are many rooms only he knows about. Sometimes I sleep in the elephant pens. They keep watch over me. There are ninety-five elephants and I know every one of them. They know me.'

'So, that's Govind and the elephants. Anyone else you can rely on?'

'Yes. There is a forester, an old man who has always cared for me. And I like the airman, Captain Mercer. He is very friendly and says one day he will teach me to fly. He lets me stay in the hangar whenever I like and he never gives me away. But my best friend in the palace is a good man who is staying with my father. A tiger hunter. He has taught me all his skills. His name is Colin O'Connor. I go out into the jangal with him as often as he will take me.'

'Mmm . . . Doesn't sound all that secure to me, roving round the jungle with a tiger hunter,' said Joe. 'You mentioned a nanny, I think? Is she still in employ at the palace?'

Bahadur's face softened. 'Yes, she is here. She is a Scottish lady, Miss Macarthur, and she is very fierce. She would fight for me with the courage of a tigress but she is a woman and she could not keep off an assassin with a parasol, could she?'

'Where are her quarters?'

'In the Old Palace. I will take you to see her tomorrow. She will be pleased to meet a friend of Sir George.'

'Another elderly conquest!' thought Joe, grudgingly. 'The umpteenth member of the Sir George Appreciation Society.'

'I'd like to see you again tomorrow, Bahadur. In fact it would put my mind at rest if I had you in my sights as much as possible every day. Stick as close by me as you can. If anyone asks why, tell them you're teaching me astronomy. Now, look, I've got to write up a report for

63

Vyvyan, bathe, dress and get myself down to dinner. Better get a move on!'

Bahadur looked at his wristwatch. Joe blinked in admiration. It was a diamond-encrusted Cartier watch and though Joe would never have remarked on another man's possessions, the look of boyish pride as Bahadur consulted it prompted him to make the anticipated admiring comment. Bahadur smiled in glee, his first genuine smile, and instantly he slipped the watch off his wrist and handed it to Joe. 'I'm so glad you like it. It was given to me by a jewel salesman from London who visited last year. My father was much impressed by the man's generosity to his son and placed a large order with him. Now I give it to you. Please take it.'

Joe's embarrassed protests were brushed aside. 'But this is our custom,' the boy said firmly. 'If a guest admires any of our possessions, we are proud to give them to him. You are a warrior like the Rajputs, I see this, so I know you must understand. Would you not want to give me something of yours if I truly admired it?'

'Well, yes, of course,' said Joe automatically, taken in by the boy's expression of earnest innocence and honour.

Too late he realized that he had been trapped. Bahadur placed the watch ceremoniously in the centre of the dressing table, turned to Joe and said, 'Well now, I really must be going. I'll return tomorrow and we'll continue our conversation, sir.'

Joe held his breath as the boy made his way to the door. Was he going to get away with it? Reaching the table by the door, Bahadur caught sight of the Browning M and raised his hands in an actor's gesture of surprise and recognition. He picked it up. It slid into his grasp with familiar ease, the scale appropriate to his small hand. 'Keep this safe, Mr Sandilands. I would be most distressed if you were to lose it because it is the most beautiful, the most comforting gun I have ever handled. Just to have such a gun as this – though unloaded, as you say – tucked into my belt, would make me feel more secure.'

He sighed.

Joe knew he'd been tricked but he recognized that the crushing fear the boy was living under was genuine, the threat real, his plea heartfelt.

He took a deep breath. He heard his own voice saying with what he thought might just be the formality and pride appropriate to a Rajput warrior, 'I would be honoured, Bahadur, if you would keep the gun.'

They smiled at each other in complete understanding and Bahadur and his Browning disappeared as suddenly as they had arrived.

Soaking in his bath, Joe was torn between rage and amusement. He was angry to have lost his gun though luckily he had had the forethought to pack his old service revolver along with ammunition. Ammunition! A sudden cold thought sent him dripping, naked, from the bath to his trunk. He tried to recollect the weight of the little gun in his hand when he had wrested it from Bahadur and could not. Cursing his carelessness, he dug around and, with a sigh of relief, found the spare clips for the Browning still where he'd placed them, wrapped up in a waistcoat.

He counted them. There was one missing.

Chapter Seven

Joe groaned. A nervous twelve-year-old was loose about the palace armed with the police commander's own gun. Not unloaded as he had thought but with eight lethal bullets up the spout. Joe imagined Sir George's comments if he ever found out. Suppose the lad went straight back to the zenana with his new toy to exact retribution from the maharanees for the attempts on his mother's life? Like a fox in a hen-coop he'd be able to kill at will.

Joe tried to put these horrifying but fanciful ideas out of his mind. There had been something about the boy that had earned his confidence. He didn't doubt his courage and he'd been impressed by his cleverness and quick thinking. Perhaps Bahadur had presented him with a true bill – he genuinely wanted to keep the gun as personal protection. Well, so be it. He reasoned that Bahadur could trust no one; he could be in genuine danger of death from an unknown quarter and, ultimately, his only defence might well be the Browning. And then, though heaven forbid, he'd be damned glad he'd given it to him. He told himself to relax and finish dressing. He had left himself only an hour in which to complete his report for Claude.

Feeling rather foolish sitting at his desk in evening gear and the promised white tie, all pressed at a moment's notice by the palace staff, Joe found supplies of writing paper and an excellent fountain pen, already loaded with black ink, and set to work. The words flowed easily, no detail was missed and he was happy with his account. He folded it in two, slipped it into his pocket and, after a guilty look at the Cartier watch, he tucked that into his other pocket, not knowing what else to do with it and acknowledging that the security of his room was non-existent. He pulled the bell and waited for his escort to the dining room. He had left a perfect ten minutes to spare.

While he waited he went to stand in front of the cheval glass to make a last check on his appearance. The evening suit, tailored for him in Calcutta, fitted well, the narrow, waist-long jacket flattered his slim figure and long legs. His spanking white shirt and tie emphasized a face darkened by almost a year of living an outdoor life in the sun. 'More of this and I'll be able to pass for a native,' he thought, tugging at his tie. 'But not, perhaps, with these eyes.' Light grey was not an Indian colour. 'Huh! Fighting elephant, indeed!'

He was confused to find himself wondering briefly what Madeleine would make of him with all the layers of dust and perspiration washed away and reminded himself guiltily that she would, of course, not be expected in any society to come down to dinner mere hours after her husband's death.

The reassuring figure of Govind appeared in the mirror behind him. 'The waistcoat, Govind,' said Joe. 'Not too fancy, I hope? What do you think?'

Govind considered for a moment. 'Everything is perfect, sahib. Exactly what is required. Handkerchief perhaps?'

They set off, retracing their earlier steps back to the Old Palace. 'The reception will be in the durbar room tonight,' said Govind. His voice took on a hushed and serious tone. 'The palace – the state – is in mourning for the young prince and this will continue for twelve days. You arrive at an unfortunate time, sahib.'

'You must tell me how I may best avoid getting in the way,' said Joe with concern. 'Mark my card, Govind, and don't let me crash about insensitively annoying people.'

'I think the sahib has the sensitivity of an elephant.' Govind smiled and gently nodded.

For a moment Joe was startled then he remembered that for these warriors who lived, worked and sometimes fought alongside elephants the animal was revered for its intelligence and discretion. He returned the nod, recognizing the compliment.

'The funeral ceremony will take place tomorrow afternoon at the samshan – the cremation ground – by the river. You and your fellow guests will not be involved. The palace has many distractions to put before you while we are occupied with our religious rites.'

'I see,' said Joe doubtfully. A situation already socially delicate now promised to be impossible. 'Are there areas of the palace and town I should perhaps avoid?'

'Yes, sahib. The mourning rituals will be performed in the women's quarters where the ruler has gone to join the maharanee, the mother of his son. The zenana will be the scene of much wailing and crying out. The women will be breaking their bangles in grief over the body of the Yuvaraj and garlanding him with flowers. This afternoon's events are most distressing but His Highness will be present to greet you and share a drink, although he is very tired and very busy as you can imagine he would be and he will not stay long. You will be able to become acquainted with the other guests, however, and enjoy an excellent meal. His Highness is concerned that you should all have a pleasant and most sociable evening.'

Joe smiled his appreciation of this piece of considerate attention. It was a sensible arrangement; he would have organized things in just the same way.

He approached the door of the durbar hall with keen anticipation. He was a sociable man and enjoyed conversation. But, above all, he was desperately hungry and hoped that the drinks party wouldn't drag on for too long. It seemed a very long time since he'd shared a railway curry with Edgar at Umballa.

Vyvyan was waiting for him at the entrance to the durbar

hall. He ran an approving eye over Joe, followed immediately by an enquiring lift of an eyebrow.

'I have it,' said Joe in answer. He produced his report and handed it over.

'Good man!' said Claude. Without giving the document a glance, he passed it to an aide who slid it into a file and moved away.

'Most of the guests are already here so you've timed it well, and the ruler himself is eager to meet you. Shall we go in?'

Joe followed him through the pair of heavy sandalwood doors, lined with ivory and held open by two servants, and he stood for a moment, stunned by the glittering scene before him.

'Like stepping into a Dulac illustration from *The Arabian Nights*, I always think,' whispered Claude, entertained by Joe's reaction.

The large meeting room was long and low and not a square inch of surface, it seemed, was without rich decoration. Fluted pillars, encrusted with coloured stones in a complex floral design, held up a ceiling shining with mica and gold leaf. The long walls were pierced by arched doorways and the intervals between were covered in expanses of mirror glass. Even the floor shone and Joe, coming out of his trance and moving forward, set a careful foot down, mindful that his evening shoes were new, the leather soles still slippery, and was grateful to reach a thick amber carpet in the centre of the room. Two crystal chandeliers, Lalique, he guessed, and ranks of white candles set on low tables in the corners of the room provided the lighting; flickering flames reflected off a thousand shining surfaces.

In contrast to the brilliant setting, the guests were a sombre group in black and white. Soberly clad in deference to the recently bereaved, they had gathered at the far end of the room. At Joe's entrance all stopped talking and turned to look at him. One of the men, wearing evening dress improbably topped off with a white silk turban in which winked a diamond aiguilette, came forward to greet him. He was leaning heavily on an ebony stick and, although a tall and well-made man, was obviously not in good health. His features could have been carved from aged ivory, the skin drawn tight over bones almost visible beneath diminished flesh. His dark eyes, however, remained full of life and were taking in his guest's appearance as he approached.

Claude, at Joe's elbow, hurried to make the introduction. 'Your Highness, may I present Commander Joseph Sandilands?'

Maharaja Udai Singh smiled and nodded but, Joe noticed, did not go in for hand-shaking.

'We are delighted, Commander, that you can be with us at such a difficult time. I understand that you have offered your valuable services and expertise to look into my son's death which you were so unfortunate as to witness this afternoon.'

Joe found Indian voices attractive and musical but, even by Indian standards, this voice was remarkable. It was deep and liquid but the formal phrases were lifeless – formulae concealing despair and pain. His speech had the quality of the heart-rending adagio of a cello concerto Joe had heard at the Queen's Hall the year after the war's end. Edward Elgar's, he remembered, and the composer himself had conducted. Joe had listened, tears in his eyes, as the music spoke to him of loss, regret and devastation. Udai Singh's voice resonated with the same emotions.

Joe bowed. 'It will be an honour, Your Highness, though a most unwelcome task,' he replied with equal formality.

'It is my wish that the cloud of grief which hangs over the palace should not be burdensome for our guests. You are not of our religion, tribe or culture and will play no part in our mourning. I am conscious that, as bereaved father, my attentions will be elsewhere for the coming days but you are my guests and will not be neglected. The palace is large and can accommodate both the sorrow we are feeling and the pleasure you may have been anticipating.'

Then, with a change of key, 'Let that be our last mention of today's events. Come and meet your fellow guests who ought to be able to put a few distractions your way during your stay. I cannot introduce you to your hostess because my wife, Shubhada, has yet to arrive. Are you married, Sandilands?' He smiled enquiringly at Joe. 'No? Well, a word of warning for when you are – for every pair of earrings you give her, she will hesitate a further ten minutes when dressing. So, the next senior lady . . . Mrs Vyvyan! Lois!'

He addressed an Englishwoman who had detached herself from the group and was looking attentively in their direction.

Well, this was a surprise! Joe had not realized that Vyvyan was married but, shaking Mrs Vyvyan's gloved hand, he decided she would have been easy to pick out as his consort in spite of the difference in their ages. Unusually, Lois Vyvyan appeared to be a year or two older than her husband. She was wearing a long black dress, a silken shawl covering her shoulders, and round her throat was a double row of pearls. Her skin was milky white and her dark auburn hair was swept up behind her ears in a twisted knot. Spare, elegant, proper, was Joe's first impression, and very English. He was surprised, therefore, when she leaned confidentially towards him and he caught a scent of something oriental and seductive on her warm neck. Shalimar? He thought so.

'Commander, we are all so delighted you could come,' she said in an attractive voice which managed somehow to give an impression of cool distance. 'Your reputation goes before you and we will all expect to be entertained by stories of your exploits on the North-West Frontier to say nothing of Whitechapel. I've never met a detective before. Do you drink pink champagne?'

With an effort Joe stopped himself from looking down to check that he'd wiped his police issue boots on the scullery mat. He thought of replying that a jar of ale would slip down a treat if it was all the same to 'er Ladyship but controlled himself. Smiling his most devastating smile he accepted a glass of champagne from a footman and looked at it critically. 'In the absence of Krug '15 a glass of pink fizz will be most welcome,' he said easily and instantly regretted his pettiness. To his embarrassment, Udai Singh had overheard his set-down but, to his relief, a thin amused smile appeared on the lips of the ruler. 'My preference also,' he said. 'I'm sure our cellar can supply?' Without a further word, the attendant moved away, Joe was sure, to pass the unspoken instruction down the line.

'As for Lois, this is a new experience for me also,' Udai went on smoothly. 'I don't believe there's any such thing as a detective in India. Though I understand there is a police force in Bengal and some of the other British Indian states. Perhaps during your stay with us you will encourage us to look into the possibility of establishing such a force? You must meet the captain of my guard. We have what you would probably consider a rather rudimentary squad which keeps the peace in Ranipur. I'm sure Major Ajit Singh will be intrigued to learn the Western arts of anthropometry and fingerprinting.'

'Western? I understand, Your Highness, that fingerprinting originated in India. And, indeed, it has been practised by the Bengal Police – along with a system of anthropometry adapted from the Bertillon method – for the last thirty years. They were fingerprinting and recording criminals in Bengal two years before Scotland Yard got around to it, sir.'

The maharaja smiled. 'You will have to work hard to convince Major Ajit Singh that there is anything to be gained by keeping an imprint of a thief's left thumb on a card in a filing system, locked away in an office, Commander. If Ajit knows a man to be guilty, that man will lose his fingerprints down to his wrist. The problems of identification, punishment and crime prevention will be solved . . .' He paused and added slyly, '. . . at a stroke.'

Joe knew when he was being baited and smiled politely.

'I suppose, Commander, you're a blend of wise man, soldier and executioner?'

'Not the last, I hope, sir!'

'But a man of action, I hear. Edgar speaks highly of you. Ah, now here's another man of action – Colin O'Connor, tiger hunter, naturalist, my oldest friend. And Edgar's mentor. Did you know that? Colin taught him all that he knows – about hunting, that is! Colin! Come and meet a policeman! I'll leave you for a moment – I must greet Sir Hector who, I see, has just come in.'

Colin O'Connor, a gaunt middle-aged man, took Joe's hand in a sinewy grip. His evening suit was a good one but much worn and faded. His lined face was deeply tanned, his brown eyes under bushy grey brows were searching and humorous. 'How do you do, Sandilands? I understand you're to be my next pupil?'

'What has Edgar been telling you?' said Joe. 'No, really, I must ask you to disregard anything he has said. I have no ambition to kill a tiger though I would very much like to see some. A day's stalking, perhaps?'

Colin O'Connor laughed. 'This is not red deer country, Sandilands! In the forest, the tiger stalks *you*. But I'm glad to hear what you say. I am, in fact, a reformed tiger hunter. It's a wonderful creature, Sandilands, perhaps the handsomest God designed, but the numbers are so reduced that I fear that by the end of the century there'll be none remaining. I hunt them, these days, with a camera, not a rifle.'

'That must be dangerous?' said Joe. 'I don't know much about photography but I do know that you have to approach within feet of your subject.'

'Yes, you have to get close to the beasts and a tigress with cubs, for instance, is likely to object to my presence – if she can detect me, that is!'

'But you're here to kill a tiger, are you not? A renegade, I hear.'

'Yes. A service I still perform when called on. These days I shoot only for the pot or to kill man-eaters, be they tiger or leopard. So, if the idea of pitting your wits against a creature that's eaten over a hundred villagers, some of them children, appeals to you, join us on the hunt.'

'In the circumstances, I'd be delighted,' said Joe. 'But won't it have to be put off until the mourning period is over? I mean, it will involve local organization and supplies, local men. And wouldn't a tiger hunt be regarded as a bit frivolous at a time like this?'

'Normally yes,' said Colin, 'but I've spoken to the ruler and he was firm about it. "My son has died," he said. "Is that a reason to stand by and allow more sons and daughters of my people to be killed each day we leave the tiger alive?" No, he's quite right, of course. Three or four dying every day in the northern villages. Everyone's too terrified to leave their home and there's work to be done in the fields, animals to graze. The hunt has to go ahead and as soon as it can be managed.

'It's usual for the population to be confined to the town for the mourning, gates closed and so on, but the ruler's given dispensation to all involved to carry on as normal. You'll find that's typical of Udai. Known him for years and I can tell you, under all that flim-flam and the layer of Western sophistication, the real force that drives him is concern for his people. You'll hear them calling him "Bappa". It means "father" and he takes the title seriously.'

Joe caught sight of Edgar on the fringes of the group, watching his exchange with O'Connor. Edgar ran a finger round his collar which, like the rest of his outfit, was straining at the seams and nodded in Joe's direction. His face was gleaming with sweat and he was clearly in some discomfort. The reason for his discomfort appeared to be a small woman who had backed him into a corner and seemed to be lecturing him.

Colin O'Connor followed Joe's glance and laughed. 'Shall we go and rescue poor Edgar?' he said.

'Who's he talking to?' asked Joe, curious.

'He is being talked to by Lizzie Macarthur,' said O'Connor.

'Miss Macarthur? You mean Bahadur's nanny?'

'Yes. I see you've been doing a bit of scouting around already? Beating the thickets of the palace jungle? Beware, Sandilands! Who knows what strange birds you may put up! Lizzie's a royal nanny, cousin of the last Viceroy but one, I think. She'll have been invited this evening to make the numbers a little more even, I shouldn't wonder. We're to sit down to dinner six gentlemen and four ladies. I bet the Vyvyans have been doing a bit of pencil-chewing trying to do the seating arrangements! Keeping separate the sexes, the married couples, the siblings and the people at each other's throats – that doesn't give you much leeway!'

'Invited just to make up the numbers?' said Joe. 'Hardly fair treatment?'

'She's not normally called on for the usual-sized dos, which can be anything up to a hundred people, but with a small gathering like this she's expected to help out. But don't waste your sympathy on Lizzie! Come and meet her.'

They made their way across the room to the ill-matched couple. Lizzie Macarthur was short and slight and somewhere in that indeterminate period approaching middle age. Thick brown hair cut short with an abundant fringe framed a pink and angry face. She was wearing a demure, old-fashioned dress which might have been dark blue or dark green or even faded black.

She turned to Joe without waiting for an introduction. 'Commander Sandilands, am I to understand you have some influence with this gentleman?' she said in tones which left no one in doubt that she considered Edgar anything but a gentleman.

'Good Lord, no! If you're having a problem with Edgar your only recourse would be Sir George Jardine who is known to have occasionally brought the rogue to heel!'

Joe noted that a corner of Miss Macarthur's mouth twitched in a not unfriendly way. 'Sir George sends his regards and asks to be remembered to you,' he lied, seeing his advantage and following it up. 'Now, Edgar, what on earth have you been saying to offend Miss Macarthur? Let me guess! She's had to correct your view that Robert Burns is possibly not the most wonderful poet in the world?'

'I can assure you our disagreements are on more weighty matters! Your friend has just been telling me that he opposes the idea of education for girls.'

'Ah . . .' said Joe, shaking his head reprovingly. He refused to be drawn into a serious discussion at a dinner party. 'Then let me reassure you, Miss Macarthur. Edgar is an opponent of education for girls and for boys alike and is himself a walking example of his policy.'

'Levity,' said Miss Macarthur frostily, 'is the last thing I would have hoped to hear spicing the conversation of a man whom I understand to be a fellow Scot, a war hero and at the spearhead of his profession.'

'Oh, I don't know,' said Joe easily. 'It helps to lighten the burden of those three dubious attributes.' He hurried on, 'But what an interesting necklace you're wearing, Miss Macarthur! Am I mistaken or are those golden stones cairngorms from the Grampian mountains? They were a favourite of my mother's. How good it is to see a bit of home in these outlandish parts – a bracing contrast with the diamonds and pearls on view at every hand.'

Miss Macarthur made a sound that might have been 'Pish!' or even 'Tush!' and added, 'A pupil of Sir George's, I see. Lesson One in the Seduction Handbook? "Oily charm and how to apply it"? But stick at it, Commander! I think you have potential.'

'Humph!' said Edgar, glad to find himself no longer her target. '"All the charm of all the Muses," that's what he's got,' he muttered.

'And, Mr Troop, I would not be standing here appreciating your quotation from Tennyson had I not myself, although a female, been properly educated!'

Joe was beginning to enjoy the sparring but his attention was attracted – everyone's attention was attracted – by a figure making an appearance at the door, though 'making an entrance' was the phrase which came first to Joe's mind.

There was something theatrical in the way the young woman paused, exactly framed in the doorway.

The prince went to greet her. 'Shubhada, my dear, come and meet our guests.'

She walked with all the grace he would have expected, shimmering in black silk down to her ankles. Her gleaming dark hair was cut in a shoulder-length bob and at her throat was a single enormous diamond on a silver chain. More diamonds sparkled in her ears. The prince led his third wife off to speak to the physician, Sir Hector Munro, and Joe settled to wait his turn to meet this beauty.

The doors opened again and Madeleine Mercer came in, escorted by a handsome young man Joe took to be her brother, so alike were they. He had hardly expected the grieving widow to make an appearance, and certainly not an appearance with quite this éclat, he thought. He was not alone in this expectation apparently; a collective gasp went up from the gathering, a gasp which was instantly suppressed and disguised by an intensification of the cocktail party chatter. The fair Madeleine had chosen to wear a white satin slip of a dress with white gloves. There could not have been a greater contrast between the two young women.

Lizzie Macarthur picked this up at once. 'White swan, black swan,' she whispered to Joe. 'Odette, Odile? Do you think they planned it? Almost looks as though it was choreographed! Now then, Commander, I see I must lose you to the prima ballerinas – which one will you meet first, black or white?'

'I don't think we have a choice,' said Joe. 'Here's Madeleine advancing on us. We have met, by the way.'

'Joe! Good to see you again!' she said, taking his arm in a proprietorial way – or was she clinging to a rock in a strange and threatening sea? Joe squeezed her arm comfortingly, stricken to see that under a carelessly applied layer of make-up she was pale and the black from her lashes had been smudged by tears. Her eyes glanced here and there amongst the company in a nervous rhythm but her voice remained confident and just a shade too loud. 'Hi, there, Lizzie.'

'Madeleine, my dear, do you think this is wise?' asked Lizzie Macarthur, concern in her voice. 'You don't have to be here, you know. No one was expecting you to come. Wouldn't you rather be by yourself for a bit? I'll take you to your bungalow if you like . . . or you could stay with me for the night. I'll sit with you if that would help?'

'You're a peach, Lizzie!' said Madeleine. 'But I can't stay by myself. I'd . . . I'd . . . just fall apart. I feel . . . safer . . . with people around me. Heaven knows, I don't enjoy cocktail parties but it beats shaving my head and wailing which is what I think I'm expected to be doing right now.'

She gave a tremulous smile, put up her chin and said in a firmer tone, 'Joe, I want you to meet my brother Stuart. This isn't the time or the place but he needs to speak to you.'

'Stuart! I'm pleased to meet you.'

Stuart Mercer was as good-looking as his sister with the same colouring. His fair hair gleamed with a suspicion of brilliantine. Smiling was an obvious strain and his handsome square face was stiff with tension but Joe caught for a second a slanting flash of even white teeth and a passing warmth in the hard brown eyes.

'Thanks, Joe,' he said without preamble. 'Thanks for being with Maddy. For doing what you did.'

'Haven't even started yet,' said Joe. 'Bad business and I'd like to hear what you have to tell me tomorrow. We'll fix a time. How about nine?'

'Sounds good to me. Nine then.'

Madeleine, holding his arm with an increasing grip, was anxious to break into this chaps' clipped conversation. 'Aren't you going to say something about my dress?' she hissed.

'You look delightful, Maddy! Dazzling, even,' said Joe smoothly, pleased to have an excuse to run his eyes over her.

'Joe, that's the whole point,' said Lizzie Macarthur impatiently. 'Don't you see what she's getting at? She's afraid that you think her choice is rather a faux pas, bearing in mind the sad events of the day. And so it is! Is that not right, Maddy?'

'Too right!' Madeleine exploded. 'And it's not my fault! I got a note just as the dressing bell rang saying that if I was planning to make an appearance it would be appropriate if I chose to wear something white this evening because white is the Indian colour of mourning. Friendly hint from my wonderful, thoughtful stepmother-in-law!'

Joe took a second to work this out. 'Third Her Highness landed you right in it!'

'I'll say! Then she comes swanning in wearing black like all the other British, making me look like a vaudeville act!'

'At least you had the good sense not to wear the red nose,' said Joe consolingly.

'Don't worry, Madeleine,' said Lizzie. 'I'll make sure that people understand.'

Madeleine smiled her thanks but remained unplacated. 'Have you met her yet, Joe?'

'No, not yet.'

'I think you should put that right. She'll think you rude if you delay any longer, particularly chatting to me. Lizzie can take you – she's over there with the doc.'

Shubhada was standing at the other end of the room in conversation with Sir Hector, her eyes flicking restlessly round the other guests. On seeing Joe approach she took from her bag a holder and a cigarette, and, at a word, Sir Hector ambled off to find the means of lighting it. She turned to Joe with a smile of welcome and Lizzie made them known to each other. Joe produced a lighter from his pocket and lit the cigarette she fixed into the black jade holder. He was amused to see that she didn't seem to smoke with any great enthusiasm or skill and judged that this piece of sophistication was being demonstrated for his benefit.

They exchanged a few pleasantries and he confided what had been his first impressions of the palace.

'You must get to know the surroundings also,' advised Shubhada. 'The grounds are quite delightful and stretch for miles.'

Her voice was low and would have been thrilling had not Joe caught an edge of condescension in her manner. Well, what else could a policeman expect from a maharanee? He'd heard much the same tone in Queen Mary's polite conversation – 'So, you're going to India, young man?'

'I should value your opinion on my husband's polo arrangements,' Shubhada went on. 'I hear you are an expert horseman and assume you play? We must arrange a game for you. If you will come down to the polo ground tomorrow morning I will present you with a little problem but I fear I will embarrass you because I will ask you to take sides.'

'Take sides?'

'Yes. You must come out either for me or for my husband since we are in the middle of a disagreement.' Her easy smile told him that this was not serious. 'Udai is planning to turn the polo ground into a golf course!' She affected a shocked tone. 'Hard to believe, I know, but he is seriously suggesting this. Golf is all the rage in England and he became quite skilled at it when he was last there. And, of course, the polo ground is extensive and of adequate size for a wretched golf course. You must help us decide what to do, Commander.'

This was party chatter. Joe knew she was not particularly interested in hearing his reply, she was just giving him an impression of her character, her position and her special influence with the ruler in the few minutes that were allocated to each guest at such a gathering. She could have summed it up in seconds, he thought: sophisticated, powerful, spoiled. Something needled him into refusing to turn this into a pas de deux.

'I can solve your problem and save your marriage in a word, Your Highness,' he said with a confident smile.

'Oh, indeed?'

'Golo!'

'I beg your pardon . . . I don't understand . . .'

'That was the word. As you say, the extent of the field required is the same for both sports. Both are played with a club. Run them together! Gentlemen (or ladies) must play golf on horseback. You can call the new game "golo". Invent a pair of trousers to play it in . . . let's call them, er, "ranipurs"! Why not? And there you are – we have the new jodhpurs! The sport will be all the go on three continents in no time at all.'

Shubhada stared at him with incomprehension. She began to edge away from him, making distancing movements and finally saying, 'I see my husband is about to leave. He is quickly fatigued. Excuse me if I go to him, Commander.'

When she was out of earshot Lizzie snorted. 'Scored an own golo there, I'd say, Sandilands! She rather hates you because you didn't take her seriously. Now why didn't you play along? Anyone would think you'd taken against 3HH?'

'I'll tell you something, Lizzie,' said Joe confidentially. 'Anyone would be right! Oh, dear! I'm not sure Sir George's training has quite taken yet. Under all this southern English slather there's a bolshie borderer lurking still.'

'I'm very relieved to hear it!' said Lizzie. 'Look around you carefully, Joe. Look at the cast of characters around the maharaja. He's dying . . . I suppose you know that . . . and his death will change everything. People will find their positions, their lives even, changed overnight. And perhaps someone is taking hold of events before the event. There's a lot at stake, Joe.'

81

'And much depends on the succession. Has Udai Singh made a statement on his decision? Dropped a hint?'

'Nothing. Not a word. And, you know, that's very odd . . . it's almost as though he's waiting on events himself. Waiting for something anyway.'

Chapter Eight

Their hissed conversation was interrupted by the arrival at their side of Sir Hector solemnly bearing a candle in a golden cup. 'I say, wasn't Her Highness waiting for a light?' he said. 'Had to go about her hostess's duties, I suppose. Young girl like that shouldn't be smoking anyway . . . ruin her throat . . . It's Sandilands, isn't it? The detective? Look. I'd rather like to talk to you. Professional matters . . . sure you understand . . . Tomorrow morning be all right?'

Joe smiled. 'Sir Hector, I'll be delighted to put you on my list!'

The moment had arrived for Claude to cough discreetly and gather the attention of the six men and four ladies who made up the dinner party. The maharaja's retirement to the zenana had left him to play host and Third Her Highness, now returned to the company, stood by as Claude paired the guests off and asked them to follow him through to the dining room.

The party moved through into a smaller but equally brilliant room where a massive crystal table had been laid for ten in the European style. The room was of double height and lit by candles and oil lamps and, overhead, an electric chandelier from the hand of the same designer struck glints from silver cutlery and delicate glasses. In the high ceiling, fans swished rhythmically, keeping the atmosphere, if not cool, at least tolerable. The illusion of coolness was heightened by the blue and white colours of the painted walls and the pale, shining beauty of the white eggshell stucco floor. Taking in the refreshing scene, Joe thought that if only they could have devised a way of reducing the temperature dramatically, he might have fancied himself in the heart of a glacier.

Joe noticed that Claude had offered his arm to Shubhada, perfectly correctly, as she was the highest-ranking lady and would expect to take her place at the foot of the table opposite Claude who would be seated at the head. Joe did not quite like to see the way Shubhada's eyes had slid over the equally expressionless features of Lois Vyvyan who was assigned to the arm of Sir Hector. Did Lois resent the perpetual social downgrading she inevitably suffered, or had she come to terms with her husband's powerful position and her own supportive but shadowy role?

Joe was thankful to be asked to take in Madeleine and hurried to clamp her trembling arm under his, sensing that, after three rapidly drunk glasses of champagne, she was hardly able to steer a straight course. As he eased her into her chair (incredibly, even the chairs appeared to be made of crystal), he glanced around the table, curious to see how the Vyvyans had managed the seemingly impossible task of seating this disparate group. He found himself between Madeleine on his left and Shubhada on his right and prepared himself for an awkward evening. His worst expectations, however, were not realized. A glance at the eloquent grey eyebrows of Sir Hector sitting opposite was enough for him to receive the message 'Watch out! Squalls ahead!' and the two men set out to be cheerful and garrulous. Madeleine soon sank into silence, wrapped in her own thoughts, and Shubhada, feeling no obligation to rival her or cut her down to size, ignored her completely and tailored her conversation to suit the determinedly jolly and inconsequential chatter of the men on either side of her.

Lois Vyvyan was on the doctor's right and directly opposite Madeleine. Completely at ease, she was managing at once to talk to her neighbours and, with discreet nods and gestures, to direct the serving team. Watching her covertly, Joe was finding himself more and more intrigued and was beginning to think he might have to revise his first unfavourable impression.

Shubhada might be sitting in the first lady's position at the table but it was Lois who addressed the guests as the first dishes were brought to table. 'You'll find we're dining in European style this evening,' she announced. 'Udai has recently engaged a chef straight from the kitchens of the Ritz Hotel in Paris and we have the honour of being the first to sample his skills. He has the reputation of being particularly inventive in his cooking of game and promises me that his smoked haunch of wild boar, which I am hoping will make an appearance later, is unparalleled. When did you last dine at the Ritz Hotel, Commander? Perhaps you will be able more accurately to judge the standard than those of us who are not so recently come out to the East?'

'I'm afraid the best I can offer,' said Joe easily, 'is the cuisine of the officers' mess in the Rue St Pierre . . . A little uneven in quality . . . Though the wild boar my sergeant killed in the Ardennes forest and spit-roasted over an open fire was good. The wild thyme we scattered on the dried mule dung we used as fuel seemed to add a little *je ne sais quoi*. Yes, Mrs Vyvyan, I'll be the judge of your wild boar.'

Conversation at once began to rumble around the table concerning the best method of killing wild boar and other luckless game and Joe again wondered what quality it was that Lois Vyvyan possessed that so annoyed him. Normally of equable character, he was not easily needled into making a brisk reply but there was something about her challenging manner towards him that made him respond like a naughty schoolboy. Could she have formed a dislike for him so early on in their acquaintance? There was some emotion, he detected, lurking behind her frosty good manners but it only extended to him. He compared her chilly attitude to himself with her concern for Madeleine who was moodily pushing her first course around on the plate with a fork and failing to eat a single bite of the meltingly delicious terrine mousseline. Quietly, Lois Vyvyan leaned forward and suggested that an omelette might be brought instead. Madeleine flushed, smiled, shook her head and made a better pretence of eating. Smoothly Lois resumed her conversation with Stuart Mercer, seated on her right and, curious to hear what these two could have in common, Joe listened with half an ear. They appeared to be talking about Paris where Stuart had spent some time at the end of the war. Typically, in her well-bred way, Lois was not drawing him out on his wartime experiences; the blood and chaos of war were unsuitable topics. They were exploring the safer territory of his post-war impressions of life in the French capital. Lois showed the correct degree of awe and disbelief as Stuart recounted how, egged on by his friends, he'd flown his plane between the legs of the Eiffel Tower. She went on to question him on heights and air speeds and appeared to understand Stuart's replies which was more than Joe could have claimed.

Joe's eyes moved with what he hoped would be interpreted as the unexceptional curiosity of a newcomer around the members of the group. His experience in Military Intelligence had taught him that valuable information was often given away by a look, a gesture, a hesitation, and he had grown into the habit of watching people interact with each other, picking up clues to their relationships and even motivations.

Half-way through the first of the dishes, Shubhada's table napkin slid from her silk-covered knee and fell at Joe's feet. Instinctively, he bent to pick it up, only marginally faster than the waiter who also hurried forward. As Shubhada herself was also leaning over to retrieve it, Joe's face, to her embarrassment, brushed her arm and they just, by a neck-breaking manoeuvre on Joe's part, managed to avoid banging heads together.

For a few minutes Joe lapsed into a surprised silence. Perhaps Lizzie might be able to give him the information he needed: had the Guerlain salesman paid a visit to the palace recently? He stored up with pleasure the thought of intriguing with Lizzie. It had been Shalimar. Definitely Shalimar. The slim brown arm had been touched with the spicy Parisian scent and he had caught a waft of it on her face or in her hair. His keen senses had caught the same perfume on Lois Vyvyan. Incongruous on the Lavender Lady, he had decided, but this perfume, exotic, yet sophisticated, a warm, mysterious cocktail, could have been created with Shubhada in mind. Were the two women aware of this clash? Perhaps they hadn't even noticed.

But surely Claude had?

Or did Claude assume all female skin smelled like that? He looked again at Claude seated between Lizzie on his left and Edgar on his right. Claude leaned towards Lizzie listening with unfeigned interest to what she was saying, smiled and made a reply which caused her to hiccup with suppressed laughter. A natural charmer who didn't even seem to be aware of it, Joe decided with a pang of envy. The best kind, the kind who had the confidence not to need to seek approval. He wondered if Claude had ever stood on a doorstep in a lather of indecision, uncertain of his welcome, shooting his cuffs, straightening his tie and swallowing? Joe couldn't imagine it. The merry blue eyes, the clever slanting smile, the mop of hair, thick and shining as a young boy's, must always have drawn attention and approval.

Though not, he remembered, from Edgar. Wisely, Edgar had been placed between Claude and Colin O'Connor so no lady had the task of making polite conversation with him. He was happily yarning with his old tiger-hunting friend and in no danger of annoying anyone.

At the end of the magnificent meal, which had indeed included a dish of wild boar that Joe pronounced 'non-pareil' and had ended with a range of sumptuous desserts including the recreation of Mount Everest in meringue, cream and chocolate, it was Lois who caught the eye of the ladies and murmured to Shubhada, 'I think we are ready to withdraw, Your Highness.' Shubhada rose to her feet and with gracious smiles led the small group of ladies from the room.

At once, bottles of port and brandy and silver cigar boxes were laid on the table and the gentlemen, left to themselves, unconsciously stretched out their legs, ran a finger round their collars and surreptitiously eased open a button on their jackets. Voices grew gruffer and more animated. Edgar launched into a not-entirely decorous story and the first subdued laughter of the evening rippled around the table.

A servant entered and spoke quietly to Vyvyan who nodded and sent him off again. 'We are to be joined,' he announced to the table, 'for brandy by the Dewan who, as I expect you are aware, has been up to his ears sorting out today's problems. Joe, you're the only one who hasn't yet met the Dewan, I think. He's the maharaja's older brother and you'll see the family resemblance. Zalim Singh is . . . I suppose you'd call him prime minister . . . grand vizier . . . he plays Thomas Wolsey to Udai's Henry VIII. Nothing much happens in the state of Ranipur that he doesn't know about.'

Did Joe imagine the slight flick of an eye in his direction as Claude said that?

'The Rajput Sir George, are you saying?' Joe began.

'Oh, not in the same league, I'm afraid,' said a deep and amused voice from the door.

Zalim Singh came in smiling, expansive, confident of his welcome. Unlike his brother who had chosen to wear Western evening dress, Zalim was impressive in a white silk coat and trousers and jewelled turban, thick ropes of pearls around his neck, golden slippers on his feet. He was as tall as his brother, being well over six feet, but more massively built, and the impression of glowing good health and strength he gave out was at odds with Joe's expectations of a man whose life of politician and courtier was lived out in the shaded corridors and antechambers of the palace.

'"Grand vizier", however?' Zalim smiled. 'Yes, I rather think I like that! I'm sure I'm no Thomas Wolsey, though I confess I am not conscious of the gentleman. Did he have a happy life?' he enquired blandly. 'Commander Sandilands?' he added, picking out Joe. 'A friend of Edgar's, I understand?'

His handshake was firm and brief, his smile warm. Joe reminded himself that the Dewan was known to have taken an excellent degree in History at Oxford. Settling companionably into the empty chair next to Joe, Zalim poured himself a brandy and accepted a cigar from Colin O'Connor. Joe had met men like this before: men who could light up a room with their presence. It was not an attribute solely of the wealthy or high-ranking: Joe remembered a private who, quite unconsciously, had had the same effect on whatever dug-out or filthy dark hole in the trenches he fetched up in. The barmaid at the King's Head in Cheapside could have written a treatise on it – if she had been able to write. Joe's housemaster would have called it 'leadership' but it was more than that. It had elements of optimism and humour and an ability to enhance the morale of any group in which they found themselves.

Joe recalled Govind's account of the lineage of the Rajput princes. They were of the Suryavansa, the Solar Race, he'd said. Everywhere on the palace walls Joe had noticed emblems of the sun: golden, smiling faces, beneficent and life-giving. He looked again at the broad cheerful face of Zalim Singh and saw a descendant of the sun god.

He remembered the plaque mounted on a shutter above the elephant gate in the courtyard. How much more convincingly the face of Zalim Singh would have shone forth from the window on an overcast day than the ascetic features of his younger brother.

Joe determined as soon as convenient to ask Edgar to fill in the background of the previous succession for him. How had it happened that such an obvious choice for leader as Zalim had been passed over for his younger brother? Did he resent it? And now that the present ruler was growing weak and his days were numbered, had Zalim decided to take a hand in deciding the next succession? With the raja's two legitimate sons both now dead, surely it was a straight run through to the gaddi for him? Joe looked again at the powerful golden and white presence at his side and a chill shiver trickled down his back as he remembered there was a third possible impediment in Zalim's path to the throne. Bahadur. His illegitimate nephew.

For a moment Joe's head spun. He felt the dizzying disorientation of being thrust into an alien culture. This was not his world. Nothing here was truly familiar. Parisian chefs, Lalique crystal, Dow's port, these were so much foam on the surface of deeply foreign waters.

His brief from Sir George had been short and unsatisfactory. 'Remember at all times, Joe, the treaty we signed with the prince of Ranipur in 1818 . . . Here – I've had a copy made for you . . . you'll find it interesting. I'm looking at Clause 8 . . . got it? I quote, "The maharaja and his heirs and successors shall remain absolute rulers of their country, and their dependants, according to long-established usage; and the British civil and criminal jurisdiction shall not be introduced into that principality." Criminal jurisdiction – that's where you come in, Joe – or rather where you *don't* come in.'

'Thank you for pointing that out, sir. I'll leave my fingerprint kit and handcuffs at home. So, I'm being sent in in an advisory capacity only?'

'Um . . . not even that, I'm afraid.' Sir George had looked uncomfortable.

'Does the absolute ruler have such a thing as a police force of his own?' Joe enquired mildly.

'Yes. But don't count on any assistance from them,' said George. 'They wouldn't recognize themselves as "policemen". They are the Royal Guard. Bodyguards, henchmen, knives for hire, assassins on request. In fact, Joe, I wouldn't be at all surprised if your target is actually among their ranks. But I mustn't say more . . . . it's all speculation at best at this distance. That's why you're going with Edgar, my boy – to keep a watching brief and report back. No need to . . . er . . . go sleuthing about the place in a visible way, you understand. Could get you into a lot of trouble.'

Joe had been running his eye down the treaty document with a good deal of interest. 'I say, sir,' he said, frowning, 'have you seen this at the end of the treaty? It says, "Done at Dihlee this sixth day of January, AD 1815." Signed and sealed by Mr Charles Theophilus Metcalfe, Resident. And the treaty is between the Honourable English East India Company and the Raja Maun Singh of Ranipur. The East India Company? Long defunct! Does this piece of paper still have relevance? Is it still legal?'

'Oh, yes. Look at Clause 1. Good opening, I think you'll agree. "There shall be perpetual friendship and alliance between the Honourable East India Company and the Raja of Ranipur. The friends and enemies of one party shall be friends and enemies of both. The British Government engages to protect the principality and territory of Ranipur in perpetuity." Well, there you have it. The government of the day took over the rights and the responsibilities of John Company on his dissolution. We, that is HM Gov., gave its word. And you don't welch on a Rajput! We've protected them and they've done much for us over the years. Did Edgar tell you how the prince of Ranipur came by his nineteen gun salute and his title of Maharaja?'

Joe shook his head.

'It was well earned and springs from their respect for the female sex. In the darkest days of the Sepoy Revolt when the British were being slaughtered by elements of the Indian army a small contingent of women and children were shipped off in boats down the river by their menfolk who were making a last rearguard stand against the native forces. A desperate measure and the pursuing rebels soon caught up with them, riding along the bank and howling with glee when they saw that the boats were awash and beginning to sink. What they hadn't realized was that they'd strayed into the territory of the prince of Ranipur. He remembered the treaty his great grandfather had signed and set about upholding his part of the bargain. He sent a rescue party out to pull the women and children to safety on the southern bank and loosed his crack troops against the rebels on the northern bank. Routed them and held the British civilians in safety until they were picked up many weeks later by a recovered British force. A very grateful British force. He was given his increased gun salute and the plain Raja became Maharaja – great ruler. And they acquired a good story to tell, one of bravery, chivalry and Rajput honour. I think that's why we get on so well with the Rajputs – we admire the same qualities.'

Joe had fought back the temptation to add, 'And Machiavellian deviousness? How about that quality, George?' He thought he knew the answer.

His eyes rested again on what he suspected was the Machiavelli of Ranipur. Zalim was eagerly inviting the company to step outside and enjoy the night air, now cooling, he promised, as it wafted upwards from the lake behind the palace. An entertainment had been laid on for them in the courtyard.

They followed him, brandy glasses in hand, along a short corridor and down a flight of steps, emerging into the dark blue velvet of an Indian night. Music and chatter, laughter and short bursts of song greeted them and, unexpectedly, a crowd of courtiers, twinkling in jewels and satins, standing around a marble-paved sunken courtyard some thirty yards across and surrounded by a colonnaded piazza. Somewhere a fountain splashed and gushed, throwing up a fine cooling spray. The air was heavy with the scent from the orangeries which lined the courtyard and from the more distant blossom trees surrounding the lake. With a gesture, the Dewan invited the dinner guests to join him, seated cross-legged on the carpets which had been spread over the marble slabs. He indicated that Joe should sit at his left hand in the centre of the group and, at his nod, the music began in earnest as a small group of musicians gathered at the far end of the colonnade began to play.

Joe detected the sound of the tabor and sarangi, a flute and a guitar whose exponent was so skilled he could have appeared with the Philharmonic. The sweet notes of the tappa filled the air, a measure of plaintive simplicity which put Joe in mind of his own native Scottish tunes. After the briefest of pauses, the music struck up again but louder, faster and more compelling.

Into the arena swirled a group of female dancers, the bells on their ankles sounding an insistent rhythm as they stamped their way forward and took up their places on the black and white squares of the courtyard. Against this sombre backdrop the bright reds, blues, purples and yellows of their ankle-length petticoats of heavy silk stood out, lit by countless flares and strings of lights hanging from the columns. Their hair, jet-black, was smoothed down in gleaming curtains on either side of their faces, the rims of their dark eyes lined with kohl.

Nautch girls, that was what he had heard them called, though Joe had not yet seen nautch dancing. Much enjoyed by the bachelors in the employ of the East India Company, these performances were discouraged by their, for the most part, married and prudish successors from Victorian England. And more fool them! Joe thought as he settled to enjoy the dance. Expressive eyes and flashing smiles enchanted him and, as they began to dance to an ever faster rhythm, he was lost in admiration for their lithe vitality. Of the dozen dancers one or two appeared to be the stars and they came forward to perform individually before the Dewan. One in particular attracted Joe's admiration. A little taller than the others, she was outstandingly acrobatic in her dancing and drew applause from the crowd. With the composure of Ellen Terry taking a third curtain call, she began to repeat her routine and Joe was intrigued to notice that whenever she came out of a turn, it was his eye she caught. He thought he must have been mistaken but no, when she rejoined the rest of the company, she continued to watch him. The Dewan himself seemed to be conscious of this. He turned to Joe with a raised eyebrow and, leaning towards him, in an amused tone whispered, 'Her name's Padmini!'

He continued to chuckle good-naturedly to himself until the dancers, with a final athletic flourish, disappeared.

Glasses of pomegranate juice and iced tea were suddenly at their elbows while the musicians wound down, playing a soft native tune. Suddenly, the Dewan rose to his feet and the rest of the audience rose also, a general stirring of excitement beginning to run through the assembled courtiers.

'At this point in the evening's entertainment my ancestors would have regaled you with a gladiatorial combat,' said the Dewan conversationally to Joe. 'But no longer, though I have in mind a contest of sorts. We Rajputs enjoy a sporting exhibition as much as the British, you know. We are hoping our guests will participate.'

Joe was beginning to feel a ripple of anxiety run through him. He hadn't quite liked the emphasis on the word 'British'. Surely they weren't expecting him to put on a show? Good Lord! – didn't they go in for bare-knuckle boxing and panther wrestling? There were lengths he was not prepared to go to even for the honour of the Empire. He waited in trepidation for the Dewan's next announcement.

'We are hoping to engage the might of Scotland Yard in a friendly – I hope friendly – round of one of our favourite Rajput games. Chaturanga, we call it.'

Joe searched his memory for a reference to this sport but drew a blank.

'You play chess?'

'Chess?' Joe could only repeat in some astonishment. 'A game which originated in India, I believe. Yes, I do . . . but – here? Now?'

'Yes, indeed, here. Look! Do you see the squares? The courtyard is laid out for an open air game.'

Joe looked again at the pattern of black and white

marble slabs and realized that they were more than merely decorative. He was looking at a huge gaming board.

'This is an adaptation of our national game, chaupar or pucheesee,' the Dewan was going on. 'Normally it is played on a four-armed grid and rather similar to your own Ludo. Pieces move around the board according to numbers thrown using conch shells.' Joe nodded dubiously. He had vaguely heard of this game. 'But my brother is very fond of chess as it is played in Europe – it leaves less to chance and shows off the players' skills – so he had the court adapted for playing this game. He understands that you are a skilled player, Commander . . .' A courteous nod and a smile in his direction did nothing to ease Joe's forebodings.

The crowd pressed forward, murmuring and smiling, the dark-suited dinner party guests distinguishable amongst but greatly outnumbered by turbaned Rajput nobles in court dress, diamonds winking and pearls gleaming against silk coats. The atmosphere was one of restrained joviality but with an undercurrent which to Joe was palpable, an undercurrent of excitement. They shuffled around the courtyard, taking up positions giving a good view of the chessboard. He tried to recall whether their interest went as far as betting on the outcome and wondered very much who his opponent would be. With sinking heart he acknowledged that this was undoubtedly a set-up and that one of these clever, competitive Rajputs had already been chosen to make a fool of the officer from Scotland Yard.

He was surprised and relieved to hear the Dewan announce that his opponent was to be Edgar Troop.

Smiling and feigning humble astonishment, Edgar took up a position on the opposite side of the square. He nodded courteously to Joe and clicked his heels. Joe did the same, his mind racing. He had no idea that Edgar could even play chess, but then, there were many facets of Edgar's character which, thankfully, had so far remained a mystery.

Reminding himself that this was just a bit of after-dinner entertainment and that with deliberate sleight of hand they had been set against each other to amuse the more skilled Indian audience, Joe determined to give a good performance. Chess, for him, was the equivalent of battle planning and he began at once to check the lie of the land. He had no idea of the local rules and assumed that his opponent did. But the Dewan was speaking again.

'Commander Sandilands has not played our national game before. I think, under the British rule of fair play, it would be in order to appoint an adviser, one to each side.'

A murmur of agreement went up.

'Claude? May I ask you to second Sandilands? I myself will undertake to assist Captain Troop. Not that Edgar needs or would pay attention to advice, I think.'

Joe noticed that Colin O'Connor was frowning and looking disconcerted. He caught Joe's eye and made a grimace Joe could not fathom. 'Bad luck, old man, but do your best,' was the nearest he could get to an interpretation.

The atmosphere was becoming increasingly tense, murmur and chatter shot through with sudden bursts of laughter, long speculative looks directed at the two players.

'Are they betting on the result?' Joe asked Vyvyan who had taken up a position at his right hand.

'Betting? No, not at all. But the outcome will entertain them . . . whichever way it goes. They're as fond of a bit of gossip and speculation as your average officers' mess,' he replied cryptically.

'What the hell?'

'Just calm down and go along with it, Sandilands. It's only a game. It'll give a lot of pleasure to a lot of people if you foul up and that's the worst that can happen. At least in this combat nobody dies. They like a good show so I'd slightly overdo everything if I were you. Play to the gallery. Now listen. These are the rules. It's very simple for a competent chess player which I understand you are . . .'

He explained the rules, which indeed appeared quite

straightforward. So simple was the whole game that Joe could not for a moment understand why the crowd was still throbbing with an undercurrent of excitement.

'This is all very well,' he said impatiently, 'and I don't want to appear demanding, but when I play chess I normally play it with chessmen . . . you know . . . pawns, rooks, knights, perhaps even a king and queen . . . I see none here.'

Vyvyan gave a knowing smile. 'Ah. Yes. The chessmen,' he said mysteriously. 'If I'm not mistaken – here they come!'

He turned to enjoy Joe's expression of stunned amazement as the crowd parted and into the arena with a tinkle of bells, a drumming of bare feet and a whirl of bright skirts came two files of beautiful girls. With giggles and coquettish sideways glances from their kohl-rimmed eyes they took up their places on the board. Joe's pawns and pieces were dressed in red and blue, Edgar's in green and yellow. Joe's astonishment turned to amusement and he began to relax.

The Dewan addressed the company again in his booming master of ceremonies voice. 'When this game was invented by the Emperor Akbar, the chess pieces were slave girls and the winner of the round was permitted to take the whole lot away with him as his own. But we live in more civilized times. The winner of this game will not, of course, make off with the beauties you see before you. But he will have his prize.' He paused theatrically, looking first at Joe then at Edgar. 'He will have his choice of one of the girls for one night.'

Under cover of the chatter and laughter which broke out, Joe spluttered his disgust to Claude. With a fixed smile Claude replied, 'When in Rome, Joe! Come on, it's not the end of the world! It's an honour you've been accorded. Try to look as though you appreciate it. For God's sake, you can always plead a headache at the last moment!' And then he added ominously, 'If it should come to that. Look at the opposition, will you!'

They both looked towards Edgar, heavy, unattractive, the worse for alcohol but smugly confident and already running a lecherous eye over the girls.

'*La chevalerie oblige*, Sandilands! Don't you agree?'

'See what you mean, sir. There are fates worse than losing at chess! And winning a night with Edgar must rank high on the list!'

Chapter Nine

Three notes on a silver trumpet called everyone to attention. The audience stopped moving about and looked expectantly from Joe to Edgar. The girls fell silent and held themselves in their positions as still as any chessmen, backs to their master, faces to the enemy, battle-ready.

Joe leaned to Vyvyan and said, 'I don't imagine, do I, that they are graded for height?'

'Quite right,' said Vyvyan. 'Your pawns are the smallest and all the same size. All got up in red skirts. The blue girls, your main pieces, are in height order. You've got two small rooks on the outside, do you see? Larger knights next door, then bishops.'

'Why do the bishops have elephants embroidered on their bodices?' Joe asked.

'Indian game, remember. Their armies were made up of four parts: foot soldiers – those are your pawns; chariots – that's your rooks, the ones with the gold wheels on their backs; then cavalry – that's your knights with the horse's head embroidery; lastly, the elephants which are our bishops. In the centre, wearing crowns, you've got the two tallest ones, the king and queen.'

At that moment the blue queen, who was wearing a silver crown, turned her head to look at him and with a jolt Joe recognized Padmini.

The trumpet sounded again, a single note. Joe caught the eye of one of his red pawns. Did he have a feeling that she was expecting to be called on? He rather thought she did and he held up two fingers. The pawn duly advanced two

99

squares and confronted Edgar's front rank. Edgar sent forward one of his yellow-skirted pawns and the battle was engaged.

Joe surmised that no one would be entertained if the game dragged on and he decided to play with panache. He remembered a move he and a fellow officer had devised in the trenches in a despairing attempt to distract from the tedium and the terror of being pinned down by German artillery, unable to move forward or retreat. They'd called it 'Haig's Mate' and if all went according to plan he should be able to close down the game in fifteen moves.

But Edgar was giving no quarter and was from the outset making clear his intention to win. He spent hardly any time considering his game, which seemed to be a style the audience and indeed the chess pieces appreciated. Joe noticed that on occasions when a player spent a little longer in thought, the piece herself, when finally called to action, was a fraction of a second ahead of the call, a slim foot edging forward in anticipation of the move.

Edgar soon extricated himself from Joe's planned sequence and the advantage moved to and fro between the two well-matched players. One by one, pieces lost or sacrificed stamped off in a tinkle of bells to the edge of the board until only a handful were left on each side.

Joe hesitated before making the next move. He gratefully accepted a glass of pomegranate juice from a footman, using that as a respite from the remorseless speed of play. He noticed that Edgar was taking another whisky-soda from the tray. Edgar had wriggled out of all the traps Joe had set and gone on the attack with a flourish. Over the rim of his glass Joe suddenly noticed that the left foot of his blue queen was tapping out a pattern. Unlike the other pieces she was not wearing ankle bells and her movements were probably unnoticed by the crowd. He looked more carefully. Five taps. In the top left-hand corner of her square. Could she be giving him a signal? What would happen if he . . .? He ran his eye along the diagonals. Blast it! How could he not have noticed! The exhausting day, the champagne, the lateness of the hour – he could think of reasons enough, but Joe cursed himself for his lapse in attention.

He signalled to his queen that she should move five squares diagonally to the left. Unleashed at last, she swooped forward with the relish of an avenging Fury, dark skirts rustling, and rounded on Edgar's king.

'Check,' announced Claude briskly.

This was Joe's breakthrough and four decisive moves later Claude shouted, 'Shah mat! The king is dead! Checkmate!'

Edgar stared at Joe across the courtyard, stiff with defiance and anger, but he bowed courteously. Joe returned the bow. To his alarm, the girls had fluttered back on to their squares and both armies now stood facing him, some looking modestly and evasively at their feet, others eyeing him with flirtatious speculation.

'Time to bite the bullet, Sandilands. Don't fuss!' whispered Claude. 'Just smile and pick a number.'

Joe caught the straight gaze of Padmini and without hesitation said, 'If the blue queen would care to step forward . . .?'

Laughter and even a little discreet applause rippled round the square as she moved through the files to stand in front of him, still smiling.

The Dewan slapped him on the shoulder. 'A good choice. And a fitting reward for a game well played. Edgar is not an easy opponent. You have had a long and exhausting day, Commander, and are probably looking forward to your bed. Padmini will escort you to your quarters. She too is a skilled performer. At chess. Perhaps you will keep each other awake practising your moves . . .' He shook with laughter, involving everyone in his mischievous good humour. 'Take care not to overtire yourself . . . tomorrow promises to be a busy day.'

'Just go quietly, old man,' advised Claude. '*Autre pays, autres moeurs*, don't you know!'

'If he reminds me I'm not in Knightsbridge now, I'll hit him,' Joe decided.

With as little ceremony as he could manage, he set off to follow the twinkling silver crown of Padmini who moved a few paces ahead of him, swaying through the thinning crowds and into the increasingly deserted corridors. They crossed courtyards silent but for a slight breeze stirring the leaves and the gentle splashing of fountains. In the distance Joe thought he caught sounds of distressed wailing and the low throb of a drum but all else was quiet.

At last, in the centre of a courtyard which he thought he recognized, Padmini paused and leaned over the basin of a fountain, dipping her arms in the cool water. Joe watched her playing with the drifting blossoms on the surface, deciding this was probably the time tactfully to tell her to return to her quarters rather than wait for the awkward moment when he would turn to face her on his doorstep. Did she speak any English? How on earth did you tell a girl in very rudimentary Hindi that, though you thought her the most arousing girl you had ever seen, her services were not required?

He joined her at the fountain, preparing his speech. But no words would come. He stared, overcome by the nearness of the girl, tongue-tied with awe for her beauty. In her clinging blue silk she was almost invisible in the dark courtyard but the moonlight caught the jewels of her crown and lit the smiling great eyes she turned to him. Joe was overcome. He was beginning to lose his struggle with the deeply primitive emotion that had him in its grip. With his last reserves of determination he cleared his throat and began to croak out his rejection speech.

'Padmini? Have I got that right? Now, look here, Padmini, I'm most frightfully sorry but . . .'

The gazelle eyes flashed with comprehension then narrowed in disdain. Angrily, she leaned forward into the fountain and smacked the surface of the water hard, directing a spray of water straight at Joe's face. With a peal of laughter to see his gasping astonishment, she turned and ran off leaving him dripping and cursing by the pool.

Bloody girl! But at least she'd taken the hint pretty quickly. With relief and disappointment in equal measure, he set off again, certain that he could find his own way back to his room from this spot. After a few paces he stopped and listened. Pattering feet were going ahead of him in the same direction.

He caught up with her at his door and rounded on her. Cool arms went up and locked with surprising strength behind his neck. He felt his shirt damp on his skin as she pressed herself to him and, standing on her toes, lifted her lips to kiss him. As their breath mingled he was enveloped by the sweet scent of the girl, attar of roses a seductive top-note to a surge of female warmth. His arms slipped of their own will around her waist. She was warm and scented and more than willing. She had attracted his attention, won the game for him and he would have said was claiming him as her prize. God! He needed this! And he'd earned it! 'Another country, other customs,' wasn't that what Claude had said? Surrendering himself to the moment, Joe groaned and lowered his face to hers.

'Aw, for God's sake, Joe! They really stitched you up good, didn't they!'

The door of his room had opened and lamplight from inside revealed the figure of Madeleine standing there, wearing a long white robe, a glass in her hand.

Joe couldn't speak but anything he said would have been unheard as the two women faced each other. Padmini hissed something unintelligible in Hindi and Madeleine replied with matching scorn. 'Same to you, sister! Now do us all a favour and beat it back to your lord and master!' She grinned nastily. 'And you can tell him you were out-played. Victim of a discovered attack by the white queen!'

Padmini whirled around and moved away, a darker

retreating shadow amongst the shadows of the court-yard.

'Hell's bells, Madeleine!' Joe gasped. 'What are you doing here?'

She pulled him inside, closed the door firmly and shot the bolt across.

'Doing a bit of lonely drinking . . . Waiting for you to show up . . . Being your guardian angel . . .'

'What do you mean? You're not looking exactly angelic from where I'm standing!'

She eyed him critically. 'You should get a look at your-self, mister! Now, you were billed as a clever feller. War hero . . . survivor. Didn't they tell me you worked for Military Intelligence? Those are smart guys. And you fell for it! Feet – well, perhaps some other part of your anatomy – first! She's a plant! She's the Dewan's trained pillow talker. Didn't you guess?'

Joe could only stare in surprise and disgust.

'This whole place,' Madeleine waved her arms around, champagne slopping on to the carpet, 'is an anthill. It's all murmurings and gossip and plotting and all the informa-tion that's going gets channelled right back to the Dewan. If you take a leak in the ghulskhana he'll hear about it before you've flushed! He's not sure why you're here but he doesn't trust the British. He knows you're close to Sir George and that means you're at the heart of the govern-ment so he wants to keep you under close surveillance. And you couldn't have closer surveillance than the watch his pet trollop was about to keep on you! She'd have stuck closer than gum on your shoe!'

Joe's feeling of foolish inadequacy was giving way to anger. 'I don't talk in my sleep, they tell me . . . I can't see that there's a problem. And,' he added defiantly, 'had it occurred to you that this particular surveillance might not have been unwelcome?'

Madeleine swept a knowing and cynical glance over Joe. 'So I see. Well, you can always go take a cold shower.

Another cold shower. That's what you British do, isn't it? Go ahead – I'll look the other way.'

Joe swallowed and tried to keep his tone polite as he spoke. 'Would you like me to ring for Govind and have you escorted back to your own rooms?' He went to the bell pull and took hold of it.

To his dismay, the glass fell from her fingers and she put both hands over her face, silently sobbing.

'Oh, Lord, Madeleine! Now what?'

'Can't you see it yet, you great lummox? I can't go back there. I wouldn't be safe. They hate me much more than they hated Prithvi. They blame me for everything! They probably think I killed him! They want me dead! And not just because I'm a white woman. Did you know all widows are unclean? If they can't get rid of them on a funeral pyre they shut them up in a little room and never let them out. How long do you suppose I'd last out there? Without Prithvi to look out for me I'm just a target! This is the only place I feel safe. You have got a gun, haven't you?'

Joe nodded. First Bahadur, now Madeleine, both seeing themselves as potential victims. And both were seeking help from an outsider who was himself insecure and exposed in alien territory.

'You can't stay here! Imagine the gossip! What about your reputation? What about my reputation . . . I mean – how do I explain this to your father-in-law?' he heard himself spluttering like a maiden aunt. 'Look, Madeleine, can't you go to your brother for help until you can both get out of here?'

Madeleine gave him another of her long incredulous stares. 'Stuart is . . . shall we say . . . otherwise engaged and would be very upset to receive a sisterly visit. He doesn't even need to play chess to get the girls! And I notice you are admitting that this is a pretty hostile environment. Did you hear yourself say "get out of here" as in the sense of "escape from"? Well, that's exactly what I'm going to do.

I'm getting out, Joe. If I have to fly one of Prithvi's planes to Delhi to do it! But I'm not going empty-handed. I gave him two years of my life and someone's going to pay for those two years. I need to stay alive long enough to talk to Udai Singh . . . come to some agreement . . . and I can tell you – I've got my ticket out of here! And if you've any sense, you'll be in the passenger seat when I take off, Joe.'

'You'd oblige me, Madeleine, if you and your brother would remain in Ranipur for a while. You yourself, if you remember, asked my opinion on the plane crash that killed your husband and the Resident also has asked me to investigate. You and your brother are vital to the investigation and you can't leave until I've been able to gather evidence and statements.'

Madeleine gave a derisive laugh. 'Oh, yeah? Didn't they tell you in Simla that the British have no legal or criminal jurisdiction in the princely states? You can detect all you like, Joe, and, sure, it would be good to know who's killing the heirs but there's nowhere you can go with the information. There's nothing you can do but report back when you get out . . . If they let you get out!'

Joe allowed himself a wry smile. 'That's an over-simple but – I have to say – incisive summary of my brief. Don't tell me you're on Sir George's payroll too?'

'Never met the guy.'

'Anything left in that bottle?

Joe's mood was becoming less buoyant by the minute. Excitement and anger were ebbing away leaving a wistful sympathy for the hopelessness of Madeleine's situation. He watched her with pity as she found two glasses and filled them clumsily with champagne. With sinking heart he guessed that she needed to talk through her grief with someone and resentfully wondered why she couldn't have taken up Lizzie Macarthur's offer of a safe haven and a sympathetic ear. But of course, he had an obvious attraction that Lizzie didn't possess: in a desperate corner, a revolver and a steady hand will always win out over a parasol and a sharp tongue.

He eyed her warily as she touched his glass with hers. 'You're a resourceful woman, Madeleine. But – tell me – what are your immediate plans?'

'You mean how soon am I going to get out of your hair?' She laughed. 'Don't concern yourself, Joe. Your virtue's safe with me! I find dripping-wet, detumescent, disapproving cops totally resistible. I'm going to sleep there – on that couch. I've stolen a couple of your cushions. I've used your bathroom – brought my own toothbrush – so – it's all yours!'

She put down her glass, kicked off her shoes and stumbled towards the couch. 'See you in the morning, Joe. Sweet dreams!'

The champagne was still chilled, still fizzing and with a sharp edge that exactly reflected his mood. He took the bottle, surprised to find that it was only half empty. There seemed to be no good reason for not finishing it. He poured himself another glass and sipped quietly, sitting on the edge of his bed, waiting. After a few minutes of cushion pounding, wriggling and muffled oaths, his guest fell silent and still. When he was quite sure that Madeleine was asleep he went into his bathroom and spent long luxurious minutes under his lukewarm shower. Belatedly noticing that Madeleine had made off with his bathrobe he wandered naked out of the ghulskhana and crept silently around his room turning out lights, checking doors, windows, cupboards and even the space under his bed. Five minutes of reconnaissance in enemy territory could save your life and he was not going to let his guard slip now. He had learned on the North-West Frontier to be perpetually vigilant and though these silken, sophisticated surroundings in no way compared with that harsh hell-hole he thought they might in their own way prove even more lethal.

He quietly closed the last wardrobe door.

'I already checked all those,' said an amused voice from the couch. 'And that's not all I've checked . . . Charming derrière, Commander!'

Chapter Ten

Joe awoke to a discreet cough at his side and the tinkle of china on a tray being placed on a table at the foot of his bed by a cheerful Govind who made his way to the bathroom and turned on the taps. Joe just managed to find his voice in time to prevent him from drawing back the curtains to let in the full searchlight of an Indian early morning sun. His brain was still in the middle of a double declutch but he felt certain there were aspects of the night he would not wish to have illuminated until he was fully in control of events once more.

He lay low until Govind had disappeared. Where to start? His headache was not as bad as he feared it might be. Even more encouraging – there was no one sleeping on his couch. Or ever had been, to all appearances. All was neat, cushions back in place and surely that was his bathrobe hanging on the door? He sat up and called out softly, dreading to hear a reply: 'Are you there, Madeleine?'

No reply.

Relief washed over him and for a moment he was tempted to allow himself the delusion that the events of the last evening had never occurred. The discovery of a still-warm place on the other side of his bed, an indented pillow and several golden hairs in that indentation brought an even more unpalatable scenario to mind. He'd drunk too much champagne but surely he would recall the intimacy implied by his finds? He felt about guiltily under the covers for other clues but found nothing more incriminating than a folded square of writing paper.

'Didn't Nancy ever complain that you talk in your sleep?' was the short message.

Almost as a signature the sound of a small aeroplane passed overhead. For a moment he thought it might be Madeleine heading off for Delhi but the plane circled and returned before flying off again towards the Aravalli hills.

There was something he had to check on, he remembered, and, scrambling from his bed, he searched about in the waste paper basket and in all the corners where she might have abandoned an empty champagne bottle. There was only the one he remembered finishing himself. Madeleine had, he calculated, in spite of appearances – the husky gin-fogged voice, the mistimed gestures – actually drunk in his presence about a thimbleful of wine. Her first glass had been spilled on the floor, he remembered, and the bottle was chill and must have been almost full when he arrived.

Madeleine was putting on a pretence of drunkenness. But why would she do that? Protective colouring perhaps? Drunks are never taken seriously. They are disregarded, an embarrassment; people look the other way when they enter a room. People underestimate them. He sighed as he realized that he had been misled into behaving like this towards Madeleine himself. And this had clearly been her intention. Poor little Madeleine, widowed and drowning her grief in a bottle. A common enough solution in India and therefore an easy deception but, if the drunkenness was a deception, what about the grief?

Joe wondered again about Madeleine's ambivalent attitude to her circumstances. She had loved her husband by all accounts whilst hating his home and family. If something had happened to upset the balance in her life . . . But, of course, something had happened. Something of earthshaking proportions for Madeleine. The oldest son had died. At a stroke, Prithvi the gadabout socialite who was quite prepared to spend the larger amount of his time living with princely abandon in Europe or America with his adored young wife was now next in line for the throne of Ranipur. Had he succumbed to pressures put on him in the weeks following his brother's death, pressures to devote himself to the serious business of ruling, to return to family traditions, take an Indian wife to ensure the succession? How secure had Madeleine's marriage been latterly?

She had the technical skill and the opportunity to cut just the right number of steel threads to send her husband plummeting to the ground. Had she grown weary after two years of the stifling palace life of a princess – and a despised and disregarded princess at that? She had said something last night that had stayed with him through the mental fog into which he had descended. 'I've got my ticket out of here!' She was going to persuade the maharaja, by fair means or foul, to allow her to leave and not empty-handed. He wondered what exactly the 'ticket' consisted of.

Perhaps her brother Stuart could shed a light on all this? Joe looked at his watch. Six o'clock and he was due to see him at nine. Time to do justice to the pot of coffee and the pile of toast Govind had just brought in. He thought he would leave the lid of the silver chafing dish which undoubtedly contained eggs in some form or another firmly in place. He'd enjoy a cool bath and then a head-clearing walk in the freshest air he would experience that day, heading out to the polo ground perhaps, keeping well clear of the women's quarters and the town. Half an hour later, he put on the white shirt, the light box cloth trousers and the riding jacket Govind had selected for him, snatched up a topee and set out.

The sun was already beating down fiercely when he walked out of the palace at seven. As he strolled out on to the verandah looking across the undulating polo ground an elegant figure in riding habit mounted on a gleaming black Arab mare spotted him, turned and came on towards him.

Third Her Highness was followed by a syce riding an equally fine horse a few yards behind. The red silk tunic

111

and turban and the black trousers he wore had been carefully chosen, Joe guessed, to complement the white jodhpurs and black jacket of his mistress. Even the white egret pecking his way in their wake across the lawn seemed to involve himself in the frieze they presented. Raising a foot, the bird offered a hieroglyphic profile and stalked forward. Unconsciously, Shubhada echoed its movements, tilting an imperious nose that would have looked impressive on a coin.

'Commander Sandilands. Good morning,' she called. 'I was surprised not to see you exercising earlier.'

'I overslept, Your Highness,' he said with a disarming smile. 'Unused as I am to Rajput hospitality I indulged too recklessly in all the good things the palace has to offer.'

Oh what the hell! If the palace grapevine was all it was cracked up to be she'd probably heard he'd defeated a Russian grand master and slept with a whole boardful of chess pieces.

'Then I recommend a short canter.' She turned and spoke to her syce who dismounted and led his horse over to Joe. 'Shall we?'

Luckily for Joe the horse was well into its morning exercise. He thought he would have had quite a struggle to control the magnificent animal coming straight from the stables.

Shubhada led the way at a canter along the polo field and Joe began to enjoy himself, thankful that he'd remembered to put on the topee against the sun. It occurred to him that he was taking part in a very unusual scene. Maharanees like Shubhada would at any time in the past and, as far as he was aware, in the present, be kept well away from the eyes of any man and yet here she was riding off with him with the ease of any Western girl.

She stopped and dismounted at the far end of the polo field in a shady grove of acacia trees and Joe joined her, hitching their horses to a branch. He was curious to know why she had arranged this time alone with him. He wondered whether she knew the true nature of her hus-

112

band's illness. He would have very much liked to know how her own future would be affected by his death. He asked none of his questions. Even in riding clothes she was regal and a Scotland Yard officer knows his place.

She went to sit on a fallen tree trunk and pointed a finger at the other end. Joe sat down and waited.

'I wonder if you are aware, Commander,' she said finally, 'of the seriousness of my husband's condition?'

Perhaps this interview wasn't going to be as awkward as he had anticipated.

'I am, Your Highness, and may I offer you my –'

'Yes, you may,' she interrupted, 'but when the time comes. You will hear more from his physician, I am sure, but we are thinking that he will not last out the summer. We ought, of course, to have moved him to Switzerland where we would normally spend the hot season but his doctor has advised against it. Udai would not survive the journey apparently. And, naturally, as ruler, he prefers to die where he has lived, here at the heart of his kingdom.'

'A devastating loss for many people,' Joe murmured.

'Far more than you can ever know,' she said. 'But the ones who suffer most at these times of change are the ruler's wives. And, of these, the youngest, childless wife has most to lose.'

He looked at her, taken aback by her sudden frankness.

She smiled. 'I think you don't like me very much, Commander. There is no reason why you should. You are a stranger here, you owe me no loyalty or affection but – I'll tell you something – I'm very glad that you're here! I was educated in Europe and, believe me, in the small academic and aristocratic worlds in which I moved in London, Paris and Geneva one came to accept the security of a well-policed community. I know you have no jurisdiction here in Ranipur but, by your presence, you remind me that the ordered world in which I grew up is still available to me should I need to retreat to it.'

What was this? A veiled request for another ticket out of the state? In a few gallant phrases, Joe encouraged her to depend on him to do whatever was in his power to ease her burden.

She smiled. 'Remember you said that, Commander! I shall!'

Emboldened by the new, more approachable persona she was showing him, he dared to ask her how she had come to meet the maharaja.

Her smile broadened. 'I wish I could tell you it was a romantic meeting . . . you know . . . his eyes caught mine across the crowded floor of a hunt ball . . . I hurried to help him up when he fell from his polo pony . . . but no. It was an arranged marriage.'

Sensing she had her audience in the palm of her hand, she continued. 'My father is himself a raja in a southern state. An enlightened man where gender is concerned. His own mother, my grandmother, ruled the state during her son's minority with frightening efficiency for many years . . .'

She saw Joe's surprise and added, 'There are one or two states where the succession is through the female line – Travancore and Cochin, for example, and women have ruled in Bhopal for generations. Indeed, the Tiger Queen of Bhopal came out of purdah the more efficiently to work with her people when the country was in the throes of a dire famine and that not so many years ago. Many ranees followed her example. My father saw no reason not to raise his three daughters – I'm the eldest – out of purdah and with all the advantages available to his sons. We girls learned mathematics, science and languages alongside our brothers. I rode and hunted with them. Indeed, I do believe I was a much better sportsman than any of them.' She frowned. 'Oh, dear! I don't know the feminine of "sportsman"!'

Joe pretended to reflect for a moment. 'I rather think it's "sportsman", Your Highness.'

She gave him a sideways look. 'So, it wasn't until I was

shipped off to a girls' academic establishment in Brighton that I learned that girls were considered a different and inferior race. I have never accepted that. More importantly, nor did my father. He had many requests for my hand in marriage and consulted me on each. He was perfectly agreeable to refusing them all as it would have entailed a life of indulged slavery. I would have disappeared into a zenana where I would have led the life of a recluse.'

Joe was stricken by the idea of this beautiful and vital young girl being hidden away for the sole pleasure of one man.

'By my twenty-first birthday with my younger sisters conventionally married off (to their satisfaction – they were not coerced) my father and I had acquired a reputation for choosiness and the offers began to dry up. Then Pa met an old friend in London. Udai Singh, he remembered, was an easy-going soul, well travelled, clever, and enlightened when it came to the position of women. My father had not until then considered him as a suitable match for me because he was of my father's generation, comfortably married with two wives already and grown-up heirs. He was not looking for a third wife. But he was introduced to me and,' she smiled at a memory, 'that was that. *Coup de foudre*. On his part at any rate,' she added bluntly. 'It was not ideal. I was destined to be more than just a third wife but . . . well . . . Udai is very rich – and, as you see, he lets me live exactly as I want to live.'

'You enjoy the best of both worlds, Your Highness,' he said and dared to add, 'But how long will it last? Is there anything in the future that could alarm you?'

'I'll say!' she said with unexpected energy. 'This freedom you see me enjoying is an illusion! When Udai dies and the men are at each other's throats fighting for their place on the gaddi what do you suppose happens to the widows? We cannot remarry, you know. In the past there was always the funeral pyre as a quick solution to the problem and I'm sure it is an option that First Her Highness would choose if the interfering British still allowed her to do that.

They outlawed the practice many years ago.' She looked at him enquiringly, wondering how far he understood India with its rules written and unwritten, its customs upheld or suppressed according to Western morality. 'Royal wives tend these days to find themselves under guard – oh, a very discreet guard, of course – when their husbands die. Udai will go alone to his funeral pyre. And rightly so.'

'But you would say that his wives will be left more than usually forlorn?' Joe prompted.

'A wife can only continue to hold on to power and respect for her position if her son inherits and she becomes regent during his minority. And now the sons of the first two wives are both dead, First and Second Her Highnesses might as well both be dead. It was always a sadness for Udai that he had so few sons. Many daughters (expensively married off!) but only two sons survived infancy and, in his own way, each was a disappointment to his father.'

She tapped her boot with the riding crop in some agitation then said, 'Udai had begun to acknowledge that neither Bishan nor Prithvi was going to please him. I think one of his reasons for marrying me was to renew the chance of filling the royal cradle with a series of strong, acceptable sons. But sadly . . .' She looked away to hide her emotions.

'And now the two main players have been swept from the board, the palace strong men are jockeying for position?' Joe said.

She laughed. 'How you mix your sporting metaphors, Commander! But, yes, you're right! Udai has many ambitious cousins here at court who would like nothing more than to be named as his heir. He has countless relations out there in the moffussil,' she waved a deprecating hand in the general direction of the desert beyond, 'to say nothing of his so able elder brother! So many players! I sometimes think this whole succession problem could be worked out on a chessboard! And never forget that more than one of the strongest pieces are representing the interests of the British Government. Sir George Jardine is definitely a player.'

'A knight! He'd be a knight!' said Joe. 'Two steps forward, one to the side, always going over your head!'

'Of course! And Sir Claude? Now he prefers to move tangentially, sneaking up on his target crabwise . . . he'd be a bishop!' she said, almost playfully, joining in his game. 'But all we plodding, powerless pawns can do is keep our heads down and sacrifice ourselves for our royal master,' she added bitterly.

Joe considered the clever face looking mournfully into the distance and wondered why she was attempting this bluff. Pawn? Plodding? Powerless? No. He was looking at a black queen. The most powerful piece on the board. And this was no nautch girl in spangled tiara pretending for the space of a game to have power. This was a diamond-crowned woman whose power came from within and he had no doubt that when her moment came she would swoop about the board in any direction she chose and weaker pieces would topple. No one would be safe from her gliding attack. Watch out, Claude!

'Is it at all reassuring to have the Vyvyans at your elbow?' he asked. 'They would seem to represent a certain security, a familiar London way of going on. Claude strikes me as being the best the civil service has to offer.'

Did her lip curl slightly as she replied? He thought it did. 'A true product of Haileybury. He does – what would you say? – everything by the book, and, yes, that, in its way, is reassuring. You always know exactly where you are with Vyvyan. But that can be a problem when you realize that where you are with him is many leagues behind his master, the British Government. Don't be deceived by his bonhomie, his easy way with the natives, Commander – he's a dog with one master. He talks with open-minded concern about the well-being of the state of Ranipur and its inhabitants, he makes suggestions for improvements to our lives but he'd cheerfully have us all shot from cannon if His Majesty's Government gave the command.'

Joe was taken aback by the sarcasm in her tone and turned the conversation. 'And Lois Vyvyan? Is it a comfort to have available the company of an educated and sophisticated woman?' Joe asked.

'Oh, Mrs Vyvyan,' she replied with a shrug, 'Lois is as cultured as her pearls!'

Startled by the casually cruel remark and unsure how to respond, he remained silent.

'Minor aristocracy fallen on hard times,' she enlarged on her remark. 'Her father was a military man . . . army, I believe . . . Sir Alistair Graham. Lois has done well for herself landing Claude Vyvyan. A well-qualified, good-looking chap like him could probably – should probably – have aimed for an heiress of some sort. I don't imagine that your government pays him much, though his prospects are good. A wealthy wife would have been a great asset to him. I fear Claude made the mistake of marrying too early in his career.'

Joe was amused. Again, the tones of Queen Mary came vividly to mind. She had discussed the domestic arrangements of one of her footmen with just the same tone of proprietorial concern.

'But you are too good a listener, Commander. I see I shall have to beware or you'll ensnare me into admitting it was I who stole the Koh-i-nur diamond! We should return to the palace where I understand you have a busy morning of interviews arranged.'

His audience was over. Joe was being dismissed. He rose to his feet and extended a courteous hand to help her up and then brought her horse over to her. She waited for him to put out his hand again to hoist her up into the saddle and with a regal inclination of the head urged her horse into a showy trot heading in the direction of the stables.

'Now what the hell was all that about?' Joe wondered.

Chapter Eleven

He followed at a discreet distance, handed his horse over to a waiting syce then began to wander back to the New Palace. From the shaded verandah on the northern side he stood and watched as a small plane hummed into sight and landed behind a group of low, one-storey buildings screened by a line of poplar trees a quarter of a mile away. Joe decided that if he set off now he would be able to greet Stuart as he was finishing his post-flight checks. A little earlier than planned perhaps but Joe liked to see the people he was interviewing in their context, even catching them off guard.

Setting his topee firmly in place before venturing again into the sunshine he made for the hangar. The pilot, who was indeed Stuart Mercer, was busy giving instructions to an Indian flight engineer in what sounded like a mixture of English and Hindi. There was a good deal of agreeing going on and this appeared to be an easy relationship.

'Captain Mercer!' Joe called.

'Oh, hi there, Sandilands! Good to see you! It's early – you had coffee? We'll have a cup of java – though out here it's more likely to be Mysore. Good, anyway, wherever it comes from!' He nodded to his engineer who hurried off to fetch more coffee.

Joe liked Americans. He admired their easy ways and their directness but above all he respected the courage and tenacity with which he'd seen them fight alongside in Europe in a struggle which was not their own. And top of the heap, for him, were the young flyers of the Escadrille

Américaine. Volunteers, and for the most part from privileged backgrounds, they had wangled themselves into the war before their country was ready to commit them, before it even had an air corps of its own, by being taken under the wing of the French air force. The original group of seven, a mixture of rich playboys, foreign legionnaires, Ivy League graduates and stunt-flyers, had trained in legendary luxury and splendour at Luxeuil in the Vosges. When finally they were unleashed, their effect was deadly. The playboy squadron fought with the unthinking bravery, the dash and skill of a troop of medieval knights, and stories of their exploits had gone like wildfire through the allied forces. Some of the original seven even survived to preside over the adoption of the squadron into the US Air Service, late in the war, in the spring of 1918.

To have served with such a unit was a great honour and must, Joe estimated, have made a considerable impression on Prithvi Singh, prince of a warrior state and amateur airman. He looked from the neat, active figure of Captain Mercer to the planes lined up behind him in the hangar. It stood at the end of a taxiway, screened by trees, and at first sight appeared to be an offshoot of the royal stables. The building combined functionality and decorative grace.

Following his gaze, Stuart gave an understanding smile and said, 'Okay, let's go have a look at the planes while we're waiting for our coffee, shall we?'

They strolled over to the hangar, enjoying the freshening breeze that blew through the open ends.

'Not a dozen, you see, as some of the society magazines would have you believe. Prithvi has – had – five. Now four. Well chosen all the same and goodness knows how much he had to lay out to locate them and have them brought here.'

As Joe's eyes grew used to the shade he focused on a familiar shape.

'Yep, that's a Curtiss Jenny like the one that crashed. We had them for training and aerobatics. Good little plane – anyone can fly it – teach you if you like? No?'

Joe peered into the cockpit fancying himself at the controls. On the pilot's seat was a small stuffed toy. A tiger with gleaming glass eyes. Joe reached in and picked it up. 'Good luck charm?' he asked with a friendly smile. 'I suppose all the Escadrille Américaine pilots carried a talisman of some sort or another? I know the British did.'

'Yes. We're a superstitious lot. But we called ourselves the Lafayette. I was a member of the Lafayette Flying Corps.' He paused and returned Joe's smile. 'I guess you probably know that . . . And the tiger ought by rights to be a black velvet cat. We all carried one. Mine got lost somewhere between France and the States. A tiger seemed an appropriate replacement. Still, I've always hung on to the other charm we would none of us in the squadron take to the air without.' He looked questioningly at Joe. 'You were in Military Intelligence – you must have heard the rumours?'

Joe nodded. 'It was generally thought you chaps tucked a lady's silk stocking under your flying helmet for luck!'

Stuart grinned. 'That's right. But it had to be freshly worn, of course. And if you had a crash it meant that the lady didn't care for you any more.'

He reached into the plane and pulled out a flying helmet. With the gesture of a conjuror, he extracted a black silk stocking. 'Can't get out of the habit, you see. But they're not so easy to come by in India. I had to pay someone to steal this for me!'

Joe didn't seek to know more of its provenance.

'But, you know, that story's all romantic hogwash! We *did* carry stockings – but not for luck!'

To Joe's surprise, in a practised gesture, Stuart pulled the stocking over his face and grinned evilly at him through the flimsy fabric. The effect was alarming. The features were no longer recognizable, the gleam of eyes and teeth only visible beneath the flattening taut silk. The leg of the stocking was knotted into a pigtail which added to the outlandish image.

121

'Face mask! Damn good protection against the cold when you're flying in winter at ten thousand feet,' Stuart explained, replacing it in his helmet. 'And, in fact, it's useful against the dust storms out here.'

They moved on down the hangar. As they went, Joe's eye was caught by a rolled-up mattress neatly propped against a wall in a small ante-room the size of a horse stall. 'I hear you sometimes have a guest for the night?' said Joe speculatively.

Stuart smiled. 'Bahadur, you mean? Doesn't take you long to work out the comings and goings in this labyrinth! I feel sorry for that poor little feller. He thinks he's in danger and I wouldn't be surprised if he's right. He's got the idea that if he's a target, then he's going to be a moving target. Speaking as a flyer who's survived, I think that's sound tactics. I help him out when I can. But, you know, Joe, if someone around here wants him dead, then dead is what he's going to be sooner rather than later.'

He spoke with the matter-of-fact acceptance of death Joe was accustomed to hearing from men who had lost comrades every day in the war and continued cheerfully enough with his guided tour. 'Parked over there you've got a Sopwith Camel and then at the far end you'll see two enemies from the war. This here's a Nieuport 17 . . .'

'That's what you flew in France, isn't it?'

'It is. The Lafayette and the French Storks, both outfits flew it. Helped us get on top of the Fokkers that had been doing us so much damage.' He smiled. 'You can imagine what we called it!'

Stuart stood by the side of the bi-plane and patted its gleaming wooden propeller. Joe could see how one could get fond of this little plane. Nearly half the size of the Jenny, with a gently rounded fuselage, it reminded him of his first pony. The compulsion to stroke its shining flank was irresistible.

'You've not been tempted to paint the insignia of the Lafayette on the side?' Joe asked, fingers trailing along the sleek grey paintwork. 'The Apache head, I mean.'

'Seminole,' said Stuart. 'It was a Seminole wearing a war bonnet. No. Some things are better forgotten.'

He strolled over to the last plane. 'And this here's the best plane built in the war years. German air force wasn't supplied with it until the spring of 1918. If they'd had it earlier . . .' He shook his head. 'I wouldn't be standing here and the whole war could well have swung the other way. You've got to admire it though. And you have to picture it with Manfred von Richthoven at the controls.'

'The Red Baron? Is this what he flew?'

'Yep. His unit was the first to be issued with it.'

Joe had never seen the Fokker D. VII close to and found himself murmuring in agreement. The single-seater bi-plane had a narrow, razor-edged fuselage and squared-off wings. Was it handsome? No, rather it was purposeful and sinister, though Joe acknowledged that this could have been the effect of the black paintwork relieved only by a stylized white imperial eagle stencilled on the fuselage behind the pilot's seat.

'160 h.p. Mercedes engine, max speed 124 m.p.h., climbs to ten thousand feet in just over nine minutes. A killing machine. But its best trick is its ability to hang on its propeller at altitude. When the Nieuport will stall or have to lose height, this baby just keeps on soaring.'

The clink of china and a musical call drew their attention back to Ahmed. 'There's our coffee! We'll go sit in the shade over there and you can ask me some policeman-style questions . . . some more policeman-style questions!' he said with slight emphasis. 'Now we've both established who we're talking to,' he added.

'Was it so obvious?' asked Joe, disarmed by the man's openness.

'No. You're good. But, then, so am I. I may take risks in the air but when my feet are on the ground I'm a careful man. And I take no one at face value either. Plenty of carpet-baggers and scoundrels around after the war; folks who'd never heard a shot fired in anger suddenly awarded themselves medals and turned con-artist. Old pros like us can suss them out straight away but most folks are easily taken in. But I guess you can't do much bluffing flying a plane! Either you can or you crash!'

His eyes clouded for a moment as he sipped his coffee with an appreciative grimace. 'But the question you'd really like an answer to is why am I still alive and why is Prithvi dead in my place? And I'll tell you, Joe, I'd like to hear some answers myself.'

'Well, whichever of you was the intended victim – and we'll examine that later – the method of killing may give some solid evidence. List for me, will you, the people who had the technical skill and the opportunity to cut through the elevator wires.'

'Four people. I would, of course. My sister Madeleine. Ahmed, the engineer you saw just now. And Ahmed's brother Ali.'

'This may sound ridiculous but I leave nothing to chance . . . Prithvi himself? Would he have had the knowledge?'

Stuart snorted at the deviousness of the question and considered his answer.

'No, I don't believe he would. He'd have been able to tell you what the elevator *did* because he used it but he probably thought it started and ended with the joy stick. I could never get him interested in the mechanics of the planes. For him, airplanes were like horses – you climbed aboard and rode 'em. You didn't concern yourself too much with the feeding and watering and the state of their teeth and tack. But I see what you mean . . . a sort of suicidal last grand gesture. Cocking a snook at his papa? "Here's how much I think of your state – I'll splat myself all over it."'

He shook his head, still thoughtful. 'Naw! That wasn't Prithvi. He could be a bit of a jerk but underneath he was all Rajput. A scrapper. I admired him. He took on his father and his uncle and faced them both down. I'm talking about his marriage now. He stood by Madeleine in the face of a lot of opposition. He had guts. The arm-twisting went on right from the moment they were married. First off Prithvi was told not to get involved with an American girl and when he took no notice and did and was rash enough to bring his bride home with him, well, you can imagine, the reception was not exactly warm. They never let up on the pressure to get him to marry some respectable Indian girl of their choice. I lost count of the princesses that were dangled before him – they were still trying right up to his death. He rejected a daughter of the house of Jodhpur only last month. All out of loyalty to Madeleine. She's a tough girl, my sister, and she knows what she wants. Made Prithvi swear she'd be the only wife. Maddy's not one to play second fiddle to anyone. Prithvi was as good as his word. And he was more than half-way to becoming a good pilot.'

Joe looked around the small airfield. 'I don't see . . . Ali – did you say?'

'No one sees Ali,' said Stuart bodefully. 'Guy's disappeared. He worked on the planes with his brother. Ali was my rigger and Ahmed my fitter. I've questioned Ahmed. First thing I did! You bet! No one's seen Ali since yesterday morning. Early. He was working on the plane as normal and then just lit out. No one saw him go. Ahmed turned up to check the engine before the flight.'

'And Ahmed failed to notice the cables?'

Stuart's jaw tightened and he squinted into the distance, unable to hold Joe's gaze. 'He didn't notice. But why the hell should he? His responsibility was the engine. He assumed his brother had left the plane ready for flight. He always had. That's what always happened. If I'd taken the flight instead of Prithvi, I might have noticed. But, Joe, I can't be certain.

'Those cables are fine – from a few feet away you can hardly see them and the saboteur had a little trick up his sleeve.'

He gestured to the hangar. 'Come and have a look.'

Coiled on a work bench were the blackened remains of the lethal cable. Joe picked up the raw edge and ran a finger over it. He considered the smear of thick black engine oil on his hand.

'Right,' said Stuart. 'He put that stuff over the cut strands so's there'd be no shine of freshly sawn metal to give him away. And I'll tell you something else. When you line this up in the position it would have occupied – and I already have – you'll see that the frayed part is right over the dark-painted part of the fuselage. Just where it doesn't show. Camouflage. Careful type.'

'Careful. Yes. And what else can we infer? What's your opinion of the man who did this?'

'Someone who knows planes, that's for sure. Someone who knew exactly how many threads to cut through. Someone like Ali.'

'Ali is your rigger, you say?'

'Yes. It's a vital job. These crates are held together with not much more than wire, string and glue and they get buffeted out of shape in the air. As soon as they land, your rigger gets going with his spanners and his levels and he trues it all up again ready for the next flight. It's a skilled job. Ahmed's taken over his brother's duties.'

'Who would have the clout to put pressure on Ali to sabotage the plane and then make sure he wasn't around to tell anyone?'

Stuart spread his hands in a hopeless gesture. 'Dozens of people. The pressure could be money or it could be favours owed or promised. Society here is very . . .' He hesitated for a moment. '. . . seigneurial. Family, tribe – it works through a hierarchy with the maharaja at the top of the pile. Everyone owes allegiance to someone above in the pecking order. Ali was quite low down the ladder and there must be, as I say, dozens of guys who could give him the run-around. And that's not counting the women! First Her Highness would certainly not have been displeased to see Prithvi plummet to the ground!'

'This is bringing us now to the question of who exactly was the intended victim. From your last remark I take it that you assume the intended victim died as planned?'

'I've given it a lot of thought and, really, in the end, I'm wondering why anyone would want to kill me. Madeleine, perhaps – they can't stand her – but me? I'm just a flying chauffeur. Not important. But Prithvi – coming so soon after Bishan and in the context of the ruler's terminal illness . . . You'd say there was a pattern to it even Dr Watson might spot, wouldn't you?'

'Tell me how Prithvi came to be at the controls. How did the switch occur?'

'We'd planned the reception display flight a couple of days back when Claude told us you were coming. Everyone knew about it. I was tempted to sell tickets! You may be wondering,' he said with a wry smile, 'how you come to merit such a salute?'

'It had crossed my mind that Edgar and I aren't exactly in the same league as the Prince of Wales!'

'Boredom! Day follows day out here and they're all the same. Hot, uncomfortable, predictable. You'll do anything to break the routine and if a half-way decent excuse for taking off and stunting about for a while presents itself, you take it.'

'Glad to oblige,' said Joe drily.

'It was a diversion, a distraction, an exercise. We worked on it together but it was always going to be my flight. So, figure my surprise, when, leaving my quarters to head for the hangar, I saw the Jenny taking off. A good five minutes ahead of schedule. I hurried over and grabbed Ahmed and asked him what the hell was going on. Well, you can question him yourself if you want to . . . He said Prithvi came over all geared up for a flight and told him he'd decided to take the Jenny up himself. You don't argue with the heir to the throne so Ahmed spun the propeller and sent him on his way . . . with an unwanted passenger aboard.'

Stuart fell silent, fighting down a shudder. His horror was felt by Joe who remembered the cartoon that had passed from hand to hand along the front line: a young aviator, jaw jutting into the air stream, going gallantly forward unconscious of the grey-shrouded figure he carried in the passenger seat.

'Death,' murmured Joe.

Stuart didn't answer. He was reliving, Joe supposed, the vital five minutes that had separated him from a premature and inexplicable death.

'And this Ali had every opportunity before the fatal flight to cut the wires?'

'Oh, yes. Anyone observing him, myself included, wouldn't have suspected a thing. To all appearances, he would just have been carrying out routine checks and refurbishment. That's how I'd have done it . . .' Stuart said, brow creased in thought. 'Yes. I'd have brought out a set of pre-cut elevator cables and fitted them in place of the existing ones. Then no one gets to hear a saw hacking away at wires just before a flight. He could have done his preparation work well away from the plane in the workshop at any time that suited him.'

He frowned again and watched Ahmed who was working on the engine of the Jenny.

'Common sense tells me, Joe, that Ali cut those wires but that's kinda hard for me to believe.'

'You think Ali was loyal to you?'

'Not to me. No. Nothing personal. But – we found this in the war – the air crew, the fitters and the riggers, identified with the plane they were supporting. The pilot was part of the package, like the wings or the engine. I've had many a bollocking from my crew when I came back to base with a damaged plane. It would go against every instinct for one of these guys to deliberately destroy his pilot and his plane. He wouldn't have killed me. And if the pilot also happened to be his future ruler, well . . .'

'You're saying that you don't think Ali did it at all but that if he did do it, an overwhelming pressure must have been put on the poor chap?'

'Doesn't make sense, does it, but that's about as close as I can get.'

'Any idea where our vital witness might have gone?'

'Sure. We've got ideas. Ahmed thinks he must have returned to his village. That's a day's camel ride from here if you want to go check. He's probably just arriving.'

'You think that would be a waste of time?'

'I do!' Stuart put his cup down carefully and squinted into the sunshine, checking that they were not overheard. 'I think Ali is at the bottom of the lake.'

'You're saying he's joined the ranks of the surplus-to-requirements assassins – like the men who supplied the panther that killed Bishan Singh?'

'Yeah. That sure was one unlucky black cat,' said Stuart bleakly.

'This village to which Ali may have fled – what's its name?' Joe asked.

'Mmm . . . let me think . . . Surigargh! That's it. Surigargh.'

'I've heard of that somewhere,' said Joe. 'Isn't it the maharaja's own native village?'

'So they say.' Stuart fell silent for a moment, eyeing Joe with speculation.

'And a whole day's camel ride away, you said?'

The two men looked at each other and grinned.

'Thought you'd never get around to asking,' said Stuart. 'Plane's ready. Be delighted to take you up. The Jenny can reduce a day to a half-hour there and a half-hour back.' He looked at his watch. 'We could be back in time for tiffin or luncheon if you prefer. We could even land if you want to go in and lean on the headman. There's a stretch of roadway we can use.'

Joe watched as Stuart gave a surprised Ahmed instructions in Hindi. Ahmed was putting a few finishing touches to the aircraft, spanner in hand, checking on the tightness of a screw, running a sinewy finger along the cables to test their tautness. Joe pictured his brother Ali performing just this ritual yesterday.

'The things I do for Sir George and Merry England,' he muttered between clenched teeth.

As they collected their flying helmets and water bottles

from the hangar Stuart talked easily about his hurriedly conceived flight plan. 'We'll do a circuit over the town – make out that we're a couple of airborne trippers, just sightseeing. Nothing untoward in that – everybody does it. Even HM Vyvyan made it known that, if invited, she might not be minded to decline the offer of a short spin over the kingdom!'

'HM?' Joe asked.

'Her High and Mightiness!' Stuart said cheerfully. 'That's what I call her! She's everything the word "memsahib" calls to mind, aren't I right? Ambitious, too. I think she thinks she's in training for the position of Vicereine . . . hope someone remembered to tell poor old Claude!'

Joe was startled. 'You're not serious? Claude as Viceroy? I don't see it!'

'Not a chance, of course! The guy's talented . . . not quite in the Curzon league – who is? – though playing the same game, I'd say. But he loses points on pedigree. You British are still overly impressed by a dukedom or an earldom and all Claude has is a father-in-law who is believed to be a baronet of some sort. Claude's grandfather made quite a fortune for himself in trade as far as I can work out. His son promptly spent the fortune and Claude hangs on to a threadbare family estate back home in Wiltshire, working his way up the ladder of foreign politics and respectability. That's the way he sees the world going.'

'How do you know all this?' Joe asked.

'Told me once in his cups – only time I've ever seen him under the influence of anything but his wife.'

Stuart's expression turned serious for a moment. 'And who's to say he's wrong? The world's changing so fast it makes me giddy! Even out here. And it's the clever and the adaptable who'll come out on top. Make your plans, Joe! I have!'

Before they came within earshot of the patient Ahmed who

stood at the ready, hand on the propeller, Joe asked, 'This Surigargh. You were saying, the native village of Udai and his brother Zalim . . .'

'Yes. That's so. And it's also the home of Udai's favourite concubine, Lal Bai, the mother of Bahadur. Lal Bai means Ruby Girl. She's known throughout the state for her love of jewellery. Has the finest collection of rubies in the land, they say. You ought to try to meet her, Joe. They say she's quite a woman!

Chapter Twelve

Lal Bai hurried down a dark corridor of the Old Palace, red skirt swirling, sandalled feet crunching over shards of broken jewellery. A pile of cheap glass bangles ceremonially broken in grief at the death of the Yuvaraj annoyed her and, impatient, she kicked them out of her way. Gewgaws! Her own jewels were safely hidden away in the toshakhana and there was no chance that she would be expected to sacrifice them according to custom. Lal Bai lived and survived by her own rules.

Why should the women of the zenana give up their pretty things in honour of a man who never visited them? They'd had little time, in any case, to restock their trinket boxes after the funeral of the first son. And Prithvi was not popular. That Angrez wife of his had kept him well away from the harem and even his mad old mother complained she had hardly seen her son since his marriage.

Now his body was being prepared for the burning ghat by the bai-bands. Before the sun set the Jats would carry the bier to the pyre of sandalwood. They would kindle the flames and feed them with cotton oil and camphor and remain in attendance at the samshan until the fire had burned itself out. Then they would remove what was left of the body and throw it into the river. Lal Bai pictured the scene in all its satisfying detail. Prithvi Singh would go to join his brother. Lal Bai smiled in triumph, hastily flicking the tail of her dopatta over her face. So near her goal she could risk no report of disloyal conduct. There were eyes everywhere in this maze and not all were dimmed by tears. She could imagine the relish disguised by false regret in the voice of a treacherous eunuch as he gained audience with the ruler: 'How it pains me, hukham, to speak of such a matter – and you will tear out my tongue if it runs away with me – but on the very day of the funeral of the Yuvaraj, your servant Lal Bai was observed laughing and dancing in the palace . . .'

She bowed her head and went on her way. Her behaviour had been correct and in accordance with her low status. She had crept in to look at the corpse, had scattered rice and marigolds over it and had even thrown in a token glass bangle or two. The room where the body was displayed was hot and uncomfortably full of women weeping and ululating. Musicians beat out a sombre hymn for the dead, drugged heads nodding in time with the insistent, repeated tune. All the palace women had passed through except for his wife. The widow should even now be cutting off her hair, putting on black clothes and preparing to retreat into an obscure room in a distant part of the palace where she would eat meatless dishes from tin thali for the rest of her life – if anyone remembered to feed her. But where was the Angrez?

Going to parties in the Old Palace with the rest of the unclean. Sharing the bed of the latest ferenghi to arrive. A spasm of hatred made her slim shoulders quiver. She would never be able to understand the tastes of these foreigners who were made so welcome at the palace. This tall dark one with the gaze like a lance and the body of a Rajput, the police-sahib whose arrival she had observed through a slatted window, had rejected the attentions of Padmini. Well-named Padmini – the Lotus, the girl she had herself trained in the arts of pleasure. Zalim had been angry but Lal Bai had defended the girl. If the foreigner preferred the company of a drunken white whore to that of the most talented girl in the kingdom he was not worth their attention. They could discount him.

And the she-camel who had spent the night in his room – what was she to make of her? While the body of her

133

husband grew cold and stiff. Shameless whore! Unholy! Lal Bai resolved to speak to Udai Singh about this behaviour as soon as she saw him again. And, after the mourning was over, she was sure she would see him again.

She was the mother of his one remaining son, after all – a girl of fifteen when Bahadur was born. Not a wife but worthy of consideration. And still worthy of his attention. Lal Bai was well aware that she remained youthful and as beautiful as any Padmini. Surely now he would see that he was wasting his time – his precious remaining time – with that gawky girl who was neither truly Hindu nor truly Angrez. The girl had no breasts, no swelling hips, and Lal Bai had laughed discreetly when a palace guard had said that the only thing Third Her Highness liked to feel between her thighs was a polo pony.

Lal Bai pattered on, enjoying the cool of the northern verandah. She had come far from her apartment on the eastern side of the zenana but there was something she was eager to see before she returned to perform puja. She had dismissed her attendant, Chichi Bai, to prepare the incense and offerings for her morning ceremony. She would make puja on this day with gratitude to her family goddess. Mahakali was due her praise. Lal Bai's prayers had been answered and now there were no more obstacles to the fulfilment of the prophecy. Soon after the birth of Bahadur, she had paid many rupees to the fortune teller and she had every day repeated every precious word he had said to her. 'The ruler will be succeeded by his third son. But that third son will be the last ruler.'

The second part of the prophecy sounded alarming but Lal Bai had put it out of her mind. So long as the first part came to pass – that was all that mattered. She had kept it to herself, fearful of arousing jealousy, but for years she had watched the ruler's wives for signs of a late miraculous pregnancy, fearing that one of them might produce a third legitimate heir. She had bribed the maharanees' maids to bring her news each month that all was well and, with time and nature, the threat had died out. But then

Udai had married a third wife. A young wife with many child-bearing years before her.

Lal Bai had been distraught. Left alone in her quarters in the zenana while her lord spent his time with his new bride, she had passed her hours in strenuous prayer and it seemed the goddess had listened to her pleading and granted her request. Month followed month and no announcement of a forthcoming royal birth was made.

And now the first two sons were gone and her lord was growing weaker each day. Surely soon he would announce his successor? Why was he delaying? It was fitting that Bahadur should become maharaja. He had been reared with that intention. Always his father's favourite, he had been quick to learn the tasks his father had set him. He had learned languages and manners from foreign tutors, he had accompanied the maharaja on his tours of the villages learning the workings of law and taxation as well as farming and irrigation. He had learned the traditional warrior skills of a Rajput prince. It had been obvious to everyone – perhaps too obvious – that Udai favoured Bahadur and Lal Bai had had to work hard behind the scenes in the zenana, paying out many rupees to informers to ensure her son's safety. And more than rupees. She had given away many of her much-loved rubies to buy his safety but the sacrifices, the scheming, the plotting against his enemies had brought success.

Now she was to have her reward. With Bahadur on the gaddi, even though it would be six more years before he would rule alone, she would be secure. The maharaja's mother commanded respect, whoever she was. Her son was twelve years old, after all. He had reached the age of the warrior. Time for Lal Bai to ease her vigilance. Time for Bahadur to repay his debt.

She rounded a corner with anticipation and stopped to stare, shielding her face from sight with a fold of her silken scarf. She was aware that her expression of envious longing would not be misinterpreted by any onlooker. Her slight body quivered with the intensity of her desire as she gazed. At her feet lay a swathe of gardens laid out in patterns as complex as the richest embroidery, a representation in flower and shrub of the four rivers of Paradise, but Lal Bai's paradise was further off and of this world. She was looking beyond the garden, to the shore of the lake where, sheltered by the dark green canopy of a grove of neem trees, the white marble columns of an elegant small pavilion rose up, seemingly from the water itself. Balconied windows with fretted white screens overhung the lake. Lal Bai pictured herself there, breathing in the cool air rising off the water, watching the animals that crept down to drink at sunset, summoning with a clap of her hands her evening meal served on a gold thal.

Bahadur would give her the pavilion.

Lal Bai's single exposed dark eye narrowed with determination. Yes, the Maharaja Bahadur would give his mother the pavilion.

When it had been cleansed of the presence of the widow, Shubhada.

Chapter Thirteen

'Now – I'm your maiden aunt, venturing on a motor car ride for the first time. Just bear that in mind, will you?' said Joe, preparing to climb into the forward passenger seat.

Stuart affected astonishment. 'Naw! Don't tell me you're a flying virgin?'

'Not quite that. I've been up a few times,' said Joe with a grin. 'But I should warn you that I had kedgeree for breakfast. And – I don't need to remind you – you're downwind of me!'

After the heart-stopping moment when the light craft tore itself away from the earth they sailed easily upwards. Joe cleared the dust stirred up by their take-off out of his nose and mouth, getting used to the noise of the engine, and began to settle into the flight. Soon he felt bold enough to lean over and take a look at the country below him. They flew straight and level for a while, building Joe's confidence, then circled lazily over the unnaturally silent town surrounding the palace. The only activity Joe could see was taking place on the riverbank and he guessed this to be the burning ghat where the funeral pyre was being prepared.

From this height he suddenly saw that there were two Ranipurs. The ancient city and a modern one. Around the Old and New Palaces clustered a labyrinth of crooked streets which terminated in a large market place. High walls surrounding the old buildings were a clear demarcation between the old and the new. The new city was spread with lavish disregard for space over the plain beyond the river. Built on a grid system with wide avenues, it sprawled towards the desert, its uniform dull red sandstone building blocks relieved by patches of green turf and parks boasting artificial lakes, now, at the height of summer, very depleted. What could be the function of these apparently deserted buildings? Joe saw no signs of life in or around what he took to be public buildings – a school, a hospital perhaps. To the north a road set out boldly towards the desert but stopped after two miles, heaps of building material abandoned on either side of the road.

Their circles grew wider and Joe noted that there were no camel trains, no traffic of any kind making its way across the desert. Everyone was apparently obeying the mourning custom of staying within the city limits but, of course, Ali, with his inside knowledge, would have left early the previous day and had had time to fetch up in Surigargh already.

It was a shock to Joe to see clearly from this height how slender and fragile was the fringe of green crop land surrounding the city. From up here it seemed that the desert was laying siege to Ranipur, and even allowing for the fact that this was the dry season and the yearly monsoon rains could not be expected for another month or two, the desert, he would have said, had won. It spread, rippling below them into the far distance, the khaki wastes criss-crossed by silvery animal-trodden tracks. The Aravalli hills to the west stood, a barrier to the encroaching miles of fluid sand, but even they were under pressure. Great seas of sand had flooded through every gap in the hills, blown through by the winds wherever they found no obstacle.

The rivers and streams which must have poured from the hills into the kingdom in the wet season were no more than dry trackways marked along their length by the occasional well and punctuated by small settlements of round straw-topped herdsmen's huts.

After half an hour of straight flight, Joe began to notice

camel trains making their way south towards Ranipur and calculated that they must be approaching their objective. A few minutes more and he had his first glimpse of Surigargh. The four white minarets of a well caught his eye, the polished lime announcing the presence of water from a great distance. Other evidences of precious water came into view, the dull gleam of a reservoir hidden beneath a magnificent stone structure ornamented with arches and domes, flights of steps leading down on four sides to the water far below.

To his surprise this was no collection of mud huts. It had all the appearance of a fortified town. Stuart poked him in the back and jabbed a finger down to starboard. Joe noted the stone wall snaking its way up a ridge to a small fort with gun emplacements. As they flew over the town Joe guessed that there must be over a thousand houses, and huddled in the centre were one or two large buildings whose purpose puzzled him. From overhead they looked as substantial and as ugly as the fortress at Verdun. One or two were built around a single square, the largest and most central had four squares. Again Stuart indicated that this was of interest and yelled something unintelligible in his ear.

They circled round and prepared for landing. The landing strip Stuart had chosen was a stretch of unfinished tarmacked road which set out hopefully from the town and then finished abruptly, swallowed up into the sand about ten miles off. As they touched down, the plane taxied to a juddering halt and was instantly surrounded by a crowd of young boys, laughing, shouting and jostling to get close. Stuart leaped out, scanning the crowd, and shouted something in Hindi. They retreated a few inches and one stepped forward. He seemed to be known to Stuart and, with much nodding of heads and a quick exchange of cash from hand to hand, it appeared that a protection squad was in operation to keep an eye on the plane. Joe guessed it was not the first time they had done this.

Joe climbed with all the dignity he could muster from

the plane and joined Stuart on the short stroll up the dusty road into the town.

'Well, you can't sneak in unnoticed in a plane,' said Stuart. 'The whole town knows we've arrived.'

People called out greetings from all sides, bands of small boys followed, chirruping, at their heels. They had to move carefully to avoid the equally inquisitive cows which wandered along the street, protected by their sanctity and free to nibble, unchallenged, at whatever took their fancy: succulent green vegetables at a market stall or the pith helmet of a visiting ferenghi. Troops of dark grey bristling pigs rooted in the dry monsoon ditches on either side of the road, recycling the town's refuse, Joe supposed. Children lined up on platforms jutting out over the ditches, small brown bodies glistening as their older sisters sparingly poured water over them from copper jugs. Old men squatted in the shade of trees drinking tea and gaming, shrewd eyes following the two strangers as they walked on and up into the centre of the town.

In a tree-lined square Joe and Stuart found themselves ambushed by a crowd of young boys anxious to direct their attention to one of their fellows who was preparing with the sole aid of a battered attaché case to put on a magic show for the strangers.

To Joe's surprise, Stuart stopped and indicated that he was prepared to watch the show. 'We artistes,' he grinned, 'have to stick together. They're good, these kids. I've never managed to work out how they do what they do. Take a look.'

They watched in delighted astonishment as the ten-year-old prestidigitator performed trick after trick with a running commentary in a mixture of Hindi and English. Small brown hands flashed mesmerizingly, performing impossible feats with the simple props of a few polished stones, copper cups, two red-painted metal balls and a greasy pack of cards. At each magical disappearance of an object they had thought was clearly in their view the child would cry out in triumph, 'Where's it? Gone to Delhi!'

The culmination of his act came with the vanishing of the two red balls from an upturned cup and the subsequent mysterious reappearance of the balls from Joe's crotch, tinkling into the cup the conjuror held up between his legs. Joe put on a show of horror followed by relief to find, on mimed investigation, that his own balls had not gone to Delhi. The audience were delighted and even more delighted when an over-large tip had them all shooting off to the nearest sweetmeat stall.

Still smiling with pleasure, Joe waited until they had run off before turning to Stuart. 'Look, Stuart, I have to tell you, the last person I'm expecting to see here is Ali,' he admitted. 'I'm glad I came but in fact I'm not quite sure what brought us here . . . Curiosity, I suppose . . . It felt right to fill in a bit of background on the maharaja . . . The whole problem seems to stem from the succession and this is where it all started.'

Stuart grinned. 'Your instinct's probably right. This whole nasty business is driven by one question – who succeeds? Did you see the large haveli I pointed out to you? That's where Udai was born and where his cousin, the town headman, still lives. His name's Shardul Singh. We'll go and say hello.'

'Haveli, did you say?'

'Yes. Never heard of the havelis before?' Stuart smiled smugly. 'You're in for a treat! They are rather special. Look, here's a small one coming up on the right.'

The buildings which had appeared block-like and drab from the air were enchanting when seen at street level. Joe stopped and stared in wonder at his first sight of one of the decorated merchants' houses that lined the main street of the town. They presented strong walls punctuated only by rows of small fretted windows and, Joe guessed, were aired and cooled by the internal courtyards he had spotted from the plane. But it was the wall decorations which stunned. As though to counteract the bleak surroundings, the painters had covered the walls with brilliantly coloured frescoes. Joe laughed to see caparisoned elephants in procession, rearing battle-ready horses, hunting scenes, prowling tigers, flowers and birds, even files of red-coated British soldiers and a childlike impression of a train.

Stuart pointed out the most interesting scenes as they walked up the crowded main street, the houses and the standard of painting growing ever more impressive. Joe paused in front of a spectacular display of artistry in a limited palette of red, brown and green, admiring the intricate floral arches outlining two Rajput warriors mounted on gaily decorated steeds. On either side of the main image were smaller pictures of Rajput women. One played with a yoyo, another held a musical instrument, a third, skirts aswirl, ran with bow and arrow and a determined expression, and a fourth, veiled this one, peered from behind her ghungat, fixing the observer with one bright dark eye, ankles and wrists heavy with jewels.

'Here – what do you make of this?' Joe asked, his attention caught by a linear pattern of red handprints running along the bottom of the wall. 'It doesn't seem to chime with the rest of the decoration?'

'Thapas,' said Stuart. 'No, a false note if ever there was one.' He shuffled his foot uncomfortably on the sandy road. 'It's symbolic of the practice of sati. All the widows of the head of the house used to go to the pyre with their dead lord. And his concubines as well. Most went willingly – it was a matter of pride and honour and an outward show of the love they bore for him. But I suppose you know all this? On their way to the fire they dip their right hand into red ochre and leave a print on the wall of the house.'

Joe looked in distress at the line of prints, some no more than child-sized, and stammered, 'But there must be . . .?'

'Never tried to count them. They go all the way around.'

Joe looked more closely. The line of prints was fading progressively as it stretched away but the last two or three seemed to him suspiciously fresh. He shared his suspicions with Stuart.

'It goes on,' said Stuart wearily. 'The British outlawed it a hundred years ago but you can't be everywhere. The last of these prints was put there three years ago, I'm told. But come on, let's go in, shall we? This is the headman's house. The house where Udai was born. They'll be expecting us.'

'Amal khaya, sahib?'

'What's he saying?' asked Joe.

'He's asking if you've had your opium today. He'll provide if you haven't had time for it yet this morning,' said Stuart.

Joe managed to find the right words in Hindi to say thank you but refuse the traditional stimulant. His host, Shardul Singh, waved away the hookah, smiled and asked for tea and pastries to be brought instead. They were seated barefoot and cross-legged on white cotton-covered mattresses laid on the cool marble floor of a verandah overlooking a courtyard filled with flowers and fruit trees. Joe wondered briefly how many buckets of water had to be carried here each day to maintain this profusion. Shardul was simply dressed in white dhoti and kurta with a yellow turban and surrounded by similarly attired smiling men ranging from very old to young. One of the younger ones was brought forward with the explanation that his English was much better than Stuart's Hindi and with great good humour the audience got under way.

The polite compliments flowed from both sides and it was some time before Stuart judged the moment right to introduce his business. Delicately he asked if he might speak with the chief's kinsman, Ali.

The enquiry was greeted with what Joe's keen eye took to be genuine puzzlement. Heads were shaken, consultations took place and questions were asked. The conclusion was that Stuart must have been misinformed about the movements of his rigger. Ali had not returned to his home since he had left it over a year ago to work for Stuart

143

at the palace. The men appeared politely concerned but not alarmed by the alleged disappearance of their kinsman. They were in fact more intrigued by Joe's presence than by Ali's absence and, it seemed to him, were impatiently waiting for some explanation of his arrival amongst them.

Stuart filled in the details of Joe's visit to Ranipur, rather overdoing his importance, Joe thought. Friend of the Viceroy? Celebrated tiger hunter? Polo player extraordinaire? He hoped he would not be expected to demonstrate any of these alleged attributes. And now Stuart was telling them that Joe was also a scholar – a great Brahmin in his own land. He was involved in research for a study of the Shekhavati region. They had all heard of Colonel Tod who a hundred years earlier had written a history of Rajputana? Well, Joe was continuing the Colonel's good work. Would they mind if he asked them a few questions on life amongst the Rajputs?

They didn't mind. They were intrigued. They were voluble in their answers. Joe took out his Scotland Yard notebook and wrote down answers to questions Stuart told him he was asking. He even interposed a few of his own, and so entertained was he by the narrative energy and the delight the men took in their folk stories and the history of their tribe that he was almost caught out when Stuart slipped into the conversation a question about the Ranipur succession. He knew Joe would be very interested to hear the story of the accession of Udai Singh.

A favourite story, obviously, as everyone was eager to offer his own version or correct someone else's. From the torrent of Hindi and English Joe teased out an intriguing tale. Udai, far from being a modest village boy, was the younger son of a well-to-do merchant but not of the royal blood. At his birth nearly half a century ago when the customary horoscope was prepared and read out, his family were stunned to hear that the baby would one day be ruler. The men remembered and recited the horoscope word for word and Stuart translated. '"The boy will one

144

day be maharaja and the father of a maharaja who will see a new sun rise over Ranipur."'

And all had gone as forecast. The old ruler had been childless and, with advancing age, and no doubt aware of the prophecy, had adopted the young Udai, taken him and his older brother to Ranipur and trained them both in the skills required to rule a kingdom. Udai had been a good ruler, they added, and had looked with favour on his native village, doing whatever he could to alleviate the tragedies that the years had brought.

Joe felt his new role of historian called on him to enquire further about the tragedies. Again the response was almost overwhelming. The seven-year drought at the turn of the century, the present drought which threatened to be just as catastrophic, the war in Europe which had killed so many of the young men who had gone off with the Ranipur Lancers, the influenza which had decimated the population, the failing of the trade routes, the unending taxes imposed by the British and the migration of the young to the cities . . . The list was long and full of pain.

As he listened with half an ear to the heartfelt, keening liturgy of loss and devastation, a terrible thought came to Joe. A thought so terrible his mind recoiled from it and he thrust it away. It returned with double force and he knew suddenly why his instinct had led him to Surigargh.

Chapter Fourteen

In the durbar hall Udai Singh heard the Jenny fly overhead and dismissed the remaining supplicants. He sent away his servants and called his brother to his side.

'Our guests are returning, Zalim.'

'As you suspected, Highness, they went off in the direction of Surigargh. The Englishman has a reputation for finding out the truth and a reputation for honesty. Edgar says he is all he appears to be and serves no one but the British Empire. He is Sir George's eyes and ears, they say.'

'But the brain, Zalim, that's what interests me. Has he got the brain to get to the heart of our problem? We must encourage our enterprising detective. If he has been sent to observe, let him observe. Make certain that the telephone line is put always at his disposal – he will need to report back to his master. The man has standing amongst his own people, I observe, and his presence here has already made them more circumspect and calmer . . . like a herd when the shepherd returns. He has no more power than they themselves have but he carries an aura, an illusion of strength which they appear to find comforting. I should like him to stay on for a while. In the days to come there may be a danger for my son, and Bahadur tells me he likes and trusts this man. So be it. Let the policeman be an unofficial bodyguard for the child. Offer him distractions . . . Though not women if the reports are to be believed!'

'He may have rejected Padmini, Highness, but he did not spend the night alone.'

Udai Singh raised an eyebrow.

'The American. Your daughter-in-law . . .'

No one but his brother would have risked passing on this piece of information to the ruler. Udai's reaction was explosive.

'No longer my daughter-in-law!' spat Udai Singh. 'If, indeed, she ever was! The woman is doubly unclean – a foreigner and a widow. He might as well lie with a road-mender! But they are foreign, casteless and have their own habits.'

'I am informed, Highness, that nothing other than conversation took place between them. It is possible that the American merely took shelter with him.'

'Perhaps his tastes lie in other directions? Find out what we can offer him. But sport – that is certain to divert him. We must get the tiger hunt under way and as soon as possible. But, for now, the time has come. Send for the detective and for Edgar. I wish them to attend me here in half an hour. Send also for the scribe in case we need his services for an adjustment to the script and we'd better have the Resident though he is well aware of what I propose. I'll perform this ceremony from the gaddi.'

He turned and walked slowly away, leaving the Dewan to clap his hands and issue commands to the flock of servants who were instantly in attendance.

Edgar and a palace khitmutgar were waiting for Joe as he made his way back to the New Palace. Edgar was not in a welcoming mood.

'Where the hell have you been, Sandilands? Galloping all over the sky today of all days? Looks a bit disrespectful, wouldn't you say? And sending that girl back last night? What the deuce was that all about? She's not some dolly in a box on approval from Hamleys, you know!'

'Just sticking to the unwritten rule of the Raj, Edgar,' said Joe patiently. 'The sahib never accepts a bribe.'

'Unless it's one of the three f's, remember – flowers, fruit or a –'

'Yes, thank you for the reminder! But I don't need it.'

'You could have caused offence. In fact, you've blotted your copybook twice already and you've only been here a few hours. Now listen! The ruler wants to see us both. Straight away. Probably going to give us our marching orders and who will blame him? So comb your hair and follow me.'

They walked along to the throne room, large and splendid and built to accommodate a thousand people. When they entered it was occupied by only five. The ruler sat in splendour on his red velvet gaddi, raised up on a silver base, his head protected by a golden umbrella held by a bearer. A wrinkled old man sat at the foot of the dais, ink pot and pen to hand. Zalim Singh stood at his brother's right hand. Claude hovered discreetly in the background.

'Gentlemen! Good morning! Delighted you are able to spare me a few moments. Wouldn't impose but I have to ask your assistance with an affair of state. It's very simple. I would like you to append your signatures to these documents.'

Udai held up two parchments decorated with several seals and many calligraphic flourishes. To Joe and Edgar they looked very important indeed.

'My will,' said the ruler. 'Or, more precisely, a written statement of my wishes regarding the succession. I have already agreed the content with the Resident.' He nodded briefly in Claude's direction and Claude looked studiously at his shiny boots. 'And it just remains for two good men and true to attest by their signatures that they have witnessed this to be my uncoerced wish.'

He beckoned to the scribe, who took the parchments from his hand and placed them on a portable desk at the side of the room. A fountain pen was produced and all awaited the ceremonial signing.

'I say, sir,' Joe protested, a prey to sudden misgiving, 'surely this should be witnessed by dignitaries of Ranipur and not by two passing condottieri? Are there not some trustworthy court officials of ancient lineage on hand?' he finished with a deprecatory smile to soften his gauche interjection.

'Trustworthy court officials?' said Udai, returning his smile. 'Contradiction in terms, there, Sandilands. And witnesses have been known to disappear, have their minds changed, even end up floating in the lake. We've made two copies of this and you're going to take one away with you. You may read it – indeed, I feel you should,' said Udai helpfully as they went over to the desk.

Edgar snatched up the pen and, briefly scanning the document, signed without delay in the spaces the scribe indicated but Joe took a few moments to absorb the contents of the will.

No surprises here. Bahadur, the natural son of Udai Singh, was to become ruler on the death of his father and two regents were named to govern until the boy reached the age of eighteen.

Joe looked with interest at the names: Claude Vyvyan and Her Highness, the Maharanee Shubhada.

Joe signed and the scribe carefully rolled up the documents and wrapped each around with a swatch of red velvet. One he handed to the ruler and the other to Joe.

'Quite a business,' commented Udai. 'And you will not be deceived, I know! This little performance is put on for the eyes of the British Empire. My own state and subjects are not so demanding and the succession is announced more simply. This evening my son, Bahadur, will eat from my plate at a public meal and, by this act, be recognized by all as my heir. Now that's out of the way, why don't we all go out on to the terrace and have a celebratory drink?'

They looked politely aside as Zalim helped his brother to rise from the gaddi and make his painful way out of the room, leaning heavily on his shoulder. Joe lagged behind, uncertain and disturbed. There was something about the composition of the will, just one small detail, that had struck him as odd. The date, 16th June, had been written into both copies in ink of a slightly different colour from the original. Stephens blue-black instead of Stephens black.

On an impulse, Joe approached the old scribe and began to help him fold up his writing table. He eyed the man surreptitiously. Obviously the man wrote in English but did he speak the language? How would he react to being asked a question? Oh, what the hell! Joe decided to take a chance on low English cunning and Indian eagerness to please. 'How good is your memory, I wonder, sir?' he said with a wide and friendly smile. 'Can you remember the exact day in April the ruler asked you to draw up this document?'

'Certainly I can remember!' said the old man proudly. 'It was the third day of April.'

Chillingly, his shot in the dark had produced an innocent piece of information which shored up the fantastical theory he'd been building since his visit to Surigargh. His first reaction was to get hold of Edgar and lay out his ideas but he suppressed it. He would never be entirely sure of Edgar.

Edgar was waiting for him in the corridor. 'Now what are you up to? Not a good idea to be seen fraternizing with the lower degrees, Sandilands. Just keep your mind on the job in hand, will you? Remember you're due to telephone Sir George this evening with a progress report. You'd better have something up your sleeve. He's not going to be impressed when you tell him you've spent your morning going up for a five bob flip around the countryside and hobnobbing with the natives.'

'You're quite right, Edgar, old man,' said Joe equably. 'But I shall have the news of the succession to pass on and that's quite something! The dark horse has come in first and it just happens to be the one Sir George has his money

150

on. That's bound to please him . . . assuming he wasn't already aware of the situation. He always seems to be one jump ahead of everyone else.'

'Not so sure he's going to like all the details,' Edgar muttered. '"Woe to the land where a minor rules or a woman bears sway," they say in Rajputana. And here, it seems, we've got a double dose of bad luck! Now, come on! We're bidden to have a drink on the terrace. Better make it a quick one, if we can. I understand you have people queuing up to see you and I have a tiger shoot to plan with Colin.'

The mood and composition of the group on the terrace was subtly changed. The maharaja and his brother had been joined by a selection of courtiers, and a man in dark blue uniform with a good deal of gold frogging had stationed himself behind Udai's right shoulder. The pop of champagne corks was echoed by a gush of congratulations. The release of tension was evident as all raised their glasses to salute the new heir, the Yuvaraj Bahadur.

All drank except for the uniformed stranger who remained at attention, motionless apart from his dark eyes which constantly moved around the group. Joe was not quite comfortable with the length of time they locked with his own. He was reminded of one of those playground staring games where the first to look away was the loser and he was relieved when the ruler called to him by name, compelling him to break off.

'Joe. Commander Sandilands. I want you to meet your opposite number in the Ranipur force. This is Major Ajit Singh.'

No hand was extended so Joe returned the formal nod of the head.

'Ajit is responsible for policing the state, and the very low level of crime we enjoy bears witness to the efficacy of his methods. I'm sure you'll have much in common and much that you do not have in common. I will leave you to exchange views. Oh, by the way, I understand you visited

151

Surigargh this morning, Commander? Ajit's home town as well as my own.'

He moved away to speak to Claude, leaving Joe face to face with the Chief of Police.

Ajit Singh's tall frame was held erect. A dark moustache shot through with silver rose in two smooth wings to tuck under the white turban. Every aspect of his uniform was immaculate and Joe was interested to note the whole impression was of a serious, even – for India – understated military presence. The most pernickety sergeant-major of any crack regiment could have taken lessons in turn-out from this man.

'We will speak in English,' said Ajit firmly.

Joe was accustomed to deep and mysterious Indian voices which made the tones of the average Englishman sound insubstantial, superficial, braying at times, but Ajit Singh's voice was distinctive even for a Rajput. Joe thought he must gargle with a suspension of sharp-sand in honey to achieve these depths – guttural but seductive.

'I do not speak well but I hear that you do not speak Hindi at all,' Ajit added blandly.

Joe smiled, conceding the first point in the arm-wrestling contest into which he had been propelled. Ajit crooked a finger and from his place at the door a young officer attired in similar dark blue, though with considerably less gold about him, came respectfully threading his way through the crowd towards them.

'Ram speaks excellent English, Sandilands, and he will help us to converse,' Ajit explained. 'He had his training with the Calcutta Police.'

'Okay,' thought Joe. 'Two points to Ajit Singh.'

The young officer shook his hand and introduced himself briefly in flawless English, and Ajit commented, tapping the man proprietorially on the shoulder, 'You are looking, Commander, at the next Chief of State Police. At the very least – for Ram could go further. His career, I fear, will call him to the capital where he will do well.'

They plunged into a surprisingly easy conversation.

Ram was eager to pick Joe's brain and questioned him closely on Western developments in policing methods and crime solving. Expressions of interest and astonishment greeted his outlines of the first Flying Squad and the proposals for an international police force. He was intrigued by the new techniques of ballistics which Joe was passionately pushing forward and listened intently to his ideas on the use of dual-microscope examination of cartridges.

Claude, who had approached to the fringes of the group, seemed equally impressed. 'And you're saying that these processes are even now available to the Calcutta Police, Sandilands?

'Not only to the Calcutta Police but to the whole country. Much of what you've heard me boasting of, I must admit, is still in the experimental stage but yes – certain analytical ballistic techniques are available to us. We can match a cartridge case to the breech face of the gun that fired it; we can match the rifling marks on a bullet to the barrel down which it came. As clear and as useful as fingerprinting. It's all early days, but showing reliable results already. Evidence collected, let's say here in Ranipur, can be sent to police headquarters in Calcutta and in a couple of days you can get your analysis back by telegraph. Crime solving is throwing down barriers everywhere and criminals can no longer hide behind frontiers. They can be pursued across oceans if necessary.'

Joe went on to talk about the use of the Woman Police Force, which amazed and amused Ram, and the improvements in the working conditions and pay amongst the ranks, which puzzled him. 'Here in Ranipur,' he confided, 'we have no need of such a large force. No one patrols the bazaars, the streets that is.'

'Then how do you control petty crime?' Joe asked.

'In each street there is an informer. An unofficial, though well-rewarded, person who acts as eyes and ears for Ajit Singh. If a crime occurs, it is first discovered locally and news comes to us at once. Action is taken. The criminals are usually known in their own street and because they are certain of discovery, you can appreciate, sahib, that the incidence of crime is very low indeed.'

'All very well for your average petty criminal, I suppose,' said Joe, 'but tell me, Ram, how would you deal with a crime committed by – oh, let's say . . .' He waved an arm around the assembled company. '. . . one of the noblemen present in this room?'

He instantly wished he could pull back his question but, too late, the young man stammered an unintelligible reply, embarrassed and looking to Ajit Singh for support.

Ajit spoke easily, a slight touch of amusement in his voice: 'What Ram is trying to say is that there *is* no crime amongst the nobility, Commander. I'm sure you understand. When did your King George last pick a pocket? Have you arrested Queen Mary yet for poisoning her cook?'

Joe smiled at the attempted humour and was relieved when Ajit himself changed the subject. 'But I understand, Commander, that we find ourselves working towards the same end, here in Ranipur?'

'I would be surprised to hear that,' said Joe carefully, 'since I am not working and would not be allowed to work, professionally that is. Pleasure only is my reason for being here.'

Ajit's whiskers twitched slightly. 'Then I . . .' He referred to Ram for help with a word. '. . . anticipate the ruler's command. He has discussed with me the possibility that you might be asked to help me to keep a protective eye on the new heir, the Prince Bahadur. These are unusual times, as I think you appreciate, and this young man may be in need of our aid. He has confided to his father that he likes and trusts you. It will give him confidence to see himself protected on all sides.'

'Is this protection squad a recent development?' Joe asked.

'In fact – no,' said Ajit. 'The boy will be unaware of it but he has been watched since he left the safety of the zenana.'

Joe wondered just how safe the zenana might be considered in the light of Bahadur's information but raised no question.

'He has chosen to spend his time in some unusual places,' Ajit smiled. 'And my staff have complained about the difficulties they have experienced in staying close to him whilst remaining unobserved. But, as you see, the boy is fit and well and no attempt on his life has been uncovered.'

Joe looked away from the magnetic eyes for a moment to hide his own expression. 'What a pantomime!' he thought.

Aloud he said, 'I shall, of course, be delighted to join you in any attempt to preserve the Prince Bahadur's peace of mind or, indeed, his life.'

Ajit bowed politely to his new colleague.

'I was lucky enough to see the town of Surigargh this morning, Ajit Singh. I understand you know it well?'

'It is my native town, Commander, and very lovely. I have travelled much . . .' He hesitated, then confided, 'I too was in the war in France. I went there with the Ranipur Lancers and survived. I have seen nothing in your continent which can compare with Surigargh.'

Joe nodded in agreement.

'But tell me, Sandilands, because I do not take you for a tourist, why you went there.'

'I say, is this official, this line of questioning?' Joe asked lightly.

'Not at all,' smiled Ajit, 'it is merely conversation. Because I know why you went there. No secret!'

'Ali,' said Joe. 'We are looking rather urgently for Captain Mercer's rigger. Mercer is finding it difficult to manage without his trained rigger as I'm sure you can appreciate. We had heard that Ali had returned to Surigargh. Not sure why.'

'You would not find him there,' said Ajit.

'No indeed. No one had seen him apparently. They had no idea where he might have gone. I wonder if you have any idea, Ajit, of his present whereabouts?'

'Oh, yes,' was the laconic reply. 'I'm surprised you didn't ask.'

Joe waited, an enquiring smile on his lips. The smile faded at the finality of Ajit Singh's next pronouncement.

'Gone to Delhi!'

Chapter Fifteen

Joe was relieved to be tugged by the sleeve at this moment and to hear Edgar's apologetic voice: 'Sorry to break up this coppers' convention, Ajit, old man,' he said affably, 'but Sandilands is much in demand this morning and is half-way through his calling list. Will you excuse us?'

Joe added his own excuses and followed Edgar from the room. 'Well, thanks for rescuing me from the Inquisition, Edgar! What a formidable man! I hope he never decides he wants to speak to me in his professional capacity!'

'Good bloke, Ajit. In his way. Keeps control. Does what Udai wants done and does it without fuss. Brave feller too – much decorated, I understand, in the war. Still – I know what you mean. Don't go annoying him, Joe. I wouldn't like to have to spring you from one of his dungeons. I don't forget I was once on the receiving end of his policing methods.'

'I'll bear it in mind. And now – in pursuit of something positive to report back – perhaps you could put me in touch with Sir Hector who is somewhere about in this warren. He asked if he might see me this morning. There's still a bit of the morning remaining.'

Edgar grunted, 'Well, you'd better make it quick. I have to pass on to you an invitation to take tiffin with the Vyvyans. Lois told me to bid you to present yourself at the Residence at twelve thirty sharp. She can't abide lounge lizards, so smarten yourself up, try to look a bit *military* if you can remember how that's done and be punctual. I'll summon Govind to take you there. Now, follow me,' he said and walked ahead.

Some minutes later they had arrived again in the New Palace and Edgar knocked at the door of a suite which appeared to be the twin of Joe's own. The old physician opened the door at once and welcomed Joe. Edgar made his excuses and left them together. While Sir Hector bumbled off to a sideboard to pour out a whisky-soda Joe cast an eye quickly around the rooms. He was intrigued to see how the doctor had arranged the accommodation to suit himself. The bed and chairs had been swept into the smaller of the two living rooms and the larger now looked like a combination of library and consulting room. Benches were stacked with files and cases of instruments, a brass microscope with black japanned base and bearing the label 'Zeiss. Jena' stood at the ready. There was even a large table in the centre of the room on which a patient, or a corpse perhaps, could have been accommodated. Piles of fresh white linen and rows of glass pill bottles gave the room a reassuringly efficient air.

'Do you have help here?' asked Joe. 'You seem to be running a small hospital . . .'

'As a matter of fact, I do have help,' said Sir Hector. 'I've got a squad of young chaps I'm training up. They're very good. Wasn't easy to recruit them though at first. They have their own system out here, you know. Ayurvedic medicine it's called. Leaves, herbs, roots and so on. I'm afraid the court physician wasn't very pleased to see me coming over the horizon, but there you are – the ruler is very Western in some of his ways. He called me in too late though. And the deaths of his two sons have sapped his will to live, you'd say. Terrible setback for any parent, lethal for a chap who's got weeks to live. To be frank, I've been alarmed at the rate at which he's sunk since his sons started dropping off the twig. Bound to drag you down, disasters like that – so unnatural for one's sons to die before one. Many of us learned that sad lesson in the war, don't you know . . .' His voice trailed away.

'Is there nothing you can do, sir?'

'Nothing. Painkillers when necessary but even that's superfluous – they have their own local supplies, as you'll be aware. In fact his Ayurvedic remedies may well prove to be the most efficacious when it comes to these last stages.' He frowned and went on, 'I'm trying to learn what it's all about and I have to say it's not all the mumbo-jumbo you might expect. Oh, no. I've seen some quite remarkable things . . . The ruler keeps a potion about the place at all times and when he feels he's *in extremis* he'll swallow it.'

'Kill himself, do you mean?' Joe was alarmed.

'No, no.' Sir Hector shook his head and smiled. 'Quite the reverse. It's something called hiranya garbha. It's a blend of pure gold – yes, the metal – goodness knows what the process might be for melting it down and making it digestible! – and ginger and other reviving herbs. If you take it on your deathbed, it's reputed to bring you round sufficiently to enable you to talk. Been used – you can imagine the circumstances! – to elicit a last-gasp answer to urgent questions of the "Where did you hide the key of the treasure house, bapuji?" type. I will observe its effects with interest, should the occasion arise. Might even write a paper on it . . . But it's not the ruler's demise I wanted to talk to you about,' he finished hesitantly.

Joe sipped his whisky and waited.

'The deaths of the two sons have concerned me. Well, of course, they've concerned everyone. And from your presence amongst us, Sandilands, I'd guess that the powers that be are troubled also. Is that right?'

Joe nodded. 'Yes, indeed, sir. And we were wondering whether you had any information regarding the deaths, any medical information perhaps, that might help us to understand the circumstances?'

'Difficult. Hindus don't go in for post-mortems, you know. I wouldn't have been expected to carry one out on the princes and, after all, the cause of the deaths was very clear in each case. But in the case of the elder prince –

159

Bishan, wasn't it? – the ruler actually asked me to inspect the body. Not the regular carve up, you understand, more a snoop around to give him the specific information he wanted.'

'Which was . . .?'

'Quite simply – did the boy suffer? That's all.'

'A reasonable request from a father?' suggested Joe.

'Yes, of course. A natural need to know. But it was the answer to the question that intrigued me.'

Sir Hector nodded towards the central table. 'Had the body brought here before we gave it over to the bai-bands. You know the circumstances of the death?'

Joe nodded. 'Savaged by a wild panther, I hear?'

'In a nutshell, yes. The body was a mess, as you can imagine. The flesh was shredded, one arm torn off . . . the beast must have been hungry – it had started to eat him. But, you're a hunter, perhaps you are aware that a panther kills cleanly? One blow would have been enough to finish him off and I think I identified the lethal blow. To the throat. Where you'd expect it. The subsequent mangling looked dramatically hideous but practically all the wounds occurred after the poor chap was already dead.'

'So the answer to Udai Singh's question would be that his son did not suffer an unduly horrifying or protracted death?'

'That's so. But there's something else. Difficult to tell with the destruction of tissue but there were signs that he'd taken a stiff dose of opium: pinpoint pupils, discoloration of the tongue. Now, Bishan wasn't a complete fool. He took opium every morning, many Rajputs do – it's hardly significant to them. Of as much note as this whisky we're both enjoying.' He waved his glass at Joe and offered to refill it. 'It fortifies them for the day. But it doesn't make them blind and deaf. On a normal day there's no way Bishan would have failed to notice that the beast's jaws were not sewn up and it still had its claws.'

'But this was not a normal day?'

'Well, it didn't make much sense to me, the whole scene,

so I called for his body servant, the chap who was always close to the prince in the morning, and questioned him. Easier said than done! These princes are surrounded by a retinue of servants, all apparently completely loyal to their master. Well, that's Rajputs for you – they'll defend their rulers whatever their faults. Anyway, I finally got hold of the right chap, gained his confidence and listened to what he had to tell me . . . I say, I hope I haven't muddied the waters?'

'On the contrary, you did exactly the right thing.'

'Good to hear you say so. Well, I asked him how much of the drug he'd taken . . . made him describe Bishan's routine. The servant confirmed that Bishan took his opium in the traditional local manner. Here . . . Look.'

Sir Hector opened a drawer, took out a small object and put it into Joe's palm. Joe studied the ball of dull yellow-grey substance with interest.

'This is how it's prepared for consumption.'

'Nothing like this at Ciro's,' said Joe.

'I'm sincerely glad to hear it! It's been cooked in milk and sugar to counteract the evil taste.'

'What on earth are you supposed to do with it?'

'You take one of these,' said Sir Hector, picking up an oval-shaped mortar. 'I say, Sandilands, don't assume that I always have the makings to hand, will you? I took the liberty of removing these from Bishan's rooms . . . You pop the opium ball into the mortar and crush it. Then you mix it with water, filter it and drink. It's a lot faster and much more immediate than smoking it through a hookah which is an alternative.'

'Where did he get it from? Who was his supplier?'

'No mystery there. It's not exactly on prescription, you know. You can get it in any bazaar but Bishan got his from a local tribe – the Bishnoi – who live further south near Jodhpur. They're farmers, pacifists, nature-lovers, tree-worshippers, if you can believe.'

'And purveyors of strange substances to the royal family?'

'For generations. Apparently Bishan had been taking a mild formula for years and appeared to be accustomed to it and tolerating it reasonably well. But then, according to the servant, two days before he died, Bishan asked him to make up his drink using a different supply. He produced a box with three balls of opium and had one made up in the usual way. From its effects the servant assumed it was a stronger formula – it put Bishan on his back for half the day.

'He recovered and, nothing loath, took a second shot at it the following morning. He was just *compos mentis* enough to follow his morning routine, including the panther wrestling, with lethal consequences. That ball of opium you're holding in your hand is the third and last remaining sample of the special batch. It would be interesting to find out how he came by them. Not, I think, from the servant who had been most helpful. When he realized what I was suspecting, he began to panic. By this time, the chap was quivering with fear, naturally. Thought he might be suspected of being instrumental in something nefarious and might expect a visit from Ajit Singh and his merry men. I think I managed to calm him down and dismissed it as nothing important – just a physician's curiosity. They all know I'm interested in Indian medicine so I think I covered my tracks.

'I brought the samples back here and tested them and – sure enough – there was a difference. The new box contained pills incorporating a dose that would have almost paralysed anyone who consumed them.' He paused for a moment and added, 'If Bishan took one of those horse pills he would have entered the panther cage flying! He would have been so high he wouldn't have noticed the beast until it tore his throat out and probably didn't feel much even then. Yes, my answer to the maharaja's question was – "No, sire, your son did not suffer."'

'But we're left wondering why the presumed heir to the throne changed his formula?'

'Exactly. On paper this is a clear case of death by mis-adventure . . . but who supplied him with the opium that dulled his senses to a point where he would walk into that cage? The panther killed him all right. But who *murdered* him, Sandilands?'

Chapter Sixteen

A name was on the tip of Joe's tongue.

The urge to answer the doctor's question and indulge with him in a little fervid speculation was almost overwhelming. He sensed that Sir Hector would have been a lively co-conspirator, perfectly willing to listen to his outrageous suggestion and talk through it with him. A vision of Charlie Carter back in Simla came to Joe and he found he was missing the superintendent's salty common sense and his local knowledge, missing his companionship and support. But silence, for the moment, was his only recourse. He fought back his own excitement at the laying of a further brick in the foundation of his theory. If he reasoned rightly, the enormity of his revelation would be such that it could only be allowed to reach the ear of one man: the man who held the invisible reins of power in India, the *éminence grise* behind the Viceroy – Sir George Jardine. But Joe was not yet so certain of the identity of the killer of the ruler's sons that he could alert Sir George.

He was aware of the danger of building on one idea to the exclusion of all others and was determined that the seductive completeness and simplicity of his theory would not cut him off from other avenues of enquiry. He was frustrated by his powerlessness to conduct an investigation by the book. His brief restricted him to cruising around this alien crime scene, picking up bits of information from whoever was willing to divulge them. And he was not deceived – some of the facts and impressions confided to him might well have been as misdirecting and distracting as the swift brown hands of the child conjuror in Surigargh.

He sighed and thanked Sir Hector for his evidence and for sharing his concerns with him. He reassured him once more that his actions had been exactly what Scotland Yard would have approved and begged his continued discretion. As he prepared to leave, he was struck by a sudden thought. 'Sir Hector, can you tell me . . . not sure how intimate you are with the royal family . . . can you tell me whether Bishan was married? What his family circumstances were?'

The old physician looked puzzled for a moment then replied slowly, 'Yes, of course, I can see why you'd want to know that and perhaps it takes a fresh eye to look at the situation from that angle. I believe he had a wife but I don't remember hearing of any offspring.' He cleared his throat and looked uncomfortable then added, 'Doesn't have the reputation of being a terribly uxorious fellow, if you take my meaning. But you'd need to ask someone closer to the family than I, Sandilands. Being a medic – you know, you get out of the habit of gossiping. Sorry, old man . . . I'd like to help.' Thoughtfully he said, 'And this means that now Udai will never see a grandchild. Pity, that. He's quite a patriarch at heart . . . they all are.'

As Joe nodded goodbye, Sir Hector, on impulse, seized him by the hand.

'Now look here, Sandilands – you will keep in mind the fact that the ruler has a third son to lose, won't you? It would be unbearable if anything were to happen to that bright young chap.'

Joe considered for a moment and then replied, 'Don't concern yourself, sir. I have a feeling that young Bahadur is safe enough. Now.'

Govind was already waiting by the door to take Joe on to his next meeting. A quick visit to his own quarters enabled him to shower and rub himself down and exchange his sweat-stained shirt and trousers for the fresh ones which had been laid out on his bed. Linen trousers, white shirt, a club tie that he could not instantly identify and a discreet blazer borrowed and adapted from Sir George's stock, he noted. This seemed to be a formal enough occasion and in England he would have arrived on Lois's doorstep clutching a bunch of flowers, but here? He wondered what was the custom.

'Govind? Should I take a small gift for my hostess? What do you think?'

'Sahib, I think Mrs Vyvyan would welcome, would even expect a small token. Not flowers perhaps as she has surrounded herself with them . . .' He thought for a moment while Joe waited expectantly for the elusive word. 'Bounteously!' he added, pleased with his adverb. 'You will see! But madam does enjoy reading. And anything that comes from Home is always eagerly accepted.' He smiled, looked calculatingly at Joe and decided to go further. 'I believe that the sahib has amongst his luggage one or two copies of books, recent ones, by her favourite author. She would be delighted to find herself the recipient of, shall we say, *Jill the Reckless* by P.G. Wodehouse.'

Joe grinned. 'Well, luckily I've just finished reading it. Good thought, Govind! And perhaps it should be accompanied by *The Indiscretions of Archie* for Mr Vyvyan?'

Privately, he wondered how many of this author's books Govind had himself devoured.

While Joe put the finishing touches to his outfit, Govind located the books and carefully tied them up with a ribbon by which they might be carried since the dark blue dye of the covers would undoubtedly smudge if they came into contact with a hot hand, he explained. Not for the first time, Joe wondered at the courtesy and high efficiency he encountered everywhere in India and asked himself how on earth he was going to manage his affairs back home in his flat overlooking the Thames. He contrasted the stately, all-knowing Govind and his impeccable arrangements with portly Mrs Jago who twice a week rolled up her sleeves, adjusted her pinny and did battle with the smuts deposited on his rooms by the neighbouring Lots Road power station.

Catching Govind's surreptitious glance at his watch, Joe hurried to present himself, noting that as they were a good fifteen minutes ahead of the lunch appointment, the Vyvyans' quarters must be at some distance from his own.

'Far to go, Govind?' Joe asked, walking smartly down the corridor of the New Palace alongside his escort.

'Quite far, sahib. But a pleasant walk. To the north of the Old Palace, between the palace and the lake is a house which was built many, many years ago as a retreat for the rajmata, the queen mother. It is now used as the Residency.'

They arrived at last in front of a fifteen foot high wall covered in cascades of pink and white pelargoniums, and Govind led the way through an archway into a garden which took Joe's breath away. He grinned. 'You said it, Govind! "Bounteous". That's the only word for this show! Eat your heart out, Wisley!'

A profusion of foliage and flowers, many recognizably English ones, clustered around a small but gracious Moghul-inspired dower house. A flight of marble steps led to a pillared portico and an open door at which stood Lois Vyvyan. Looking for all the world like a Staffordshire figurine, was Joe's impression, as he took in the light afternoon dress of lilac, the trug spilling over with marguerites and dahlias that she held on her arm. Catching sight of them, she handed the trug to a servant standing by, dusted off her hands and came forward to greet Joe.

She aimed a smile at a spot a fraction over Joe's right shoulder. 'Welcome to the Residency, Commander.'

She dismissed Govind with a nod and indicated that Joe should install himself in one of the rattan planter's chairs which stood on the verandah. 'May I get you a drink? We have sherry, champagne, hock . . . ' she said vaguely.

167

'The idea of a glass of hock is suddenly appealing,' said Joe affably and another servant was sent off to fetch the drinks tray.

'We are well provided for, you'll find,' she said. 'Anything – well, most things – one has at Home is available in Ranipur. You just have to ask. Udai is very generous. The only thing the Residency lacks, in fact,' she smiled and arched a carefully plucked eyebrow, 'is the Resident! Claude! He works too hard. The cry of the memsahib all over India, I know! But it's true. Always one more document to complete, one more letter to dictate, one more petitioner to see . . . He will be joining us shortly.'

'Where does your husband do his work? Here at the Residency?'

'No. This building is very lovely but hardly commodious. We have four reception rooms and six bedrooms and that's quite small for India. Claude has his office in a bungalow down by the lake. A good arrangement. I would not care to have my house trampled through by all and sundry. Oh, excuse me – may I take your parcel?' she asked, catching sight of the bundle of books.

'You may indeed take it,' said Joe. 'And keep it. It's a small gift for you and the sahib. Govind assures me that you appreciate Wodehouse.'

As he handed over the books he was struck by a sudden doubt. Had Govind got it right? Did this stiff Englishwoman have a sense of humour? But her reaction was spontaneous and certainly not a snort of disgust.

'You are too kind! But what a treat! Oh, are you sure you can spare them?' she said, unfastening the ribbon with eager fingers. '*Jill the Reckless*. Oh, good! I haven't read it.'

'It's very new,' said Joe, pleased at last to feel he was living in the same world as Lois Vyvyan. And to pass the time until the arrival of the drinks, 'I've just finished it. It's the usual story of a pretty young girl who loses her fortune and has to go, penniless, across the ocean to find herself a congenial, rich man . . . I think you'll enjoy it,' he finished hurriedly, not at all convinced by Lois's arching eyebrows that she would.

But perhaps his doubts were a delusion as she replied in a friendly enough tone, 'I'm sure I shall. And what have we here? For Claude? *The Indiscretions of Archie*?' For a moment he had a clear notion that if Lois were capable of a giggle she was attempting to repress one. 'Commander, are you trying to convey a message?'

The drinks tray arrived at that moment and Lois did not wait for his answer but busied herself checking its contents.

'Here's your hock. A good one, I think. Seltzer for you? No? Why don't you bring it through to the drawing room? I hear you have quite an eye for architecture, Commander, and you must be curious to see the interior. It does not disappoint!'

It didn't. Joe thought he could live out his life in this pretty house and count himself blessed. By Indian standards the rooms were, indeed, small but Lois had chosen to furnish them appropriately in pieces lighter than the usual Western, overstuffed, oversized, dark wood relics of the Victorian age. Unusually for a memsahib, she had introduced one or two items of Indian workmanship; a long low white upholstered sofa was scattered with piles of silk cushions in lime, purple and magenta and in pride of place was a white-painted grand piano.

Joe walked over to it and ran a hand over the keys. 'Do you play, Mrs Vyvyan?'

'Yes.' She smiled. 'Not well, but with more skill than you, apparently. What was that? I didn't recognize it.'

'Not entirely sure the composer would have either,' said Joe. '"Elite Syncopations". Scott Joplin . . .'

'Ah. I'm not familiar with jazz,' said Lois. Her tone made it quite clear that she sought no greater familiarity.

Joe turned his attention to the ranks of framed photographs methodically lined up on the piano. Some were in sepia, some in black and white, all were formal portraits. In prime position on the front row was an army man so like Lois, Joe asked without hesitation, 'Your father?'

She smiled sadly. 'Killed in France. He should have retired years before but,' she shrugged a slim shoulder, 'you know how it is with military men, Commander. When your country needs you, you make yourself available. And my father was army to the core.'

Her pride was evident. Joe looked more closely at the uniform, trying to identify the rank. 'Brigadier-General, I think? Your father did well.'

'At whatever he attempted,' was the brief reply.

Joe's eye was caught by a distracting detail of the Brigadier's uniform and he turned his face away from Lois, unwilling to reveal his fleeting expression of interest and surprise. Could he have this right? he wondered and checked again discreetly. Yes, it was small but there was no mistaking the insignia.

He could have commented on it, shown an informed interest in the wreath of oak leaves surrounding the letters RFC, asked a polite question, but he decided, on impulse, to keep his observation to himself. Enough to note that Lois didn't consider it worthy of comment.

'Your rank intrigues me,' Lois went on. 'Commander? It has a naval ring to it?'

'Yes. And quite deliberately so. You are intended to be impressed by it. You are intended to think, "My goodness! If such a young and dashing chap can attain the rank of Commander, he must be of high ability and of some consequence in the force."'

He had attempted a light, self-deprecating tone but Lois was ready, as usual, with her barbed comment. 'Or perhaps, "Here is a young man who has stepped into dead men's shoes"? Many gaps in the ranks after the war. Too many green young colonels in the services. I suppose it was the same with the police?'

In all his time in India, Lois Vyvyan was the first to question him about his rank. She seemed genuinely interested and well informed, if annoyingly rude. Did she choose deliberately to ruffle his feathers? Joe was reminded strongly of a little Angus terrier he had owned before the war. It had hated strangers and would approach them, tail wagging with every sign of good humour but the moment a hand was extended in friendship, that hand would receive a nasty nip. Joe knew the dog couldn't help it. He set out to be welcoming, he knew he ought to be friendly but he just had to bite first.

'Well, I left the army a green major,' said Joe, 'and not being a dyed-in-the-wool military man I was very ready to transfer to the police force.'

'Strange decision?' said Lois. 'Wasn't it? Did no one advise you against it? Pounding the beat and apprehending small boys stealing apples must have seemed rather tame after four years of battling the Kaiser?'

'Delightfully tame,' said Joe with a broad grin. 'I was never a career soldier. But I was promoted quickly from apple-scrumping arrests. There are in normal times two commanders for the London area. I was appointed a third with special duties.'

Lois was listening with genuine interest so he carried on. 'After the war, many officers were turned loose on the civilized world to make their way in it again. Many had had their lives destroyed, their position in society usurped, their wealth dissipated, their fiancées stolen . . . And what were they left with? With a carefully nurtured ability to kill and to survive and a coarsened sense of morality on which to base their future existence. You will be shocked but perhaps not surprised to learn that some of these trained killers took to a life of crime and violence.'

Lois nodded.

'And who was there to apprehend this new breed of villain – the upper class crook? Not a bumbling, blue-caped bobby, wobbling along on a bike! Imagine, will you, arriving at a large country house or at a flat in Albany to put a question or two to the Right Honourable Fruity Featherstonehaugh. A bobby would be expected to present himself at the tradesmen's entrance, wipe his boots and, if he was lucky, the butler might inform his master of the presence of the Law below but in the meantime he would be welcome to a cup of kitchen tea and a slice of cook's Dundee cake . . .'

'Naturally. But a commander, well-born and educated, arrives at the front door able to speak *de couronne en couronne* to His Grace or whoever is suspected of some dastardly wheeze . . .' said Lois with a flash of insight and enthusiasm.

'Exactly! I have a department chosen by me and a wandering brief from the Commissioner, Sir Nevil Macready – who, by the way, is a close friend of Sir George and very like him in style.'

'I see it all,' smiled Lois. 'But what on earth are you doing in India? I'm sure you are much needed in London. How can they spare you?'

'I was lent to Sir George for six months to advise and train the Calcutta Police,' said Joe. 'A two-way process as it turned out! I learned as much from them as they learned from me. But my secondment seems to have stretched beyond the original spell. Sir George keeps finding me cases to clear up.'

'And is that what you're doing here?' asked Lois with a sweet smile. 'May we expect you to drag one of us away in manacles?'

'No. I'm off duty. Sir George has granted me a week's leave to watch a tiger being bagged.'

'Oh, I think you're planning on doing more than watch, Sandilands,' came Claude's voice from the door. 'I've seen your gun! You could shoot the eye out of the Man in the Moon with that! Don't be deceived, Lois, by this chap's modesty. I had someone check his file for me – I'm a careful man, Commander! – and he's quite a fire-eater. Watch out, Lois! If you've been cheating at bridge, he'll find you out!'

This was the first time Joe had seen the Vyvyans reacting with each other and he was intrigued to note the sudden gentleness in Lois's tone as she enquired about her husband's morning. Her expressive face could not hide an unspoken question underlying the words and Claude

172

responded to this with a reassuring smile and an impercept-
ible nod. He answered succinctly and lightly, involving
their guest in his replies, and his eyes, Joe noticed, followed
his wife as she moved about the room. He would have said
their relationship was one of respect and affection.

With Claude's sunny presence, the conversation, which
had been limping along, took on a lighter tone and a faster
pace. After a while Claude said hesitantly, 'I don't believe
you'll mind, Sandilands, if I tell Lois the news of our little
ceremony with the ruler earlier? So much to do as a
consequence of all that, I haven't yet had time to inform
her of his decision! My dear – it's Bahadur!'

'Well, of course it's Bahadur! But how good to know that
officially at last!' was Lois's delighted reply. 'And . . .?'

'And yours truly is to be co-regent. I must say I look
forward to working with that clever young man! Quite the
best thing that could have happened for Ranipur and for
India. Why don't I have a glass of that hock to celebrate,
my love? I don't often indulge in the middle of the day but
this is a special occasion – I'm sure you'll understand,
Sandilands? A lot of hard work and planning has gone on
behind the scenes to get to where we are at this
moment!'

His comment fell with an almost audible clunk between
them, a comment wide open to misinterpretation by anyone with a devious mind and quite obviously that was
exactly what Lois Vyvyan had. Surprisingly, she chortled
into her glass and looked at Joe with merriment. 'Gracious,
Claude! Do have a care! The Commander is reaching for
his notebook! He'll be asking you for a confession to two
murders if you're not more circumspect!'

Joe grinned affably back and Lois went on in the same
light tone, 'But who's your partner-in-crime, Claude? You
said co-regent? My money's always been on Zalim . . .'

'No. Rather a surprise, I have to say. It's Third Her
Highness. Shubhada. The lad's stepmother.'

Lois's amusement died. 'Ah. Not such good news. Now
why on earth would Udai go and do that?'

'Makes a certain sense when you think about it,' said Claude. 'The girl's intelligent and ambitious. I think she'll take the position seriously. And don't lose sight of the real reason for naming her. Udai's very much in love with her and very much under her thumb, you'd say. He knows that his death will strip her of all official position in the state. She will be reduced to an insignificant and very dull existence indeed when he pops off. By making her co-regent he enhances her power in princely India.'

'Power, you say? Just how much power are we considering, sir?' Joe asked.

'It depends on Bahadur himself,' said Claude. 'He may want to get his hands on the reins of government as soon as possible, which would be at the age of sixteen – eighteen if he's not so keen. The intervening years, the years of his minority, will be vital for us. We'll send him to Mayo College or, better still, to England if that's what he would prefer, and run the show while he's off playing cricket and learning French and geography. Tricky times, as you're aware, Sandilands. Politically, we're walking through a minefield. No one is sure what the role of the princely states ought to be in the larger context of the continent – many different opinions. All we can do here is keep the lid on until further orders are issued.'

'And the day-to-day running of the state?' Joe pressed further. 'Will you and Her Highness have a hands-on role to play or will the authority be in name only?'

'Oh, very much hands on the reins,' said Claude. 'We'll have to supervise the organization of the state, the finances, the taxation. We'll be the literal keepers of the treasury! What about that, Lois! There's a sort of ceremonial handing over of the keys to the khajina . . . I suppose they've got a spare set . . . Should check on that . . .' he murmured.

Joe smiled to see the civil servant so near the surface. The excitement of his new situation was not going to override the meticulous attention to detail that kept Claude's ship afloat.

'Khajina?'

'Very mysterious and romantic,' Lois joined in. 'Oh, Claude, do you think they'd let me in – just for a quick peek? It's a little stronghold in the hills, Commander, a mile or so to the west. And – can you believe? – it's where the rulers of Ranipur have always kept their treasure. Gold, precious stones . . . worth goodness knows how much! They say the loot is stacked deep in the stone coffers that line the room . . . You can plunge your arm in up to the armpit and encounter nothing but jewels!'

'They all have them, you know. The princes. Banking and Western methods of storing and moving money around are quite unknown to most of them and certainly not encouraged by HM Government. Hyderabad could buy out the whole of Europe probably and still have change. And heaven knows how much there is stashed away in the Ranipur treasury,' Claude said with an air of intrigue.

'Isn't it, er, vulnerable, up there in the hills?' asked Joe. 'Looks like bandit country to me – I flew over it this morning.'

'Nothing's ever disappeared from the treasure house, I'm told. It's guarded by a family of indigenous hill people. They will only let in the keeper of the keys. Udai says they let him in occasionally to run his fingers through his goodies but they don't exactly encourage visits. It's not like viewing the Crown Jewels in the Tower of London at tuppence a go!' he said, shaking his head in mock warning at Lois.

A servant arrived to announce that luncheon was served and they made their way through to an airy dining room facing on to a northern verandah aired by a slight breeze blowing in from the lake. Joe paused, admiring the view framed by the open stone arches.

'Wonderful, isn't it?' said Lois, following his gaze. 'I never tire of looking at the lake. You must come in the evening, Commander, and see the animals. The strangest creatures come down to drink. All kinds of deer, some predators even and wild camel. And the flocks of birds are quite magical! When the duck fly in, they're so thick you can't see the opposite bank!'

'I see your neighbour over there has an even better view. Is that pretty little pavilion inhabited – the one that seems to be growing out of the water? The white, Moghulesque house with the fretted windows?

'It certainly is,' said Claude. 'The ruler gave it to his third wife as a marriage present. Shubhada insisted on having her own accommodation when she came to live here – the zenana was no place for her. And there she lives, discreetly away from the hurly-burly of court life, in some seclusion which, I can tell you, is hard to come by in the palace. Smart move! And the girl's had the good sense to surround herself with her own staff, mostly recruited in London and Paris and all intensely loyal. Not a whisper of gossip comes from those quarters, I can tell you! Shubhada could be planning the next Indian Mutiny over there and we'd not be aware of it.'

Lunch, to Joe's surprise, was Indian. Lois explained that they both had a fondness for it and they happened to have an excellent Indian cook, a Pathan from the northern provinces who had the skill of producing spiced and delicious dishes which were not over-hot for an English palate. As Joe sampled the array of fragrant piles of lamb, chicken and vegetables in rich sauces presented on silver thalis he agreed that he had never tasted better.

'Tell me, Sandilands,' said Claude as they lit up thin cheroots and accepted cups of coffee at the end of the meal, 'what made you dash off to Surigargh this morning? Am I to think the copper has a deep interest in the domestic folk art of Shekhavati?'

'As a matter of fact,' said Joe, 'yes! I have! Though I had no idea what I would see before I got there. Amazing stuff! Very special and, I do believe, quite unknown outside the region?'

'So I understand. The havelis are rather remote – unapproachable to those who don't have access to a camel or a plane. But what a disappointing response! Try harder!

I had hoped to hear you were straight off like a bloodhound on the trail of whoever is killing off the heirs.'

'Not my job,' said Joe firmly. 'In spite of your appointment. I was accompanying Captain Mercer who is very anxious to locate his rigger, Ali. His favourite for the wire-cutting sabotage, which was very neatly done! Captain Mercer was told that he'd gone back to his home town. We were hoping to catch up with him.'

'Any luck?'

'I'm afraid not. No sign. I'm told by none other than Ajit Singh that our lad has "gone to Delhi".'

Claude sighed. 'And we all know how to interpret that! Sounds to me as though poor Ali has gone to feed the crocodiles in the lake.'

'Crocodiles?'

'Yes. There's a sort of scavenging squad of the ugly brutes at large in the lake. Their numbers are carefully controlled. I'm sure they perform a useful function,' he added bleakly. 'But, look, Sandilands, I'm not happy with the way things are going. I do detect a pattern and I don't like the look of it. I'm fond of my new charge – Bahadur – and I would like to see him flourish. I wouldn't like to see him ending up a *bonne bouche* for the crocs and it does look as though the ruler's announcement may well have made him a target.'

'It's possible,' said Joe. 'It's certainly possible. And that would imply that a superior power is at work here. Two murders which could well have been passed off as death by misadventure or accident were cleverly worked out and perpetrated, and not only the victims but the hired help were removed. It takes a lot of clout in any society to bring that about. And anyone that powerful is not likely to be scared off committing a third murder by two honest English observers standing by exclaiming, "Oh, I say! That's simply not cricket!"'

Joe would rather have been drawing Claude out on his observations and impressions but he sensed an anxiety about the man, an anxiety he appeared to want to share with a congenial fellow countryman.

Claude was nodding, his eyes on the glowing tip of his cheroot. 'Just what I . . . we've been thinking. And I'd be prepared to draw up and share with you a list of – three? Yes, perhaps three.'

Lois nodded her agreement.

'But of course, we won't actually articulate any of them – walls have ears, you know, and our home-grown Ko-Ko is well served.'

'And I think if we were to compare we'd see the same names come up,' said Joe. 'But I have thought, Vyvyan, that we may not be dealing with something as straight-forward, as obvious, as the elimination of all the heirs. Has the thought come to you that ends may already have been achieved? That perhaps the accession of Bahadur may be the ultimate aim of whoever is behind all this?'

Claude looked puzzled for a moment and then hopeful. 'You're thinking we could all shout "Gone to earth" and go home to our tea? I must say, it would be a huge relief to come off watch.'

'Good Lord!' murmured Lois. 'We'd all been con-centrating so much on the idea of all the potential heirs being wiped off the slate . . . But who then? . . . The boy has a good number of people in his corner, including Claude – including me if it comes to that . . .' She stopped in some embarrassment.

'Yes,' said Joe, 'the two murders do seem to have brought about a good result for the state . . . and for British interests. But look here, I'm just theorizing out loud. I've only been here two minutes and I could have it wrong. I'd be glad to hear from you, sir. Oh, and by the way – so would Sir George! He was complaining that he hadn't had your report on the death of Bishan. And with the next one due now – well, better not let them pile up, eh?'

Vyvyan was silent for a moment. 'I sent off a report as soon as I was certain of the facts,' he said carefully, 'about a week after the death. You're saying that it never reached

Sir George? I did wonder why he hadn't taken action – until he dispatched you, that is. I kept a copy. Keep a copy of everything. You can see it if you want to.' He stirred uncomfortably. 'Must say, that makes me feel a bit . . . what? Overlooked? Besieged? Look, as a precaution, why don't you carry a copy of my report on each of the deaths back with you in your saddle bag when you return to Simla? Just in case.'

'I'd be pleased to do that,' said Joe. 'Look, sir, is there any chance – before we all get swept up on to elephants and off into the wilderness to try conclusions with this tiger – that I could have a word with Zalim Singh? On a purely unofficial level, of course.'

'Shouldn't be difficult to arrange,' said Claude, stubbing out his cheroot, 'but there's someone else who's asked to see you. Again. Bahadur in his new role of Yuvaraj wants to have a word. Said I'd take you along after lunch.'

'I'd like very much to see him again. Our first interview was short and impromptu, you could say. But where's he got to? He seems to be an elusive presence around the palace. Like a ball of quicksilver!'

'That's a pretty fair description,' said Claude. 'You never know where you're going to stub your toe on him. He's with Lizzie Macarthur for the day. She's tutoring him in the natural history of Rajputana, I believe. Oh, she's much more than a nanny. Studied at Oxford and a good teacher. Bahadur is devoted to her and she's a steadying influence on his rather, um, volatile character.'

'Quite a contrast between the two female influences in the boy's life?' suggested Joe.

Claude grunted. 'You're right there. His mother is totally uneducated, illiterate even, and that's normal for village girls of her age but she's a clever woman. Well, she'd have to be to retain such a hold over the ruler for so many years, I suppose. It would give her enormous consequence if – I mean when Bahadur inherits. If he didn't she'd be left with nothing. Reduced to the ranks, you might say. And I suppose that's already occurred to you?'

'Yes, and I'll tell you something else. The main players all seem to have one thing in common and that's Surigargh. What are we looking at, sir? A sort of Mafia set-up?'

'Oh, very like that,' Claude agreed. 'Family connections, ruthless ambition, power struggles, vengeance . . . the Sicilians don't have a patent on that, you know. And I can think of a few Scottish clans who would give the Rajputs a good run for their money,' he added slyly.

'You don't annoy me with a remark like that, sir,' said Joe easily. 'I'm a Lowlander from the Borders. We rather look down on all that "wild Heeland" stuff. But Lizzie, now, she's a Macarthur from . . . the shores of Loch Awe, I think. She'd understand!'

'And she'd go a long way to protect that young charge of hers,' said Claude. 'In determination, I do believe she'd be the equal of that most famous of Rajput nursemaids . . . Do you know the story, Sandilands?'

Joe thought that he did but shook his head. He was enjoying hearing Claude, teasing information out of him, assessing his views, his alliances.

'One turbulent night,' Claude began, launching himself into the story with relish, 'the palace of a Rajput princeling – and he no more than a baby lying in his cradle – was invaded by his wicked uncle and his bunch of cut-throat followers intent on killing his nephew and claiming the throne for himself. Not an unusual story but the next act in the drama was unusual – very. The nursemaid felt honour bound to defend the prince in the only way that to her seemed possible against such odds.' He fell silent for a moment, the power of the well-known story still able to make him pause in the telling. 'She snatched the prince from his cradle and put her own baby in his place. The murderous mob arrived and stabbed the nurse's baby to death. The real prince was smuggled out of the palace and years later when he came of age he presented himself and eventually reclaimed his kingdom. The nursemaid is much honoured in Rajputana for her loyalty.'

'Terrible, terrible story,' murmured Joe. 'And, yes, I can quite imagine it being told in the Gaelic round a turf fire of an evening!'

He eyed Claude covertly. In his easy conversational way, the Resident had presented Joe with four – or was it five? – potential heads on a platter. Joe watched him clap his hands and order more coffee to be brought. How could Joe describe the man's mood? More than relaxed, he decided – elated, celebratory. But, after all, he had just been handed a significant position. And the key to the state treasury. An uneasy thought came to Joe: with the other heirs removed, Claude's path to the regency was clear, with all the power and prestige that would flow from the position. Sir Claude and Lady Vyvyan? It sounded fitting. And after that? A governorship? The next Viceroy but two? Small wonder that the Resident and his wife were concerned for the welfare of the new Yuvaraj: Bahadur himself was the key which would unlock Claude's glittering future.

Chapter Seventeen

A change had already come over Bahadur. The shadows had lifted and the boy's good humour was beaming through.

'Commander Sandilands!' he exclaimed when Joe arrived, escorted by Claude, at Lizzie Macarthur's rooms in the Old Palace. 'I was hoping to see you! Tell me, sir, have you heard my good news?' While he spoke he struggled out of the dark green laboratory apron he had been wearing and threw it impatiently on to the floor.

'Indeed I have, and I congratulate you on your forthcoming elevation. The state of Ranipur is lucky in the choice of its successor,' said Joe with a polite bow.

'I have already conveyed my congratulations to the Yuvaraj,' said Claude. 'A happy day indeed!'

'Well, if you two have finished clicking heels and playing courtiers . . .' said Lizzie briskly, 'there are matters I have to discuss with the Commander.'

'Yes, indeed. Thank you, Mr Vyvyan, for escorting the Commander,' said Bahadur. 'We needn't detain you.'

Claude flicked a raised eyebrow at Joe, smiled, bowed briefly in farewell and left.

'Bahadur, my lad, why don't you make yourself scarce for a while? Buzz off with Jaswant, why don't you?' She indicated a silent elderly Rajput dressed in the drab uniform of a royal forester who was standing in a corner of the room. He was unusually small and dark-skinned for a Rajput and such was the stillness of the man that it was some moments before Joe had even become aware of his presence.

Joe glanced around the book-lined room. Benches at work height took up three walls and Lizzie and her charge had been seated at tall stools surrounded by open books, bell jars, specimen cases and metal trays carrying rows of scientific implements. The ruler must have placed a valuable order with Zeiss, Joe thought, noting two further microscopes standing to attention on a bench. A blackboard in one corner carried a chalk drawing, showing, he guessed, the circulation of the blood. Joe smiled to see the recreation in miniature of what must have been the familiar academic surroundings of Lizzie's youth.

'Half an hour, that's all, then we must get back to our specimens!'

With dignity Bahadur replied, 'Certainly I will allow you to confer with the Commander, Miss Macarthur. I will return shortly as I wish to speak with him myself. Meanwhile I will go with Jaswant.' He glanced at the forester patiently standing by. 'Jaswant is our animal collector, Commander,' Bahadur explained. 'And he reports a hatch of kraits in the locality. I have never seen one. I should like to see one.'

He preceded Jaswant out of the room.

'Ah!' said Lizzie flatly. 'Growing up, you see! Growing into his new position. Quite right too. Twelve years old now. That's a man by Rajput reckoning.'

'Lizzie! Didn't the boy mention a krait?' said Joe, alarmed. 'I don't know much but I do know that's the most dangerous snake in India! Is this safe? I mean, ought you to let him . . .'

Lizzie smiled. 'Don't concern yourself, Joe! He's perfectly safe with Jaswant. He's a local man from the hills – a tribal, as some would have it – and no one knows the region better than he does. The two of us have practically raised that boy by ourselves with the occasional spurt of interest from his father or his mother. Jaswant won't let him run into danger. He'd give his life for him.'

'Like the Rajput nanny I heard about?' suggested Joe.

'Oh, that dreadful old story! Well, I've never had a child of my own so I suppose I can't reliably comment but, yes, I too would go a long way to protect Bahadur. I've known him since the day he was born.' Her eyes clouded but she went on crisply, 'But then, he's grown now and rather eager that we should all acknowledge the fact. So be warned, Commander! Though, I think you possibly got there before I did,' she said with a sly sideways look.

She picked up the discarded apron, folded it and put it away then offered him a seat on a battered old sofa and while he settled himself, poured out glasses of whisky, Talisker, he noticed, casting a quick glance at the label. He had been about to refuse the customary whisky-soda pleading a surfeit of hock at lunch time but there was no refusing neat Talisker in a Waterford glass.

'Slàinte mhath,' she said, using the Gaelic toast.

'Slàinte,' he replied. He admired the pale liquid gold before taking a reverential sip. 'Does this transport you to the shadow of the Black Cuillins of Skye, Lizzie?' he asked.

'Not really,' she said prosaically. 'Dashed good malt, though, don't you think?'

'The best! No expense spared, it would seem, in Ranipur?' he ventured.

'I'm afraid so, Joe. And it goes against all my frugal Scottish instincts. Excess, extravagance – can't be doing with it. Apart from this indulgence, of course! And when you consider the poverty that exists side by side with the riches of this vast country, it does raise your hackles. I'm sure people will have spoken to you about the poverty, Joe? Europeans are full of advice, aren't they? ". . .Well, of course, you just have to ignore it. Give it six months, old boy, and you won't even be seeing it any more. Beggars? What beggars?" Idiots! Anyone with a heart goes on seeing it!'

She paused for a moment, her flash of anger dissipating. 'In fairness, I should say that Ranipur is rather exceptional.

Udai is an example to all. He's put a good deal of his resources into schemes to improve life for the common man, and there are no stories of reprehensible excess linked with his name. You must have heard the sort of thing . . . you know . . . a conversation overheard between two maharajas – "So difficult to decide with what to fill one's swimming pool! Champagne, obviously, but should it be brut or sec?"'

She laughed. 'Not sure that's true but it just could be.'

'I had heard that the Ranipur welcome for the Prince of Wales last year was somewhat lavish?' said Joe tentatively.

'It had to be! There was a lot riding on it. Prestige, face . . . whatever you like to call it. Each prince trying to outdo the rest in the lavishness of his hospitality . . . Magnificence and spectacle were heaped before Edward Windsor. I only hope he appreciated it,' she sniffed disrespectfully. 'And, yes, you're right – Udai had electricity installed and by that I mean from the generators upwards, culminating in rows and rows of fairy lights, if you please, outlining the palace. But they had the sense to offer the royal tourist sporting distractions as well – you know – pig sticking, duck shooting, camel racing.'

'No chess?'

'No. No chess! A huge outlay, all the same, for a two-day visit. Though nothing like the sixty thousand pounds they spent in Bharatpur on a single night-pageant. I have to say, Udai did well. Even I was stirred by the sight of the youthful British prince (for so he appeared to me) being carried by six stalwart Rajputs to the banqueting hall in a ceremonial chair, his fair hair lit up by the golden glow of thousands of oil lamps and bonfires and the palace outlined in silver light behind him.'

'Hold hard now, Lizzie!' Joe teased, putting on a Scottish voice. 'Tha's no a Stuart ye're talkin' aboot!'

'No indeed. And I'm no admirer of the House of Windsor! But the lad made a good impression all the same. Even though it has left India counting the cost.'

She looked at him closely for a moment and said

shrewdly, 'You've already begun your inquisition, haven't you? Well, I wonder what I've given away? Is there any other light I can shine on your problem?'

Joe laughed. 'Just talk to me, Lizzie! I'm fumbling around in the dark. Be my torch!'

'And here we all were, hoping the detective was going to tap Ajit Singh on the shoulder and have him consigned to his own deepest dungeon awaiting transport to the gallows in Delhi!'

'Not the way it works, Lizzie. Even if I *could* find out for certain that Ajit Singh had killed off the two heirs, I have no powers to do anything about it. If he came to me with a signed confession in several languages I'd merely be able to comment, "How interesting. Now don't do it again or HM Gov. will start to get a bit hot under the collar."'

'Pity! We'd all like to see the back of *him*. The sooner he's replaced by that nice young lieutenant, the better!'

'But if he's involved at all, he's only the instrument, Lizzie. It's highly likely Ajit's behind the killings. But who's behind Ajit?'

'Oh, anyone with influence or cash,' said Lizzie thoughtfully. 'He'd take a bribe. He's been known – well, strongly rumoured – to have performed many services for the ladies of the zenana. A useful extension of their power.'

'But what about a European, of either sex, requiring to whistle up a little skulduggery? Suppose for instance *you* needed someone to push old Edgar off a cliff?'

'Huh! That's a job I'd gladly do myself! Why give someone else the satisfaction? And – believe me, Joe – no one, not even *you* would find out that I'd done it. But yes . . . yes. I think I could make it worth Ajit's while to oblige . . . What about it, Joe? Shall we?'

He smiled at Lizzie's attempt to lighten the discussion and seized the moment to invite her to indulge with him in a little gossip and speculation.

'Delighted to do that,' she said, pouring out another generous measure of whisky.

Feeling rather foolish he asked, 'Have you had a visit from a Parisian perfume house recently, here in Ranipur?'

Lizzie frowned and smiled uncertainly at the same time, assessing the seriousness of his question. 'No,' she replied decisively. 'Jewellers, grocers, couturiers, purveyors of tinned soup, tobacconists, candlestick makers . . . No perfumiers. There are always attar-wallahs selling their wares to the purdah ladies but I don't think that's what you have in mind, is it? Why are you asking?'

Joe explained, pleased to see that Lizzie also was intrigued but unable to account for the shared taste in perfume of Lois and Third Her Highness.

'Shalimar? Can you be certain?' said Lizzie, disbelief in her voice. 'I'm not aware of it but I can imagine. Sort of thing that Shubhada would wear but – Lois? She wouldn't buy anything but Yardley's so someone must have given it to her. And who would do that but Claude?' She giggled naughtily, pleased with her solution. 'Claude! Well! What have you uncovered, Joe! Perhaps our upright Englishman has a secret penchant for oriental mystery? "Here, Lois, old gel, try a spot of this behind the ears, what!" Sorry, Joe. I've no idea. But I'll see what a bit of female gossip can reveal. Not really my style but in the interests of detection . . .' She hesitated for a moment then said suspiciously, 'It *is* in the interests of detection, I hope? Purely a professional enquiry? Not been getting too close to Lois, have you? You begin to worry me, young man! Sniffing, all too literally, around your female suspects! Are you an expert in scents? A . . . what do the French call it . . . a nose?'

'Just one of my surprising skills,' said Joe, smiling. He sniffed the air, stagily. 'And you, Lizzie? Now let me see . . . Mmm! Got it! Eau de formaldehyde! Very alluring!'

Too late he realized that his flippant remark had not amused Lizzie. She looked away and busied herself arranging the glasses on the tray but he caught a sudden expression of sadness and distance in the lively brown eyes. He decided to move to safer ground.

'Tell me, Lizzie, what brought you to India?'

'Elopement,' she said at once, and sat back to enjoy his surprise.

'Ah. Elopement. Now, are you going to enlarge on that or are you going to leave me squirming with embarrassment and framing my next question which will undoubtedly be about something of undeniable tediousness like the weather?'

'I ran away from a rather dour Scottish home in the company of a young man who loved me. He was taking up a post in India and I came with him. We were intending to marry – I suppose that makes it an elopement.'

Joe nodded. 'And what became of your young man, Lizzie?' he asked quietly, unable to dodge the question, though fearful of the reply.

'Henry had been offered a position of assistant surgeon in Bombay – a very lowly position, not at all what my father had in mind for me. When we landed there was an outbreak of the cholera and what would Henry do but roll up his sleeves and pitch in? And what would I do but help him? He died. I survived,' she said bleakly. 'I was actually then quite glad firstly of my father's forgiveness and secondly for his influence in getting me a position here in the royal household. Though I was not unaware that by this gesture he effectively ensured that his disgraced daughter would stay on the other side of the world for some years, if not for ever. My stipend is generous and I've managed to save enough to ensure I have a comfortable return. I shall buy a little tile-hung lodge in the Home Counties, grow wisteria over the door and breed spaniels.'

'Lizzie! I forbid you to do any of those things!'

'Well, perhaps I may concede on the wisteria-hung, dog-infested cottage but the return home at least is not something I'm prepared to give way on. My job here, as you've noticed, is just about completed. I don't want to be discovered in a few years' time mopping and mowing in my dotage in some remote cubicle of the palace warren! And

– tell me – what choices does a thirty-four-year-old spinster have in post-war Britain?'

Joe was prepared to give this question his best attention and they discussed for a while the depressingly narrow range of occupations open to a clever, unmarried woman. Under the warming influence of Lizzie's large brown eyes and the no less large measures of her whisky, Joe was on the point of suggesting that she marry him and allow him to make her the happiest of women but on running the phrase through his mind again he thought he might not have got that quite right.

Before he could commit himself the door opened and Bahadur came back into the room ostentatiously consulting, Joe noticed, another impressive wristwatch. He was shadowed by Jaswant who was carrying a linen bag at his side. Half an hour had passed quickly in Lizzie's company and, alarmingly, Joe calculated that, allowing for study or – heaven forbid! – capture, a family of dangerous snakes must be at large within a ten-minute walk of the Old Palace. He looked again at the bag Jaswant carried. He saw something stir in the depths.

Bahadur looked rather put out to find his nanny and his British bodyguard side by side on the sofa sharing a convivial whisky and said with some asperity that if Miss Macarthur could spare the Commander he was ready to take him to a further appointment. Another glance at the watch underlined his eagerness to be off.

'I have a feeling,' Joe muttered in Lizzie's ear, 'that someone's playing Pass the Parcel with me!'

'Keeping you on the move, at any rate. Perhaps there is a thought that a rolling policeman gathers no information? Where are you taking him now, Bahadur?'

'We are working in accordance with the Commander's expressed wishes,' said Bahadur loftily.

Joe wondered whether the 'we' was the royal we or referred to some company of which Bahadur now considered himself a part.

He took his leave of Lizzie and set off to follow a pace

or two behind the heir to the throne, thinking that couldn't be wrong. After a few yards Bahadur waited for him to draw level and continued at his side.

'You will miss the heat and the beauty when you go away to school in England, I think,' said Joe conversationally.

'I shall not be going away to school,' said Bahadur. 'I have decided to stay here in Ranipur where I am needed. I can have tutors sent out to me to continue my education and I have no desire to learn to play cricket.'

Joe smiled to himself. This young Rajput promised to be a challenging ward for Claude.

'I understand you would like to speak to my uncle, Zalim Singh?'

Joe agreed.

'Well, he is anxious to see you and to conduct you to the zenana. An honour, sir. My uncle is the only person who has the authority to admit you and he only does this because an audience has been requested by First Her Highness. You will not forget what I told you about Their Highnesses?'

This last was not so much a question as a command. Again, Joe agreed.

'Their grief and anger will have redoubled on hearing that I have been named Yuvaraj. I myself will not accompany you to the women's quarters. It is full of their servants and who knows with what orders they may have been issued?'

They seemed to be working their way into the deep centre of the Old Palace and it was some minutes before they arrived in front of a pair of highly decorated doors flanked by two Royal Guards who promptly stepped forward and barred their way. Bahadur spoke up sharply and Joe caught his own name in the exchange. Moving with synchronized efficiency, the guards opened the doors and one of them stepped inside and announced him. Joe looked around for Bahadur but, disconcertingly, the boy had quietly slipped away.

'Sandilands! Do come in!' a welcoming voice boomed

out and Joe stepped into the room that he guessed to be the command centre of the state of Ranipur. Indian rooms in Joe's experience were sparsely furnished: often merely carpets and cushions were added, perhaps with the thought that nothing else was required to compete with the lavish decorations to walls and ceiling, perhaps in the knowledge that anything more substantial risked attack by armies of ants or some sort of tropical fruiting body. Joe had heard both explanations. This room was an exception. Although it had the customary hangings, a silk carpet held down at its four corners by carved lumps of precious stone and many breathtakingly lovely Rajput paintings, the largest part of the floor area was occupied by desks, tables, bookcases and racks of ledgers: all the accoutrements of an office in Whitehall were here. Clerks were busy. No fewer than three were tapping away at typewriters, the very latest American models. In pride of place was another up-to-the-minute piece of equipment – a Bell telephone, its black and gold splendour holding its own against the Eastern glamour of its surroundings. Electricity had been installed even in this far corner of the palace. The air was stirred gently above them by electric fans and the working areas were lit by pools of shaded light supplied by Liberty lamps.

Poised and welcoming and obviously at the helm stood Zalim Singh, radiating efficiency in the centre of the busy scene.

'Come in and take a seat, Sandilands! You discover me in full flow. Even on this sad day – no, I would say *particularly* on this sad day – there is work to be done. The funeral itself has thrown up a good deal of organizational matters which demand our immediate attention. I expect it is much the same with state funerals in London?'

'Exactly, sir. And, I hope, having interrupted you, I will not long divert your attention from more urgent matters,' Joe replied.

'Oh, what could be more urgent than a murder investigation?' Zalim said, a smile just failing to sweeten his blunt remark. 'For I gather that this is what you are conducting under our noses, as you might say. But let me be frank and to the point, Sandilands.' He waved a hand at one of the clerks. 'I am even now dictating a report on the death of Prithvi Singh for the British authorities in Simla. As a matter of courtesy, you understand, for we are dealing with a purely internal, domestic matter. I will tell you now, Sandilands, as a trusted envoy of Sir George . . . would that be a fair description of your role? . . . that there is no mystery here. My report will state that the first two sons of Udai Singh have both died as a result of misadventure. There is nothing one could consider as sinister or worthy of further investigation in either death.'

'As you say, sir,' said Joe. 'And if, when you have completed your report, you would like me to carry it back to Sir George in Simla I can guarantee its safe arrival,' he added blandly. 'Along with that of Mr Vyvyan.'

Zalim inclined his head, acknowledging the thrust. 'Thank you. I shall be pleased to do that. Now, may I offer you a cup of tea?'

The door had opened to admit a servant carrying a silver tea tray and Zalim indicated that they should sit on divans at a low table to continue the discussion. He dismissed the three clerks and Joe found himself seated, alone, face to face with the real power in Ranipur.

The two men regarded each other over the rims of their Meissen teacups for a moment then Zalim burst out laughing and put his cup unsteadily down. 'Shall we stop circling round each other like a pair of over-cautious wrestlers?' he suggested. 'Look here – unofficially I'm prepared to admit there are inconsistencies in the details of the deaths of the first and second sons but I'm certain Sir George would encourage us all to focus on the point we have arrived at and not let our eyes linger on the water that has passed under the bridge. And we have reached a position which I think is acceptable, even welcome, to the British as well as to the state of Ranipur. Do you agree?'

'I do,' said Joe. 'But tell me, sir, are you content with the arrangements for your own future? Would you not have preferred to operate as regent within the state?'

Zalim looked as though he had anticipated the question. 'A regency lasts for a few years only and, knowing Bahadur as I do, I can tell you, Sandilands, that it will not be long before he has dispensed with the services of his regents. We are being open with each other now – I speak to you as I would speak to Sir George.' He gave a slight bow as though conferring honorary governorship on Joe. 'The appointments were, as you have guessed, of a cosmetic nature. Her Highness Shubhada is thereby guaranteed the consequence she desires and the British Government through its agent, Vyvyan, feels itself included in the future affairs of the state and remains our ally.'

'But *we* know that the ship of state goes sailing on under the same steady hand?' suggested Joe and Zalim's broad smile encouraged him to add, 'But, tell me, sir, was there ever a moment when you have thought that perhaps the helmsman deserved to be captain?'

Joe held his breath. He knew he had gone too far. Zalim affected to look puzzled for a moment then his expression cleared and he replied calmly, 'We Rajputs have little occasion to use maritime metaphors, Sandilands. Perhaps I can answer your impertinent query with an ancient saying of ours? "The Rajput's kingdom is the back of his steed." My ambitions are – have always been – circumscribed. I seek no further than my own saddle. I am more . . . able . . . than my brother in some respects and these skills I gladly deploy for him and the state. Allegiance to the head of state is the first of all the Rajput's virtues. My head and my sword are always at his command and now, of course, at the command of the Yuvaraj. Fidelity is the source of honour in this life and of happiness in the hereafter.'

He paused and for a moment appeared to be surprised by his own frankness. 'I learned long ago that ambition is a corrosive thing and our religion teaches us that worldly wealth and consequence avail us nothing in the end. Udai approaches his end fast now and let me tell you what will happen when the moment of death arrives. He will be lifted, as he dies, from his bed and placed on a heap of straw on the floor. He will take his last breath as he took his first – in simplicity, taking nothing from the world as he brought nothing in.'

'And the horoscopes – the prophecies – will have been fulfilled?'

'Yes indeed. They are always cast at the birth of a child and never prove wrong. My brother was correctly identified as a future ruler although a most unlikely candidate for the gaddi and, as predicted, he will be succeeded by his third son. Events are not in our own hands, Sandilands, and we try to no avail to twist the arm of Fate. But there are some . . .' he paused and sighed, 'who find themselves unwilling to accept the unrolling of Fortune's carpet and I fear that I must ask you to submit to an audience with the mother of Bishan, First Her Highness. She has asked to see you and she is not accustomed to being denied. I will take you to the zenana myself. You understand our custom of purdah? The women's quarters are guarded and no man but the prince and I may be admitted.'

He rose and summoned the clerks with a clap of his hands, issued further orders and set off with Joe.

After five minutes of striding along a pace behind Zalim, Joe was fancying himself Theseus but without the life-saving thread. And what dark presence awaited him at his destination? The endless corridors, the rustling of unseen people concealing themselves behind doors and in alcoves as they progressed were disconcerting and disorienting. He reminded himself that he was heading for an encounter, not with a fearsome man-eating monster but with an elderly princess with little knowledge of the outside world, a mother whose only son had died less than two months before and who was clutching at straws in her unwillingness to accept the hand dealt her by Fate. He sighed. Perhaps the monster was to be preferred.

A distancing courtyard alive with doves and chattering monkeys separated the women's quarters from the main body of the Old Palace and Joe blinked in the harsh sunshine as they emerged from the shadows. Such was the onslaught of the afternoon sun he began to think that crossing the open space to the entrance to the zenana might tax his endurance too far and he looked with wonder at the tall spare figure standing straight as a lance to attention in full sunlight guarding the door.

Elderly, magnificently bewhiskered and hot-eyed, he was obviously a military man of some distinction. Already well over six feet, he wore a turban surmounted by a high red cockade. His waist was hung about with several leather belts to which was attached a medley of weaponry. As they approached, the guard, ferocious white whiskers bristling, drew a slender curved sword from its scabbard and held it before him at the ready in a theatrical but nonetheless purposeful attitude.

Zalim greeted him and ritual exchanges were made in Hindi.

'My cousin's father-in-law,' explained Zalim. 'A nobleman and keeper of the zenana. We have made special arrangements for your audience with Her Highness. These arrangements will include the services of an excellent interpreter as Her Highness speaks no English.'

He called out a name and a figure which had been waiting unseen in the shadows of the doorway came forward. A girl, a tall girl with long black hair, large darkened eyes and a red rose at a jaunty angle behind one ear greeted Joe in a low and seductive voice. She was wearing, not the traditional Rajput petticoats and tight bodice, but long voluminous trousers and a tunic in a floating, gauzy fabric. Bangles chinked on her ankles and slim brown arms. She wore no veil or dopatta and looked Joe boldly in the face, curious and speculative.

Zalim gave a few words of instruction to the girl and

195

made to take his leave of Joe. 'Well, off you go. I leave you in the care of Zafira. If there is anything you require . . . anything at all . . .' he said, his voice purring in unmistakable conspiracy, 'he will be delighted to accommodate you.'

'Another of the Dewan's pillow-talkers?' Joe wondered, remembering Madeleine's scathing phrase.

It was a moment or two before the significance of Zalim's remark hit him. He followed thoughtfully behind the sinuous figure of Zafira who walked along singing and clapping his hands every few paces as though in warning. 'Watch out! Here comes . . . what? . . . a foreign policeman and a palace eunuch,' Joe supposed. 'Strange pair!'

Intrigued, he had a thousand questions he would have liked to put to his guide but fearing his interest might be misinterpreted he asked none of them, following silently until they reached a colonnaded central courtyard. Here another paradisal garden spread its four green squares thick with lilies, orange blossom trees and bougainvillea and alive with the sound of piped water tinkling down decorative chutes and splashing from a central fountain.

Peacocks stalked and scolded amongst the greenery but the living birds were outshone by the brilliant representations, tails proudly unfurled, captured in mosaics of lapis lazuli, turquoise and gold which decorated the walls of the zenana. Balconies overhung the courtyard and Joe was aware as they crossed the garden of scrutiny from many pairs of eyes behind the latticed shutters. He guessed that in normal times this place would be alive with chattering, laughing groups, with music, games, and perhaps dancing but today, a funeral day, all was still and silent apart from the mournful calls of the birds.

They arrived at a shaded corner of the colonnade where a screen woven from split bamboo had been erected. On the outer side had been placed a stool and Zafira invited Joe to sit on it. He assured Joe that he would translate fast and accurately; he was accustomed to performing this service for Her Highness. There was a slight movement behind the chik screen, a faint waft of attar and Joe's audience had begun.

What had he expected? A shy, indistinct murmuring? Female curiosity? An outpouring of grief? All of these.

'You are very handsome . . . for an Angrez!' The voice was firm, clear and attractive. 'Tell me, young man, are you as clever as you are handsome?'

'Clever enough not to be seduced by compliments, even though they come from the highest lady in the land,' he replied diplomatically.

A burst of laughter from behind the screens made him wonder if, after all, he might begin to enjoy the conversation.

'I pay no compliment; I merely tell the truth.'

Joe felt disadvantaged by the unequal situation between them: she could catch every nuance of his changing expression whereas he could only guess at hers. Rather like performing on stage, he decided: actors, blinded by the footlights, saw little of their audience yet were able to feed somehow on their responses. Very well, he'd be an actor.

He turned his head and presented his profile but also the war-damaged left side of his face. 'Perhaps only half the truth, Your Highness. I have it on good authority that I bear more than a passing resemblance to the famous Yashastilak.'

'I had observed your wound,' came the calm reply. 'And it is to be honoured. It is a sign of courage and hurt taken face to the enemy.'

A bursting shell knows no compass direction but if she wanted to believe he'd received a sabre-cut in hand-to-hand fighting, he'd happily go along with that. He raised his chin, narrowed his eyes and tried to look at once noble and fierce.

More gurgles from behind the screen.

'Yes! I see it now. Definitely Yashastilak!

'But you must be wondering why I have asked you to come and talk to me, Sandilands? Of course, it is always a

197

pleasure to meet an attractive young man and I wish we could converse in more auspicious circumstances.' Her voice had taken on a businesslike tone. Clever Zafira, Joe noticed, was managing to convey this in his rapid translation.

'My son, Bishan,' went on the princess, 'should even now be preparing to take his place on the gaddi but that will never be. They tell me his death was an accident but I do not believe this. My purdah prevents me from finding out the truth. In the zenana we hear only what the outside world chooses to tell us. I hear from Edgar who has long been my friend that you go after the truth like a hound. When you have found it I would like you to come again and whisper the name of my son's killer. You will be well rewarded.'

What could Joe do but politely commiserate with the grieving princess and promise that he would tell her the truth which she deserved to know when he was in a position to reveal it?

'But there is one matter you could clear up for me,' he said hesitantly. 'I don't wish to intrude on family grief but it would be useful to my enquiries to know more precisely what were Bishan's immediate family circumstances. Was he married? Did he have any children? I have only just arrived in Ranipur and things that are common knowledge to others are not yet known to me.'

Her voice became cooler but she answered swiftly enough. 'He was married. His wife is about the place somewhere in the zenana. They were married when they were children as is the custom. My daughter-in-law is a princess from a southern state. And, no, Bishan was not blessed with children. My daughters between them have many children but we were still waiting for Bishan's good fortune . . .' Her voice trailed away and Joe sensed that his question had disconcerted her.

'But your thoughts, Sandilands, follow mine down a well-trodden track. If Bishan had had several sons, my husband would not have been reduced to the disastrous choice he has had to make in the matter of his successor. I hold Bishan's wife, dull little mouse that she is, much to blame. If she had compelled his attention as I continually urged . . .' Regret and rage cut off her words.

It seemed the right moment to take his leave and Joe extricated himself as smoothly as he could, blindly following Zafira's swaying hips and clapping hands through the corridors. As he plodded on he felt a weight of sorrow for the disregarded mouse and wondered to what dark corner of the zenana she had fled to hide her shame and to escape the scorn and anger of her mother-in-law.

Chapter Eighteen

Predictably, the lowering features of Edgar Troop greeted Joe as he emerged from the zenana.

'There you are, Sandilands! And here I am, you see, on sheepdogging duty,' he said with an awkward laugh. 'After the day you've had, Joe, I expect it will be nothing but good news to hear you can stand down now.'

Well, this was a surprise! Insightful sympathy was not a trait Joe easily ascribed to Edgar.

'Not that, officially, you were ever on duty, of course. I don't lose sight of that,' he murmured. 'We've arranged to have a portable meal served in Colin's quarters – just the three of us – and we can spend the evening planning the tiger hunt. Colin got down here a few days before us and he's been able to do a bit of reconnoitring. He'll fill us in on his plan, assign duties, check the armament . . .'

Joe smiled to see Edgar's heavy features suffused with the joy of anticipation. This was his world: an evening spent in unbuttoned but purposeful ease with like-minded men, competent and keen. The barracks not the brothel, after all, appeared to be his natural habitat.

'Did you manage to have much talk with First Her Highness?' Edgar asked casually when they had distanced themselves from the zenana.

'Incredibly, it was more in the nature of a mild flirtation,' said Joe.

Edgar scowled. 'She likes her distractions. It entertains her to make a fool of gullible young Englishmen. Never underestimate her. You can't see *her* in the shadows behind that screen but it's always strategically placed with you a little way away sweating it out in the sunshine. She sees *you* all right! Every shifting expression!'

'Yes,' said Joe. 'I'd worked that one out! Thinking of introducing a similar technique to the CID when I get back. We too find it useful to catch the shifty expressions.'

'What did she want with you? Apart from the chance to view your manly features?'

'What everyone wants: find out who killed her son and whisper the killer's name to her.'

'And did you turn up anything interesting?'

'I found that Bishan was a most unsatisfactory first son. He was a neglectful husband and produced no children.'

'*I* could have told you that! In fact, I rather think I did. Out of his brains with something or other most of the time. Rumoured to have been interested in boys but I don't think there was any evidence. Neutered tom, I'd have said.'

Joe was very prepared to take Edgar's estimation of sexual orientation as professional and reliable.

'No loss!' Edgar added, echoing Sir George. 'His mother mourns him but no one else.'

'A different character from his brother, Prithvi?'

'Well, remember they were *half* brothers. And yes, Prithvi was a much more likeable fellow. Got on much better with his father. Was trusted by him, you'd say. Good-looking, charming, bit of a drinker but he got that under control. Playboy. Madeleine wasn't the first girl he got involved with but she was certainly the last. It was obvious to all that he was head over ears in love with her . . . But in all other ways he was a bright chap. You'd have liked him.'

Emerging from the palace buildings, Edgar stopped and pointed ahead. 'But forget all that for the evening. There's Colin's bungalow – over there, half a mile away at the north end of the Long Pond. Do you see it?'

They followed a hard-beaten lakeside path, glad of the shade of fringing willows and the cooler air rising from the water. The sun had sunk behind a ridge of the Aravallis, turning the sky into an upturned copper bowl reflecting itself in the waters of the lake. A few birds, moorhens, he judged from their movements, were sculling about on the burnished surface but all was otherwise silent. Two grey, hunch-shouldered herons stood poised at the fringe, their frozen silhouettes emphasizing the deep stillness. It would be an hour or two before the animals would gather in twitching unease, making a fragile truce when they came down to drink as night fell. Joe noticed a small boat on the lake making for the shore. An Indian was rowing but Joe could not identify the other figure in the stern.

Following his gaze, Edgar commented, 'Third Her Highness. She's a keen fisherman. All-round sportsman in fact. She'll be an admirable regent for young Bahadur. Set him a good example and perhaps a challenge! I'd like to see her weaning the lad away from the influence of that nanny of his. Too much store set by subordinate clauses, Bunsen burners and Plato's views of the universe. What the lad needs is some experience of real life!'

The bungalow was built to a blueprint of the civilian accommodation designed by Edwin Lutyens. Practical, constructed to catch every air current that could be caught and, best of all, predictable. After nine months in India, Joe could have found his way around it blindfold. Colin's welcome was warm and brisk. Without preamble he led them to a table on the verandah overlooking the lake. It was laid with sheets of paper, pencils and bottles of mineral water chilling in silver ice buckets and they settled to something very like a military briefing.

'I've only had four days to chase after our tiger, a week would have been better, but at the rate at which the creature is killing villagers, I don't feel inclined to wait any longer than necessary. Two or three are being killed each day or having narrow escapes. It was difficult to get any of the local people to accompany me, armed though I was with the latest Lee-Enfield. They're scared stiff and hiding for most of the day.'

'Why so many casualties?' Joe asked. 'I know nothing of tigers, of course, but isn't that a high strike rate?'

Colin looked down at the table and said thoughtfully, 'A tiger needs a given amount of flesh per day to sustain life . . . Thirty pounds or so. His normal kill: chital, sambur, pig, buffalo, he can sit over for two or three days. To be blunt – there's not a great deal of flesh on some of these villagers.'

'Yes, of course,' said Joe hastily, feeling rather foolish.

Colin sensed his embarrassment and added, 'Claude asked the same question.'

'Claude? Will he be of the party? Funny, I hadn't expected him to be the slightest bit interested in tiger hunting.'

'He isn't. His interest lies in looking over my shoulder to make certain I've taken all precautions to ensure the safety of his protégé – Bahadur. As you can imagine – Claude is very involved with the lad's continued good health! He came along with me for two of the days. Sensible chap, gets things done. We managed to buy up a few goats and stake them out. The tiger took the bait and we were able to follow the blood trail and the spoor. I think, in the end, Claude was quite intrigued by the process!'

'Is that when tigers hunt? In the daytime?' asked Joe.

'Yes, daylight hours. Leopards attack at night.'

'What sort of area are we looking at?' said Edgar, examining a sketch Colin passed to them.

'Well, you know that tigers are territorial?' Joe sensed that Colin was setting out the problem in terms that he, a newcomer to the jangal, could understand. 'Each one establishes supremacy in a particular area, kills within it and defends it from other tigers. This one has three villages on its shopping list. Here, look.' He drew a line around the outer edge of his map and pointed out the three settlements inside the line. 'Oh, by the way, not *tiger*. It's a tigress. I've heard accounts from some of the people who've sighted it and I've seen its tracks. It's a big female. Possibly as much as ten feet over curves. If she's got cubs hidden away somewhere she will be very bad-tempered.'

'But why does a tiger take to eating people?' Joe asked. 'They don't do that naturally, do they?'

'No, the tiger's a gent. He'll go out of his way – but not *far* out of his way (he's proud, too) – to avoid humans. But sometimes the rules of nature break down. As in this case. The tracks I found near Dilakot show she's been wounded in some way. The front right paw is turned in, practically unusable. Whatever happened to our beast, it produced a creature unable any longer to run at and attack its usual prey. Not got the speed and strength any more. To survive, she turns to easier, slower-moving creatures unable to defend themselves. We think she started out as a cattle-lifter then, as her debility increased, she took to killing men, women and children.

'There have been no reports of hunters wounding and leaving a tiger to its own devices in the forest which is the sequence that usually creates a man-eater so we must assume that she got her wound in a fight, or a trap. Oh, there is a complicating factor: about a fortnight ago, a village woman threw a sickle at it – it had just killed her daughter – and she's sure she hit it in the eye. So what we have is a half blind, limping tigress. Sounds a piece of cake, doesn't it? But it's these wounds that are making her desperate and cunning and making her seek out ever easier targets.' He paused. 'Five children were killed last week. The villagers are terrified. But more than terrified, they are grief-stricken and angry. The men have agreed to turn out and act as beaters when the royal hunt at last arrives with all its pomp and circumstance to help them.'

Joe caught a note of disapproval in his voice. 'Aren't they doing the right thing, Colin?'

'Let's say I'd do it another way! I'd go in quietly with Edgar – wouldn't even take you, Joe! – and a handful of picked bearers, take our time and finish the job cleanly. The most efficient way to get a tiger is to simply locate his kill – not difficult if you've provided the goat or the young buffalo yourself – follow the drag and sit over it until he comes back for the rest the next day. It doesn't always go according to plan – tigers are clever and their senses are about ten times more acute than ours. You start out in the forest with the assumption that they are tracking *you* and they are much more skilful at it.'

'Sounds terrifying!' said Joe, unable to restrain a shudder.

'It can be. And I'll tell you the most frightening thing – when you've gone alone into the forest after a man-eater, your senses are telling you he's close and you're following his tracks . . . you wind around between rocks and suddenly you realize you've been led in a circle because there, in front of you, are your own prints. And – superimposed on the top of your prints are the tiger's own. He's behind you.'

'I think I'd prefer the maharaja's way,' said Joe. 'A hundred elephants and a division of heavily armed sportsmen.'

Colin grimaced. 'It goes against the grain to attempt what should be a surgical operation with all the panoply of a staged royal hunt. They've prepared the elephants and sent them off into the forest already. All the gear and supplies went with them. Your gun case is even now being lovingly put into your tent, Joe! Along with the Fortnum & Mason's hamper. We're to go out by motor car or horse – take your pick – and meet up with the elephants a mile or two from what I think must be the tiger's hiding place.'

'We're to *camp* there?' Joe asked. 'Out in the jungle?'

Colin laughed. 'Edgar, didn't you tell me this chap had

survived four years on the front? After a damp dug-out in the Flanders mud, Joe, I think you'll find you have nothing to complain of! Your own tent, cooks and stewards on hand and no one shooting at you. They're well used to putting on shows like this. The Viceroy himself sometimes spends a week here in March between his stints in Delhi and Simla.'

He began to draw on the map. 'Now, look, this here's a sort of funnel, wide end to the west.'

'A nullah?' offered Joe.

'Right. It's a narrow valley within striking distance of all three villages. There's a stream from a spring in the hillside running down the middle and it widens out as you go . . . to about a hundred and fifty yards. Steep banks to north and south. It's about a mile from beginning to end and thickly screened by tall grasses on either side. Elephant grass – reaching twelve feet in some places. This tiger has chosen well. Beyond the grass there are trees. A fringe of large trees. Now at this narrow eastern end, twenty yards across, no more, there's a sort of rocky ledge with an overhang right by a water-hole and that's where I'm guessing the tiger has its den. Tigers don't relish the heat – they like to cool off with a good wallow, like anyone else. And water's essential to them – I've known tigers drag their kill for miles to take a drink before settling down to eat. I began to follow the tracks of this one up the valley but had to leave off because the light was going but I'll bet my boots that's where she is. It's within earshot of the villages. She can hear when the buffalo are being led out, she can hear the women chattering to each other in the fields, she can hear the children shouting.'

'Colin, I don't think elephants crashing about in this small area are going to be much of a help,' Edgar said.

'No, they're not. I thought we'd join them in camp, admire their decorations, go for a ride to impress Joe, take a few photographs of him lording it in the howdah for his mates back home. Then we'll tether them and go in on foot.'

He pointed to the trees he'd drawn along the sides of the valley. 'I've had some machans fixed in the trees. That's a wooden shooting platform, Joe. Well above tiger-leaping height and giving good cover. Beaters will be here . . . here . . . and here . . . covering both sides of the valley and the narrow end. They'll start well away from the guns and will close in slowly, making a hideous racket!'

He gave each of them a meaning look and went on, 'I'm sure you both appreciate that this outing has its political aspect and we have to accommodate that, so the placing of the participants is somewhat sensitive. I've put Bahadur in the first tree over here nearest to the den so that the new heir can have the first shot when the tigress, disturbed by the noise, starts to escape down the nullah. I've put Shubhada on the same machan. She's a good shot and very cool-headed. He won't feel he's being patronized and protected if he's sharing with a woman but she will be quietly looking out for his safety, you can be sure.'

'Is that entirely safe?' Edgar asked.

Colin grunted. 'Nothing's ever guaranteed in a tiger hunt but I was firmly told by Udai no less that it would be a very good idea if Bahadur were to come back from the outing with his first tiger skin. And bagging this particular one will go down very well with the people of course. Be an auspicious start to the reign and all that. Ajit Singh was not best pleased either and insisted on sharing the platform with the heir but he's been overruled. I suspect by Bahadur himself. Anyway, I've put Ajit on the machan opposite . . . here. It's about a hundred yards away across the nullah.'

'And who's this here on the tree to the left of Bahadur?' Edgar asked.

'That's Claude – I have checked all this out with the Resident, by the way. He's a good shot, they say, but not experienced with tiger. And opposite Claude – and you'll notice the machans are all a little splayed so no one is shooting directly at anyone else (don't want any nasty accidents) – I've put you, Edgar.'

'So this last one at the end of the nullah on the south side is my tree?' said Joe.

'Yes,' said Colin, pencilling in a J. 'Look on yourself as backstop. If the five other guns fail you'll have to uphold the honour of the Met. But I'm not expecting it to get past Bahadur. Just to the left of his machan, you see . . .' He drew in a dotted line running from the stream bed to the south side of the nullah. '. . . is a game track. It joins the bank where a landslide has fetched down enough rubble to make a neat little exit out of the valley. I'm betting our tiger will try to sneak out of the valley by the nearest path the moment the balloon goes up. Either way, Bahadur will get a good shot at it.'

'And where will *you* be, Colin? We seem to have run out of trees.'

'Oh, here, there and everywhere. I'll be on foot, co-ordinating the beaters. Plugging any gaps . . . nervously checking she doesn't surprise us all by doubling back and breaking through the cordon, with dire results . . . that sort of thing.'

He smiled encouragingly at Joe whose concern was beginning to show. 'I'm not going to say "Don't worry" – that would always be the last piece of advice I'd give! Worry like hell! A desperate and clever tiger on the loose, six guns pointing God knows where and half a village out, armed with sticks and old swords . . . I can tell you, Joe, it's a nightmare! All I can say is – I've never yet had a fatality or an accident, however slight, on one of my shoots. That's as far as I can go with a guarantee, I'm afraid.'

'That's good enough for me,' said Joe, instinctively trusting the old hunter and liking his honesty. 'And, who knows? I might surprise you all! There might be a head labelled "Sandiland's Tiger" in the trophy room or wherever they keep them before the week's out.'

'There's a whole wall of them in the silah-khana. Show him the armoury, Edgar, on your way back through the palace. Might encourage him. Now, a nightcap before you go? I'm planning an early start tomorrow morning, by the way. In the cars, wheels turning by seven o'clock. I expect the ruler will be very relieved to see the back of us for a few days. It's been difficult for him, this last bit. And the thing he needs least at the moment is a contingent of Europeans cluttering up the palace.'

'Send them off into the moffussil!' said Edgar. 'And the fewer who return, the better!'

'Something like that,' said Colin uncertainly.

It had been a good evening, Joe thought. He had said little, content to be entertained by the two old friends who yarned the hours away retelling well-known stories for Joe's benefit, but at last he set off back along the dark lakeside path, Edgar steering his way by the light of an enormous amber moon and the small, twinkling lights of the houses along the water's edge. Joe paused, holding his breath to see the magical white lamplit outline of Shubhada's pavilion reflected in the still water. Forest creatures were about and he heard their furtive movements, their occasional throaty warnings. He stood, entranced, listening to the unexpected song of a night bird, a liquid golden stream of sound from the branches overhead.

'Himalayan song-thrush,' said Edgar, prosaically. 'Always the first to say good morning and the last to say goodnight. Now come on, Joe, step out! If you want to take a look at the armoury before you turn in.'

Edgar threw open the door of the armoury and switched on the lights with the confidence of one who had the undisputed entrée and, with a wide gesture, invited Joe to inspect the room's contents. It seemed to him to be half trophy room, half museum of Rajput militaria from a bygone age. He commented firstly on the rows of tiger and leopard heads since this seemed to be expected of him. Rank upon rank and, apart from a small marker identifying the hunter and the date of the kill, indistinguishable one from the other, they glowered down at him. All snarled defiantly, all had bright glass eyes which reflected back the light bulbs from their black pupils, following him around the room in a disconcerting way.

The centre of the room was occupied by the stuffed body of a superb tiger, its coat, in spite of its experiences at the hands of the hunter and the taxidermist, deep and thick, shining with an illusion of health. Joe could not hold himself back from running a hand along the sleek pelt, wondering at the massive size of the animal.

'Winter coat, that's why it's so thick,' said Edgar. 'Udai shot it himself a couple of years ago. His last tiger. Big one – ten foot six, nose to tail.'

'I can see why Colin prefers to go hunting with a camera,' said Joe to annoy Edgar. 'It's against nature to turn a gun on such a fine creature for no good reason.'

Edgar looked at him, disbelieving. 'Hunting's a good reason,' he commented briefly. 'Come and look at the weaponry. Imagine having to face one of these without the advantage of a big-game rifle and a hundred yards between you. Up close, staring it in the eye, thirty stone of powerful muscle launching itself at you, feeling its breath on your face and nothing more than one of these in your hand!' He pointed out the rows of lances lined up along a wall. To Joe they looked fearsome enough. And the displays of vicious curved talwars, longswords and pig-sticking spears made him shudder.

Edgar gave a sly grin. 'Not your scene exactly, is it, Joe? All right. I'll let you off the other exhibits!' He waved a hand at a series of large glass cases. 'Torture instruments, bits of gladiatorial gear. All in use until a few years ago, I'm told. And all very interesting. Rather far-sighted of

Udai to preserve it, you'd say. Would have been all too easy to dispose of it in the name of modernity but that's Rajputs for you – very conscious of their past and proud of it.'

They turned the lights off and left. Joe shuddered, his imagination telling him that this was not a room in which he would have enjoyed finding himself alone after dark. But his tour was not yet over. Remorselessly, Edgar opened the door of the next room along the passageway. 'Here you are, you see, in complete contrast – could you have anything more up to the minute than this?'

'This' was a lavishly decorated shrine to the game of snooker. In the centre of the room, standing like a huge altar, a snooker table (though the word was inadequate for such a structure) gleamed in gold-embossed mahogany. In an echo of the ranks of lances next door, snooker cues were lined up against the walls in racks and scoreboards were fastened to leather-lined panels.

'Most impressive,' said Joe. 'We must have a game sometime. And I'll wear Sir George's jacket in deference to the sumptuous surroundings. Anything less sartorially sensational would smack of disrespect!'

'Do you *have* to talk like a music hall MC?' grumbled Edgar.

'It must be all this mahogany and red plush,' Joe muttered.

'Well, thanks, Edgar, for the tour,' said Joe as they arrived in front of his suite. 'Now go and get an early night, old man. Remember we have a brisk start in the morning.'

With a sigh of relief he went into his room, loosening his tie, kicking off his shoes, hurling his jacket in the direction of the wardrobe and making for the bathroom. He was glad he'd had the forethought to tell his valet to stand down; he didn't feel up to an appraisal by Govind's bland but all-seeing eye. There were many things he was unable to come by in India and solitude was one of them. With pleasure he ran his own bath and wallowed in the water, then stood naked and dripping wet on the marble floor for several minutes until he could imagine himself cool again before drying off.

There was a light tap on the door. Joe sighed and tucked a towel round his waist. He waited, expecting Govind to come in to check he had all he needed. The tap was repeated. Cursing to himself he went to the door and opened it. There was a rush of scented air as Madeleine ducked under his arm and dashed into the centre of the room. She looked excited and determined and she was holding out a brown foolscap envelope for him to see. Joe groaned.

'Got it! Didn't I tell you I'd do it! But you weren't really listening, were you, Joe?'

'Good Lord, Madeleine! What have you got there? Your "ticket out of here", I think you said . . . you see, I *was* listening! Is that it? I want you to tell me quickly and then buzz off, will you? You've already ruined my reputation irreparably!'

Madeleine rolled her eyes. 'Your reputation! Joe, you squeal louder than a virgin in the Black Sox dressing room! No one saw me come. I was very careful. And I thought you'd be interested to see what I have here!'

With shining eyes she handed over the envelope. Resentful of his own curiosity, Joe opened it and slid out several printed legal documents. It was a few moments before he could work out what he held in his hand but when the import of the papers hit him he sat down abruptly on the edge of his bed, clutching them in a damp hand.

'What the hell, Madeleine!'

'Thought you'd be impressed!'

He leafed through the package silently adding up figures in his head.

'A million? Have I got that right? A million dollars' worth of bearer bonds, stock certificates, title deeds . . . All instantly negotiable, I notice. Now . . . the question is – do I want to know how you came by them?'

'Well, since you ask so prettily, I'll tell you! The ruler gave them to me this afternoon. I think he's glad to pay me off and get rid of me.'

'And what did you offer to do in return?'

'It's what I offered *not* to do that got his attention and triggered his generosity!' she grinned.

She left Joe riffling in disbelief once more through the documents and poured out two glasses of tonic water from the tray laid ready. She handed one to Joe and sat down by his side. Her triumphant good humour was hard to resist.

'Let me guess . . . you promised not to reveal what Prithvi had been getting up to in the States, I begin to think most probably with his father's connivance?'

She looked at him in some surprise. 'Why . . . yes . . . something very like that. Say – you really *can* put it together, can't you?'

'Let's start a bit nearer the beginning, shall we? I did wonder exactly what Prithvi was doing in an obscure part of the southern states . . . Texas, was it? . . . when he met you. Now, looking at these, I think I can guess!'

She nodded. 'He'd been in Florida. Know where that is, Joe?'

'Vaguely. Carry on.'

'He'd been sent over to the States as his father's agent. His financial agent. Things had not been going too well, cash-wise, in Ranipur for years.' She paused, wondering how far she should confide state secrets, he guessed.

'I *had* worked that out,' he said encouragingly. 'Years of drought, the mines running out, crippling of the lucrative trade routes, depopulation, over-taxation, enforced contributions to the war in Europe . . . I could go on! The signs are all there to be read by anyone with eyes to see. In an earlier century they would have taken up arms against another state on some pretext or none and simply stolen

213

their treasure but this is no longer an option allowed under the Raj. And the clues that indicate the coffers are bare are the unfinished projects and the calculatedly spectacular pieces of extravagance – hocus-pocus to hide the true state of the princedom.'

'You're a hard man to fool, aren't you?' she murmured. 'Yes, you've got it figured right. They cashed in their reserves of jewels and Prithvi came over to the States – via Paris, Switzerland and Amsterdam – to invest in the future. They decided that instead of sitting by watching the last reserves be depleted year by year until the treasure house ran dry, they'd invest and get a return on their money. And, Joe, it's working! These guys own Florida!'

'Own Florida? Is that good?'

Madeleine sighed. 'Prithvi was interested in golf and polo and that's what originally attracted him to the place. He realized that what *he* thought attractive, others did too. Americans were taking vacations . . . foreign tourists were arriving. Suddenly real estate was hot! People were buying up mangrove swamps before breakfast and selling them as building plots before tea. For fifty times the price! Prithvi got in on the deals right at the beginning. He did well.' Her face was animated with humour and affection. Joe didn't interrupt.

'His family wasn't always *royal*, you know? Merchants, that's what they were from somewhere on the trade route north of here.'

'Surigargh,' said Joe.

'That's right, and I guess it's in the blood – dealing, I mean. Prithvi was good. Very good. He diversified. He invested his Pa's money in lots of things. He was bright, he was lucky. He followed his nose. One day he was in the crowd that listened to the Dempsey-Charpentier fight. The whole thing, well, all four rounds of it, was described from the ringside and put out all over the country by wireless-telephony. Prithvi wanted a part of it so he bought Westinghouse stock and you know what's happened to wireless-telephony?'

214

'We call it radio broadcasting now,' said Joe. 'Clever old Prithvi!'

'He just went with his own enthusiasms. He was mad about automobiles – he bought General Motors stock. Aeroplanes – he took shares in the Curtiss company. That's how I came to meet him. He was thorough. He didn't just get carried away. He heard we were flying Jennys so he came over to see the show and talk to Stuart about the aircraft before he invested.'

'Well, I can really admire what Prithvi achieved,' said Joe. 'But tell me how you managed to turn the screws on poor old Udai Singh and make off with these?' He tucked the sheets back into the envelope and handed it back to her.

'He's kept very quiet about this new way of financing the state. Zalim knows, of course, and possibly Claude, but no one else I think. It's very, well, medieval still in its thinking and customs – you've noticed – and most people here don't travel. They haven't much idea of the world over the pond. For them, the wealth of Ranipur is in its state jewellery and reserves of precious stones, stashed away safely in the khajina. If they were to find out that it's been almost emptied and the new wealth is a few dozen sheets of paper locked in the safe in the ruler's bedroom, things might get a bit uncomfortable for the ruler and the Dewan. "Questions," as you British might say, "would be asked."'

Joe looked at her, grim-faced. 'So you threatened to broadcast the fact that the state coffers are bare, that they've been systematically looted by Udai Singh? That the man proud to be father to his people has sold his inheritance for a stack of papers printed in a foreign language? No wonder he's eager to get rid of you! I'm amazed he hasn't had you fed to the crocodiles!'

She turned large, frightened eyes to him. 'And that's still a possibility. Don't think I don't know that! I've got Stuart to keep the planes trimmed and fuelled up and ready to go. Come with us, Joe! We could be off tomorrow at first

215

light. First stop Delhi – next stop, anywhere in the world! Why not?'

'Can't be done. I have an appointment to shoot a tiger in the morning.'

He heard his crisp, dismissive British officer's voice replay in his head and was ashamed. 'Oh, for God's sake, Madeleine, I'm sorry! What a pompous thing to say!'

She squeezed his arm. 'You've been hanging around with Edgar Troop for too long! Never a good idea, Joe. But at least you do see why I'm creeping about looking over my shoulder the whole time?'

'Yes, I do and I won't wrap it up, Madeleine, you could have brought down a wasps' nest on your head. You shouldn't have meddled. You don't know what's been going on under the surface . . .' he added distractedly.

'And you *do*?' she asked immediately, seizing on his uncertainty.

To tell her? To confide in her? To hear her down-to earth reaction, telling him his fears were ridiculous? For some time Joe had felt himself in possession of the appalling truth behind the deaths of the two heirs but unable to seek rebuttal or support for his theory from anyone else. So unpalatable was his suggestion, he had hidden it away in a corner of his mind but, piece by piece, layer by layer, information, opinions, intuition had snowballed around the core of his idea until he was desperate to let the whole thing out, and hope that someone would shoot it to bits.

She took his face gently in her hands and turned it towards her. 'You know, don't you, Joe? You know who killed Bishan and Prithvi?'

Taking his silence and downcast eyes for an answer she persisted: 'Tell me! Prithvi was my husband! I have a right to know! I must know!'

He held her hands in one of his and put his other arm around her shoulders.

'It's all right, Joe,' she said. 'I'm not going to scream and stamp about or chase after anyone with a carving knife!'

He swallowed and opened his mouth to speak, thought

216

again and looked away. Then, remembering Lois with her admonition – 'The walls have ears', he turned and put his head close to hers. Through the lily-scented curls he whispered, 'They were killed on the orders of Udai Singh. Their father.'

Chapter Nineteen

Madeleine's shoulders began to shake with horror and he held her tightly for a few moments until she grew steadier. Her mind was whirling, he guessed, tracking his own on its unwilling journey down the dark corridors of palace intrigue. She took her time.

'Okay, Joe,' she said finally in a calm voice, 'I'm prepared to go along with this . . . to a point . . . but first, tell me – why?'

'Well, so long as you remember that this is purely speculation. And I've only been in the palace –'

'Get on with it, Joe!'

'Udai's people call him "Bappa",' Joe began simply. 'And there you have it. He is father to the tribe and nothing in his life is more important than this role. He discovered he was dying about two months ago and what will a dying man do but put his house in order? The survival of Ranipur was his first consideration. Above everything, he knew that his first son would be a disastrous ruler and unable to pass on the state to his own children because he had none and there was no prospect of there ever being any. I believe he looked at his three sons and decided that the third, Bahadur, was almost perfect for the job – would have been perfect had he been legitimate – but acceptable all the same. Everyone likes him, he's an able boy and the choice would please the British whom he values as an ally in these troubled times. They're in favour of preserving the autonomy of the Indian princedoms after all and to that end the politics of Ranipur and the Empire march together.

'Shortly after he realized death was imminent he made up a will – more in the nature of a statement of succession but I'll call it a "will" for simplicity. The document was left undated until today. I've got a copy. That will named Bahadur as heir. So we know this was his plan before the deaths of Bishan and Prithvi. But he kept it quiet. From his own experience of being named Yuvaraj he knew that the potential for blood-letting was there. Had they guessed his intentions, the older sons would have taken action to divert the course of events.'

'Wait a minute! Just wait a minute! "Divert the course of events"? What the hell are you suggesting? One of the "older sons" was my husband, for Christ's sake! Are you suggesting that Udai expected Prithvi to take his brothers for a ride like some Leftie Louie or Alphonse Capone?' Madeleine pushed him away angrily.

'I'm not conscious of those gentlemen but if I take your meaning – yes, that's exactly what I'm suggesting. And don't shoot the detective, Madeleine! I'm just trying to work out which way the snakes are wriggling in this nest of vipers. Udai knew his sons, after all, and for longer than you had known Prithvi. He was "all Rajput" according to your brother and might well have reverted to a Rajput way of dealing with an unsatisfactory succession. Udai had decided on Bahadur and he removed, I believe, the potential obstacles to the boy's inheriting the throne.'

'But Udai got on well with Prithvi. He sent him to the States last year as his representative . . . He trusted him . . . Prithvi thought he was certain to be next up for the gaddi,' she objected.

'Yes. And seeing a sample of the evidence tonight,' Joe tapped the envelope, 'I would say that's a true picture of the situation at that time.' He fell silent, not quite knowing how to go on.

'And then I came on the scene,' she said bitterly. 'Is that

219

what you're not saying? By marrying me Prithvi was effectively putting himself out of the running . . . scratching himself from the contest?'

'I'm afraid so. No child of yours could ever succeed and Prithvi repeatedly refused to take a second wife. He and his father must have had a deep, irreparable split over that.'

'They did have a few pitched battles,' she admitted. 'Prithvi had a short fuse. So – I signed my husband's death certificate . . . is that what you're saying?'

His silence answered her.

'Is that a bottle of whisky over there?' she asked forlornly.

'Yes, can I get you one?' said Joe. 'I'd gladly have one myself.'

'Disgusting stuff,' she commented. 'But thanks.'

He poured out two glasses, adding a large measure of soda water to Madeleine's.

She took a sip of her whisky, grimaced and took another. 'But look here, Joe. Let's take this a step at a time. Could any father no matter how much he disapproved of the life his son was leading – I'm thinking of Bishan now – arrange for him to be eaten by a wild panther? I'm not buying it!'

'Well exactly! And that's why it was such a good cover. Udai did check with the doctor that his son didn't suffer. The doc thought this normal parental concern, and parental concern it certainly was but not normal. Bishan's death was, in fact, quick and relatively painless.'

Joe told her about the opium dose and the killing methods of panthers and Madeleine listened wide-eyed.

'But why would Bishan change his opium dose just like that?' she wanted to know.

'I asked myself, Whom would he trust sufficiently to accept an enhanced dose from him? His father? Perhaps after a discussion on the lines of "Why have you not presented me with a grandson yet? Having problems?

Here, take a dose of this. It'll make a man of you . . . put ink in your pen" or whatever the Rajput equivalent is. Speculation, of course, and how will we ever know? But the ensuing "accident" as staged was convincing.'

'But who was he trying to convince? And why wouldn't a knife in the ribs have been as effective? Or just an overdose of the drug? Why the fancy footwork?'

'No. With the British Empire looking over his shoulder in the sleek shape of Claude Vyvyan, urbane, friendly but all-noticing, it would have to look as much like a genuine piece of misadventure as possible. And the opium and panther-wrestling routine was such a well-known and regular part of Bishan's life it was feasible. But sharp old Claude must have become aware that all was not on the square. He wrote a report for Sir George, a report that never got through. There must have been something in there that Claude inadvertently or perhaps even deliberately let slip that they didn't like the sound of. Sir George knows that Claude is nothing if not efficient and he would certainly have reported the death to him. His twitchy old nose began to smell a rat.'

'And he stuffed you down the hole to see what you could discover?'

'Something like that.'

'And Prithvi had to die too – again apparently by accident – to clear the field for Bahadur. That I can't stomach!' she said, downing the rest of her whisky. 'That creeping little coyote!' She burst into a fit of sobbing.

Joe was disconcerted. 'Not a member of the Bahadur fan club, then?'

'No! Way too slippery! He despises me – well, don't they all! – and he's forever down by the planes, hanging around Stuart, watching . . .'

She fell silent and the silence stretched between them.

'Joe, she whispered finally, 'he could have done it! Bahadur knew enough about the planes to have cut the elevator wire. And we were all so used to seeing him holed up down there, feeling sorry for the poor little guy, we didn't notice him any more. He'd had a couple of lessons with Stuart . . .'

'But it was Ali who disappeared.'

'Of course. Fall guy. They got rid of him so they could put the blame on him. He wasn't around to deny it if things went wrong for them and their handiwork was discovered. Stuart never thought he would have done it, you know. Perhaps they asked him and he refused . . . Riggers don't . . . couldn't bring down their plane and their pilot.'

'I had wondered why on earth Prithvi should have taken up the plane Stuart was meant to be flying. And, again, I can only think, "order or suggestion from above" and there aren't all that many people above Prithvi in the hierarchy if you count them. Just one. His father. So we're back to paternal machinations.'

'Not quite sure what you mean but I can tell you that Prithvi did have a long talk with his father that morning. Do you think that's how it happened? "Why don't you demonstrate your ability for these Britishers? You're as skilled as that Yankee pilot by now, aren't you?" He knew Prithvi never could turn down a challenge. Do you think that's how it happened, Joe?'

He nodded. He deftly put down his glass as she threw herself towards him, sobbing into his chest.

'God, I'm stupid!' she hiccuped. 'I thought I was being so clever! "Give me my dues and perhaps I won't tell the world about your naughty dollar deals!" Like an infant threatening to poke a grizzly in the eye!' She tugged at a corner of his towel and dried her eyes. 'I'm a target now, aren't I, Joe? And I've brought my danger to your door. Look, let's think this through. If Udai – and it's still "if" as far as I'm concerned – is behind all this, he didn't do it alone. Oh, I don't just mean the ones who changed over the panther and sawed through the elevator cable, I mean I bet he had help at the planning stages. Certainly Ajit

Singh and his men were there at the sharp end, the executive branch you might say, but also I'm guessing . . .'

'Zalim?'

Madeleine nodded. 'And I don't forget young Bahadur, curse him! Believe me – *I* don't forget him!'

Joe sighed. He went over to the door and drew the bolt across, switched off a light or two then returned to sit by Madeleine on the bed. 'So, with the present ruler, the future ruler, the Prime Minister and the Chief of Police and the Palace Guard all eager that we shouldn't get out of here and start talking to anyone,' he said, 'we have quite a problem. Suddenly your planes begin to look very attractive. Tell me – if you were to take off, where would you head for?'

He was quite sure she had no intention of revealing her plans but it was worth a try.

'You could get to Delhi easily. But you might want to avoid a reception committee at the airport. These planes can land anywhere that's firm. A road will do. Pick your point of the compass.'

'And continue by rail perhaps? Rail leading to a port? Bombay? Madras? Calcutta?'

None of the names raised a flicker of response on Madeleine's face. 'Yeah. Could be done,' she said noncommittally.

'And all this leaves us with the night to get through,' Joe began.

She reached for his hand and turned to him a face softened by something which in the half-light might have been affection. It could also have been pity or even need.

'Joe . . . I could . . . we could . . .'

An uncertain Madeleine?

He stroked her shining head, put his arms around her and gave her the reassuring hug he reckoned she had been craving. 'You'd better spend the night here again,' he said gently. 'My turn for the couch, I think.'

Chapter Twenty

Joe reported early for duty at the elephant gate, his packing done by Govind in the time it took to eat his breakfast. All traces of Madeleine had been removed as best the two of them could manage in a frantic ten-minute bustling about before the sun came up. Retrieving her envelope from underneath her pillow, she had grinned, 'You'd wonder how I could sleep so well with my head on half Miami!' and it had made its way down the front of her blouse. She took in her belt a notch to hold it firmly in place. 'So long, Joe. See you in the jungle.'

'What? You're going too? This is turning into a charabanc trip!'

'You didn't think it was to be just a chaps' outing, did you? Eight gents in velveteen coats, yarning over the angostura bitters? Sorry, Joe – we're all being encouraged to go. To clear the palace for a few days, I'd guess. And, honestly, I'd rather take my chances with the wild tigers than the palace ones. I'll feel safer out there with the snakes and the scorpions – no kidding! I think Lois and Lizzie are staying behind because they don't approve of shooting animals but everyone else will be there.'

And here they were, milling about in the courtyard, some anxious and excited, others phlegmatic, even bored. Last minute instructions were given to the servants, forgotten items were urgently sent for from the palace. Everyone checked places assigned in the motor cars. It was going to be a two-hour journey and no one wanted to be put to sit next to Ajit Singh.

Joe stood back, silently admiring the forethought Colin had put into the planning. Heavy camp equipment which included iron water-tanks of drinking water had been sent off days earlier by camel and bullock cart and there remained only the ten members of the shooting party and their personal items of luggage to be distributed among the motor cars. Nothing had been left to chance, not even their placing in the fleet. Three passengers were allotted to each with a uniformed driver and Colin effortlessly ushered the guests into their places, hearing no argument. The first, a Rolls Royce, set off with Bahadur, Edgar and Ajit Singh, and the second, a Hispano-Suiza, with a perceptible lowering of the anxiety level, followed with Madeleine and Stuart and Sir Hector, firmly refusing to be separated from his medical bag which he insisted should travel with him.

Joe was invited to sit in the third motor car, a Dodge, one of three, with Colin and Claude, and with a further four cars carrying the baggage they set off, waved at by Lois and Lizzie.

'Don't shoot one for me, Joe!' said Lizzie.

'Darling, do check your boots for creepy-crawlies, won't you?' said Lois to Claude.

Joe looked round, concerned. 'Colin! I don't see Her Highness . . .'

Colin pointed ahead. 'There she is, half a mile up the road. Shubhada elected to go on horseback accompanied by her grooms. It'll be a point of honour with her to get there before we do. But she won't find it *that* easy – the ground's hard and dry. Good going for motor cars! We should make good speed.'

The drive along the forest road with the sun slanting through the trees awaking clouds of acid-yellow butterflies was magical in the early morning, though the approach of a seven-vehicle motorcade frightened away any animals they might have encountered. Some hinted at their presence by the occasional warning cry. On the last few miles to the camp site Joe noticed that the surrounding land was growing more rocky and broken and there were signs of ancient civilization on every hand. A crumbling sandstone fort looked grimly down from its hilltop, heavily ornate Hindu temples nestled in patches of jungle, and here and there they caught the grey-green gleam of lakes in valley bottoms.

Shubhada was already installed when they drew up, sitting on a folding camp chair, a half-read novel on her lap. Teasing, she waved a teacup at them and looked at her watch. 'Oh, good. I was hoping you'd be here in time for tiffin,' she said. 'I hope you don't mind but I've already settled in. First to arrive has choice of tent, you know!' She pointed to one at the end of the double row of white canvas tents pitched in a clearing. She had chosen the end nearest the jungle and furthest from the supply and cooking tents.

This did not please Colin, who had been about to place the two ladies protectively in the centre of the group, Joe guessed, but he smoothly reassigned the tents and all disappeared gratefully into their accommodation to smarten up and wash away the dust of the journey. Shubhada was in her element, striding about the camp in jodhpurs and riding-jacket issuing orders. He wondered what kind of a shot she was as he watched her fussing over a camp servant charged with unloading her gun case from the Rolls. It looked very splendid, he thought, as it disappeared into her tent, and he wondered whether she had been allowed to borrow her husband's Purdeys for the occasion.

Everyone else's guns had been delivered to the camp the day before and Joe's Holland and Holland duly made its appearance. He welcomed the Royal as an old friend in this strange place. He took it out, held it to his shoulder and squinted down the barrel. He checked his ammunition and satisfied himself that all was well with the gun. He was not allowed to put it to more serious testing as all shooting had been banned by Colin. Now that everything was in place, he didn't want to risk alerting the tiger to make off for a hunting ground farther afield.

A holiday spirit seemed to have invaded the group. Free of the crushing atmosphere of the palace and happy with their outdoor accommodation, they settled in the filtered sunlight of the glade to enjoy each other's company over constant cups of tea and glasses of iced (now how had the khitmutgar managed *that*?) lime juice and soda. They sat down ten to lunch in the open at a table lavishly supplied by a field kitchen already in bustling order and manned by several palace cooks. The male guests were kitted out in khaki shirts and shorts and had good-humouredly adopted the Australian army bush hats Colin provided for them. No bright white pith helmets were to be worn on the hunt – a quiet camouflage was the order of the day. Bahadur and Ajit Singh conformed by agreeing to wear turbans of dull green. Everywhere, Joe was aware of teams of men cheerfully at work to support this enterprise from the twenty mahouts and their elephant handlers to the splendid major-domo figure who was organizing the valets and maidservants.

But Joe was uneasy. He strolled with Edgar a short way into the forest for a companionable after-lunch cigarette. 'Nothing like it since the build-up to the Somme,' he remarked to Edgar, pointing to the scurrying squads of servants. 'And all for one tiger! Where on earth are they all sleeping?'

Edgar pointed to the south. 'A hundred yards away in the next clearing there's a sort of tent city. And the elephants are corralled down by the lake. And all this is not just for the tiger – as well you know! – it's supposed to be an entertainment, a bit of relaxation for us Europeans. In the middle of his troubles, Udai is providing a distraction from the awfulness we've got caught up in. Typical piece of courtesy from the ruler and it would be very nice if you stopped sneering and questioning and set about having a good time. Why don't you pick up Colin, take an elephant and go out and have a look at the countryside? Calm your nerves a bit.'

Thinking perhaps that he'd spoken a little sharply, he added, 'Look, Joe, if it's concern for Bahadur that's making you so twitchy, you can relax a little. Not too much, mind! We're both still on duty. But he's away from the palace now and surrounded by people who have his welfare at heart. When he goes up that tree he'll be feet from Shubhada and yards from Claude, both of whom have the strongest reasons to keep him alive. Across the nullah there's his father's man Ajit and he's not done a bad job of protecting the lad so far, you have to agree. Then there's you and there's me. That adds up to quite a protection squad!'

'You're right, Edgar, but I get a bit nervous in a scene like this – high-powered rifles everywhere you look, a man-eater lurking somewhere in this dense scrub, elephants to fall off, trees to fall out of and heaven knows what else! Place is a minefield!'

Joe made to sit down on the stump of a tree but was hurriedly caught by the arm by Edgar. Edgar thrashed about with his stick removing leaves and debris from the roots and then, satisfied with his efforts, said, 'Never sit down anywhere that you haven't checked for snakes, Joe. These woods are crawling with hamadryads . . . That's all right. You can sit down now.'

'Thanks, Edgar! Thank you very much!' said Joe. 'But I've changed my mind. Let's get back to camp.'

The rest of the day passed equally smoothly, to Joe's relief. Determined to make the most of this break from palace routine, the group, hunters and spectators alike, took on a cohesion and, he would have said, an identity. Perhaps this was what happened in the Boy Scouts or on a Chapel Outing. It was certainly what happened on the battlefield. But a shared deprivation did not feature in their experience under canvas. The guests were eager to share their approval of the rich appointments of their tents. No ground sheets here – they trod on silken Persian carpets. The folding campaign furniture was made luxurious by tasselled cushions, and those who had been dreading the discomfort of a latrine were pleased to note the provision of a personal, mahogany thunder box.

But, against the current of satisfaction and bonhomie, Joe felt, for no obvious reason, a thrill of unease as he looked round the lively faces gathered over the supper table. Colin, behind whom everybody had instinctively rallied and whose word everyone obeyed without question, had been entertaining them with tales of shikar. But the tales were more than entertaining and amazing, Joe realized, they were instructive and, in the best tradition of storytelling, the audience felt its own experience had been widened, its sensibilities deepened and perhaps its point of view adjusted.

Surprisingly, Ajit Singh, instead of being the inhibiting presence all had anticipated, joined in the after-dinner campfire storytelling, picking up and running with Colin's accounts, adding a Rajput view or explanation, occasionally telling an ancient folk story of his own.

Stuart, who had never been on a tiger hunt before, was all flattering attention, joining with Joe in asking the right questions of the right person, bouncing the conversation along. This young American, Joe thought, would have been an asset at the dinner table of the Vosges château where his squadron had trained in notorious and enviable luxury during the war. His sister, however, was less congenial.

In the overwhelmingly masculine gathering, Madeleine was uncharacteristically restrained and staying firmly in her brother's protective shadow. As she was paying no more than casual attention to Joe, he could almost have wondered whether he had imagined the intimacies of the previous evening. Madeleine was making no female alliance with the only other woman present. Rebelliously wearing a bush shirt and divided skirt topped off with a cowboy hat, she presented an interesting contrast with Shubhada who glimmered in a little dinner dress of midnight blue silk. Voluble and excited, the maharanee seemed to be enjoying the company of the men. Though her behaviour was never less than scrupulously correct, there was a quality about her which intrigued and puzzled Joe: an energy, an elation or satisfaction perhaps. The girl was certainly in a good mood. The thrill of the chase? She was said to be a keen hunter.

Bahadur too was enjoying the chance to be with a group of men he admired, and though not entirely confident of his status amongst them, his companions, by their conversation, let it be understood that all were gathered there in the lamplit clearing miles from civilization for a levelling and urgent purpose. No one felt it his duty to tell the young Yuvaraj it was past his bedtime and he sat on, listening with obvious pleasure until finally he summoned up his own body servant and declared his intention of turning in, recommending that the others follow his example.

Most were only too pleased, after their long hot day, to use this as a trigger for their own departure and soon, after much genial calling of 'goodnight', all had retired to their own tents, their way lit by the glow of the sinking fire and the torches of the night watch. Joe stayed awake for a long while, alert to the sounds of the forest around him and to the sleepy sounds of the camp settling down. He smiled to hear the doctor, whose tent was immediately opposite, gargling heartily before, with a final trumpeting noseblow, settling to his bed. Bahadur's tent was to Joe's right, sandwiched between him and Colin and opposite Ajit. Joe heard him stirring about for quite a time after he had gone to bed, chattering with his servant and even sending the man off to the supply tent on some errand or other. Judging by the subdued snort of laughter on the servant's return, Joe guessed he was clandestinely laying in a personal supply of the Swiss chocolate he appeared to have taken such a fancy for and he smiled indulgently.

The last muffled yawns and creaks petered out and Joe felt himself at last to be the only one of the party awake. The way he liked it to be. He was lying on his light-framed charpoy bed with its cotton-covered mattress, naked and damp from his tub wash, alert and anxious. He listened to the plink of frogs from the lake and the occasional yelp of a jackal. Twigs snapped and undergrowth rustled as night creatures moved stealthily by, skirting the clearing men had invaded. It was ridiculous that after the relaxed conviviality of the evening he should be left coiling with tension. Each time he tried to identify the cause of his disquiet he came back to the same disturbing thought: in his eagerness to arrive at a solution he had broken the first of his own most compelling rules. He had reached and even confided a conclusion before all the evidence was in. His suspicion of Udai Singh's role in his sons' murders was no more than that – and an outrageous suspicion! This was twentieth-century India after all, not fifteenth-century Turkey with the savage princely blood-lettings that accompanied every sultan's death. The British Empire held sway, not the Ottoman. He had been over-hasty and all he could do now was hope that Madeleine would have the good sense to keep silent about the theories he'd confided to her. She'd only half believed him anyway, he told himself hopefully.

And if he'd supposed wrongly – and he rather thought he had – what did that imply for Bahadur's security? 'Bahadur, old chap, are you all right?' he wondered silently. He also wondered if Colin and Edgar and Ajit were, like him, on watch. 'Ceaseless vigilance, Sandilands!' he told himself with a stabbing memory of a similar night on watch in Panikhat. He was still trying to turn it into Latin when he fell asleep.

In the depth of the night he woke, listening intently. The sound that had woken him – where had it come from? He feared for a moment that Madeleine might be crazy enough to pay him a visit but no one pulled aside the flap of his tent. In a moment Joe was on his feet and into his dressing gown and standing in front of Bahadur's tent. He listened carefully and could have sworn that the odd noise he heard was Bahadur giggling.

'Bahadur! Sir! It's Joe Sandilands. Is all well?' he called in a low voice through the flap.

'Joe? Of course. Go back to bed! Much to tell you in the morning! When my trap has been sprung you will call me Bahadur the great hunter!' More stifled laughter followed the puzzling remark and Joe crept back to his tent.

Emerging late the next morning, Bahadur looked subdued and avoided Joe's eye. He avoided everyone's eye. He joined them at the table with polite greetings all round but seemed unwilling to pursue a conversation. Joe would have put the bilious appearance down to a surfeit of chocolate had not Bahadur tucked into his breakfast with some eagerness. The boy brightened up a bit when Colin began his briefing, the last before the hunt began.

It was mostly standard advice about the necessity to constantly check one's rifle and take care not to point it at other hunters but contained more useful pieces of information on the most vulnerable points of a tiger's body and the preference of sideways or head-on presentation of target. Ever mindful of the safety of the group, Colin unsmilingly handed to each a railwayman's whistle on a string and ordered that it should be hung around the neck. It was only to be sounded in dire emergency. 'It's not a toy. It's not to be used for entertainment or pranks,' he said stiffly. Joe noticed that he was handing out Bahadur's whistle as he said this.

They were to approach downwind of the nullah, ceremonially making the last part of the journey on elephant back. Cameras appeared and a file of elephants duly paraded, looking majestic, their hides painted with swirling patterns in bright colours, rich velvet cloths draped about their backs and golden ornaments hanging from their foreheads.

'Joe, Edgar! You take this one,' Colin called and they stood on the mounting block and scrambled, one at a time, into the cane-sided howdah. Joe looked about him with delight to see the lavish equipment packed into the small space: gun racks, cartridge pockets, bottles filled with lime juice, bottles filled with tea, a sun umbrella, a spare shirt, a pair of gloves, a skinning-knife, a camera and a block of Kendal mint cake and, most puzzling in the heat of an Indian summer's day, a large blanket.

Catching Joe's look of surprise, 'Bees,' Edgar said. 'In case of attack by. Just roll yourself up in it.'

The mahout turned to them with a grin and announced that the name of their elephant was Chumpah and she was the senior elephant in the herd. As they lurched about uncomfortably, dipping and swaying at once sideways and back, Joe concentrated on imagining the grandeur of an earlier age when a hundred of these magnificent animals would have taken part in the hunt, encircling the tiger, bringing their riders within spear shot of the beast and sometimes being leaped upon and killed. With a sharp cry and a dig behind the ear with his toes, the mahout persuaded Chumpah to move faster onward into the forest and the hunt had begun.

Standing on the fire-step counting the seconds before going over the top produced the same sort of tension. Joe licked his dried lips. He wiped his sweating hands on the seat of his trousers, one at a time. Nine o'clock and already the heat was unbearable even up here amongst the foliage. He thought of Sir George high in the Simla hills, probably sipping tea on the lawn in the shade of the deodars with a refreshing breeze knifing in from the Himalayas. He checked his rifle. He'd checked it three times in as many minutes. A section of the steel barrel which had been in full sun burned his hand. Even the rifle was overheating.

He'd need gloves to handle it soon. So that was what they were for! He wondered nervously if the heat would affect its performance. Had Colin mentioned that? He looked down from his perch fifteen feet up in a tree to the south of the stream bed and tried to catch a glimpse of Edgar opposite. There was no movement from the tree cover which hid Edgar's machan. Nor from Claude's to his right. Colin had chosen his hide-outs well.

He refocused on the hundred or more yards separating the edges of the nullah. He saw a tapestry of golden grasses, some shifting in a breeze he could not feel, some standing spikily to attention and taller than a man's head. With her striped coat she could be anywhere in that under-brush and they wouldn't catch a glimpse of her until she decided to break cover. Here and there, where the grass grew less plentifully, were patches of earth, reddish sand, stretching for yards along the dried stream bed. Joe decided he only had a chance of getting the tigress in his sights – assuming she had successfully run the gauntlet of the five other guns – if she appeared in one of these gaps in the vegetation. He narrowed his eyes and looked care-fully at the nearest gap, assessing its size and judging how large his target would look in the setting. Would she come creeping stealthily along like a domestic cat or would she be bounding angrily through her territory like the Queen of the Jungle that she was? He knew so little in spite of Colin's constant coaching.

The forest was surprisingly silent. In the far distance an elephant trumpeted, even the gang of langur monkeys overhead who had at first registered a chattering protest at his presence in their tree had settled down to groom each other quietly. Joe's ears were straining for the sounds of the beaters. Was Colin having a problem with the squad of villagers, over-eager volunteers, all anxious to settle old scores with the tigress?

He checked his wristwatch, surprised to find that he'd only been in his tree for half an hour.

A small herd of sambur wandered into sight, then seeing

something it was uneasy with, one of them belled and flicked its tail, startling the others into a nervous run down the nullah. To Joe's right a short warning call rang out – a monkey? – alerting the troupe above his head. They peered, chattering, about them, then, deciding there was no cause for alarm, settled back to their preening.

Joe knew that on many days Colin had sat up in the branches of a tree without the comfort of a machan on tiger-watch for hours on end, once overnight in the Himalayas in a downpour, a situation from which he had to be extricated, all limbs locked rigid, by his men in the morning. Joe had only been aloft for an hour and he had the benefit of a stout platform and a ladder if he needed it. Suddenly the temptation to climb down for a pee and a cigarette was almost overwhelming.

A single blast on a silver bugle released all his tension. The hunt was under way. Colin's choreography was beginning to be played out. Distantly, voices called, sticks clashed rhythmically together and drums began to beat. The men were advancing slowly on all three sides of the funnel-shaped draw and the stage was set for the appearance of the main player. Joe's blood was racing. She would have been alerted by the first bugle blast and would even now be starting to cover the mile separating her from the open end of the valley and freedom. Eyes fixed on the stream bed, he counted the minutes. Unless she had veered off course to climb the scree slope to the left of Bahadur's tree she would be level with the guns at any moment. Joe listened, expecting to hear gunshots from his right. Minutes went by, the noise from the beaters grew louder but no shots rang out. Nothing from Bahadur? Nothing from Ajit Singh?

'Oh, God!' Joe cursed under his breath, 'This trap's empty! She's not here! And we'll have to do the whole bloody thing again somewhere else tomorrow . . . or the next day!'

A single shot from Claude's position steadied his nerves.

Something was moving, then. He waited, scanning his sector.

Then she was there, in the spot where he'd looked for her. Outlined against the sandy patch on which he'd been concentrating, she stood, stealthily sniffing the air. A huge beast, gleaming red-gold and black in the harsh sunlight, she was magnificent. The monkeys above his head barked a tiger warning, dancing about with outrage and fear. A shot cracked out from Edgar and she reared on her hind legs roaring a protest. Seemingly unharmed, she swung about and plunged into the cover of the grasses. Was she wounded? Had Edgar missed? He'd fired with the tiger sideways on to him. An easy target but not the best of shots when it came to placing a killer bullet. Joe watched the waving of the grasses as she came on at a bounding run towards his tree. Swallowing nervously he tracked her as she forged forward.

'Go for the throat,' Colin had said. 'Don't try for a head shot. More difficult and tigers often survive a head wound. The throat shot's the stopper.' But how the hell did you shoot a tiger in the throat when you were fifteen feet above its head and it was charging straight towards you? By the laws of geometry the throat would be an impossible target if she got any nearer. With sinking heart he acknowledged that, incredibly, everyone else had missed their shots and it was up to him. Hands steady on the gun, he waited. Instinct, calculation, luck, they all played their part: suddenly she was clear of the grass, her throat a target for the duration of one more stride. He pulled the trigger. Her forward dash stopped abruptly and she stood still, looking up at him, with, he could have sworn, a slight smile on her face, then she crashed to the ground.

Movement below Edgar's tree told Joe he was already running towards the kill. Joe climbed down, still clutching his rifle, his head a whirl of mixed emotions with something very like elation bubbling to the top. As Colin had taught them, he picked up a stone and threw it at the body to check for signs of life. It seemed to him a mean act but

236

tigers apparently dead had been known to leap roaring to their feet when inexperienced shikari had approached to place a conquering foot on their necks. There was no movement so he moved forward to apply the second test. He tugged the end of the tiger's tail and, still seeing no response, he waved his rifle in triumph as Edgar ran towards him.

When Edgar reached the open ground he stopped. His body tensed, he dropped his hat and yelled something which Joe could not possibly hear over the continued noise of the beaters and the now hysterical monkeys.

Joe could make no sense of what was happening but his blood chilled to see Edgar's gun go up and train steadily straight at him.

'Edgar! What the hell?'

Joe was looking down the barrels of a 500 express rifle and one of them was still loaded.

Holding his rifle one-handed, Edgar raised his left arm and in a well-remembered soldier's silent warning his hand chopped down savagely twice. In instant response, Joe spun around to cover his rear and looked straight into the open red jaws of a tiger.

A tiger only feet away, very much alive, full of rage and on the point of springing. Colin's voice sounding in his head, and his instincts allowing for the change in height as the beast leapt, Joe swung his rifle upwards. With no time to shoulder it, he fired from the hip. The recoil of the big gun threw him backwards and sideways away from the twenty-stone body hurtling towards him and he fell, out of the path of the tiger as it collapsed, twitching and thrashing, over the prints of his own feet in the sand. Its hot breath swept his cheek as it crashed down; the claws of one outflung paw raked his forearm.

The monkey chorus leaped about, angry little black faces gibbering and screaming, throwing pieces of wood at the body of the tiger. Joe scrambled to his feet and was glad of the support of Edgar's arm as he rushed forward and held him upright.

'Sorry, Joe, couldn't get a clear shot at the bugger! You were right in my line of fire. But what the hell! Where did *he* come from? Are you all right, old man? That was a nasty surprise!' He released Joe and went to examine the tiger. 'Fine shot! Right through the throat!' He straightened and began to laugh. 'Two tigers, with two bullets, in two minutes! This is a story that'll be told at campfires for years! Two Shots Sandilands! I can hear it now.'

Edgar's attempt at jovial insouciance did not deceive Joe; it covered a depth of trembling agitation. At last Joe managed to get his vocal cords in gear. 'Edgar – thank you. Thank you very much. Again.'

Edgar raised his revolver. 'Mustn't forget the all clear in all this excitement!' He fired three swift shots. 'We'd better get the doc to have a look at that arm but meanwhile I'll put this round it.' He produced a large handkerchief. 'Can't have you dripping blood everywhere in that dramatic way.'

'What in heaven's name is going on here?' Suddenly and silently, Colin was at their elbow, rifle over his arm. 'Oh, no! Good Lord!' He read the scene in front of him at once, needing no word of explanation from Joe or Edgar. 'Two of the creatures! How can I have missed that? What a bloody fool! Joe, are you all right?'

Joe reassured him. 'The tigress did everything you expected her to do, Colin, right on cue. But where the hell did this other one come from? It was right behind me!'

Colin shook his head slowly. 'Her cub? Most likely her cub. Fully grown as you've noticed. They must have been hunting as a pair . . .' His face contorted with anger and regret. 'If only I'd had more time to examine the area I might have come across a second set of pug marks. This was very nearly a disaster.'

'Explains why so many villagers were being taken,' said Edgar practically. 'Feeding two of the buggers!'

A band of villagers, beaters judging by the sticks and drums they still carried, approached warily, then less warily as they saw the two bodies lying motionless. They

238

shouted exultantly at Colin, clashing their sticks together in triumph. One approached the tigress and began to pour out invective on the dead animal.

'"This shaitan of a tiger",' Edgar translated with a grin. 'Just giving you the flavour of this now . . . They're glad it's dead. He's naming all his friends and relations who've been killed . . . it's quite a long list.' He turned to the hunter, who was still unable to join in the celebrations. 'Come on, Colin, cheer up! All's well that ends in two dead man-eaters. It's a double triumph for everyone.'

Slowly Colin allowed himself a slight smile, then, catching the relief of Edgar and Joe and the good humour of the beaters, a wider smile.

As the noises died down, they all grinned at each other in satisfaction over the body of the tiger. They were still grinning when, a moment later, an insistent blast of a railway whistle sounded to the east. It sounded again and again.

Chapter Twenty-One

They ran, blinded by sweat, lungs heaving a protest at the heat, drawn on through the scrub by the note of panic in the whistle.

It led them to Bahadur's tree.

Shubhada, stiff with fright, dropped her whistle as they crashed through the remaining bushes and pointed with an unsteady finger towards the thicket separating her tree from the one to its left, that of Claude Vyvyan. Joe looked and looked again.

'Where's Bahadur? Your Highness, where's Bahadur?'

Again she pointed. Shrilly she said, 'I don't know! He got down to have a . . . to answer a call of nature . . . sometime before the bugle blew. I told him to try not to . . . it was only nerves . . . but he insisted. Then the beat started and he still hadn't come back. I didn't know what to do. I stayed on the machan trying to cover the nullah and the game path. I didn't want to whistle in case it brought the tiger down on us.'

Colin nodded in approval but he was looking grey with anxiety.

'I never saw her. And Bahadur's still in there! He must have heard the all clear but he didn't come out so I started to blow my whistle. Vyvyan got here just before you and he went in. He hasn't come out either!' Her voice rose to a peremptory scream. 'What are you waiting for? Go and help him!'

Edgar held her ladder in place and she climbed down

and made to dash into the undergrowth. Edgar barred her way.

'Help! Colin! Over here!' came Claude's voice faintly.

On unwilling feet they made their way in single file following a pathway of flattened grasses into the heart of the thicket. Claude's rifle lay abandoned to one side of the trail. Shoulders heaving, Claude was kneeling over a small form lying on its back. Hearing them approach, he got to his feet and stood, arms dangling hopelessly at his side. His khaki shorts and shirt were patched and dark with sweat and blood, tears ran down his face and he dashed them away with a bloodstained hand.

'Too late. He's dead. Bloody tiger got him!'

In silent horror they crowded round the body of Bahadur, shock anaesthetizing them from the destructive emotions of fear, guilt and regret which would lay ambush to them later.

'Don't touch the body.'

At the quiet command from Joe, Edgar and Colin held back, eyes devouring the scene. Somewhere behind them there was a stricken cry from Shubhada and Claude went to her side, murmuring. With an automatic assumption of authority, Joe bent to examine the body. Unable to bear what he saw as a look of astonishment and horror on the boy's face, Joe gently closed the eyelids and turned his attention to the fatal wound.

The throat had been torn out, raked by the claws of a tiger, and the boy had doubtless died from loss of blood and perhaps the shock of the attack. Further claw marks were visible on his chest where his tunic had been torn away.

'His rifle?' asked Joe.

'He left it on the machan,' said Shubhada.

Joe remembered his own horror on being attacked and he'd had the comfort of a Holland and Holland rifle ready to hand. He could not imagine the terror that must have filled Bahadur's last moments. Looking down on him with pity, Joe noticed something odd about the posture of the child's body. The right arm was bent at the elbow and the lower arm and hand were concealed underneath his hips. Carefully Joe raised the slight form an inch or two and pulled the arm free. A small black revolver clutched in Bahadur's hand was dislodged and fell at Joe's feet.

With a gasp, Joe turned his face away until he could regain a measure of control. Finally, he looked back at Colin and Edgar. 'My revolver,' he said. 'He admired it so much I gave it to him. For protection. Poor little sod! He was trying to defend himself with my little pop-gun!'

'Wouldn't have been much use against a tiger even if he'd managed to draw it in time,' Edgar commented, picking it up.

'You'd use a toothpick if it was all you had to hand,' said Colin bitterly. He was looking about him at the trampled grass, at the ground around the body.

'Keep everybody back!' Joe snapped out a command, hearing a crowd of beaters and hunt servants congregating at the fringes of the thicket, and Edgar went to pass on instructions and post a guard.

No guard was strong enough to keep back Ajit Singh who arrived a moment later, his confidence momentarily shattered by what he saw. He stalked straight up to the body, distraught and angry.

'Sandilands, what has happened here?' he demanded. 'Vyvyan, I can't believe that this could have happened under your very nose!'

He listened carefully as Joe filled in the details, his eyes moving constantly around the scene taking in, Joe could have sworn, the position of every blade of grass.

'Probably not the right time to ask, Ajit,' said Claude boldly, 'but I should really like to establish – while it's fresh in all our minds – the sequence of events. Tell me, why didn't you take a shot at the tigress when you had her in your sights?' He turned to the others and added, 'Saw her clearly from my machan. She drew level with Ajit Singh – perfect target – but we heard nothing from him. I remember being rather puzzled. Nodded off, had you,

Ajit? I waited until she moved along into my sector and I fired. She cantered off, tail up. Missed, I'm afraid. Not a good shot. Well, Ajit?'

What had been Madeleine's phrase? 'A baby poking a grizzly in the eye'? Perhaps the stress had unhinged Claude? Joe could think of no other reason for this suicidally bold and unnecessary challenge. His hand went automatically to hover over the grip of his revolver as, slowly, Ajit turned on Claude.

Ajit did not draw a dagger and cut Claude's throat as Joe half expected he would. Instead he unleashed a smile with the fine edge of a surgical scalpel and spoke in a tone of purring menace.

'Why did I not fire when she presented herself as you accurately describe? My prince . . .' He gestured reverently at the body at his feet. '. . . was to have every opportunity to claim her head. The tiger is a royal beast and should be shot by princes not the common herd. I held back, waiting for the shot from his machan, but it never came and the tigress passed into the sights of others.'

The smile intensified in its devastating politeness. 'But do tell us, Vyvyan, why we see you here, covered in the royal blood? Your machan was yards from this scene of slaughter. Did you see nothing that could have alerted you to the danger?' His voice began to grate with an emotion increasingly difficult to hold back. 'How gladly would I have leapt between my prince and the tiger's jaws!'

Joe believed him.

Vyvyan drew himself up and seemed about to unleash another ill-timed volley at Ajit when Shubhada intervened. 'Vyvyan!' Her voice was sharp, calling him to heel. 'There is no reason to hold Ajit Singh accountable!'

Colin, who had been inspecting the scene, straightened and came to stand between Ajit and Claude. 'Her Highness is right. Nothing either one of you could have done,' he said. 'It was the *young* tiger that got him. It must have been lying up here when we put everybody on to their machans. When Bahadur climbed down and strolled all unawares into the shrubbery he surprised it and it turned on him. A normal tiger would have crept away and he wouldn't even have known it was there but this one was a man-eater and they've lost all respect for humans. Then the bugle blew, the beating began and it sneaked out by the back door.

'Here, look . . . and here. There are one or two paw prints if you look carefully but the ground is so trampled I can't work out exactly where it broke out.'

'So – while we were all watching the nullah,' said Edgar, 'it made its way towards the exit by Joe's tree and, frightened and angry, did what man-eaters do and went for Joe whose back was presenting a perfect target.'

'*Young* tiger, did you say?' Claude's voice was bemused.

'There were two. Mother and full-grown cub. The cub killed Bahadur and then almost got Joe,' said Edgar, indicating the bloodstained handkerchief round Joe's arm.

Claude put his head in his hands and groaned.

'How useful it would have been,' Ajit turned his glare on Colin, his anger still seeking a target, 'to have been made aware of the presence of two tigers. Had we known there was a second lying up, no one would have risked his life alone, without a rifle on the forest floor.'

'Time! If I'd been allowed the time I asked for . . .' Colin began to protest.

Through his shock and grief, Joe was conscious of the struggle for power or at least the struggle for the avoidance of culpability that was raging over his head as he knelt and continued his examination of the body. He listened and watched, knowing that he ought to call a halt to the recriminations before he had a further killing on his hands, but a professional interest kept him silently observing and it was Edgar who put an end to the ugly scene.

'Stop this!' he said firmly. 'I've heard jackals make sweeter noises on a kill!'

His blunt remark calmed tempers sufficiently for Joe to rise to his feet and extend an arm, unconsciously his own claw-raked left, and seize Ajit's bunched fist. 'Ajit, Edgar's right. This is no place for arguments. We must have Bahadur taken back to camp. You and I will need to take statements from all who were here. A most regrettable accident and we must look into the circumstances of it and try to understand it.'

Ajit nodded solemnly and, acting on the cue Joe had offered, began to stride about assigning duties to the servants and telling everyone to follow Colin back to camp and to remain in their tents. They were instructed not to emerge until asked to do so by either Ajit or Commander Sandilands.

A slow and mournful procession trailed after a bier hurriedly assembled from saplings, bearing the body of Bahadur. More saplings were cut to transport the bodies of the tigers and these brought up the rear.

Sir Hector, Madeleine and Stuart came out to meet them, eager for news. They had heard the shots and were expecting a triumphant appearance of successful hunters and their quarry. They were devastated by the grim cortège which wound its way into camp. Joe outlined as briefly as he could the events leading to the tragedy and silently they absorbed the horror of their situation.

The doctor was the first to recover his aplomb. 'Look – take the boy to my tent, will you?' he said. 'There's a large table set out in there . . . well, you never know . . . I was prepared for incoming wounded.' He looked at Joe's arm. 'And I see it was not in vain. You'd better come along, Joe.'

Joe followed Sir Hector to his tent and watched as Bahadur was laid by the bearers on the table. The doctor dismissed everyone and the two men were left alone with the body. Hector opened his black bag and took out a tray of gleaming silver instruments. 'The living before the dead, I always say, however important the dead may have been. Show me your arm, Joe. Mmm . . . you've had a lucky escape but you don't need me to tell you that. So far. Have to hope it doesn't go septic in this heat. Always the danger.'

To Joe's surprise, he uncorked a bottle of Swiss mineral water and poured it over the wound, flushing away the dried blood and dirt into a copper basin. Joe winced and gritted his teeth and waited for the next part of the process.

'Now the gore's gone I see that it's not too formidable. I think we can get away without stitching it if I bandage it carefully but it will need to be disinfected. You'll have another interesting scar to impress the girls with, Joe.'

He took a small phial of yellow liquid from his bag, broke off the top and trickled the viscous contents over the tears in the flesh.

'What's that?' Joe asked.

'Haven't the faintest idea! I get it from Udai's court physician. Works a treat – much more effective than potassium permanganate,' he said confidently and proceeded skilfully to bandage up the arm. 'Now, before the body gets snatched away from us and started on the undertaking process, why don't we have a look at it?'

'I've had a look,' said Joe repressively. 'Throat torn out by a tiger. Small throat. Large claws.'

'All the same,' Hector persisted, 'indulge my professional curiosity for a moment and approach with me, if you will, Commander.'

With dire memories of Madeleine making just the same formal use of his title before the enquiries into Prithvi's death, Joe accepted the change in his role. No longer the patient, he was now the police commander being invited to witness an autopsy. Reluctantly he went to stand on the other side of the pathetic little corpse and watched as, with a face devoid of emotion, the doctor selected a slim instrument and proceeded to examine the wound.

'Yes. No doubt about that. Tiger killed him with one, possibly two blows right to left diagonally across the throat. Death from immediate gross loss of blood. There's something here . . . sand . . . bits of vegetation . . .'

'From the paw,' said Joe, impatiently.

Hector glanced quickly at Joe. 'Yes . . . paw. I say, didn't Colin tell us last evening that tiger kill their prey with their teeth?'

Joe was impressed by Sir Hector's perception. 'Yes, he did. And so they do, I understand. Water buffalo, large deer and so on. But Bahadur was hardly prey – more in the nature of a small, fragile nuisance who'd blundered by mistake into the tiger's thicket and disturbed his midday snooze. Swatted him away.'

Sir Hector looked more closely at the wound, adjusting his spectacles as he probed. With a grunt of satisfaction, he selected a pair of tweezers from his kit and took out a white object, dropping it with a plink into a small china dish.

Joe peered at it. 'Tiger's claw?'

'Yes.'

The doctor looked up from his work, set down his scalpel and spoke thoughtfully. 'Joe, I want you to go over the whole thing again. Everything. Sorry to be so tedious but I want to hear what happened from the moment you got into your tree until the moment you found Bahadur in the thicket. Miss nothing out.'

To Joe's further puzzlement, he took out a sheet of squared paper and began to draw a plan of the nullah, marking on it everyone's position. He took a red pencil and, as Joe's story progressed, he marked the paths the tigers had taken, the tigress moving in a straight line from right to left across the page, the cub lying up between the trees occupied by Bahadur and Claude and, having dispatched Bahadur, circling round to the south to attack Joe from behind.

He asked one question: 'Is there any chance that the old tigress could have made a detour and herself have killed Bahadur?'

Joe considered this. 'No. I would say – no. Ajit spotted her in the centre of the draw on her way down from the den. He tracked her as far as the next sector – Claude's stand. From there she was in view tree by tree until I put a bullet in her.'

'Thank you, Joe. You're very patient. And clear.'

'Sir Hector, is there a point to all this?' Joe asked uncertainly.

The old doctor came close to him and shot a swift anxious look at the door flap. He paused for a moment, listening, before he answered.

'I think we've got another one of those, Joe,' he said.

Chapter Twenty-Two

This was the last thing in the world Joe wanted to hear and for a moment his mind refused to take in what Sir Hector was saying. He stifled the automatic objections that leapt to his lips and instead sat down, silently absorbing the doctor's assertion, made carefully, unwillingly and fearfully. It was not an assertion he could dismiss out of hand.

'You mean you're not happy with the circumstances of the death as reported?' he asked. 'Surely nothing could be clearer?' He pointed to the claw in the dish. 'He even left his calling card.'

'And there's the problem,' said Sir Hector. 'Just follow a thought through with me, will you, Joe?' He sighed and tugged at his moustache in his anxiety. 'I'm sure you'll say I'm being unnecessarily pedantic and after all, if you look at the line-up of witnesses closely involved – two top police officers, the best tiger hunter south of the Himalayas, the Resident, the maharanee, Sir George's trusted hatchet-man . . . well, who am I to throw a spanner in the works and tell you you're all deluded?'

'And is that what you're saying? Come on! Out with it! What *have* you seen?'

'Unfortunately, I haven't got my microscope to hand . . .' He rummaged in his bag and produced a hand-held lens. 'I use this for removing splinters and suchlike. It will have to do.'

He leant over the table and examined the claw again

with the aid of the glass. 'Ah! Yes! I was not mistaken. Here, take a look yourself, Joe.'

Joe looked and blinked and looked again.

'Could you perhaps wash the rest of the blood off, Sir Hector? We need to be quite certain about this . . . Thank you. Yes, that's even clearer.' He spoke slowly. 'To my inexperienced eye, this claw has a slight striation along the length of it which might be a split or crack; it has a chip at what you might call the business end and the whole claw has a yellowed appearance.' He looked up at Hector. 'In fact it reminds me of nothing so much as my great-aunt Hester's teeth in her declining days. Hector! This is the claw of an *old* tiger!'

Hector nodded. 'Colin! You must fetch Colin!'

It was pitiful to see the change that had come over the old hunter in the last two hours. Like a man just hanging on to the threads of consciousness after a stunning blow to the skull, Joe thought. Colin was going through the remembered motions of polite response but his spirit was somewhere beyond reach. Blaming himself for the whole fiasco, Joe realized, and he acknowledged that in his place he would have reacted in the same way. He guessed that Colin would have seen in Joe's eyes a reflection of his own pain and guilt had he been able to focus on anything other than his inner turmoil.

He followed Joe without question back to the doctor's tent. Joe handed him the magnifying glass. 'Look at this object in the dish and tell us what you see.'

Colin studied the claw and then said with a note of puzzlement creeping in, 'A claw. Tiger claw. Well worn . . . chipped . . . judging by its colour I'd say from a mature if not aged beast. What is all this?'

Joe and Hector looked at each other. 'That's what *we* thought. Would it surprise you to hear that I've just extracted it from the boy's throat wound?'

'Yes, it would. The old tigress went nowhere near the

thicket where Bahadur was found. He was killed by the cub,' said Colin patiently. 'And, anyway, I've never come across a claw being left in a wound before. Just doesn't happen.'

'Colin,' said Joe gently, 'that's a claw I've just witnessed being taken from Bahadur's throat.'

Colin was beginning to rally and recover his old sharpness. 'Something wrong here . . . I think we should have another look at the wound, don't you? Sir Hector, would you . . .?'

They gathered around the body, taking care to leave elbow room for Sir Hector as he retrieved his instrument. Joe held up the magnifying lens in position for him as he worked. Suddenly he stopped and grunted. 'Pass me that probe, will you? Third item from the right, top row . . . There it is. I'm sure I'm not mistaken. Oh, good God!'

'There's *what*?' hissed Joe.

'Deep wound to the jugular. Severs the vein. And not delivered by a tiger's claw. Much, much deeper than a claw could penetrate. It's straight . . . slim. Insignificant surface entry marks and these camouflaged by subsequent laceration administered by the claws. Two sharp edges, clean cut. The skin has retracted over the mouth of the exit making a very small wound indeed. Very easy to miss. Stiletto? Isn't that what those Italian blades are called? Went in at an angle, so delivered by someone taller than the victim. But then, who isn't?'

He put down his probe. 'I'd say the lad was killed by a stab to the jugular. It could have been delivered from behind. There's the faintest bruising on the jaw. Here, Joe, kneel down for a second, will you?' He demonstrated, advancing on Joe from behind, grabbing his chin and holding his head firmly. 'Not a good idea to pull the head up too far – you can lose the arteries behind the windpipe but that's not generally known. We'll assume our man pulled upwards. Such a small throat, he wouldn't have had a problem.' He raised his scalpel and Joe cringed as he brought it down sharply, the point hovering over his exposed throat. 'Clear run at the neck, you see, and that way the jet of blood is directed away from you and you don't emerge from the undergrowth covered in blood. There would have been a lot of blood . . . And the boy was standing at the time, as you see from the blood trails on his clothing.'

'But the claw wounds, Hector? What are you saying about *them*? Were they inflicted before, at the same time as or after the insertion of the blade? Did the tiger come across him as he lay dead? Can you tell?'

Sir Hector sighed. 'Speaking generally, post-mortem wounds are diagnosed by the absence of signs of vital reaction. If a wound is made while the victim is still alive, tiny blood vessels are ruptured and the heart – if it's still beating – forces blood into the tissues around the damaged area. The blood clots and it's difficult to remove by washing. Pass me the water and that sponge over there. I'll see what I can do.'

He worked on, muttering about microscopes, white cells and leucocytes, only half expecting Joe to follow. Finally, he put down his instruments and washed his hands, saying thoughtfully, 'Difficult to believe but the claw wounds seem to have been inflicted at the same time as, or as near as makes no difference, immediately after, the stab to the neck.'

Hector shook his head. 'The poor chap appears to have been mangled as he was dying by an elderly tiger with a loose claw but that's as far as I can go with the medical evidence. Beyond this point I'm out of my territory. Sorry, but it has to be over to you and Colin now. I've done all I can and probably said more than is warranted – or safe.'

'Hector, thank you! You've been most meticulous. No one else would have noticed there was anything wrong and what fools we would have been. Look, can I ask you both to say nothing of what we've seen for the moment?'

Colin and Hector nodded their agreement and Joe went

on, 'And I'm sure you'd understand the reason if I were to suggest that the next step might be a second autopsy?'

Hector began to look affronted but Colin nodded. 'I see where you're going with this, Joe. You wouldn't have been about to call for an autopsy on a tiger, would you?'

'Exactly that!'

'Oh, er, I'm afraid you'll have to count me out, old boy. Not my area of expertise at all,' Hector demurred.

'It's all right, Hector,' said Colin. 'You're looking at a world-class dissector of tigers! I always remove the paws, the head and the pelt, sometimes with nothing more than a penknife. It's expected. No one will think anything of it if I go and do that right away. In this heat, the sooner the better. Will you come with me, Joe?'

They found the tigers where the bearers had left them in a small clearing next to the supply tent. Many men had gathered round to marvel at the size of the beasts, to gossip and to commit to memory every detail of their deaths at the hands of the scarred sahib. And here was more excitement. The eagerly anticipated moment when O'Connor Sahib would skin them. Murmurs of encouragement greeted Colin and the freshly bandaged Joe as they approached to examine the bodies.

'Start with the young one, shall we?' said Colin briskly. Joe found he could in all honour not look away when all the eyes of the admiring crowd were trained on the swift silver knife as it worked over and through the body. He found it helped to concentrate on Colin's matter-of-fact commentary delivered in Hindi and English. Off came the paws with a cursory examination. 'Trace of blood on the right front. Healthy young beast. About three years old, I'd say. Not much wear on the claws. All five on each front paw intact and four claws on each of the hind paws.' Catching Joe's flash of interest, he added, 'Tigers only have four claws on the back paws, Joe.' He turned his attention to the head. 'Do you want this prepared to hang over your desk at Scotland Yard, Joe? It's yours by rights!'

The head was set on one side to be collected by the palace skin-curer and the pelt followed, Colin rolling it up carefully. 'They say a diet of human flesh is bad for tigers but I must say I've never found any evidence of that. Always seem to be in perfectly good condition. This one certainly was. The other one now?'

He moved over to the tigress and the crowd murmured savagely under its breath. They knew who was the real villain. They knew it was the tigress who had become a man-eater and terrorized their villages for months, killing their children, their parents, their cousins. Teaching her cub to become a killer. Colin began methodically to carry out the same procedure, talking to Joe as he worked. 'Always a good idea to do this when a man-eater's involved,' he commented. 'Physical flaws can often explain why the creature's taken to the unnatural habit of preying on men. I note that this one has been blinded in the left eye but I understand that is a recent wound and not the reason behind her change in diet.'

Three paws were removed then, detaching the fourth, he held it up to the gaze of the audience. 'And here you have it. Porcupine quills. Must have come off worst in a fight with a porcupine.' He counted. 'Eight, nine, ten quills have penetrated the paw to quite a depth. In fact some have worked their way in, hit the shin bone and done a U turn. Must have been painful and incapacitating. I think this tells us why she took to catching slower, feebler prey. All claws in all four paws in place and I would judge that she wasn't all that old. More than ten, less than thirteen years perhaps? Weight? A good size for a tigress . . . I'd say 350 pounds or thereabouts. And the pelt . . . Fine coat rather ruined by two bullet holes. Looks as though Edgar got her in the side before you finished her off, Joe. Look, old man, would you mind very much if I offered this to the head-man of the local village?'

'I think that would be very fitting,' said Joe and the pelt was carried off with whoops of triumph.

They made their way back to Hector's tent. All signs of the autopsy had been cleared away, the body covered in a white sheet, and Hector was sitting quietly on watch. He listened with raised eyebrows to Joe's account and then said simply, 'Well, your experts have given their forensic opinions and evidence, Joe. We can go no further. Nothing more we can do here. Does anyone have plans for the body? There's no way we can get it back to the palace before dark today and you know they cremate their dead within twenty-four hours.'

'It's all right, Hector,' said Colin. 'Ajit's dealing with that. A pandit has been summoned and the cremation ceremony will be carried out by the villagers at first light. We'll take his ashes back to Ranipur to be scattered in the river.'

He approached the body and looked sadly down at the torn features. 'Poor, poor little scrap,' he murmured. 'And when someone dies, aren't there always things you regret? Things you didn't say . . . things you did say . . .'

There was something underlying Colin's sadness that invited Joe to ask, 'Something *you* said, Colin?'

He seemed relieved to be prompted to say, 'Yes, you all heard me. Ticked him off in front of everyone. Last thing I ever said to him. Told him not to fool about with his whistle.'

'Sounded entirely reasonable to me,' said Joe. 'The lad was a bit overexcited . . . could have caused havoc. But was there something behind the warning?'

'Yes, there was. He'd been larking about in the night. Surprised you didn't hear anything, Joe?'

'I did hear . . . things,' said Joe. 'Go on.'

'Well, I'd taken the precaution of leaving a night watch on duty. Oh, they didn't enter the camp – their brief was to discreetly patrol the perimeter. So I was surprised when

255

one of the chaps woke me up at three in the morning. He said there was a problem in front of the tents. Couldn't work out what it was but a large patch of something white, shining in the moonlight, had caught his attention. He thought I ought to investigate. We went along and found that the ground between Claude's tent and the one opposite – Captain Mercer's, I think – an area of four by four yards – had been strewn with flour.'

'Flour?' The doctor was astonished, Joe less so.

'Did you alert anyone?' he asked.

'Yes, we did. Got poor old Claude out of bed. Couldn't understand what was going on but when he twigged, he was prepared to put the blame on Bahadur for a particularly pointless practical joke.'

'What steps did you take?'

'Sent for a broom and brushed it away as best we could and then, egged on by Claude, we did something I'll always regret. Turned into schoolboys ourselves. Must have been the full moon, the spirit of camaraderie . . . I don't know what. It was Claude's suggestion. He was spitting angry and determined to teach the boy a lesson but all the same I should have put the lid on it.'

'Colin, what did you do?'

Colin swallowed, his head drooped and he said softly, 'Claude took the flour we'd swept up and spread it in front of Bahadur's tent. Then we faked up a trail of enormous tiger paw prints marching straight up to the door – the old pebble in hanky trick.' He looked at Joe, stricken, tears in his eyes. 'It wouldn't have fooled him for half a minute! He'd been out in the jungle with me many times and I'd taught him all I know about tracking – even the tricks! He would have recognized it as such in no time at all and, I would have thought, erupted with laughter. That would have been normal. He liked a joke.'

Joe's mind was absorbing these details, unpleasant with hindsight, and linking them with facts he remembered himself from the night before. 'Colin, was anyone else aware of what you and Claude had done? What Bahadur had done?'

'Hard to say because I was rushing about liaising with the lead mahout by then and not really thinking about practical jokes. The lad got up late and by the time he came to breakfast I think everyone must have seen it. Assumed it was one of his own pranks, I suppose, rolled their eyes and passed on – I'm describing the actual reaction of – Madeleine, I think it was . . . yes . . . Madeleine. She laughed and said, oh, something like: "I see the man-eater dropped in for a midnight feast." Surprised to hear the detective hadn't noticed though?'

'I was more wakeful at the other end of the night,' said Joe. 'And I too made a late appearance. He'd had time to get rid of it by then.' He was reconstructing Bahadur's puzzling remark. Something about springing a trap set by Bahadur the great hunter, he remembered.

'You shouldn't put on a hair shirt for all this, Colin,' he said. 'Not your fault. But it is *someone's* fault. Someone who very nearly got away with murder and who, if it hadn't been for Hector's thoroughness, undoubtedly would have done. Because you were fooled, Colin, Edgar was fooled and I was fooled.'

'Fooled you may claim to have been, Joe,' said Hector, 'but it's going to be up to you to make some sense of all this. I must say I can't make head or tail of it. All I know is that the third heir is dead in our care and there'll be hell to pay when we get back!'

Chapter Twenty-Three

Riders had been dispatched ahead of the rest of the group to break the news at the palace. Shubhada had insisted on going with them, claiming it was her duty to speak to the maharaja first. No one was eager to contest this dubious privilege though, dutifully, Claude offered to escort her himself. His services were finally accepted with rather bad grace, Joe thought, and the advance party set off in the grey dawn.

The return journey was uncomfortable, spent tête-à-tête with Edgar who went over the previous day's events again and again, trying to work out why it should all have gone so hideously wrong. Was it possible to mistrust a man who had saved your life twice in as many months? Joe wondered, his instincts to confide the minimum to Edgar very strong. In the end, Edgar's repeated expressions of concern for his old friend Colin and the damage the death of Bahadur might do both to the man and to his reputation, persuaded him to tell Edgar about the doctor's findings.

'So you see, there was very little Colin could have done to prevent it . . . if, indeed, it was a case of murder as Sir Hector has made out. Can a hunt manager be expected to take as a factor in his arrangements the possibility that one of the shikari will murder another one? I don't think so. The shoot went according to plan – well, almost.'

'And, apart from the inquisitive doctor, the murder too. Admit it, Joe, that was a piece of ice-cold planning combined with a recklessness that makes your hair stand on end. Who the hell would have been able to do that? Who

258

is so ruthless that they'd stab a child in the throat? Who would have had the opportunity? You and I had each other in our sights for the whole time from the bugle to the whistle, you might say, so we can rule each other out, I think.'

'It's not quite that clear,' said Joe grimly. 'I heard what I thought was a langur bark a warning about half an hour before the bugle blew. But, thinking about it later, I realize that the monkeys in my tree didn't respond. They knew it wasn't one of their own tribe. I think it may have been Bahadur's attempted call for help . . . or his death cry. If someone killed the boy well before the hunt started, he would have had plenty of time to get back to his tree . . . or his position . . . not everyone was on a machan . . . before the tigress started her run down the nullah. Let's imagine the scene, Edgar. Now, let's assume you're the villain for a moment.'

Joe brushed aside his spluttered protests. 'You get up into your tree, having had the forethought to take up there with you a pair of gloves and a blanket – standard issue on each of the hunt elephants – and immediately everyone is settled you climb down again armed with these bits of equipment and a knife of some sort – not the skinning knife from the howdah, I think – too broad. Then you weave your way, easy for a tracker like yourself to do (I believe even I could have managed), between the clumps of tall grasses back across the nullah. With everyone's eyes glued to their own sector, you could have done it. Half an hour is plenty of time to get to Bahadur's tree. You call up to him to come down on some pretext. He trusts you and comes down while Shubhada's back is turned. Perhaps it's your lucky day and you don't even need to trick him into coming down; perhaps, nervously, like the rest of us, he becomes obsessed with the idea of having a pee and comes down for that purpose –'

'Joe, I won't interrupt again but I have to say – there was a patch of damp soil near the body as though someone had

259

done exactly that. I thought at the time it corroborated Shubhada's story.'

'So you were already thinking at that time that people's stories might need corroboration, Edgar? That's interesting.'

Edgar grunted in a non-committal way and Joe went on, 'So, the kid is standing in the undergrowth with his back to you. With your gloves on and the blanket tucked in front of you to soak up any blood splashes, you aim to put a hand over his mouth and plunge the dagger into his neck. Aware at the last moment that something's not right, the lad screams and tries – almost makes it – to pull the revolver out of his waistband. But you prevail. When you think he's dead you roll up the blanket and gloves – if you've been careful you might not have needed them anyway – and, and what . . .?'

'Throw them away in the underbrush? No one searched the area more than ten feet away from the body and they were never going to – no reason. Stow them away on a tree, bundle them up, take them away with you and put them on the campfire? I'd have hidden them at the bottom of Bahadur's funeral pyre,' offered Edgar helpfully.

'Yes, you would,' said Joe. 'And in London I'd have a squad of blokes checking whether those items went missing and whether any of the howdahs had traces of blood in them, but how the hell at this distance do we find out? The men will be half-way back to the palace or dismissed and gone home to their village. So little time at the crime scene because, as far as everyone's concerned, it's *not* a crime scene. Perhaps we should have made Ajit aware?'

'I'm sure he never travels without his thumbscrews. You know very well why you didn't tell Ajit!'

'Yes. The murder was committed either by a European or by Ajit himself. An investigation likely to give even him pause! He might, for the sake of appearances, have aggressively interviewed a few beaters, roughed up a cook or two . . . who knows? . . . some poor sod might have been given a free one-way ticket to the capital.'

Edgar replied thoughtfully, 'You underestimate Ajit. And that's always a mistake. But let's look again, shall we, from the obvious angle. Who had the opportunity?'

'Anyone who was within a mile at the time,' said Joe despondently. 'So that's the five people mounted on the machans, Colin who was roaming around . . . Madeleine and Stuart? Where were they, by the way? Back in camp? If so, that rules them out.'

'No. In fact, they came along too. I heard them arguing about it before we all climbed aboard our elephants. Stuart wanted to see the action and asked for another elephant to be brought round. Madeleine didn't want to go but he was persuading her, I think, by the time we all set off. They could have been cruising about anywhere in the vicinity. A word to the mahout to let one or both of them down for a minute . . . Problem – now why on earth would Stuart or Madeleine want Bahadur dead? Doubt they even knew him and they could in no way profit from his death.'

With vivid memories of his night with Madeleine, Joe was silent and it was a moment before he replied. 'Of course, we'd know more if anyone had bothered to interview the mahouts. But how could you? This is Ajit's territory and we were investigating a tiger slaying after all.'

Edgar asked thoughtfully, 'And aren't you inclined to think that's exactly what we *are* dealing with? Joe, you don't suppose the doc could have got this wrong, do you?'

It was with strong feelings of foreboding that Joe passed in the Dodge under the elephant gate and into the courtyard. Govind was waiting for him holding a slip of paper on a silver tray. A summons! Already! His heart sank.

'A message, sahib, from Sir George Jardine. He has been trying to contact you by telephone and sends strict instructions that the moment you arrived back you were to speak to him on this number.' Joe took the sheet of paper.

261

'I'm coming with you,' Edgar announced and, despite Joe's objections, insisted on accompanying him.

They followed Govind to the communications room, where a telephone sat in splendour and state in the centre of a mahogany table. Govind pushed a chair towards Joe, found another for Edgar and bowed out of the room. Joe set out his police notebook and a pencil on the table, wiped his sweating palms on the knees of his trousers and picked up the handset. He asked the voice at the other end to connect him with the Simla number. Moments later Sir George's voice erupted down the phone. Joe winced and held the receiver a little way from his ear. He wondered whether he would ever find the words to convince George that loud-hailer techniques were not necessary when using this modern equipment. He realized that Edgar would be able to hear every word.

'There you are, my boy! Glad you could at last get yourself to a telephone. Now Edgar managed to find the ops room three days ago or I wouldn't yet know that Prithvi Singh had all too literally bitten the dust.'

'I'm sorry, sir, it's been rather hectic over here . . .' Joe embarked on an embarrassed apology.

'So I hear. Those chess moves tax a fellow's stamina. Lucky that Edgar found the resilience and the time to file his report.'

'Before we go any further, sir, I should perhaps tell you that Edgar is himself at my side as we speak.'

'Well, that's nothing but good news. Saves me making a further phone call. I'll speak up. Now then, suddenly, this morning I find the news of Prithvi's death presents me with rather a problem. A problem of etiquette.'

'Etiquette?' said Joe, startled. 'We too have our problems not unconnected with Prithvi's death, sir, but I wouldn't have said that protocol featured particularly in our –'

'Yes, I'm sure, and you can tell me all about them in a moment. Now listen, Joe. On Tuesday night the good Edgar telephones me saying that the second heir to the throne has been killed. Now – not sure where you've got to down there but it's Friday in Simla – yesterday, while you were all away chasing tigers, I received a missive from the maharaja. Sent, quite properly, by special messenger. It had been sealed and dispatched the day before Prithvi died. Quite extraordinary and – I'm sure you'll agree – significant. It contained official advance notice of the betrothal of the prince's second son Prithvi Singh to . . . what's the girl's name . . .' Papers rustled and George began again, 'Princess Nirmala, one of the daughters of Mewar state. Sensible move. An alliance between Ranipur and Mewar would, of course, always be interesting to His Majesty's Government. Preliminary announcement and all that to assess our reaction to the forthcoming marriage. A fixture set for next month, I'm informed. Polite of him to let me know . . . all very correct . . . but you see my problem, Joe. Do I reply to this, causing hurt and offence, or do I tear it up and send my condolences on a death of which I have not yet been officially informed, possibly causing hurt and offence. Advise me.'

'George! I had no idea! No one has mentioned this, not even his first wife . . .' said Joe, reeling at the information.

'Ah, yes, the fan-dancer. Is she still about the place?'

'She is.'

'Well, they couldn't have kept it quiet for much longer but as the poor chap died before anything could come of it, they'll want to keep it to themselves for the princess's sake. Very Rajput. Wouldn't want her name spoken of in harness with that of someone who's no longer with us – could be damaging to her future prospects. With a bit of luck they'll have been able to cancel the invitation cards. Anyway, I'll hold fire for a day or two, see what transpires, what? Now tell me what you've been up to.'

Wearily, Joe started on his concise account of events since his arrival in Ranipur. Sir George listened so quietly Joe once or twice had to check that the line had not been cut. Finally George asked, 'Is it too early to ask if by any chance you've come up with a solution to these mysteries? Three deaths? Any idea who's behind all this?'

'Yes. I have. Yes, I really think I have,' he said. 'Now that the evidence is in. I'd like a little more time to clarify things,' he finished uncertainly.

'Quite a puzzle, I agree,' said Sir George, 'but, look here, I think at least I can help you out with 3 across. Still got Edgar with you?'

'Yes, he's here.'

'Right. He's just the chap you need. Put him on for a minute, will you?'

Joe passed the earpiece to Edgar but heard every word of Sir George's commands before he signed off.

'Edgar, can you find your way to the silah-khana?'

'Of course, Sir George.'

'Then take young Sandilands there at once. You're to show him the baghnakh. See if it gives him a few ideas.'

Edgar hung up the receiver with a hand shaking with excitement, his expression one of stunned amazement. 'The baghnakh! The bloody baghnakh! That's how he did it!'

In the irritating way of a conjuror who is determined to hang on to his surprise until the last dramatic moment, Edgar would say no more but hurried along the corridors until they arrived at a door Joe recognized. The armoury.

They slipped inside, having checked that they were unobserved, and Edgar switched on the lights. 'Now, Sandilands, remember turning down my invitation to view the gladiatorial exhibits, the other night? This time you can't refuse. George's orders.'

'Stop being so bloody mysterious and get on with it!' Joe snapped.

Edgar approached a glass case and lifted the lid. 'Ah. Both still in there, I see. Probably nothing in it but you can see what George was getting at. Hideous, hideous things! Baghnakhs! Sorry but there's no word for them in English.

Wouldn't want one. The sound of the Hindi says it all, I think.'

Joe was looking at twin objects. Two huge paws of a tiger had been mounted on short thick handles. Joe shuddered. 'What the hell are they for, Edgar?'

'Well, they're not back-scratchers. They're for killing. What else? They were used as weapons in gladiatorial combats. There's a rather lurid account by a Western traveller, top-brass, staying as the guest of a maharaja who staged some fights for his entertainment, boxing, wrestling and so on. For the grand finale, a couple of stout chaps appeared armed with these things and started hacking chunks out of each other. The guest was so sickened by the performance, especially when he was hit in the face by a gobbet of flying flesh, that he called a halt.'

Joe was not deceived by Edgar's insensitive delivery. He thought it masked a horror he would not have been capable of articulating. He took one of the weapons from its place and turned it over. They looked at it carefully. 'Good Lord – it's the size of a dessert plate but nothing untoward there, I think,' said Joe. 'Seems to have all its claws. Try the other one.'

'Ah. One claw missing.'

'We've got to get this to the doctor. He's got a microscope in his room, perhaps he could compare these claws with the one we found in Bahadur . . . yes, I kept it. And who knows what he might find traces of, unless it's been thoroughly cleaned and there hasn't been a great deal of time for that, I'd say. But how in hell do you transport something like this to the hunt? And back? Without someone noticing. Servants packing and unpacking . . .'

'Same way we're going to take it out of here,' said Edgar with a grin. 'See that gun case over there? Empty it, will you, and we'll stuff it in there. Nobody looks twice at anyone carrying sporting equipment about in this place!'

As they passed the ranks of ceremonial daggers, jewelled hilts twinkling, they both stopped, turned and looked.

'Something here for every taste and purpose,' said

Edgar. 'From castrating an elephant to paring your toe-nails. Take your pick. What about this?' he said, pointing to an evil-looking Afghani punch dagger. 'Easy to hide about the person.'

'No, too broad in the blade,' said Joe, looking carefully at it, 'and the blade's triangular. Wouldn't match the wound profile. But, yes! Look! Over there.'

Six slender knives with plain undecorated steel hilts were mounted in a row.

'Never noticed those before,' said Edgar. 'No winking jewels set in the hilts to catch the eye, I suppose. Medieval? European, would you say?'

Joe sighed. 'This is where I click my finger and summon up a sergeant who arranges for the whole lot to be wrapped in a handkerchief and taken away to the labora-tory. And an hour later they ring me on the telephone and say suspect item number five has traces of human blood recently deposited and a complete set of fingerprints on the hilt. But – for now, for here . . . let's just note, shall we, that number two from the right is shinier than the rest so it's probably been recently cleaned,' muttered Joe. 'Pop it in the box, would you, Edgar?'

They walked on nonchalantly through the palace, Edgar carrying the gun case, until they reached the rooms of Sir Hector Munro. He was supervising the unpacking of his effects but sent his servant away immediately he caught the expression on the faces of his two callers. It was enough to open the case and show him the contents. With an intake of breath and a shudder of revulsion, he under-stood what he was looking at and what was required of him. He carried the weapons to a bench, checked and adjusted his microscope and set to work.

'I hardly need to inspect the dagger,' he said. 'An exact match with the wound, I'd say. Been cleaned and polished.

Can't say I can see a trace of anything but smears of Brasso on it.'

Tweezers and swabs took samples from the paw and these went under the microscope. Joe offered the claw he had preserved wrapped in a handkerchief and they set to wait for Sir Hector's findings. Several times he called them over to look down the eyepiece and verify a conclusion and finally he said, 'That was well done, both of you! However did you manage to come up with this? I'd never seen or even heard of such a thing. But it's certainly the tool that was used in the killing of the Yuvaraj. The missing claw is a match for colour and general state of wear.

'The object has obviously been preserved for many years and been put to active, er, martial use which has resulted in the claws being less solidly attached than those of a live tiger. Not surprising that one of them worked loose and became embedded in the wound.' He paused for a moment. 'Of course, it could have been deliberately extracted from the foot and placed in the wound as a clinching factor. You yourself referred to it as a "calling card", I think, Joe.'

'Over-egging the pudding, wouldn't you say?'

'I would. Colin certainly would. Any expert would. You did – with hindsight and a hefty nudge. I think our perpetrator wasn't expecting to have a scientific searchlight shone on his handiwork. Just as interestingly, the matter I've found between the claws and on the pads is flesh and hair and, I'd say, not animal but human. And it's not been there all that long. I wouldn't say it's been left over from the last combat even if that were last week which it wasn't. It's relatively fresh. Someone's given the thing a good brush or comb down, a thorough job, and one which would deceive the human eye – unaided. You couldn't identify it without a microscope.

'I say – would you like to take that thing away with you?' he finished, distaste in his tone.

The baghnakh had safely been stowed away in the gun

267

case when a servant appeared at the door. Trembling and anxious, he delivered his message. The doctor's presence was urgently required at the ruler's suite. The Maharaja Udai Singh was dying. He wanted to see also the two sahibs, Troop and Sandilands.

Chapter Twenty-Four

They were escorted with urgency through the New Palace to a north-facing wing projecting out into parkland, the lake a distant gleam between crowding trees. Two rows of the Royal Guard were lined up along the corridor leading to the prince's apartment, and although the men made not the slightest movement Joe passed between them with a shudder.

As they arrived, the carved sandalwood doors opened and an Indian woman came out. A young girl dressed in blood-red Rajputana silks, her black hair was parted in the centre and a jewelled ornament hung very precisely in the centre of her forehead. Her arms were covered in ivory bangles from shoulder to elbow and gold anklets gleamed as she walked. Head erect, a smile on her face, she came on towards them. She glowed. She pushed ahead of her an almost palpable bow-wave of triumph.

Joe, Edgar and the doctor stood aside, gazing.

'Shubhada?' Edgar finally managed to ask.

Her glance flicked from one to the other. They were hardly worth her attention; she did not attempt to greet them.

An anger beginning quietly to burn in him pushed Joe to stand in front of her, blocking her path. Two of the guards took a step forward, hands on sword hilts. At a gesture from Shubhada they stood back. She waited for him to move aside, tapping her foot, the chink of anklets expressing her irritation. Her eyes remained fixed on the top button of his jacket.

His voice when he spoke was so soft she had to lean slightly towards him to hear what he said.

'Shah mat?'

'Shah mat. Though I think I prefer the English saying: "The King is dead. Long live the King." She smiled. She seemed amused. 'It always pays to look to the future, Commander.'

'Perhaps that is all one can do when the past is full of dishonour and death . . . and guilt!'

She was unable to meet his scorching gaze and stood, motionless, until he stepped aside and released her to flow on down the corridor.

'Now what the hell was that all about?' muttered Edgar.

The doctor at that moment was ushered into the state-rooms and Edgar and Joe were left to wait outside in the courtyard.

'And why is Third Her Highness got up in that outfit, do you suppose?' he persisted, with an anxious look at the guards to ascertain they were out of earshot. 'Are you going to tell me what on earth was the meaning of all that gibberish? Whatever you said, it certainly took the wind out of her sails!'

'An accusation of murder usually has that effect,' said Joe.

'Murder? Shubhada?' Edgar whispered, disbelieving. 'Are you barmy? Who's she supposed to have murdered? Not . . .?'

'Yes. It sickens me to say it but yes. Bahadur.'

'Then you *are* barmy! She of all people needed the boy alive, you idiot! She was going to be regent – years of power ahead of her to establish herself. Who knows,' his voice reached a new depth, unwilling to hear himself pointing a finger at Udai's wife, 'perhaps she had it in mind to milk the treasury? She's got expensive tastes. It has occurred to me that she mightn't have balked at helping herself to the goodies.'

Joe nodded. 'And those aren't the only goodies she was planning to help herself to, if I've got it right.'

Edgar considered. 'You've lost me, old chap.'

'The Resident.'

'Don't follow. Claude's the other key-holder, so to speak. Are you saying she was planning on suborning her co-regent?'

'Not suborning. Seducing, more like.'

Edgar whistled under his breath. 'You can't mean . . .'

'Yes. She's in love with him. If they haven't already embarked on a liaison, it's certainly on the cards. Part of the lady's look towards the future.'

'Absolute nonsense!' Edgar tried to splutter quietly. 'Total fantasy! Why, I'd have sworn she doesn't even like him . . . Good God, man! You've got me gossiping like you . . . just like two old maids at a Simla tea-party! What possible evidence do you have for such a scurrilous suggestion?'

Joe sighed. 'None you would accept, Edgar. A boat on a lake . . . a trace of perfume in the air . . . what indeed?' He shook his head. 'It does sound mad but, believe me, I'd place no weight on mere glancing suspicions if they weren't themselves given strength by the circumstances of Bahadur's death. Listen! Claude works (till all hours according to the memsahib) in a bungalow down by the lake.'

Edgar nodded.

'A short way along the shore is Shubhada's secluded pavilion, staffed by her discreet and devoted servants. She has a boat. We actually saw her being ferried about on the lake when we visited Colin. Where had she been?'

'Fishing of course!' said Edgar. 'We all understand she's a keen fisherman but you're saying it's not just lake trout she's got her hooks into?'

'No proof at all – I'm just asking you to follow a trail and see where it leads. I'm talking about possibilities. I don't

271

know how this intrigue – let's call it that, shall we? – started or who started it.'

'Well, a royal Indian female would not be Claude's natural prey, no matter how hungry, if you understand me. Way beyond his reach. Inviolate!'

'Yes, I would agree with that,' said Joe, 'were it not for the fact that this would not be the first, nor the hundredth, not even the thousandth love affair between an Indian and a European. And Cupid's been known to scatter his darts a little carelessly sometimes. But I take your point. I don't think Claude would have set out to ensnare Shubhada. Charm, perhaps, but not ensnare. It was most probably started on Shubhada's initiative or it was a simultaneous *coup de foudre* – the words do feature in her vocabulary. She grew up in the West – must have absorbed the usual romantic notions. May even have read *Monthly Moonshine Magazine* under the covers in her Brighton dormitory. And, let's admit it, shall we – though I'm sure it annoys us both – Claude's an attractive chap.'

Edgar's lip curled in distaste but Joe persisted. 'No, come on! I can imagine a girl being struck by a thunderbolt at the sight of him. Anyway – let's say they start on an after-hours association . . . Lois gets fretful. "Do you *have* to work so late, Claude? And what's that strange smell?" Can you imagine?'

Joe told Edgar about the French perfume. 'A very memorable scent,' he concluded.

Edgar was intrigued. 'So – he gives a bottle of the same stuff to his wife, and whichever girl he's been necking – as Stuart would say – he comes up smelling of Shalimar, so that's all right!' said Edgar. 'Hah! There's chaps in Simla would thank you for the tip! And with the maharaja dead and the pair of them made co-regents they can get their hands on power, money and each other! Very well. All that I can imagine – because I have a lively imagination – but what I can't accept is that, on the brink of this good fortune, Shubhada would throw everything away by killing Bahadur. Without him she has nothing.'

He fell silent and then said quietly, 'And there's the rub. *You* can't get around or past that, can you, Joe?'

'You're right, Edgar. There's something missing . . . something I haven't seen. A piece of this jigsaw's fallen on the floor and no one's noticed. But it doesn't stop us building up the rest of the picture.'

Doggedly, he went on, 'She didn't do it alone, you know.'

'Claude? I had wondered.'

'I think he did the killing. As soon as everyone was installed on their machan I think Claude came down to the thicket. Shubhada found a way of getting Bahadur to climb down. May even have told him to take the opportunity of having a last pee in a nanny-ish sort of way. While she takes the baghnakh out of her gun case – it didn't travel with the other luggage, she kept it with her all the time – and throws it down, Bahadur goes or is dragged into the thicket. He has time to cry out once and attempts to draw his revolver. No good against tiger but it would have stopped Claude in his tracks if only he'd been faster. Claude kills him. A quick stab and then he rakes over the small exit wound with the claws.'

Joe hesitated for a moment, ordering his thoughts. 'And this is what chills the blood, Edgar – he took the precaution of pressing the device into the ground a few times to create spoor in case anyone should be looking, so when Hector examined the wound . . .' Joe's voice trailed away.

'He found bits of sand and grass? Nothing if not thorough, the Resident.'

'As you say. Then the baghnakh and the knife disappear back into the gun case and Claude goes back to his tree. He shoots and misses the tigress to establish that he's there in position and the hunt progresses. As soon as she hears the all clear, Shubhada starts to whistle and when we come bursting in we see Claude, bloodstained, dishevelled and distraught. And every reason to be.'

'Distraught yes. But calculatedly so,' said Edgar. 'Remember the mad way he went for Ajit? Makes sense now. He was establishing in our minds the assertion that Ajit had been away from his machan or failing to shoot at the vital time. Spreading suspicion of neglect. It would have worked.'

'It was meticulously worked out,' said Joe thoughtfully, 'and yet . . . and yet . . . it could all have gone desperately wrong. How thrilled and surprised they must have been when a second tiger strolled on-stage unexpectedly. Played right into their hands!'

'I'm surprised Claude didn't take the easier way out and just shoot his victim,' said Edgar. 'Easy enough to fake a shooting accident. Heaven knows – they crop up naturally all the time!'

'I had noticed that Claude was paying close attention when I was telling Ram about ballistics. I think he even questioned me on the ease with which we could now obtain bullet profiles by simply sending the evidence off to Calcutta for analysis. I can almost feel sorry for him! He'd probably planned an accidental death by stray bullet and then, suddenly finding a smarty-pants police officer was going to be up the next tree, had to change his plans dramatically.'

'All the same – with the help of Shubhada and her acting abilities they damn nearly carried it off. Would have done if it had been left to you and me, old boy!' said Edgar. 'They hurried off before everyone else – with every appearance of bad feeling, did you notice? – to replace the weapon in the armoury having given it a good cleaning the night before. But why? It still leaves me asking – why the hell should they do this?'

'I'm nearly there. Tell me, Edgar, did you see the joke Colin played on Bahadur to teach him a lesson? The tiger's paws in the flour outside his tent?'

Edgar smiled. 'We all saw it. Just the sort of thing the lad appreciated. *Would* have appreciated. Didn't seem particularly amused on this occasion.'

'That's because his own trap had been discovered and

dismantled before it could be sprung. He was disappointed and sulking.'

'Trap? What trap?'

'I heard him stirring about in the night. He sent his man off to the supply tent for what appears to have been a sack of flour. When I asked if he was all right – I heard him laughing and checked on him – he said something mysterious about Bahadur the hunter's trap being sprung and he'd tell me about it in the morning.

'What he did with the flour was creep about spreading a layer of it outside Claude's tent. He thought that he'd get up early in the morning and check for spoor.'

'Good God! He was expecting to find a trail of footprints from someone else's tent to Claude's! Shubhada. She was at the end of the row . . . she'd have had to cross the flour to reach his tent – had she been stupid enough to try! Do you suppose Bahadur suspected something was going on before you did?'

'Yes, I do. He'd spent the last few months living rough about the palace, sleeping here and there, hiding in corners. He was clever and pretty devious himself. He'd learned all about life and intriguing – survival too – from the zenana. I think his mother must have been a bigger influence on the boy than people allow. Perhaps she even marked his card. If anyone could have observed an intrigue and known how to interpret what he saw correctly, he was the most likely. And having guessed – well . . .'

'Blackmail. Power,' said Edgar.

'No wonder he was so full of confidence immediately after he was declared Yuvaraj. Not only was he Prince in Waiting, but he had his prospective co-regents where he wanted them. And I'm sure he made them well aware of it. No waiting involved for Bahadur. I think he told them what he knew and what he intended to do about it if they didn't toe the line. They made their plans well before the hunting trip. The flourish with the flour was a bit of naughtiness – a practical demonstration of the power he had. Now what would have happened if he'd carried out his threat and told his father what was going on?'

Edgar's shoulders quivered with exaggerated horror at the question. 'Rather not think about it, old man! Yes, perhaps they did the only thing they *could* do. Committing a murder and losing their potential power would have been infinitely preferable to the appalling consequences had he spilled the beans to Udai and been believed.'

'But there's still something I can't get at,' said Joe.

'That missing piece? It'll come. Let's concentrate on putting what we've got on the table into some sort of order.'

An unwelcome thought struck Edgar. 'And what about the other deaths? Bishan? Prithvi? You're not suggesting that –'

The door opened and their names were called. Sahibs Troop and Sandilands made their way in to have their last interview with a dying prince.

Already in an agitated state, Edgar hurried forward, his grief obvious, in response to the wide gesture of Udai's outstretched arm.

'Edgar, my friend! Time to say goodbye, I think. Not *much* time – though I must agree with . . . is it Tagore? . . . when he says, "The butterfly counts not months but moments and has time enough." How trite death makes all such pronouncements sound, even the simple heartfelt ones!'

Elegantly clad in an achkan of white brocade, pearls draping his silken turban, he was lying on a divan, a glass of whisky at his elbow, looking, Joe thought, as bright as a bee, as urbane and welcoming as the hostess at an eighteenth-century literary salon. Voltaire himself must have been greeted in the drawing room of Madame du Deffand with just the same charm, full of subtle flattery. In the place of the small group of musicians gently playing a keening melody, Joe almost looked for the young Mozart at a harpsichord. But the image dissolved at the sight of the symbolic pile of straw by the window and the two Rajput footmen who stood grimly by to place their prince on it when his last minutes came. In a far corner, the old scribe turned from his table to smile and nod.

In attendance stood three courtly figures: Zalim Singh, for once expressionless and unsmiling, Sir Hector and an elderly, distinguished Rajput whom Joe took to be the palace physician.

'And Sandilands, how good of you to come,' said Udai. Before Joe could speak, he held up a hand. 'Please say nothing to me of the disastrous hunt. No one can struggle against Fate though we all try to the last. Indeed, you see me here, still struggling. I have said I would like Bahadur's ashes to be scattered on the river with mine. We spent little time together in life but we will make the great journey together in death.'

A tear escaped from Edgar's eye and embarked on the hazardous journey down the rough terrain of his cheek.

'My men of medicine you see . . .' He indicated the two still forms standing at the head of the divan. '. . . have administered the hiranya garbha and already I begin to feel its effect.' He turned to Sir Hector. 'Now, I know you're interested, Hector, so I'll tell you – I feel the predicted inner warmth, my pain has reduced by, oh – eighty per cent – my vision has cleared and my thoughts are sharp. Quite remarkable! But then – I must try not to confuse the physical effects of the pill with the mentally uplifting effects of my happiness.'

Joe and Edgar looked at each other, fearful for the ruler's sanity. His happiness? Was this was the speech of a dying man who had learned that morning that his last son had been killed by a tiger?

'Whatever the agent producing this effect, it gives me the energy for two last requests. Will you approach, Sandilands? You have been enquiring into the deaths of my first two sons. Before I take my final breath I should like to hear your solution to these mysteries.' Catching

Joe's hesitation and his wary glance at the others in the room, Udai smiled. 'You may whisper the information if you wish.'

While the others turned and tactfully spoke quietly amongst themselves, Joe went to stand close to the ruler, bent and murmured into his ear. Udai Singh closed his eyes, smiled and nodded.

'You repeat what Major Ajit Singh said to me half an hour ago. And I must believe my pair of hunting hounds when they are each pointing in the same direction. What a pity you will never work together, Sandilands! You must put up the quarry for others to shoot down. You see, Edgar – we plan our last hunt together! And now, my friends, I will impose upon you to perform a last service. I would like to ask you to witness my will.'

The old clerk stepped forward and handed parchments to Joe and Edgar.

'Read it. It will look familiar. I would like you to sign the document exactly as you did before. I want you to take one of the copies away with you and present it to Sir George. You will note that the wording is the same, only the date has been changed. We now see that on today's date, I, Udai Singh, Prince of Ranipur, name as my heir and future ruler of the state, my third son, Bahadur.'

He smiled to see their confusion. 'It seems the astrologers had it right, after all!'

Chapter Twenty-Five

They looked helplessly at Sir Hector for guidance. What were they witnessing? Euphoria? Madness? Some mental state of delusion brought on by the drug Udai had consumed? Hector gave a reassuring smile and made a fluttering sign that all was well.

The energy of the dying man was burning itself out rapidly and no one was more aware of it than himself. With shining eyes, he was watching and enjoying their reaction, Joe guessed. A strange piece of deathbed manipulativeness. When he had relished their discomfiture sufficiently, he smiled and spoke breathlessly in a voice beginning to lose its clarity.

'An hour ago my world was ending,' he said. 'Ending in misery. My three dear sons were all dead. The succession come to nothing. And then my beloved Shubhada came to see me. She is not Rajput by birth but she has the spirit of a Rajput ranee! And she came to tell me that she carries a child. A son. My son who will grow under her care to be a prince of Ranipur. I have asked her to name him Bahadur. The prophecy will be fulfilled, you see!'

Joe was the first to collect his wits. While Edgar murmured congratulations and shed another tear, Joe looked hurriedly through the parchment he'd been handed. Not much time. There was no way he could wrap up in courtly phrases what he had to say.

'Your Highness,' he said, 'we will be delighted to sign these documents but may I suggest one amendment . . . as

I see we have the scribe in attendance, this will be easily done?'

The maharaja looked puzzled and with a wave of the hand invited him to continue.

'When we come to the clause concerning the appointment of regents for the Prince Bahadur until he attains his majority – you name, of course, his mother Shubhada but also the person of Mr Claude Vyvyan. We are looking at a span of possibly more than seventeen years. Who knows, with the way promotion is going in the Empire at the moment, where Vyvyan will be in so many years' time? Would it not be more circumspect, sir, to strike out the name of Vyvyan substituting simply "the current Resident of Ranipur" and allow the regency to go along with the office and not the individual?'

Udai looked to Zalim for guidance, his mind beginning to fog, Joe calculated and he held his breath. Zalim was quick to respond. 'Splendid idea, Sandilands! A piece of diplomacy worthy of Sir George. How very thoughtful.' Udai nodded his assent to the clerk who made the necessary alterations. These were initialled by Udai with his last strength. Joe and Edgar signed the documents and the ceremonial red silk ribbons were attached. With a sigh, Udai nodded to his footmen who came forward and gently lifted him from the divan and placed him on the straw.

At a sign from the doctor, Joe and Edgar tiptoed from the room.

'Where are we going?' said Joe as they walked back down the corridor.

'No idea, old man. I was just following you,' said Edgar, and Joe realized that if he were ever to see true emotion in Edgar's ugly features this was the moment.

'Poor old Udai!' said Joe. 'But at least his last hour was a relatively happy one. Sorry – what a commonplace thing to say! – but he dies with his eyes not on the past but on the future and full of hope. And, surely, that is an unusual and blessed state?' A sideways glance at Edgar showed that his attempt at consolation had gone wide of its target. He chose another approach. 'But, come on now, Troop! We still have work to do. There are people about in this place who deserve their comeuppance. By the way, did you hear the click as the last piece of the jigsaw went home?'

'Click? Deafening report more like! Shubhada pregnant? And how the hell does she know it's going to be a boy?'

'She doesn't, of course. The astrologers do though, and their predictions cut some ice in Ranipur, especially with the ruler who is quite desperate for this piece of news. Extraordinary! That Udai should be succeeded by his third *legitimate* son!'

'Well, at least it explains why she's taken to walking about in full Rajput regalia,' said Edgar thoughtfully. 'She's showing the ruler and the whole court that she's the new Rajmata. She's going to be mother of the next maharaja as well as regent for the next eighteen years. And she's really entering into the role! She has, after all, an unquestionable stake in the kingdom now. And, you know, Joe . . .' Edgar's furrowed brow creased a little more as he struggled to order his thoughts and speculations. 'I begin to wonder whether this new maternal princess might find her interest in the Resident is beginning to wane? Perhaps it already has?'

'But her news explains why Bahadur had to die. The moment she announced her pregnancy to the ruler, Bahadur's claim to the throne would disappear like smoke and what could they expect him to do but rush to his father with his story? No more playing around with threats and practical jokes!'

'And what would be Udai's reaction? Could this story about Shubhada possibly be true? Was there a sinister reason for her sudden pregnancy? The proof of the pudding, of course . . . only time would tell . . . nine months to be precise before anyone would see who the child favoured. I'd bet my last shilling that it's Udai's child but, the seed of suspicion once sown . . . And Udai was under pressure – he had only days not months to come to a decision. There was a strong chance that he'd play safe and denounce Shubhada, send Claude away, his career in ruins, or simply feed the pair of them to the crocodiles . . . I don't know.'

'Could be arranged,' agreed Edgar. 'Ghastly accident while out fishing one evening, brave Resident hears screams, dives in to lend assistance. Snip! Snap! Gone to Delhi.'

'And the fear of this retribution signed Bahadur's death warrant.'

'Yes . . . The boy was damn dangerous and no longer of any use to them. They didn't need an unruly little Yuvaraj with a dubious claim to the throne when Shubhada was about to produce a legitimate heir. I think you're right, Joe.'

'And that's a bad sign, Edgar! You've stopped arguing with me. We could be talking ourselves into a most embarrassing piece of jumping to conclusions. You may not know where you're going but I'm heading for Lizzie Macarthur's rooms. No, don't groan! We need . . . I need a spot of Scottish scepticism and good sense. I also want to offer her my sympathy for her bereavement. She loved Bahadur, you know. Very much.'

Lizzie looked surprised and not at all pleased to see them. She invited them to come in and take a seat in a voice that was only just polite. Her hair was dishevelled, her face pale and her eyes still swimming with tears.

They sat down awkwardly side by side on the battered sofa. Lizzie didn't make the customary offer of a drink which, for once, Joe would have been glad to hear, but eyed them balefully, settling down on a lab stool opposite. Joe had felt similarly intimidated in his housemaster's study twenty years ago.

'Don't blame us, Lizzie!' he plunged straight in. 'Hear what we have to say, will you? You must be thinking that we're the most incompetent pair of bodyguards to have let Bahadur die. That's not what happened. The child was murdered. His killing was arranged in the most cold-blooded way.'

She listened in chilly silence but without interruption to the tale which Joe and Edgar between them hacked out, correcting and reminding each other as they went.

Finally, she looked at Joe directly. 'You are telling me that Bahadur was killed by Claude and Shubhada, working together?'

He nodded.

'What a clever chap you are, Sandilands! You gallantly shoot dead a pair of man-eating tigers but a pair of hunting humans is too much for your capabilities? You sent the boy out . . . no, you *staked* him out like a goat and they tore him to pieces almost under your nose!'

'That's unfair, Lizzie!' said Edgar. 'Calm down, for goodness' sake!'

She made a visible effort to rein in her anger and, with a return to her usual cool tone, commented, 'And Lois? What are we to think of her? She too a victim of two selfish people's unthinking rush towards power? Poor, poor Lois! And tell me now what you propose to do with your information?'

'I shall, of course, make Sir George aware of our suspicions and he will no doubt deal with Vyvyan in a discreet way. As for Shubhada, she is the mother of the future Prince of Ranipur and, as you know, the treaty we have –'

'Shut up, Joe!' said Lizzie. 'Edgar, pour us a whisky and let's think about this.'

'In all this excitement, I hope you haven't lost sight of the two previous deaths of heirs to the throne?' said Lizzie. 'Are we to suppose that Claude with or without the help of 3HH has been cutting a swathe through the royal family to achieve his ends? Three killings? Each one exposing him

283

a little further? How dangerous! How mad! It's hard to believe. And he's such a charming man.'

'No, as a matter of fact, I don't believe Claude had anything to do with the first two murders. I think he and Shubhada saw the advantage they created for them, reducing the obstacles between them and the regency to one vulnerable but threatening young boy. They seriously thought they could pass the murder off as a further arranged misadventure, one of a series. I'm sure we were all meant to think that Zalim Singh was behind the clearing away of contenders for the throne, using his agent, Ajit Singh. If anyone enquired, he would discount any involvement by Claude because he truly *was* remote from the first two. It's always misleading to assume that killings that occur in the same place or within a framework of time have necessarily been committed by the same man. No, I think Claude used the opportunity offered by the first and second deaths and hoped that if anything went wrong everyone would jump to the conclusion that another domino had fallen over – pushed by the same finger.'

'Very well,' said Edgar, 'but have you stopped to think why he bothered? Risking his career, his reputation, his *neck*, for goodness' sake . . .'

'For what?' said Joe crisply. 'For the key to a fortune? For the inside of the bend to high office? For the love of a beautiful and powerful woman? No, hardly worth the effort, you'd say.'

'Just doing what colonial powers have always done,' said Lizzie thoughtfully. 'Every provincial Roman governor expected to make three fortunes out of his stint abroad: one for Rome, one for himself in retirement and one to pay off the judges back home when he was charged with malpractice. I wonder how soon Claude was contemplating retiring? Tell me, Joe, is he still free to come and go about the palace? Or is he under restraint?'

Edgar and Joe exchanged a look. 'Free as the breeze for all we know,' said Edgar. 'Apart from ourselves, you're the only one who's aware, Lizzie. Even Udai has not been told. He thinks Bahadur was killed by a tiger.'

'And if, as you say, Claude has nothing more on his conscience than the death of Bahadur, who *did* kill Bishan and Prithvi then? Are you just showing off or have you really worked it out?'

'I've worked *something* out,' said Joe. 'Something in which Ajit Singh appears to concur if the ruler is to be believed. But I have yet to push the murderer into revealing himself . . . or herself. I may be wrong. I've been wrong once already. It had occurred to me that . . . sorry, Edgar, this will offend you, I know . . . I had thought that the sons had been removed to make way for Bahadur. Removed for the well-being and security of the princedom by their father.'

When Edgar's explosions of dismay and disgust had rolled away, Joe patiently explained his reasoning. Lizzie nodded several times.

'Edgar, do be quiet!' she said, finally. 'Joe, are you sure you're not right? It sounds very convincing to me. We all know – even Edgar knows – that the good of the state was Udai's main concern. He would have put it first every time. And to be honest, I wasn't in the least bit sorry when Bishan died. We all heaved a sigh of relief.'

'But Prithvi was different. He would have been acceptable had not one vital flaw ruled him out as far as Udai was concerned, and that was his obdurate refusal to marry a second wife,' said Joe. 'But then Sir George tore the most almighty hole in my neat theory this morning when he told us that the British Government had been given news of the forthcoming marriage between Prithvi and a Rajput princess. Very hush-hush and before it was made public Prithvi had died.'

Lizzie's eyes were growing rounder by the second. 'How extraordinary! No one here knew of that!'

'I think at least one other person must have known. The main player so to speak. Madeleine. And if she knew, she'd have told Stuart. They would both have seen it as a betrayal. I think everything changed for Madeleine when the older son died. Her husband was certainly in line to be named Yuvaraj. He was growing ever closer to his father and they saw the economic future of Ranipur with the same eyes. You yourself wondered, Lizzie, why the ruler was delaying naming his heir. Could it have been that he was very prepared to ink in the name of Prithvi but with the proviso that he agreed to marry a princess of Mewar?'

'Yes, I think so. And if your account of the dealings on the stock market is accurate, it would have made better sense for Prithvi to have succeeded. Bahadur was talented . . .' Her voice wavered for a moment then she recovered her balance and went on, 'but he would not have understood those dealings. Like his mother, he placed great store by wealth you can hold in your hand. He had, in fact, a very traditional approach to life. All those years in the zenana . . .There would have been a period of turmoil at the worst possible moment for the state. Zalim Singh would have been hard pressed to keep the ship of state on an even keel, I think. Poor Madeleine! She was battling the family, the court, the whole Ranipur way of life.'

'And she was fighting for her own chosen style of life. She had anticipated glittering tours of European capitals on the arm of her rich and handsome young prince but had discovered that she could expect no more than a life in a city she hated, the unwanted foreigner who was proving an obstacle to his succession. And if she learned that a second, royal Indian princess was to become his wife she saw a bleak future living with people who resented her and a husband whose affections she must have begun to doubt.'

'You're saying that *Madeleine* sawed through the elevator cable?' said Edgar in astonishment. 'Well, I have to say – nothing that girl did would surprise me but . . . but . . . well, we both saw her reaction when she pulled the flying helmet off the dying pilot and saw it was her husband. Could *anyone* feign such shock?'

'If anyone could, Madeleine could. She's rather good at feigning.' Joe cleared his throat and forced himself to continue. He wasn't finding his theorizing easy. 'But I agree with you, Edgar. She didn't know Prithvi was about to die.'

In the silence that followed, Lizzie stirred uncomfortably then said, 'Stuart did. Her brother did. He would have done anything for Madeleine. If he knew that her role in Prithvi's life was going to be diminished and thereby his own, incidentally, I think he would have taken it upon himself to think and act on her behalf. Cut and run. And after all – who better placed? He could saw through the wires at any time that suited him. Perhaps Ali the fitter became aware and had to be got rid of? And who but Stuart would be able convincingly to send Prithvi up in his stead? We only have Stuart's assertion that he was supposed to be the pilot – Prithvi could all along have expected to go up.'

'Stuart's a trained killer. He's looked pilots in the eye, kids his own age, his mirror image if you like, and calmly pulled the trigger and shot them down in flames. Twenty notches or whatever they are on his fuselage, don't forget. Another one seems insignificant,' Edgar added.

'Well, Stuart's done the cutting,' said Lizzie, 'why didn't they do the running as soon as they got their hands on a million dollars' worth of bearer bonds? Why did they go out to the tiger hunt with everyone else? They could have stayed behind and taken off in the Jenny when you were all looking the other way.'

'Ah. Yes. Good point, Lizzie,' said Edgar helplessly. 'Any ideas, Joe?'

Joe shook his head, thinking furiously.

To cover his colleague's embarrassment, Edgar burbled on. 'So, what comes next? We have no jurisdiction in the state, no power of arrest. Chap's American, anyway. What a diplomatic tangle! Do we ring Sir George? Ask his advice? Do we drop the word to Ajit and wait for him to make an arrest? That's two for the dungeons – Claude and Stuart.'

'You're forgetting Bishan,' said Lizzie. 'The first murder from which all this stems, it seems to me. Who arranged *his* death? Can we expect a third culprit to join them in the cells?'

'No,' said Joe, finding his voice. 'The first murderer? Good Lord, it sounds like the cast list of a Shakespearian tragedy! No. There can be no expectation of the first murderer ever being arrested. He is well beyond even Ajit Singh's reach!'

Chapter Twenty-Six

'I hope you're not still banging on with the idea that Udai had Bishan killed?' Edgar's voice had an edge of menace but he collected himself at once and added shamefacedly, 'No, of course not. Sorry, Joe. Hardly likely to have whispered his own name into the ear of a chap as he lay dying.'

'It was almost as difficult to give him the name he was seeking. The confirmation (because I'm sure he already knew) that his first son had been murdered by his second son was the last thing a dying prince wants to hear. Prithvi. I think he'd finally decided to behave in all things like a Rajput prince and use his skills for the benefit of the state. And his first task was to clear his own path forward. I think it was Prithvi who talked Bishan into taking the stronger than usual dose of opium and used his authority to order the replacement of the panther. He must have strongly believed in his ability to save the country from the economic disaster that is threatening it.'

'A disaster that has already overtaken one or two princely states,' said Lizzie. 'But I don't think anyone here has the faintest idea how near the brink we might be. What a mess . . .' She sighed. 'Suddenly my little tile-hung cottage begins to look very attractive.'

Her sigh was interrupted by a peremptory knock at the door. When Joe went to open it he was alarmed but not surprised to see the handsome and agitated features of Ajit Singh's lieutenant, Ram.

'Sahib, I am pleased to have tracked you down!'

Not the effort he was implying, Joe considered, as he was quite certain that their every move was shadowed.

'Ram. Good to see you again though the circumstances are hardly auspicious,' said Joe. 'Won't you join us?' he added vaguely, doubtful that inviting him into the room of a memsahib was the right thing to do.

Ram shook his head. 'Forgive me. I must ask you and Captain Troop to accompany me at once to the office of the Dewan where he and Major Ajit Singh await you. The memsahib's presence is not required,' he added with a polite nod to Lizzie who had appeared by Joe's side.

The guard at the door of the Dewan's office when they reached it appeared to have doubled, Joe noticed, but at the sight of them no challenges were rapped out. The doors were opened instantly and they were ushered inside.

No clerks on duty this time; the room was occupied only by the Dewan and Ajit Singh. With a gesture and polite formulae they were invited to take seats at a low table opposite the two Rajputs, and Ajit Singh began in what seemed to Joe to be the middle of the story. He spoke fast and bluntly. Time, apparently, was of some importance.

'Were you tempted to lie, Sandilands, when the ruler asked you for names?'

'Of course,' said Joe without hesitation. 'But it would have been impossible to get away with it. He would have known. He *did* know . . . I'd swear even before you gave him your opinion. He'd worked it out.'

'And here we are in possession of the identities of two killers. One is outside our jurisdiction but the second, Captain Mercer, remains on our list so to speak.'

'What have you done with him?' asked Joe alarmed. 'The chap's American, you know, not English.'

'I am aware of the man's nationality but the legal aspects of this case are interesting. What are we to do if a foreign national commits a capital crime on Rajput soil? What

290

would you do if this were London? Of course you would arrest the man and he would stand trial at the Old Bailey. If I can lay hands on this man he will spend some time in my dungeons before he is taken to Delhi to be held to account.'

'What do you mean – *if* you can lay hands on him? Surely you have him in custody by now, Ajit?' said Edgar.

Ajit stirred uncomfortably and the Dewan spoke up. 'Unfortunately that is not the case. Devastated as he was by the death of the Yuvaraj, Ajit, on the return journey, failed to notice that one of the cars, the Hispano Suiza, had been taken by Captain Mercer and his sister. They had packed it with their effects and, unbeknown to us, several spare cans of petrol. At a bend in the road they veered off into the forest and the rest of the cavalcade continued without them.'

Joe fought down a quite reprehensible stab of exultation and managed to ask, 'But where on earth . . .?'

'They had planned well. This car had been toughened for use on hunting trips. Nevertheless it will prove to have been an amazing vehicle if it does what they require of it.'

'Bloody hell!' Edgar exclaimed. 'They're making for the Grand Trunk Road. But over that country . . . no roads, not even tracks out there. They'll never make it!'

'I confidently expect to hear from our foresters within the next month that vulture-picked remains have been discovered in a little-known corner of the kingdom,' Zalim said with relish.

'Then you don't know Madeleine Mercer,' said Joe but only to himself. Out loud he asked, 'But why did the pair go along with the rest of us on the tiger hunt? I can't understand why they didn't just sail off in the Jenny. Why spend a few miserable days with people they didn't like on an activity they despised when they could have been getting away to Delhi or Bombay while our attention was otherwise engaged?'

Zalim and Ajit shared a conspiratorial glance and Zalim waved a negligent hand to encourage Ajit to speak.

'It took less effort for me to get to the truth of Prithvi's death than you, Sandilands. I simply took Ahmed into custody. No notebooks, no fingerprints, no slanted questions were necessary.' He smiled pityingly and paused.

'I'm not going to ask what *was* necessary,' Joe decided. 'Not going to give him the satisfaction.'

Ajit went on, 'As one Rajput to another, he confided that his brother had taken a large sum of money from Captain Mercer before the fatal flight and had made off in line with Mercer's suggestion, to set himself up in business as a driver of taxi-cab vehicles in . . . Delhi.' He gave a rumbling laugh. 'He really *had* gone to Delhi, you see! Not difficult to establish that the dashing air ace had set up the plane to crash with the heir apparent at the controls. A matter of honour, we are to assume. Revenge and loss of career prospects also come into the story along with the disappearance of a substantial amount of wealth in bearer bonds from the possession of the ruler. But the mystery is – why did he not simply kill Ali?'

Joe was angered by the look of genuine puzzlement on Ajit's face. 'You mentioned the word "honour". Captain Mercer may be a killer but he is not an indiscriminate killer. Ali was his rigger and Mercer entrusted his life to him every time he took off. There is no way he would have broken that trust. Perhaps Ali saw something he shouldn't have seen, perhaps Mercer needed a distraction, a bit of hocus-pocus to confuse anyone who might become suspicious. He planned meticulously, which makes it all the more odd that he should –'

'Ah, yes. You are right when you say they should have instantly taken flight but . . . ah, me!' He gave a theatrical sigh. 'This had been rendered impossible.'

Joe and Edgar looked at him in surprise and he enjoyed this for a moment before going on, 'With the assistance of Ahmed, I had all the planes drained of fuel and the reserves carried away. Captain Mercer is nothing if not careful. He constantly checked the planes and it did not escape his attention that all was not well with them. He and his sister had little alternative but, like antelopes, to seek the safety of the herd when danger threatened. By mingling with the other Europeans they felt themselves more secure than they would have been if they had remained behind at the palace. They were not wrong,' he finished baldly.

'Ajit, may I ask you,' said Edgar tentatively, 'to share with us your thoughts on the death of Bahadur?'

'The prince was killed in a manner I have yet to establish, by the Resident,' said Ajit firmly.

'Well, here we can trade information for information,' said Edgar. 'Tell us why you suspected Vyvyan and we'll tell you how he managed it.'

'For some weeks my men had been following Bahadur around the palace, as a means of protecting him. We were determined not to lose a third Yuvaraj. I think it was Ram who noticed . . . Bahadur was observed to be observing! He spent many hours tracking Vyvyan around the palace, watching his bungalow when he worked late into the night. It was not long before Ram realized what his interest was and of course he brought his problem to me.' For a moment, Ajit's confidence seemed to glow less brightly. 'A delicate situation,' he said.

Zalim took up the tale. 'Delicate is an understatement! Diplomatic dynamite! Policing Westerners with Vyvyan's power and position is difficult and there was always the necessity to keep hidden the nature of his offence which even now I will not name. What could I do when Ajit came to me? Well, what would *you* have done?' he asked with a disarming smile. 'I telephoned Sir George.'

'Sir George?' The surprise was all Joe's. Edgar was silent.

'We discussed the matter and he said he would send someone to clear up the mess. I was advised to take no direct action which would sour relations between our countries.' He looked at Joe and beamed again. 'So, Sandilands, I fear the time has come for you to live up to your reputation. You must arrest Vyvyan and take him away and dispose of him as you will.'

'Right now?' Joe asked.

'Yes. Time is, as you would say, of the essence. He is on the move. We had been expecting him to enjoy his new position of power, grow into his role, line his pockets, but his movements suggest this is not what he intends.'

'Tell me what you have observed,' said Joe.

'His household stewards report that discreet preparations are under way. Nothing too obvious. It's my theory he intends to go quickly and travel lightly. We have the motor cars and the stables under guard. He will not get away.'

'But why now and why so hurriedly?'

'He has already acquired the key of the khajina. He exercised his right to claim one immediately on the death of Udai Singh. It is my suspicion that he intends to remove treasure from the strong house and attempt an escape.'

'Ah. Now look here . . . I'm not sure how far I should reveal my knowledge of Ranipur's economic affairs but, well, how certain can we be that it will avail him anything to attempt to ransack the coffers? Will he find anything of interest to him? Bit of an empty gesture perhaps, waving the key around?'

Again Zalim and Ajit exchanged a look which Joe was gratified to see.

'Not quite empty,' Zalim replied. 'A significant amount of Ranipur's resources have been traded for more portable modern representations of wealth but some remains. The state jewellery is still in the khajina. The people call these pieces "hamara" – "ours" – and they do indeed belong to the state and not to the ruler. Udai would never have contemplated disposing of the regalia that graces state weddings and durbars. Would your King George sell the Crown Jewels? I think not! They are still locked away and Claude is aware of this.'

'We expect him to move very soon,' said Ajit. 'We require you, Sandilands, to accompany us to the khajina when he goes there and arrest him when you catch him in the act. If he is going to make his move, when better than during the mourning for the ruler? The palace is in upheaval at the moment and he has the sense to profit from the disturbance. But there are constrictions even on crime. It is mid-afternoon . . . if he is to allow himself hours of daylight in which to get away he must act soon.'

'You will stay here with Ajit,' said Zalim, 'and hold yourselves ready. I will have tea and refreshments sent to you.'

With a smile and a nod, he left them watching each other warily.

Before the promised tea had arrived there was a tap at the door, which was answered by Ajit. After a brief and whispered conversation he waved them to join him.

'He's moving!'

They followed Ajit's man through the palace and out into the hills to the west. Their path was narrow and led through scrubland offering little cover. Joe was concerned. Either they got up so close to Claude he would be bound to see them or they would have to let him get too far ahead. He confided his worry to Ajit.

'The door keeper is one of the hill tribe. He has been told to prevaricate and hold up the Angrez as long as possible,' was the confident reply.

After a mile of scrambling through bleached vegetation, every leaf of which seemed to harbour a thorn, they arrived some thirty yards from a small red sandstone building in the heavy Hindu style. Carved elephant trunks made up the massive lintels which held up the impregnable stone roof. There appeared to be no windows and only one very solid wooden door. On hearing a sharp cry abruptly cut off, they hurried forward, fanning out, guns in hand.

Ajit was first to reach the old man. A dark-skinned man of the hills, dagger drawn, was lying motionless in the middle of the path a yard or two from the door. Ajit leaned over him then looked up and shook his head. His expression was fierce, his voice rasping as he hissed a command to Joe. 'Sandilands! You know what you have to do!' He pointed to the door, which stood slightly ajar.

Chapter Twenty-Seven

Pistol in hand, Joe and Edgar went silently to stand on either side of the door. They heard no sound. Edgar pushed the door and went in first. Joe slipped in behind him. Instinctively they put some distance between themselves, crouching back to back, each covering a sector of the room. In the darkness they could see nothing save for the small oil lamp that burned at the far side. As Joe's eyes adjusted to the gloom he saw that the lamp was standing on a carved stone counter which ran around the circumference of the room. The flame reflected off the metal lids of three coffers built into the stone but if they had expected to catch the Resident with his hand in the honey pot up to the armpit, they were disappointed.

They crept further apart, peering and blinking at the shadows.

'Guns on the floor! Now!' a voice behind Joe commanded. He felt the cold kiss of a revolver barrel in the nape of his neck.

'Move together!'

Joe heard the finality with which his Browning and Edgar's smacked against the stone floor as they fell. As soon as Claude had herded them close together he would kill them with two quick shots. And inside this stone coffin who would hear? Ajit would and he would lay siege but he would not intervene in a shoot-out between Westerners.

Joe's only weapon was words and a psychological understanding of Claude. He wanted to goad the icily calm killer at his back into responding to him and he thought he knew just the formula to annoy.

'You do know that they'll scrub your name from the honour roll at Haileybury?' he said in an easy, conversational tone. 'A man like you, Claude? Why would you do this?'

'Quiet, Sandilands! Move over towards the lamp. Both of you!'

'Why risk everything? You have power, position, the love of a beautiful woman and a glittering future. Enough for any man, I'd have thought. Why gamble all that for a fistful of baubles? You must be mad!'

But Claude was not to be drawn into a discussion. Before he took a step further from Claude, Joe resolved to throw himself backwards on to the gun. If he absorbed the first bullet it would give Edgar a chance to act. He tensed his muscles. Feet slightly apart, he eased his weight on to the balls of his feet. And then he heard a cynical bark of laughter from behind.

'Power? Love? For how long? This is a sinking ship we're all on! Haven't you worked that out yet, Mr Detective? Have you any idea what the rewards are in this post? An insult! I may earn a little more than they pay a second-eleven character like you for keeping the streets of London clear of filth but not much. Rise as high as you like – it's hardly worth the effort. And what do we look forward to when the Raj finally packs its bags and slopes off back to the West? A small pension, a modest house overlooking the South Downs? Perhaps I could call it Ranipur Lodge and have an elephant's foot umbrella stand in the hall next to the Benares brass dinner gong? I would treat my friends to a chota peg before tiffin and bore them rigid with stories that start, "When I was in Poona . . ."' He spoke with bitter emphasis.

'No. That's not for me. My horizons are wider, my ambitions deeper. But I see it's for you, Sandilands, or could be if you had any time left. Edgar – he's too old a leopard to change his spots so I won't make the mistake of making him an offer. What would you like? A bangle each to look the other way for an hour? Easier to shoot you both dead and be done with it.'

'It's not too late. Give me the gun and I'll arrange for you to withdraw discreetly,' said Joe. 'It's not as if there was anything in those pots anyway. And when you leave, empty-handed, you'll run into Ajit Singh who's waiting outside.'

An impatient sigh greeted this attempt. 'Clown! Two hours ago when I came to check, there were emeralds and rubies the size of pigeon's eggs and that's for starters.'

Now that he had his targets standing close together on the opposite side of the room, Claude, still covering them, moved over to the coffers and tapped the lid of the central one. 'You can plunge your arm into a king's ransom. Far more than I need to complete my plans.'

'Sorry, old man!' said Edgar, gloating. 'That was two hours ago. You don't think Ajit Singh stands still, do you? A good deal can happen in two hours. The whole lot has been carted off. Why do you suppose they only left one elderly guard by the door? It's a trap to lure you in! And here you are – trapped! Don't be a bloody fool and give up everything for a not-so-lucky dip into an empty bran-tub!'

Sneering, Claude lifted the lid with his left hand and plunged it into the coffer. They watched, fascinated, as his sneer turned into a grimace of astonishment and then a rictus of horror. He pulled out a hand dripping with precious stones which caught the flickering light and reflected it back in a dazzle of colour. With a shuddering cry, Claude dropped the necklaces on the floor. One item remained hanging from his hand. Not glowing. Not reflecting the light. A wriggling dark shape. About a foot long.

The boom of the small Browning M was ear-shattering in the small space. Eyes riveted on Claude, Joe had barely noticed Edgar's quick snatch to the back of his belt. The small black gun which he had last seen clutched in

Bahadur's hand was hardly visible in Edgar's huge fist but its fire power was undeniable.

Claude stood, his body shaking with horror, his eyes unable to leave his left hand which still clutched the remnants of the object shattered by Edgar's shot. Finally he found his voice. 'What the hell was that?'

'A krait,' said Edgar calmly. 'Looked like a krait to me. Young one. But just as lethal.'

'Help me, for God's sake!'

'No one could help you. You know that,' said Edgar without expression. 'Ten times as venomous as a cobra. You've landed right in the mulligatawny, old man.'

'How long have I got?'

'Ten minutes? A quarter of an hour?'

Claude staggered to the door. Raising his revolver he fired three shots into the air, paused and then two more. He came back into the room and faced them, waving his gun carelessly. He smiled his lopsided boyish smile. 'One shot left. Whose shall it be?' he asked. The barrel wavered over Joe and then over Edgar and finally he raised it to his own forehead. 'Fifteen more minutes of your company, gentlemen? I think not.'

With an agility Joe had no idea he possessed, Edgar leapt on to Claude and knocked the gun from his hand.

'Edgar! What the hell!' said Joe. 'For God's sake, let him go cleanly!'

'Sorry, Joe. I'd much rather he didn't have any bullet holes in him when we haul his carcase back to Delhi. Death by natural causes, misadventure, whatever you like to call it. Anyone can get themselves killed by a krait out here. No explanation necessary. Just stay put for a few minutes. We'll wait for him to die.'

Seeing his implacable face Joe understood Sir George's game. Send in Sandilands to sniff out the troublemakers and leave it to Edgar to make sure they are not left lying around in an untidy state to embarrass the Raj. Udai Singh had suggested as much before he died. 'We plan our last hunt, Edgar.'

'No. *You* can wait for him to die! Those shots he fired were a signal. I'm going to find out who was listening for them.'

Joe ran with Ajit back towards the palace, panting out an explanation as they ran, ashamed that although he had twenty years of youth on his side, he could barely keep up with the Rajput's loping stride. With lungs that threatened to implode at any second, Joe was relieved to be called to a halt by Ajit.

'Listen!' He pointed to the airfield.

'A plane? Starting up? But who the hell?'

'So that is how he was planning to leave!' said Ajit triumphantly.

'But Ajit . . . didn't you say you'd drained all the fuel out of the planes?'

'That is true. But . . .' He paused and looked consideringly at Joe then with a narrow smile went on, 'I left enough in the two-seater, if anyone were careless enough not to check, or in too great a hurry, to allow the pilot to take off and fly . . .' He hesitated again and then finished, '. . . for a mile or two.'

Anger and despair sent Joe running on again, screaming uselessly to the pilot to stop. Of course he could not be heard above the din of the engine and the whirring of the propellers but he went on, shouting and waving his arms. As he neared the airfield, the plane gathered itself to make its dash down the runway and he looked on hopelessly as the figure in the rear seat caught sight of him and gave back a laconic wave. A black stocking mask covered the head, the obscene pigtail streaming out behind as the plane gathered speed.

Ajit had been joined by Ram and a squad of men who ran about quietly and purposefully. In no time saddled horses appeared and Ajit invited Joe to ride with him into the desert stretching ahead of the plane. Dry-mouthed and exhausted, Joe hung on, for the first time in his life unable

301

to enjoy riding a horse. After one mile at a gallop the horses were still going strong but the plane was getting well ahead of them. Joe found he was praying that by some magic it would stay in the sky. Perhaps a store of spare fuel had been found? There was no change of engine note, no sound of distress from the plane. Joe would have liked to call a halt to this mad dash into the desert but Ajit rode on, firm as a rock in the saddle, the gleam of the hunter in his eye.

A further mile out and the horses were beginning to blow when Joe heard the sound he had dreaded. A cough from the plane ahead. A splutter of protest and it began to fall from the sky.

'Glide it down, for God's sake!' Joe muttered under his breath. 'Come on! Pull the nose up, you bloody fool!'

But with an unshakeable inevitability the plane continued its downward dive. It crashed on to its nose half a mile ahead of them.

They tethered their horses and approached the wreck carefully, one from each side. They had nothing to fear from the pilot who was lying across the fuselage, neck at a deadly angle. Joe knelt by the cockpit and gently began to roll back the stocking mask, no longer alarming but pathetic. As he tugged it away, the auburn hair of Lois Vyvyan spilled out to cover her bloodstained and shattered face.

Chapter Twenty-Eight

As they rode slowly back to the town Ajit, who had been wrestling with his thoughts, finally asked, 'Memsahib Vyvyan? But why? How?'

'The how is more straightforward than the why, I think,' said Joe. 'Her father, an army officer, was also a member – a founding member, I should guess – of the Royal Flying Corps. The pioneers were mostly army men, amateurs all. He wears the insignia on his army uniform in a photograph she has. She probably learned to fly some years ago in England. She kept it quiet but had a refresher flight or two with Captain Mercer. They tell me it's quite easy to fly one of these machines . . . But why? Not so easy. She was working with Claude – in fact she could have been the instigator. Think of them as a hunting pair of tigers about the palace, shall we? Disillusioned with their circumstances, fearful for their future prospects and just plain greedy. I think they were prepared to take risks to get away with a fortune and prepared to deceive others along the way.'

That was as far as he was prepared to go in the delicate matter of the involvement of the widowed Third Her Highness. He could feel no pity for the manipulative princess who had, he thought, been used by the Vyvyans. He remembered his first night at the palace and Lois Vyvyan's behaviour. While Shubhada had sparkled at the head of the table, Lois had remained quietly in charge. Claude it was who had a reputation for thoroughness but Joe wondered how much of the reputation had been earned for him by his determined and ambitious wife. And the scent which had so intrigued him? Lois herself, he suspected, must have had the cool head to think of taking the precaution of wearing the same perfume as the girl who was intriguing with her husband. She must have been very certain of him, Joe thought. And now, too late, he could understand her behaviour towards himself. Sir George's envoy and a London policeman at that! Suspicion and anxiety had been bubbling below the surface in all her contacts with him. Small wonder that her tone had been brittle at times.

They were hailed on their way back by Edgar riding out, accompanied by Ram.

'Who the hell?' Edgar wanted to know.

Joe greeted him coldly.

'Lois. It was Lois. So, Edgar, if the krait hadn't got him, Claude would have crashed with her in the desert. Very satisfactory outcome for His Majesty's Government, I'm sure you'll say.' Edgar turned his horse and, as they rode back, knee to knee, Joe asked angrily, 'Now perhaps you can tell me what precisely were your instructions from Sir George? Follow Sandilands, wait for him to put up the game and shoot it down?'

Edgar remained impassive. 'Something like that. Couldn't be doing with a bright young spark like Claude, Indian Civil Service at its best, dragged off to Delhi for a show trial. If one Resident can misbehave – how can we ever trust the others? Could ruin the career of many a good chap. Set the hives buzzing in the Chamber of Princes . . . which, I understand, is about to form up for a very important meeting in the near future. A very important meeting. The timing would have been most unfortunate. Political nightmare. Better this way. Satisfactory outcome.'

'Do you think so?' Joe could not keep the anger out of his voice. 'From the death of Udai Singh have flowed so many other deaths.'

'Better than the dozens it would have been some

decades ago,' said Edgar crossly. 'And all can be accounted for in the most plausible way. Accidents do happen in India, after all. Damn dangerous place, I always say. And two of the killers were Westerners, never forget. Accounted for two heirs to the throne and that's quite a bill to pay. Lucky we have some leverage . . . a few good cards in our hands. We're fortunate also in that Zalim Singh is left at the end to pick up the pieces.' He paused but, receiving no response or encouragement from Joe, carried on, 'But, if it's luck we're talking about, I must say I'd like to know the odds on Claude's putting his thieving hands all unexpected on a krait snake. Lurking in a jewel coffer . . .'

His voice was heavy with suspicion. He looked at Joe, waiting for a comment.

Joe thought of Lizzie's avowal that she would go a long way to protect her charge, Bahadur. He remembered the trust with which the boy had gone off with the hill man, Jaswant. Would their love for the Yuvaraj extend also to revenge when he was beyond their protection? Joe thought it would.

'Yes, wasn't it?' he replied. 'Quite a piece of luck, I mean.'

Chapter Twenty-Nine

Lal Bai was already awake when her maid came to rouse her. She crept to the window, pushing aside the curtain of khas-khas matting, and looked down on to a milky-grey landscape lit only by the sinking moon. It would be two hours before the sun's rays poured back heat and colour into the world, two hours before the flames of her lord's funeral pyre leapt skywards to meet and mingle with them.

She stood for a moment, feeling at one with a world drained of colour, relishing the deep stillness. Across the river a wild dog called from the desert and was answered a moment later by its mate. In two hours their calls would be unheard, swamped by the deluge of sound that would pour from the palace. There would be howling and wailing as never before; the crowds would chant, 'Ram nam sat hai!', The name of God is Truth!; drums would beat and the pyre at the burning ghat would be lit at the very moment the sun rose, to the accompaniment of the ruler's last cannon salute. Nineteen times the big guns would boom out from the elephant gate. Nineteen times, for Udai had been a maharaja, a great ruler. Lal Bai resolved to count the blasts as far as she was able to count.

Chichi Bai anxiously reminded her that all was ready for her prayer ceremony but first, before puja, she must wash and dress. Silver bowls and copper vessels were laid out, filled with fragrant oils and waters, and numbly Lal Bai offered her head and then her limbs for the ritual cleaning and scented massage. That complete, she put on the bright red silk skirt her maid held out, then the tight bodice and the ganghra. One by one ivory bangles were slipped over her upper arms and gold anklets passed over her hennaed feet for today she chose to appear in the costume of a bride. Finally, Chichi Bai clasped about her mistress's throat the most precious of her ruby necklaces.

A thread of saffron intruded into the grey shot silk of the sky. 'It is the time,' whispered Chichi Bai and she left her side to glide to the door. An escort of palace servants had assembled outside and formed ranks, silent but sorrowful and agitated. Her maids, in tears, withdrew and went to stand with the other women at the latticed windows. Lal Bai placed herself in the centre of the group ready to join the procession down to the river bank. Once she was safely shielded from the eyes of the interfering ferenghi, they began their funeral chant.

'Ram! Ram!' Lal Bai began her own chant as the cortège moved forward.

When they reached the courtyard the little procession halted, held back for a moment by the wave of sound that met them. The whole city was assembled in the courtyard and on the staircases down to the river to pay a loud, grief-stricken farewell to Udai Singh. At the burning ghat below them, a torch-bearer stood by the pyre awaiting the body of the ruler. They watched as the bier passed through the elephant gate. Lal Bai's eyes shone with excitement and longing as she caught her last glimpse of her lord, lying, regal, in ceremonial costume and garlanded with marigolds. All was ready.

Not quite all. There was one last ritual gesture to be observed before they could move onward. A footman moved forward holding out a pot of ochre. Without stopping her chant, Lal Bai put her right hand into the powder and withdrew it. To the accompaniment of an increasingly fervent chanting from the crowds of mourners who stood back in awe and respect for the determined slight figure, she solemnly went to the wall of the palace by the elephant gate and pressed her red right hand firmly on to the smooth white surface.

The first of the cannons crashed out its salute and Lal Bai began to count.

Extract from *The Bee's Kiss*, the next Joe Sandilands mystery, published by Constable in September 2005.

'Sir! Commander Sandilands! This is a piece of luck! We've been trying to get hold of you. Something's come up. All too literally, sir! There's a couple of River Police here won't go away until they've seen you.'

Joe approached the desk in puzzlement and the sergeant opened the office door behind him, calling, 'Alf! George! Got him! He's all yours!'

Alf and George slammed down mugs of cocoa, bustled out of the office and stood, giving him a slow police stare. They were wearing their river slickers and naval-style peaked caps and very purposeful they looked. The leader glanced uncertainly from Joe back to the duty officer who swallowed a grin and said, 'Yes. This is who you've been waiting to interview. Commander Sandilands.'

'Off duty,' Joe muttered, aware that he looked as though he'd just strolled off-stage from his bit-part in a society farce at the Lyric. 'Sandilands it is. Tell me what I can do for you.'

'What you can do for us is identify a corpse, sir. It's down at the sub-station by Waterloo Bridge. It's a fresh one – only been in the water an hour at the most. A suicide.'

'I'd like to help, of course,' said Joe, stifling his irritation. 'But suicides are not my department. Can't you just go through your usual channels?'

'Regular channels no use, sir. It's you we have to see. Just to take a look at the body before it goes off to the morgue. Won't take a minute.'

'Why me?' Joe shivered. The evening's euphoria had evaporated, leaving him full of cold foreboding.

'No identification to be found, sir. No documents, no labels on clothing, nothing at all. Except for one item in her pocket.'

'*Her* pocket?'

'Deceased is a young female, sir.' He fumbled under his cape and held up a small white object.

'We were lucky we got there before the printer's ink ran. You can just make it out. He read from the card: '*Commander Joseph Sandilands, New Scotland Yard, London. Whitehall 1212.*'

'It's your calling card, sir.'

For a moment, Joe's face and limbs froze. When finally he found his voice it rapped out with military precision. 'Waterloo Bridge. We'll never get a taxi at this time of night. Half a mile from here? We can run it in five minutes.'

He was sprinting out of the door before the River Police had pulled themselves together. They pounded after him, boots thumping, capes flying.

As the door swung to behind them, the desk sergeant caught the eye of a passing constable who'd loitered to witness the strange scene. ''Struth! That got 'im moving! D'you see 'is face when the penny dropped? Wonder how many girls the old fart's given his card to lately?'

'Sounds like a case of unrequited affection to me,' commented the bobby sentimentally. 'Probably got some poor girl up the stick.'

Joe pounded along the Embankment, evening shoes giving him a perilous grip on the wet pavings. He looked ahead through the half-grown trees lining the river to the shimmering line of pale yellow lamps studding the bridge along its great length. Cleopatra's Needle. More than half way there. He tore off his tie and cracked open his collar. He pushed on, glad to hear his escort panting and cursing close behind.

Three young females. He'd given his card to three and that only yesterday. With dread he listed them. 'Audrey,

310

Melisande . . . And her baby . . .' His heart gave a lurch which threatened to cut off his breathing as he added, 'Little Dorcas.'

He could have asked the sergeant one simple question which would have reduced the choice to one: blonde, auburn or black hair? He knew very well why he'd not asked. One answer from the list would have been more than he could bear and he could not risk breaking down right there at the reception desk.

It must be Dorcas, he decided. Driven to distraction by her grandmother's cruelty she'd run away to London, swelling the numbers of waifs and strays who fetched up on the cold streets of the capital in their thousands. He'd been kind to her. Armitage had paid her flattering attention. Perhaps she'd been trying to contact one of them? He ran on. Without a word spoken, they all stopped and, hands on knees, gasping for breath, they tried to gain a measure of control before they entered the dismal little rescue room. The older of the two officers flung him a wounded look. 'It's all right, sir. She's not going anywhere, whoever she is. Five minutes is neither here nor there for the deceased.'

'It's a bloody eternity for me,' said Joe with passion.

A tug hooted mournfully, echoing his words. A sickening stench of decay belched from the ooze below. It was low tide and several yards of stinking mud fringed the sinister black slide of the river.

'Let's get on with it, shall we?'

They exchanged looks, nodded and went inside.

A third river officer was sitting over his tea, a brimming ash tray on the floor at his feet, filling in the crossword on the back of the *Evening Standard*. He shot to attention as they entered. In the centre of the room on a still-dripping truckle bed lay a white-shrouded figure. The cocktail of carbolic and Wimsol bleach was almost a relief after the river smells. As Joe advanced to lift the sheet he started in horror to hear a voice behind him intoning:

> *'Take her up tenderly,*
> *Lift her with care,*
> *Fashioned so slenderly,*
> *Young and so fair!'*

Joe turned and addressed the sergeant angrily. 'Who or what in hell is that?'

The sergeant's voice was a placatory whisper. 'Witness, sir. He was on the bridge when she jumped.'

A bear-like figure shambled forward into the light shed by the solitary electric bulb and presented himself.

'He's a down-and-out, sir. Harmless. We know him well. Came forward with information and we asked him to stay in case a statement was required. Name of Arthur.'

Joe turned to the man. 'Arthur? Thank you for staying. And thank you for your sentiments. Now, gentlemen, shall we?'

The constable moved reverently to turn the sheet back. Joe stared.

'Young female,' the elderly sergeant had said. And, in death, wiped clean of coquettish artifice, her doll's face framed by a mop of curling blond hair, Audrey had shed the years along with her life.

'Known to you, sir?' the sergeant enquired gently.

Order other books in The Joe Sandilands murder mystery series

No. of copies	Title	Price	Total
	The Bee's Kiss	£16.99	
	The Damascened Blade	£6.99	
	The Last Kashmiri Rose	£6.99	
	Ragtime in Simla	£6.99	
	P&P and insurance		£3.00
	Total order		£

Name: _____

Address: _____

_____ Postcode: _____

Daytime Tel. No. / Email _____
(in case of query)

Three ways to pay:

1. **For express service telephone the TBS order line on 01206 255 800 and quote 'CRBK'.**
   Order lines are open Monday–Friday 8:30am–5:30pm

2. I enclose a cheque made payable to **TBS** Ltd for £ _____

3. Please charge my ☐ Visa ☐ Mastercard ☐ Amex ☐ Switch

   (switch issue no. ....) £ _____

   Card number: _____

   Expiry date: _____ Signature _____
   (your signature is essential when paying by credit card)

Please return forms (*no stamp required*) to: Constable & Robinson Ltd, FREEPOST NAT6619, 3 The Lanchesters, 162 Fulham Palace Road, London W6 9BR.

Enquiries to readers@constablerobinson.com

Constable & Robinson Ltd (directly or via its agents) may mail or phone you about promotions or products. Tick box if you do not want these from us ☐ or our subsidiaries ☐.